EUROPE

ASIA

Vet

China

Himalaya Mtns.

India

Indonesia

Sumatra

AFRICA

Java

Madagascar

AUSTRALIA

Maintenance
Compound

Scale: 1 inch = 1/3 mile
1 sq. inch = 71.1 acres

Ponds

Connecting Bridge

FINAL
REFUGE

Also by James L. Haley

FINAL REFUGE

A Novel of Eco-Terrorism

James L. Haley

St. Martin's Press ⚘ 1994

All characters are products of the author's imagination, and any resemblance to persons living or dead is purely coincidental.

Production Editor: David Stanford Burr

Library of Congress Cataloging-in-Publication Data

Haley, James L.
    Final Refuge / James L. Haley.
        p. cm.
    ISBN 0-312-11275-0
        1. Wildlife refuges—Texas—San Antonio—Fiction.   2. Terrorism—
    Texas—San Antonio—Fiction.   3. San Antonio (Tex.)—Fiction.
    I. Title.
    PS3558.A3577F56   1994
    813'.54—dc20   94-21901
                                                                            CIP

First Edition: October 1994

10   9   8   7   6   5   4   3   2   1

To Brent and Paul

1

ERIC JACKSON had his own theory about rhinoceroses. Every wildlife book he had read called them vicious and unpredictable, the deadliest of all the big game in Africa. That was true of Cape buffalo, maybe, but rhinos—Eric Jackson was certain they were just insecure. He had known this since June of 1986.

The zoo in San Antonio then had five of them—two big white ones, imported from the Umfolozi Reserve in South Africa, that lumbered and snuffled about their paddock and seemed as big as buses; and three of the smaller, more agile black ones, a bull and a cow, who had produced a calf. At the time Eric made their acquaintance the calf was about one-third grown, not fully weaned but old enough to be offered the prepared zoo biscuits that plopped metallically out of the jerky, dirty-glassed, pull-knob vending machines at seven or eight for a quarter.

The old bull was kept in his own enclosure, where mostly he dozed, or got to his feet to munch on some new alfalfa hay, or saunter importantly over to his special corner, by the locked gate that connected to the cow's paddock. There he would sniff the limestone wall that was bleached and exfoliated by years of the repeated ritual, and then do a kind of turnabout, like a long car on a narrow road, and raise his tail, and shoot a jet of urine splattering onto the wall, as straight and strong as a wide-open garden hose. Sometimes he would peek through the steel-barred gate to see if she had noticed, but most times he would simply plod over to his other special corner, at the low end of the paddock where it made an acute angle between the kudu paddock on the south and the public viewing wall on the east, where he could look up out of his grotto and all day long see, dimly, the curious humans point at him and make their funny little baboon noises that sounded almost like home.

In this other special corner he would mill about, nosing the dirt until he found the right spot. Then he would execute another careful turnabout, raise his tail again, and flop out round brown turds the diameter of volleyballs that hit the hard-packed dirt and flattened out with heavy wet splats. And no sooner did each hit the ground than the old bull would lift a hind foot and boot it as far behind him as he could kick it. Zoo visitors who saw this for the first time were universally amazed at how that nasty-looking little sphincter could balloon out to such a capacity. It never occurred to them that this elastic anus was also a danger to the animal, and it was the reason why a black rhino was fed only the finest grade of hay. Usually it was alfalfa, about forty pounds a day, with a topping of bread and leafy vegetables. Sometimes the kitchen would substitute timothy or clover for the alfalfa, if the price was right, but whatever he got, the keepers sifted through each bale to make sure there were no stems or stalks. If he got a batch of coarse food the rhino could suffer a rectal prolapse as easily as a salesman gets hemorrhoids.

But, as long as the keepers could keep his butthole from turning inside out, they knew they could depend on the old bull to always dump on the same square yard of earth, year in and year out. He was easy to care for.

The calf was standing in the center of its adjoining paddock, to the north. He weighed about six hundred pounds, and had lost the worst of that wizened squint newborn calves always seem to have while they register the sights and sounds of the world for the first time. From the very tip of his flat, shovel-like snout there rose a small horn, an inverted cone the size of a small motor-oil funnel, and immediately behind it was a hard white nub where the scalp had begun to crust. Soon another genetic trigger would fire, and stiff, gray-white hair would begin to grow from the scaly lump, cemented together by a kind of resin secreted from within, that would mat the hair into a rock-hard cone. Perhaps by instinct and perhaps only because it itched, the calf would learn to whet and sharpen the horns on abrasive rocks until, with time and more growth and more resin and more whetting, the horns would curve into fearsome stilettos, the forehorn growing to sometimes a yard in length, backed by five thousand pounds of power. In Africa Eric's guide had shown him, within the thickets, long trenches plowed into the ground—black rhinos browse mostly on leaves, but they also use their horns to dig for roots, and he had seen deep furrows ripped into hardpan that a tractor couldn't have scratched. In the early days of settling East Africa, when the first railroads threaded through the thick bush, rhinos sometimes ambushed and derailed locomotives with the muscle behind those horns, which were their glory and curiosity—and had now become their peril.

Different zoos utilize different philosophies of caring for wild animals. Those headed by "purists" discourage public interaction with the animals and forbid their feeding by the public. Others, like San Antonio, regard contact as an important part of visitors' education, and vend specially prepared foods for people to give them. But in all the years he had been going to the zoo, Eric had never seen anyone try to feed the rhinos. You feed the monkeys, because they reach through the bars with their black little humanoid hands for a pellet or biscuit, then chatter and make faces, and try to steal it from each other. Then they drop it so they can scratch their balls, and reach out for more. You feed elephants, because you feel honored that they so ponderously condescend to reach out with their great brown trunks where you can hear the air whooshing through and you wonder how they can taste anything as small as a peanut or zoo biscuit. Then you realize they don't chew every one, they wait, and collect eight or maybe a dozen to make chewing worthwhile. You feed the bears, because they've learned to sit up and beg with their paws, which isn't dignified but everybody makes them do it and the bears go along—except for the old silver-back grizzly. When you wave a biscuit at him he throws his head back and sort of sneers with his right upper lip. That's as far as he'll go.

But Eric Jackson had never seen one person try to feed a rhinoceros. Maybe it was the vicious reputation of these animals that prevented visitors from leaning over the wall into their grotto and getting too close. Maybe people figured they were too stupid to eat from your hand. If you just threw a biscuit at them, they were too blind to see where it landed. Then they couldn't find it, or didn't bother to find it, and people said they were stupid. He didn't know.

The calf was standing about fifteen yards away, and beyond him another ten yards, his mother lay on her belly in the cool, dun-painted cinderblock rhino house, partly concealed by its heavy metal sliding door. The limestone wall where he stood rose two and a half feet above the sidewalk, and dropped down seven feet on the other side, into the grotto. With two baggies of biscuits in his hand, Eric knelt by the wall, but the gravel bit into his bare knees and he took off his well-beaten khaki bush hat and knelt on it instead. He figured the calf was too nearsighted to see him clearly—at fifteen yards he was probably a blur atop the wall—so he reached into the grotto and slapped his open hand onto the wall and called to him.

The startled calf jerked his head in Eric's direction, and out of the corner of his eye Eric saw a convulsive movement inside the rhino house. When an alerted rhino jumps to her feet, she does it so quickly you don't quite catch how it happens—she just seems to blow off the ground, all four thousand pounds of her, as if in recoil to the force of her snort, and suddenly her stubby, in-curving legs are under her and she is sizing you up, or trying to, with those round, wrinkled, expressionless little eyes.

In another second the mother bucked through the door of her house, her head up to get the scent, her respectable-sized horns cleaving the air before her brow. Eric felt the stone wall vibrate with her tread as she galloped to the center of the paddock, placing herself between her calf and the wall where he was leaning partway in. She snorted again and adjusted her stance.

All the books say you should never, ever, mess with a rhino cow when she has a calf with her. That's elementary footage to every white hunter movie. Yet, there was something about her as she stood there, partly clumsy but partly, thanks to her chunky Louis Quatorze legs, oafishly delicate. Dim-sighted and irritable and protective, she blocked Eric's view of the calf, seeming not vicious, but—what?—suspicious, perhaps, but in a yearning sort of way, like a brutalized child who reaches out, only to clench a fist. Perhaps it was because the apes which millennia before she had chased from the waterholes had during their long absence grown tall and pale and hairless, and now they abused her and repeated things about her, and mocked her for being clumsy and stupid. Perhaps she was hurt more than people imagined by an evolution that cheated her of grace or intelligence, and her personality was perhaps twisted now by the eons of derision, the shooting out of lips and the shaking of heads at her.

The north end of the paddock cornered into the sidewalk, where there was a locked metal door to the keepers' access. There the grotto looked to be only five feet below the walk. Eric soothed her in the only Swahili he could remember from his Africa trip, hoping that the soft, aspirated monosyllabic singsong would calm her suspicion. He figured she probably wouldn't know he was telling her that the souvenirs cost too much.

Slowly Eric got to his feet and, taking the rumpled bush hat from the ground, walked to the keepers' gate, maintaining the soft, reassuring babble. The cow watched his movement intently, pacing a quarter circle around her calf to keep him shielded from sight. At the gate he knelt again on the hat, reached down into the grotto and patted softly on the rock with his open hand. Suddenly—inexplicably, he didn't know how—he began to remember what he wanted to say. *"Uta-penda kula nini?"* What would you like to eat? He reached into the plastic baggie and tapped on the wall with a grainy brown walnut-sized biscuit. *"Kuna biskiti!"* Here is a biscuit. *"Je, unaumwa nini?"* Come on, now, what's wrong?

Imperceptibly at first, the cow rhino stretched her neck in his direction, her head up, and he wondered if she could smell the biscuit at that distance. The sun was out, reflecting off the limestone walls of the paddock and magnifying the all-too-apparent odor of her morning dung, and the humid southerly breeze carried the unmistakable zoo-smell of a hundred other species whose enclosures would be hosed down during the afternoon. What a waste, thought Eric. They ought to compost it and sell it for fertilizer. You can't get more organic than that. Probably some federal rule against it, though. He tapped the biscuit on the wall again and waited. Indeed she probably was able to strain out its faint nutty aroma from the many others. He was downwind, but the walls of the grotto would swirl the breeze; their sense of smell was uncanny.

San Antonio was one of the finest zoos in the country, famed around the world for its breeding successes with snow leopards and rare antelopes. But like all zoos it was expensive, in many ways wasteful, and its older exhibits, the pits and cages built as a result of the WPA programs of the 1930s, were inherently cruel in their cramped accommodation of the animals. Somewhere, Eric Jackson thought, somehow, someone must conceive a zoo that reaches the potential of what they can be—insurance for the survival of endangered species, affording a spacious, natural life for the animals and an outdoor education experience for the urban public that would make them want to enter and be thrilled and enchanted, without having to pander to lure them inside. The great zoo "revolution" that is now taken for granted had only just begun. Since the early days of the royal menageries, the dominant philosophy had been to exhibit specimens from as many different species as could be amassed, with little regard for the needs or contentment of the animals. The growing public outcry against this, sharpened by ecological crises all over the world, was prompting zoos to espouse a new purpose, for the study and breeding of rare and endangered species, and for their safekeeping until they could be safely returned to the wild. This retooling, by which public amusement was made secondary to caring for the wildlife, was enormously expensive, and in most zoos was undertaken only as capital development funds could be raised. But until then—look over there, he thought, video games in the snack bar, for God's sake. The rhino cow's ears twitched, and Eric's attention snapped back to her as if on a rubber tether.

She leaned toward him, and as he held his breath she took a step, then two, then halted, lowering her head in threat.

"Eh, msichana nzuri sana!" Oh, that's a good girl. Somewhere deep within her mystery she was overcome, and she picked her way over to him as delicately and timidly as a deer. Jesus God, he was touching her! She was smelling his hand. He held the biscuit right against her bristled, wrinkled muddy nostril so she would be certain what it was. She sniffed, and when she exhaled it sounded like the wind sighing from a

cave. Then she raised her head as far as she could, limited by the thick folds of hide that rippled back from her neck, and she opened her mouth, her lips parting with a wet smack, exposing a wedge-shaped, incredibly soft, shiny, brilliantly pink tongue. He put the biscuit right on the edge of it, brushing her upper lip as he withdrew his hand, for a second disgusted by a sheen of slimy, greenish alfalfa drool that webbed his fingers. He ignored it, and fed her two and then three more biscuits, each one of which she chewed leisurely with hollow, resonating crunches that echoed up through the sinuses and chambers of her heavy skull. He hadn't expected that—he heard it, not from her mouth with its soft tongue and thick, insulating lips, but through the top of her head. Sound, of course he had learned in physics, travels faster through solid material.

Eric Jackson patted the side of her face. *"Hujambo, bibi kifavu?"* How are you, Mrs. Rhinoceros? She lolled her head to the side and scraped her foot-tall gray-white forehorn on the limestone; Eric looked down and saw from the streaks on the wall this must be her regular whetstone. He felt her horn, where it joined with the leathery skin of her nose, sprouting innumerable stray hairs that frayed and curled out from it, and gazed down into her dim brown eye. That was the moment he gained the certainty, the full assurance, that rhinos are not vicious. They are merely insecure.

He had all but forgotten the calf, which grew forlorn standing alone in the middle of the paddock, and now walked uncertainly over to join his mother. Eric pulled back to see how she would react, but she merely nuzzled the calf, then looked back placidly up at him and smacked her lips open for another treat. With his heart pounding against his chest, Eric lay on top of the wall, fed her a biscuit and reached far down to the calf. He was vulnerable now—she could gore him, in the arm or shoulder, if she wanted to, and pull him in; he would never be able to jump back in time. But, to his sheer amazed delight he fed and pet them both, scratching their ears, pulling on the long fleshy hooks of their upper lips to see if they really could grasp with them. They could, and with greater strength than he had sup-posed.

"Hello, junior," he said softly. "Hello, junior."

Only at the sound of other voices did he look up and see a dozen other visitors, pointing at him from the east wall and taking pictures.

Eric stood up, his left hand dripping green alfalfa slobber. It was thirty yards to the nearest drinking fountain, past the cluster of people. He walked by them, keeping the sticky hand away from his shorts. A teenaged boy in a black family shook his head. "Man, you crazy. I ain't touchin' them things."

Eric had noticed before that ethnic minorities made heavy use of zoological parks, for reasons both practical and cultural, but which were difficult to explain without sounding like a racist. Without making a value judgment, black and Hispanic families are often larger than white families, and the admission price of an average zoo gives a whole day's outdoor recreation for an affordable price. And, they enjoy it. It seems to have become an Anglo burden to have to read all the information on how endangered an animal is, or how its habitat is being devastated, and look on with a sense of guilt and grief. For some reason it seemed to Eric that minorities, not necessarily because they cared less about environmental issues, preserved a greater willingness to simply enjoy experiencing a form of life unfamiliar to them.

As he rinsed his hands a little girl ran up to him. "My mama said you forgot your hat." She gave it to him. When the others had moved on, Eric returned to read over the signs at the paddock, hoping they said what the rhinos' names were.

> BLACK RHINOCEROS (Diceros bicornis)
> 4th Largest Land Mammal
> Average Height: 5 feet   Average Length: 11 feet
> Average Weight: 4,000 to 5,000 pounds
> Record Horn Length: 53 Inches

Why the hell is that last one there? People don't need to know that. Don't egg them on, for God's sake, this isn't a trophy case. He read on: *Habitat: Africa, south of the Sahara Desert*

Yeah, right. Behind the glass there was a series of maps of the African continent, showing the range of the black rhinoceros in successive decades—1900, 1920, 1940, 1960, 1980. With each one the brown blotches of their habitat got smaller and smaller like a healing pox, until in 1980 they were barely visible. In the glass he saw his own face reflected beneath his bush hat, gazing sadly at the 1980 map, at the tiny brown wedge he knew was Amboseli. That was where he had seen them, the previous year, a couple of live ones, in the distance, crashing through thornscrub like snorting, unstoppable locomotives, but mostly dead ones, bloated and streaked white with vulture droppings, the reeking stench carrying their agony to the high dome of heaven, the blood-crusted craters on their snouts showing where the poachers had hacked out their horns for the black market.

If it was in him to kill anything, he thought, he could kill a poacher. But killing was not in him—he ran over a dog once and cried for three days. He longed for justice, but he could not be its sword.

Beside the maps and the statistics was the outline of a springbok head, the international sign for an endangered species, and beneath it the legend: ENDANGERED. That is one fucking understatement, he thought bitterly. A text went on to explain the loss of habitat in Africa, and the hateful rhino slaughter by poachers who sold their horns on the black market to become status-symbol dagger handles for rich Arabs, and useless stupid "aphrodisiac" teas for rich aging Chinese dandies who felt their sexual performance beginning to wane. Rhinos, the signs read, might well be hunted to extinction in ten years for the value of their horns.

But—there was no sign with their names. Then it hit him, in a rush: the old bull with his homely, dependable eccentricity, and the cow with her trusting, stocky gentle geniality, reminded him of Fred and Ethel Mertz from the old "I Love Lucy" television series. The names fit so precisely he started laughing, hard, out loud, and he returned to the bench by the drinking fountain until he could stop, but every time he looked up he saw Fred and Ethel Mertz, and he'd start again. He didn't worry about the calf, Junior would do, but in his own heart he named the pair Fred and Ethel.

He returned to the paddock where Ethel had remained, and

reached down and pet her again. "Why are they killing you, *Bibi Kifavu?*" he asked softly. "Do you know they are killing you?" For Eric Jackson, that was the beginning.

In the eight years since that June of 1986, he had returned once or twice a year to San Antonio, most recently for breeding conferences with the director, but really, he knew, really to see Ethel, and she never failed to come out and greet him. He even brought Liz Ann up a few times, but after he fed Ethel she wouldn't let him touch her until he went into the men's room and scrubbed with soap.

2

ONE OF THE ATTRACTIONS of the San Antonio Zoo is its variety of topography. From extensive, well-shaded flats along the San Antonio River, which contain hippopotamus pools and duck ponds and a boat ride through the children's area, it slopes up sharply to the west in a series of terraces, which creates a wide variety of exhibit areas. Along the high end, on the west, where the zoo borders the U.S. 281 freeway, high limestone cliffs provide a naturally rugged backdrop to an African diorama filled with different species that can be shown together without worry whether they will quarrel for space or injure each other—ostrich, eland, roan antelope and zebra. They are Grévy zebras, which are quite distinct from the common species and are desperately rare, but ninety-nine visitors in a hundred don't know the difference. Zoos are used to that, used to the idea that most of their important conservation work involves species that indifferent people never give a second look at.

At the northwest corner, screened from public view by a green thicket of bamboo, is a machine shop and equipment yard, which sits at the corner of U.S. 281, on the west, and Hildebrand Avenue, on the north. In this yard are stored construction materials, and here is parked at night the small fleet of dun-painted golf carts used to haul food for the animals. The outside perimeter of this yard is a six-foot-high fence of dog-lopped cedar boards, just like a backyard privacy fence, painted green. If you're driving north on the freeway and get off at the Hildebrand exit, you see two fences—an outer fence of six-foot chain link topped by three-strand barbed wire, and the green board fence within that. There is about six feet of space between the two, where a thick growth of weeds and mesquite brush has sprung up.

Hildebrand is a busy exit, but after midnight nearly all the traffic turns west, toward Trinity University. Hildebrand eastbound, along the zoo fence and then Brackenridge Park, is practically deserted in the quiet watch of predawn. Along this fence is a stretch about thirty yards long where the mesquite thicket has jumped the chain-link fence, and the stubby trees and brush crowd in a tangle right to the curb.

It was two o'clock in the morning when a long, dark blue Oldsmobile pulled off 281 onto the Hildebrand exit. There was no speed trap set up, no parked cars. It turned right onto Hildebrand along the north fence of the zoo. Juan Barilla checked the rearview mirror, and saw a pair of headlights top the bridge behind him and wait at the light where he had turned. Barilla drove on, all the way down the hill to Broadway, where he turned right, then right again on Mulberry Avenue, then right onto 281 again.

Luís Barilla sat next to him, his eyes turned unfocusing out the window as the blackish green foliage and light gray limestone caliche blurred slowly by. He didn't like what they were about to do, but he could not fight it.

Anglo people think Hispanic families are so tight, so close-knit. And they are, but it's not that easy. When you are taken in and raised by relatives, it is not easy to make your place. You must show some amount of independence for yourself or the older men will not respect you, but you dare not disagree with them about anything that really matters, or they can make your life unbearable. Gringos don't have a clue what living on that kind of tightrope is like.

And Luís Barilla wanted things out of this life. Perhaps if he had grown up in the interior, where nobody had anything, he would not have hated poverty so viscerally. But he didn't, he grew up in Nuevo Laredo, in the shadow of those who had plenty, watching rich bitches wiggle into their girdles and waddle like so many fat ducks across the bridge to shop in the malls on the American side. There they could feel free to badmouth people like himself, how lazy and useless they were, what an embarrassment they were. And when they got home they almost exulted in employing people like him to trim their hedges and wash their cars. It was bad enough to take that from white people, but to take it from your own was beyond endurance. They took out on him their frustration and bile at not being able to attain the one luxury they really ached for: pale skin.

And Uncle Ramón was just like them. By almost anyone's standards, Uncle Ramón was a success. He owned, not some taco stand, but a fine importing business with a showroom in Houston's Gallería. Ramón had brought him to Houston when Luís's mother died, and given him as close to an American life as could be obtained. Yet to Luís it seemed, somehow, tatty. Take Ramón's car—an Oldsmobile, just bought, three years old—new enough to impress some relatives, but old enough to afford.

Uncle Ramón had courted and married an Anglo woman. He whored around only with Spanish women, but would never in a million years admit he had married for social advantage. And now he expected Luís to emulate him. Whenever a really cute white girl came into the store, Uncle Ramón would push him. "You go help her. She like you. I can tell." Sometimes the girls would go out with him; more often they looked at him like he had stepped way out of line—out of his league, out of his color. He hated it, being pushed into the whole lower-class feel of it, and behind him Uncle Ramón was always grinning, always chiding, like he thought it was so cute. "Go on," he would say, "you can help her. You got what she want."

Luís glanced into the left rear seat at Uncle Ramón, at his sharp dark eyes and sharp nose, his iron-gray hair blown back dry in an out-of-fashion razor cut, his dark blue windbreaker hanging loose around a yellow guayaberra shirt. He touted his membership now in the Republican party; to his family he was Ramón Barilla—to the Jaycees he was Raymond Berry. There was something contemptible in that, thought Luís, something false and pitiable. But when a man feeds you and clothes you and gives you a job, it limits your right to criticize. He has earned not just your loyalty, but the right to presume your loyalty. He owns you, in a way. Luís was sure his Aunt Ellen felt the same way about Ramón; Luís was sure she must have known about the other women. But Ramón treated her well, treated her respectfully and sometimes even affectionately. Aunt Ellen had made her decisions, and lived by them, without complaining. As for Uncle Ramón, loyalty was the only love he needed.

Juan Barilla turned again onto Hildebrand, but this time two cars approached in the opposite direction, and they had to circle the section again—down to Broadway, over to Mulberry and back to 281. It struck Luís as funny, how closely you can stalk a place without anybody noticing. The world never even notices that it doesn't notice. He smirked; maybe he should be a poet.

Ramón's younger brother, Esteban, sat in the backseat next to him, old enough for Luís to have to respect, and young enough to show signs of a fading athleticism. Uncle Esteban would go over the fence with him. He owned a part of the importing business with Ramón, but he was a decidedly junior partner, both financially and in toughness. And then there was Juan, Esteban's son, four years older than Luís. Luís watched Juan turn the long blue Olds around the dark deserted corners. Like chickens, thought Luís, we have our own pecking order.

Luís had long sensed that the Barillas did not always operate within the strict limits of the law, but he had also spent enough time in México, and seen how things worked down there, to know when not to ask questions. If his uncles ever wanted him in their confidence, they would invite him. It was enough for him to do as he was told. At least, he knew, they didn't sell drugs. Not that they were above selling drugs, but if you dealt drugs, there was always somebody tougher than you, somebody meaner, who already controlled the authorities with bigger bribes than you could offer, somebody who would kill you. Ramón's older sister's husband, Joaquín, had tried to make his fortune with drugs, back when Ramón and all his brothers had lived on their father's ranch up in the Sierra Madre. Joaquín had gone down into Saltillo and dealt drugs on the street for a while, but that was small time, and when he tried to go commercial, to play with the big boys, he ran afoul of the existing power structure. That territory was claimed already, and like the map of the globe, there is room for no new nations. It was Ramón who had found him, on their own ranch, strung up naked in a piñon pine tree, gagged, the rope tied tightly around his chest, his wrists bound, his body welted by cattle prods and whips. Under him he found a car battery and jumper cables, one alligator clamp biting into a big toe, the other into his foreskin. Only one of the cables was connected to the battery; the other had been merely touched to its terminal off and on to watch Joaquín dance up in the piñon pine. It must have taken him hours to die.

Now that Ramón was in Houston, he found the drug scene complicated by Asians and Jamaicans, and wanted no part of it. Importing was pretty safe. He was a small-timer and he knew it, and he chafed under it; he knew he could only rise so high in the Anglo business world. It had even made him chuckle sadly when he came to America and discovered that there was a Small Business Administration that lent money to small-timers like him. Of course he wanted money and power, but he lacked the relish for truly violent competition. What they were about on this night's business was in some sense a small crime, but it was a way to earn a sum of money he was comfortable with, that would get his family ahead but not entail a great deal of risk. Ramón could play, but he was cautious, treading between the law on one side and the truly dangerous characters on the other.

What they were about to do was wrong, but Luís reasoned as he gazed out the window that he had suffered much injustice as well. His mother, the Barillas' baby sister, dead too young—he carried in his billfold a yellowing snapshot of her, candlelit in her coffin, forever young, her wrinkles and the ravages of cancer whited out by the Kodak flashcube. His father—shit, who knew where he was. Luís's uncles glared at him if he asked questions about him. To please them he had dropped his father's name out of his own, but still they called him his father's son when they were pissed off at him. That really cut him.

"Get ready," hissed Juan. They had turned onto Hildebrand a third time. They saw no cars anywhere, and slowed as they passed the place where the mesquite brush grew right out to the curb. You couldn't see the chain-link fence within it, let alone the green board fence beyond that. Luís unzipped four inches of a lumpy satchel and reached in, and removed a pair of wire cutters. He closed the zipper, and held the satchel and cutters together in his left hand, his right hand on the door handle. He glanced back at Uncle Ramón, who was gazing impassively into the mesquite. The road grade was cut into the hillside, and it was about a three-foot jump from street level up to the ground.

"Here," snapped Ramón.

Juan braked. The two right-side doors flew open and Luís and Esteban hunched with their bags up into the dark mesquite with a dry crackle underfoot of years of fallen twigs and loose caliche. They flattened themselves on the ground against the chain-link fence.

"All right," said Esteban. "Cut it."

Luís stood and quickly snipped the three strands of barbed wire, which popped and curled into the mesquite branches, quite invisible from the street. He tossed the satchel over and climbed easily after it. Esteban threw his bag over the fence and Luís caught it. There was a glimmer of headlights.

"Down!" wheezed Esteban.

They both hit the dirt, covering their faces, peeking to see the car motor evenly past. They never even notice that they don't notice, Luís thought again.

Esteban followed over the chain link. They hunched through to the board fence, when headlights came again. Esteban pushed Luís to the ground. "Down! Shit!" As it approached they made out the cherries atop an SAPD cruiser. "Shit!" Esteban repeated.

It rolled by, heedless. Luís boosted his uncle to scan over the wall, and once they saw it was safe, they scaled it before another car passed and dropped into the ghostly pale gravel of the shop yard. Luís turned his ankle on a rock as he landed, but it wasn't bad.

The chain-link gate into the zoo grounds was latched but not locked. In a crouch, they let themselves in, and closed the gate behind them. They knelt in the bamboo screen and watched; it was a commanding position, one from which they could see the whole upper section of the zoo, from the petting corral on the north down to the gibbon house on the southeast. They watched carefully for several minutes, but saw nothing.

"Okay," said Esteban. "You follow me close." The area below the maintenance yard was undergoing construction. From the bamboo they slid down a steep grassy slope, past an open, thatched roof gazebo that one day would be some kind of overlook. They landed on a narrow asphalt walk; to their right, beyond a fence, was a grassy yard where cheetahs roamed during the day. Ahead of them was a door, fitted with chicken wire between double panes of glass, and a sign that read, JUNGLE WALK. High metal rods with netting stretched between them arched outward beyond the door; it was a walk-through flight cage.

The door was unlocked, but it led only into a vestibule. There were two other doors, one into the flight cage, which was locked, and one out to the right, back outside, onto a raised companionway. This door was unlocked, and they passed through. The cheetah yard was back on their right, and on their left, beneath an eight-foot drop, two huge white rhinos lay sleeping among scattered piles of hay, breathing slow and deep.

Asleep on the hay—it struck Luís like a surrealistic nativity, and he wondered what kind of savior would be born in such a stable.

"Goddamn," hissed Esteban. "We can't do it out in the open. It takes too long." He thought for a second. "Come on, we try the others."

First checking around corners for security guards, they ran in a crouch past this paddock and turned left, downhill past the big diorama with the different animals in it, left again past the black rhinos' paddocks, which were empty, and finally left still again, up a smaller walkway that dead-ended at a six-foot board gate, padlocked, with a sign that read, PERSONNEL ONLY.

Making sure they were not followed, they scaled this gate, which rattled under their weight, and once on the other side, hunched their way to the locked metal door of a squat-looking concrete block building.

As Esteban squinted into the shadows, Luís extracted from his bag a long-handled pair of lock snips, fit the blades tightly against the loop of the padlock, and began to squeeze with all his might, one handle of the snips against his meaty chest, both hands pulling down on the other. He grimaced hard before the snips chewed their way through, and the broken lock flopped against the door with a small hollow bang. Luís put the snips back into the satchel and removed a flashlight.

He opened the steel door a few inches and leaned in, shining the light around. "Is okay," he whispered.

Esteban thought he heard something. Quickly he pulled from his own bag a machine pistol fitted with a silencer and a 50-round clip, which he snapped into place as he jogged silently back to the wooden gate. He saw nothing when he peeked through a knothole, then carefully chinned himself to look over. Nothing. He ran back to the rhino house.

Luís had entered, and Esteban followed, closing the door behind him. They shined the flashlight about, and found they were in a service area about eight feet by twenty. Opposite the door, the whole width of the building, was a barricade of metal pipes, four inches thick, set two, four, and six feet off the ground, running through concrete posts six feet apart. The cow rhino stood opposite them; she seemed calm. The only people she had ever seen inside her house were the keepers and the vet. She was curious, but not afraid.

Esteban saw a door off to the right and tried it; it was unlocked, and led to the adjoining quarters for the bull. He had heard the commotion and gotten to his feet; Luís looked quickly in, too, and saw the bull looking at them from the gloom behind his own barricade.

"All right," Esteban said quietly, "we got to hurry."

For just a second the beam from Luís's flashlight searched out the calf, standing stock still against the side wall, his head instinctively down, uncertain what it all meant.

"No," whispered Esteban. "We leave him alone. Shine the light over there, on her." He stood on the lower pipe of the cow's barricade and aimed the machine pistol over the top of it. She faced more toward him than Luís, and in this square-on stance he could not kill her with a single shot.

"Okay, we do it the hard way," he muttered. As Luís held the flashlight on her he fired a short burst that peppered her from the withers down to her chest, the muzzle flashes lighting the interior like a fast strobe, eerie, violent, with a sound like firecrackers stuffed under a pillow.

The flashing rips of pain caught her unawares and she staggered into the wide steel sliding door that led out into her paddock. The delicately clumsy legs that curved in under her gave her no breadth of stance, and she hit the door with a resounding bang of the wheels in their tracks. "Shit!" spat Esteban, "you wake the whole place up!"

The bullets shredded her upper lungs but hit nothing instantly mortal; she looked through the bars dumbly and painfully and without comprehension. She opened her mouth in her labored breathing and coughed out great black clots of gore every few seconds, as some of the breath she sucked in sobbed through the holes in her side, making the blood bubble through before it collected in drops big enough to roll down to her chest.

She saw the beam of light wobble as Luís mounted the pipes, and turned her dim eyes to follow it. As she did so she exposed her neck, and Esteban fired another burst, severing her spinal cord. The stark sudden limpness rippled through her body, as visible as a pebble tossed into still water. She fell straight down in a sudden heap of limp meat, two tons of her that hit the floor with a sickening whump, straight down onto her feet, which tucked under her as delicately as a cat on a doormat, and she groaned and yielded up her ghost.

Esteban slapped Luís on the butt and motioned him over the barricade. "Go on. I get the other one."

Luís landed on the other side in a soft shallow mat of alfalfa hay, unzipping his bag as he approached the body, all the while with his eyes steadily on the calf, ready to vault back over the barrier if it so much as twitched in his direction. It didn't; with it's head still down it backed up, first one step and then two and three, until its rump wedged into the corner. "Good," said Luís softly, "you just stay there." He had moved all the way over to the cow's body before he looked down at her. Goddamn, he thought, why couldn't she have fallen on her side? Her head was too close to the door for him to get behind it, much too heavy to move and too awkward to straddle—no way was he going to park his *cojones* over a rhino's horns and just hope she was dead while he worked on her. There was no choice but to squat right in the slop of blood and shreds of lung tissue around her mouth. You're a poet, he thought derisively, it's your own kind of justice.

From his satchel he pulled a hacksaw, and set the bag down a couple of feet back, out of the blood. Trying to gain some footing in the slippery gore about her head, Luís squatted and felt the base of her forehorn, trying to feel where to begin, but it joined the skin so smoothly he didn't know how deep to go. He had never done this before. Finally he thought, Hell, it's worth so much a few ounces one way or another can't make any difference. Setting the blade right at the join he pulled it toward him four times, starting a groove, before sawing in earnest. He was nervous at first, looking toward her open eye, half afraid she might not be dead after all, that she might have one toss left in her and do to him what he had seen in a couple of movies. Out of the corner of his eye he saw the door to the other room light weirdly in a half-dozen quick flashes, again the report of muffled fire-crackers. Even a silencer can only do so much.

As the hacksaw bit deep into her horn he lost his fear and concentrated on the work. It took twenty minutes to get through both of them, the blade too hot to touch by the time he was finished.

Esteban finished with the bull five minutes before he did. Its horns were smaller, and his uncle kept a nervous watch out the door, urging him to hurry up. Just as Luís stuffed the rear horn and the hacksaw in his bag, Esteban shushed him. "Somebody comin'!" he whispered.

Luís froze, his glance darting to the calf to make certain it was still rooted in its corner, as Esteban squinted out the door, the machine pistol poised over his shoulder. Very faintly Luís heard footsteps, un-hurried, hard-soled shoes that crunched on bits of caliche gravel. The sounds came from outside the gate, as the night security paced his rounds in the cool spring night. The guard had been on the downhill side of the gibbon cages when he heard the hollow clang of the rhino's barn door echo through the paddocks. It didn't alarm him. The rhinos butted their doors a few times every night, when they wanted out to pee or take a dump. Their toilet places were outside, by the east walls, and they hated soiling the inside of their houses. The guard looked forward to summer. When the nightly lows got above seventy degrees the black rhinos could stay out in their paddocks if they wanted. The big white rhinos were out already, as they were hardier to the chill, and he turned up the walk to check on them. Usually he would linger there awhile, enjoying the sight of them at night, chuffing slowly pale gray around their paddock, and when they slept, their nostrils blew up little white clouds of caliche dust, evoking their ancestors painted on the cave walls at Lascaux. He could watch them sleep, and know what the last Ice Age looked like.

They hadn't disturbed the lock on the keepers' gate when they jumped it, and the guard shouldn't have noticed anything amiss. From his crack in the door Esteban watched him cross to the left, above the "Jungle Walk" flight cage, and watched him lean casually on the limestone wall above the white rhino paddock. When he finally moved away he went downhill, past the big diorama with the giraffes and zebras, down past the elephants. Esteban slipped outside, motioning Luís to follow, and stood on a fence to keep sight of the guard until he descended the steps at the gibbon house and turned out of sight.

"Let's go!"

They jumped the gate again, Luís first, who caught the bags that Esteban tossed over, and fled uphill, past the thatched gazebo, back into the equipment yard. Esteban covered their getaway like a guerrilla, the machine pistol over his shoulder. They peeked over the green board fence to look for headlights, before climbing out the same way they got in. Flat on their bellies in the mesquite thicket, they looked down into the street. Esteban picked up a small pebble, waiting for Juan and Ramón to drive by again.

Two other cars passed before the dark blue Oldsmobile approached; Esteban tossed the pebble onto it and watched it cruise on by. On the next pass Juan Barilla checked both directions carefully. "Is okay," he said.

"Stop," said Ramón.

The instant they saw the car slow, Esteban and Luís jumped from the thicket down into the street, and into the car. It took less than five seconds.

"What you get?" Ramón asked Esteban.

"We couldn't get the big ones, they were out in the yard. The little ones were in their houses, we got both of them."

"Let's see." He reached forward and Luís passed his satchel back to him.

Juan crossed Broadway and turned right on New Braunfels, all the way down to I-10, and headed east, back toward Houston.

Ramón snapped open a copy of the *Houston Post* and laid it across his lap. Zipping open both bags, he set the four severed horns on the newspapers, their bloody bases smearing over the sketched skinny models of a double-page Foley's ad. He picked it up. *"Aí, María,* I say maybe ten kilos, altogether."

"How much you think he give you for them?" asked Esteban quietly.

Luís turned around to listen, but Ramón glanced up at him and he knew he shouldn't have appeared so anxious.

"Is hard to say," said Ramón. "Maybe sixty, maybe eighty thousand."

"They're worth double that. Maybe more."

"Well, he got a market for them. We don't. He gotta make some money, too. We doin' all right."

Luís turned back around to the front. Ramón would buy him some nice things for this night's work. Splendid things—a watch, maybe a car, spending money. But Ramón would not pay him real money, not a share. Uncle Ramón would take care of him, but real money was independence, and that was the one thing he dared not want yet.

3 🔥🔥🔥🔥🔥🔥🔥🔥🔥🔥🔥

ERIC JACKSON heard the alarm radio click on, and creased open one eye to see the digital red 6:30 peering unforgivingly back at him. He reached out and turned the volume down—Frescobaldi, the G major Toccata from the church sonatas, an exalted piece of music that made him feel serene and complete, as though—he drifted back to sleep— he were lying in state in an abbey. Candles lit at the corners of the bier; cowled monks praying within their dim gothic vaults. Ever so gradually the chords of music grew and shifted, like different angles of jeweled high sunlight through tall stained glass. When its last echo faded, Eric Jackson breathed in, deep and renewed. Life was fast and confused. It was important to cling to what serenity he could.

Eric got out of bed, stretched a pair of shorts over his muscled thighs and hips and twisted into a bathrobe. He emerged from the hall and started across the den to the kitchen when he caught sight of the crucifix on the wall. There was a small footstool under it, cushioned in red velvet. He had almost passed it, but stopped and knelt quickly, crossing himself. "Heavenly Father," he whispered rapidly, "thank you for another day of life and the possibility to be your servant. Humbly I ask the help of Saint Francis in my work this and every day. Increase my awareness of the sanctity of all life, and especially the many lives given into my care. And Lord, guard my wife; help us to reconcile our differences, and live together once more after your holy ordinance. *In nomini patri,*" he crossed himself again, "*et fili, et spiritu sancti.* Amen."

He made, as it were, breakfast, sliding a frozen Weight Watchers packet into the microwave. As he did now every morning, after prayer, he inspected from the high battlements of his mind the arguments for and against having separated from Liz Ann. He had committed to her, he had a history with her and was comfortable, more or less, with her. But she had sought to be not his helpmate, but his life's work itself, and when he found his own life's work, her disinterest in it, her jealousy of it and her constant setting of herself in competition with it, had so undermined what he had once felt for her, that his marriage became unendurable. It may well have been a mistake to marry before his life's work became clear to him; certainly he had seen it among his college buddies, that they married too young, because they were horny or were terrified of growing old alone, or because after an intense and mostly childish campaign they'd managed to get a real babe to give them a second look. But they married, and discovered only later as they grew older and grew apart, that they were all wrong for each other. But Liz Ann's departure had thrown into the sharpest possible relief the difference between his life's needs as they pressed on him now, and the tenets and requirements of his religious background.

As a boy Eric Jackson had never set foot in a public school; the sisters had taught him everything. They were sharp and they were good teachers, and Eric respected them, but neither they nor his parents, while taking care that he develop a sound faith in God, had ever let a real-life threat approach close enough to challenge the precepts he was assimilating. He had been, in a word, sheltered, and it left him unprepared to deal with something as devastating as the prospect of divorce.

Other men would have turned Liz Ann out without regret, but for him—perhaps it was his year in the Jesuit Seminary in Louisiana, which gave him direction but also taught him that he could not live without a woman, or perhaps it was only that he was less hard and cynical than other men, but whatever it was, it was important to him to know that he had done a right thing, or more to the point, done right by her as well as himself.

After breakfast he sat in his study, staring uncertainly at the telephone before punching in a number. "Hi, babe."

There was just enough of a pause to let him know he shouldn't have called. "Hello, Eric."

"How you doing?"

"All right."

"I just wanted to ask—today's a big day out at the park—can you be there?"

Again she didn't answer for a second. "I don't know," she finally said. "I'll try."

"Liz Ann—" Oh, God, he thought, here we go again. It's too early for this. "I really wish you could."

Six years they had been married, until his slavery to The Refuge had finally broken her. Today was its christening—his triumph, she knew, but a ceremony that could only punctuate her own defeat. She thought, Why can't he understand that? He had to wait again before she said, "Richard and I are meeting a client at ten to go over a reception. Maybe we can swing by after that."

"Does he have to come?"

"It's the best I can do, Eric. We won't be able to stay very long."

There was no quick way to get to work; the shortest distance was the most tedious. From the suburbs at the far west end of Westheimer, near the intersection of Interstate 10 and State Highway 6, he drove south on State 6, stopping and starting and stopping his new, silver-green Saturn at the traffic lights for more than twenty miles. Houston angled away further to the northeast and then north as he continued through the sumpy flats between Oyster Creek and the Brazos River bottoms, as depressing a strip of mobile homes and bait shops and auto salvage yards as you could find in the entire South. Well, the bait shops weren't so bad; at least he had found a way to turn them to his purpose. Still, it was Eric's habit to look beyond them, into the salt-grass prairies and marshes and winding creeks that blanket the Texas coast for fifty miles inland from the Gulf. In them, even screened as they were by that spotty collage of frowzy roadside enterprise, he could renew himself, take heart in the vaulting flight of a heron as it pumped its way up and up on those huge white gleaming angel's wings, take refreshment from a stiffening southerly breeze that bent down waves of saltgrass before it and which still carried the far faint smell of the sea. Many humid mornings during summer he seemed like the only one on the road without his air conditioner on, the windows all down and the salt breeze whipping in warm, quick eddies through the car.

In the little town of Arcola he turned south on Ranch Road 521, skirting the winding oxbows of the east bank of Oyster Creek. It was here, in this countryside neither used nor useless, amid the smattering of people neither urban nor rural who mostly wanted only to escape from it, that Eric Jackson had found his refuge, a place he and his animals could escape to.

Two fences appeared along the side of the road, one inside the other, chain link topped with barbed wire, separated by a moat fifteen feet wide whose water shined like silver as the morning light bounced off it. The place had been a prairie, threaded with marshy bayous, until they drained it, and dug the ditch along the road and scooped out extensive ponds, some of them twenty feet deep, and piled up the dirt to use in landscaping the islands. What lay within the fences was obscured by a high, thick green planting inside it of shrubs and vines and creepers. The outer fence was a stout ten-foot deer fence, the inner one six feet high, topped with triple-strand barbed wire. Every fifty yards they had wired signs to the outer fence:

DANGER/WILD ANIMALS

PELIGRO/ANIMALES FIERAS

Eric turned right—west—on a linking road that bounded the south edge of the property, as the moated double fence continued straight as a ruler along the right shoulder of the road. After a mile and a half he turned into a broad driveway that spanned the ditch. Spinning by his left as he turned was the sign, in plain black metal letters anchored in white marble veneer, that read:

FINAL REFUGE

WILDLIFE FOUNDATION

The two fences narrowed together at a small, open-windowed kiosk, from within which a uniformed guard electronically rolled aside the gate. Eric hardly had to slow as he motored through, trading waves with the guard. He proceeded up a broad asphalt drive bordered by swaths of emerald-green deep-pile St. Augustine grass, and beyond that, a further thick planting of shrubs that obscured the fence behind them. At the head of the drive was a building of the same marble veneer as the sign. It was two stories high, the bright white broken at intervals by perpendicular full-length windows of black-tinted glass.

From the drive a spur curled off to the left into a five-level parking garage. As he approached it Eric glanced upward at its top, and saw arching away from its other side still-higher parabolas of a flight cage webbed with blue plastic-coated chain link. By backing the flight cage right up against the parking garage, they had saved money in the construction, created a superb facility for breeding Andean condors, and, by installing one-way windows looking into it at each level from the garage, engaged visitors' interest in the program before they even got out of their cars. It was Eric's own idea, and it was being written up in the next *Interzoo Yearbook,* but it was only one trick he had devised— the whole of The Refuge was a monument to his multiuse philosophy. Waste not, as they said, want not.

Inside the garage he bypassed the ramp to the upper levels, stopping instead at a striped barrier. When he inserted a passcard into the metal box in front of it, the barricade jerked upward with a hum and he drove into the staff lot nearer the building. He parked, pulling his briefcase out of the car after him, and walked up the sidewalk toward the building. He was wearing safari shorts and a khaki shirt, athletic socks and sneakers, with his briefcase at his side, exulting in the privilege of underdressing in a world where the boss is supposed to wear a suit.

He had designed the handles of the black glass doors himself— looping cast-bronze cobras, modeled after the ones he had seen at the herpetarium in Ft. Worth. He grasped one of their coils and passed into a black-floored loggia, rest rooms to the right and left, and in front of him two turnstiles between flanking cash registers and glass display cases. There was nothing in them yet but there would be tomorrow. The loggia was two stories high, the full height of the building, and from the doors he could see curving up the back wall a staircase of open stone steps, the same black as the floor, with an aluminum balustrade and slick mahogany banister.

They had decided on khaki uniforms for all the staff, whether they were involved directly with the animals or not. Behind one of the registers stood a young attendant, and on the counter by him were three stacks of descriptive pamphlets. Eric greeted him and set his briefcase down. "They got here. How do they look?"

"Pretty good." The kid was tall and affable and sandy-haired, a student at Alvin Community College. The Refuge was really closer to Alvin than it was to Houston, and hiring some students from there allowed Eric to remind the civic groups that the park benefited the local economy as well as world ecology. He spoke regularly and often at Lions and Kiwanis club lunches, and if anything, considered them at least as important as the round of public school and local talk show dates that are an important bloc of every zoo director's calendar. Business is where the money is, and businessmen inured to the idea that anything to do with conservation is a drain on commerce, needed to see that it could generate jobs, too.

The brochure folded out like a road map. On the front side were panels with photographs and explanatory text, with visiting hours and admission fees. The back side was a map of the grounds; the three thousand acres of former prairie had been graded, following the natural contours of the bayous that drained the tract, into five large islands and several small ones, connected by long metal bridges or catwalks. What this created was a map of the world, in small. The islands were the continents—South America on the lower left, just outside the administration building; Africa at the lower middle, Australia on the lower right. North America lay on the upper left, Eurasia at the upper middle and right. The world's large islands with important wildlife, such as Madagascar, were represented in The Refuge by smaller islands, like way stations along the catwalks, at their natural places in the geography.

Eric nodded his head slowly. "Yeah, this looks good."

Not shown on the map, but equally important to running the park, were facilities located at various places around the edge of the grounds. The veterinary hospital and quarantine areas were isolated in the northeast, beyond Japan, as it were. The sewage-treatment facility, power plant and pumping stations were in the southeast. A western extension contained a two hundred–acre farm, where they were able to grow nearly all the food the animals needed. The farm had its own gate, which opened onto a road that looped around the entire periphery of the place, just inside the double fence. All five of the major islands could be serviced from this road, so that the animals could be cared for without disrupting the natural vistas that the tourists would have from the other side.

Eric folded the brochure back up and put it, with several extras, in his briefcase. "Make sure everybody gets one. Is the mayor here yet?"

"Nope. I got my eye out for her, though."

"Good." Eric passed through the turnstile. "When she gets here, send her up to Stephanie. She can go to the press conference with me." As he headed up the black stone staircase, Eric glanced back out the glass front wall and saw other cars beginning to arrive, turning into the parking garage. Coming up the walk, almost to the door, he saw a sharply dressed young brunette; with her was a fellow shouldering a video camera with NEWS AT 10 stenciled on the side of it.

He walked back to his left through the upstairs corridor, opening a glass door with tall white painted letters reading RECEPTION. "Good morning, Stephanie, how are you?"

His secretary was a short woman with long, bushy, platinum-blond hair bunched into a pony tail. She was not fat, but stocky in a healthy and ruddy sort of way, as though she had grown up milking cows and got the prettier for it. She handed him his messages; he glanced at the empty mailboxes and surmised the staff were all in.

"Pinch your cheeks, doll," he told her. "The VIPs will be here any minute. You might dance for them or something until we get finished."

At the end of a short back hall he entered a large board room soft with deep blue carpet. Eight people sat around the flat, grained expanse of a mahogany conference table, chatting amiably.

"Good morning, I hope I haven't kept you waiting." Eric poured himself a cup of coffee from a pot on a long, low credenza along the side wall. At his place at the head of the table lay a photocopied spread sheet of the previous months' finances; he picked it up and strolled to the window, pretending to read it over. The long wall opposite the door was glass, floor to ceiling, untinted but tilted outward to kill the glare. This was the back wall of the building, and looked down onto the grounds. On the world map of The Refuge, the administration building was near the east coast of South America—on the pampas, as it were. The Andes Mountains, with the condors' flight cages that adjoined the garage, were to the west. To the north were the Gran Chaco, the rain forest, and the Guiana Highlands. Beyond them, Central America opened like a funnel into the Mexican Desert and then North America—just like on the map of the real world. Visible down to the right was a long metal catwalk, a hundred fifty yards across the open water of the pond that represented the South Atlantic, to Africa. A puff of wind ruffled the surface of the water, scattering a rush of brilliant pinpoints where the sun struck the wavelets.

The Refuge was not as farfetched nor improbable a concept as one might think at first. Crowded urban zoos had off-loaded onto spacious rural acreages ever since the London Zoo opened Whipsnade Park in 1931. San Diego now had more tourists going through their out-of-town Wild Animal Park than through the original zoo itself, wonderful as it is. The Bronx Zoo had opened a research and breeding station that covered a whole one of the Sea Islands off the Georgia coast, and they didn't even allow visitors. The Refuge was only a little bigger than those, but more broadly conceived, organized to combine research, breeding, and educational exhibits, as well as commercial sales to other zoos.

Eric put the spread sheet and his messages together in his briefcase to examine later, and sat down. "Jake, you want to go first?"

"Well, everything's pretty quiet just now." The chief veterinarian was a curly red-haired fellow from rural central Texas with an accent that could hurt your ears. "The only thing I really need to mention is, that Arabian oryx dropped her foal yesterday but got a prolapsed uterus. That's pretty unusual for an antelope but probably ain't no big deal. I poked her back together and I wouldn't breed her for a couple of years, but she and the calf are both all right. Bouncing baby boy."

Eric looked up at a balding black man of about fifty, seated directly across the table from Jake Teal. "Roman, do we have any offers for him?"

Roman Franklin and Consuela the personnel manager were the only ones at the table not wearing khaki. Franklin wore instead an impeccable black suit with a silver chain connecting the collar buttons of his shirt. "The Memphis Zoo wants to buy him as soon as he's weaned. They have a herd of six, but their buck is getting on in years."

Eric wrote a note on his pad. "Anybody else?"

"Baltimore will trade us buck for buck to freshen the blood lines."

"Jake, what do you think?"

"Both our bucks are pretty vigorous and they're both founders— I'd hold with what we got and take the cash."

Eric looked back to Roman. "How is Memphis? Can they give him a good home?"

"They're above average. I mean, they're not the best, but they're on the way up, and they've got a pretty good antelope program going."

"All right, Roman, set it up. Who keeps the stud books? Phoenix?"

"No. They got famous for being the first ones in the country to breed them, but the program now is managed out of San Diego."

"Oh, yes. Right. Have we run it through ISIS yet?"

"Nope," said Jake. "Lucy will check the computer this afternoon and make sure we're not sending him to his aunts or something."

ISIS, thought Eric. The International Species Information System. Computers, networks, data links—God, breeding animals used to be so easy. People see baby animals in a zoo or a wildlife park and they think, animals hump, and make babies. They have no idea. With so few specimens available from the really endangered species, to breed them in such a way as to maintain their genetic viability almost takes a frigging calculus degree. "Jake, any other mothers we need to talk about?"

"Naw, everybody's doing pretty fine. Except maybe Lakshmi. She needs to drop her calf pretty soon now. I'm gettin' a little concerned about her 'cause she's gettin' old and actin' kinda grouchy, but I got Lucy checkin' on her."

Eric wrote himself another note. Lakshmi was a stolid old cow Indian one-horned rhinoceros they had taken in on a compassionate care basis. Her history was not a happy one. An accredited zoo had rescued her from a roadside tourist trap where she had lived in virtual isolation for as long as the then-owners could remember. The zoo had believed her too old to breed, and the shortage of zoo space for Indian rhinos had become critical. When a breeding pair became available to them through the SSP—the species survival plan—they were faced with the choice of either finding her another home or euthanizing her. Eric had seen the zoo's announcement on the data net and snagged her for freight cost. Jake and Lucy had considered implanting an embryo from the freezer to see if she could carry it, but life in the more natural environment of The Refuge had rejuvenated her to the point that she mated with their bull. But still, she was old, and the pregnancy had been hard on her. "Do you think we ought to pull her from the exhibit?"

"You mean Lucy?" There was laughter around the table. "Oh, you mean Lakshmi; aw, hell no, she's a trouper. If she starts gettin' too hinky we'll just stick her in maternity."

"Roman, we have any other business?"

"We got a letter yesterday from the Edinburgh Zoo; they want some black rhino semen as soon as we can get it available."

Eric looked up. "Why don't they get that from London? They have a bull and they're a lot closer."

"They want fresh blood." He grinned suddenly, revealing a picket of bright white teeth. "That's what we got for sale, man, good American genes."

Jake Teal now wrote himself a note. "Well, I'll get ol' Junior lined up to give us a donation tomorrow afternoon. That's about his favorite activity, anyway. Boy, I mean to tell you, he just gets a whiff of them rubber gloves and that KY jelly, he starts gettin' a hard-on before we even get him in the squeeze cage."

There was more laughter around the table, not so much at Jake, but because they all knew how lucky they were to have Junior. Of all the species from whom semen samples can be obtained by electrode stimulation, the great pachyderms—elephants and rhinos—are not among them, not just because of their size but their difficult-to-reach, undescended testicles. Bull elephants would not tolerate manipulation by human hands, but rarely, very rarely, a rhino was found who was amenable to the procedure. Ever since they put the word out in the *International Zoo News,* orders had been regular. Junior was a gold mine.

Things got quiet again, and Eric looked around the table. "Anybody else? Keepers?" The head keeper and four senior keepers looked at each other and shook their heads. "Jake, no word from Stan about the Javas?"

"Not yet."

Eric ran his fingers through his hair, light brown, thick and wavy. In an age of styling mousse, he wore his dry and loose and natural. "What do you think is keeping him?"

"Maybe it rained and washed the trails out," said Jake. "That's what happened when we were there, remember? It's only a hundred miles from the reserve up to Jakarta, but there's no road hardly at all west of Malingping."

"Yeah, I guess so." The Javan rhinoceros was the most critically endangered large mammal on earth. Only about fifty remained alive, every one of them in the Udjung Kulon Reserve, on the western tip of the island of Java, in the Republic of Indonesia. Not a single specimen, let alone a pair capable of breeding or donating gametes to the freezer, existed in a zoo anywhere as insurance. Any one of a number of calamities—flood, volcano, disease—could wipe out most or all the animals in that last wild refuge. Representatives from zoos and game parks around the world had lobbied the Indonesian government for decades to send at least a few of those last fifty abroad for safekeeping, but thus far they had labored without success. The Indonesian authorities felt their prestige was at stake, that in their own eyes they could not give in to the pressure without admitting they could not adequately safeguard the last Javan rhinos. They also resented the impression they got that the zoos, especially zoos in the West, seemed more excited at the possibility of exhibiting such rare treasures than they were intent on fulfilling a mission of biological salvation. It was a suspicion made all the worse by Indonesia's long and dismal history of colonial exploitation. Anti-Western sentiment there was still high— strong enough that local authorities could not give in to Western pressure, even pressure from biologists, without losing face at home. And in their culture, death—even the death of the last Javan rhinos on Earth—was preferable to seeming to cozy up to Europeans or Americans.

One American zoo had tried to show their good faith by providing the game guards at Udjung Kulon with badly needed short-wave radios, but the gesture had backfired, handing the opposition the argument that the guards were now better equipped than ever to protect the last Javas where they were.

Eric Jackson had met with officials in Jakarta four different times, and was sure he had them on the verge of acquiescing. He did not emphasize the inadequacy of the protection in the reserve, but in his own mind that was still an issue, for the mere existence of Udjung Kulon had not prevented the beautiful Javan tiger from slipping under the dark waters of extinction. Rather he stressed the danger posed by natural disasters; the peninsula was a coastal lowland susceptible to typhoon or tidal wave—and the distinct possibility existed that an epidemic of rinderpest or some other disease could wipe out the wild stock before steps could be taken to save them. He had shown them blueprints for a special enclosure being built for the rhinos in The Refuge, where they would be housed with other native Indonesian wildlife, not just animals but plants of their natural diet as well. When Eric was able to show them the breeding successes he had obtained with Indian rhinos—even old Lakshmi—using the same technique, the government gave him permission to send his chief ecologist, Stan Over, to Udjung Kulon to track rhinos and record their specific diets.

The possibility of spiriting a pair of Javan rhinos out of the hazards of Udjung Kulon was at this moment at the center of Eric Jackson's existence. Stan Over had been gone for three weeks, and it was time for him to report back.

Roman Franklin tried to reassure him. "If he's back in Jakarta we'll probably get a fax in tonight. No, wait, that'll be Sunday over there. Maybe Monday."

Eric still looked sullen. They all knew how important the Javas were to him, and how he worried over them—worried that something might queer the deal. "Well, he'll be fine," Eric said at last. "Consuela, your people ready for tomorrow?"

"I think so." Consuela Estevez was the personnel manager, a quick-moving matron of fifty. She had six children herself, and mothered the staff and employees with a chemistry of compassion and tyranny, just like they were more of her own. "The only thing," she said, "those stories in the newspapers have been really good. We may get hit with more people that we expected. You know, we don't want to hire more help than we need, but we don't want to get caught short, either. Trouble is, we just don't know how it'll go. We've never let the public in before."

"Roman, what do you think?" asked Eric.

"Well, where do you think you might run short?"

"Concessions," said Consuela, "grounds keeping, that kind of thing."

"Unskilled-type people."

"Right."

"Maybe you could call a couple of temp places, and clear the way to get us some help p.d.q. in case we do need it?"

"That'll work," she agreed. Once again Consuela gave silent thanks for where she worked. When Eric found her she was running a fast-food franchise near the Astrodome. Her district manager was a real self-improvement, pyramid-marketing–type jerk half her age who got bent out of joint if she ever understaffed, but even worse if she scheduled more help than she wound up needing. Like all franchise managers, she'd learned to hide the expense of temporaries in her meat cost to keep the "wiener," as she called him, from finding out. But there was none of that here. The whole operation was experimental, and no one on the support staff could know exactly what they were getting into until they got a routine going. And even after that, she knew Eric would keep all his people even-tempered and supportive.

The intercom buzzed sharply and Eric pressed the button. "Yeah, Steph?"

"The mayor and her people are here, sir."

"Thanks." Her people—Well, boy, he thought, she brought an entourage. Eric leaned back and looked around the table. "Okay, it's show time." They started putting their papers away. "I don't need to tell you what an important day this is. So just remember, politicians get the front row and lots of applause."

Roman Franklin scowled, his cultivated business voice reverting suddenly to an angry, honest ethnicity as he pushed back from the table. "Yeah, well, they ain't given us bean dip to help us out so far."

Eric stood up. "I know. But maybe they will yet." He put his hand on the doorknob and whispered urgently, "And for God's sake, don't let anybody get away with calling us a zoo."

4

THEY FILED THROUGH the narrow corridor into Stephanie's reception area. Eric was well acquainted with the mayor, a short, middle-aged woman, wiry and feisty, who possessed all the enormous energy and enthusiasm required of a populist city politician. She strode over to him and pumped his hand with a strongly self-confident grip. "Well, your big day is finally here. Congratulations."

Beginning with, "How great to see you, I'm so glad you were able to come out," Eric melded into the persona that, (while he knew it was a charade) he had perfected as a necessary tool of his business: he schmoozed. Stephanie had utilized her time well, fitting the VIPs with name tags, and now that the staff were out, she circulated and sometimes interrupted conversations to plaster the tags on the staff as soon as she wrote them out.

The keepers, though, felt out of place in this scene and made their way downstairs as soon as politeness allowed. People who care so passionately for animals as to invest their lives in caring for them very often do so at the expense of social skills that their institutions could use for public relations. Animal-oriented people who can really work a room of politicians and moneybags are an avidly sought commodity. Eric usually excused his people from this duty and shouldered it himself, though in this instance he retained Jake and Roman so that none of the mayor's people should lack for attention. And the mayor had brought a car full—the Houston Zoo people had come separately, but she was attended by her parks director and her city personnel manager, a public relations aide, who toted a camera, and an older Asian man who did more listening than talking. She also made a point of introducing Eric to a liaison from the Houston public schools, who expressed interest in bringing more keepers and animals in contact with students, and arranging field trips to the park.

As they moved downstairs, the mayor took Eric's arm with an air that a confidence was about to be exchanged. "You never told me that your business manager is an African-American."

"It never occurred to me. I only hired him because he's good."

"I wish I had that luxury." The mayor's short, curly blond hair bounced to her tread on the stairs as they descended. "Our personnel department is under constant pressure to recruit and promote more minorities. We've just added a bunch of people to the Board of Directors of the Zoological Society to reflect more community representation. My friend Albert Chu down there is one of them. Let me catch him, I want you to meet him. He's interested in your work out here—" she leaned closer and whispered, "—plus he's got more money than God. I'm sure you'll want to know him." She released him and went more quickly down the stairs.

"Her friend, my hiney!" Eric suddenly felt Roman Franklin's big black hand encircle his collar, and his growling whisper was right in his ear. "He finances her campaigns and she keeps the cops out of his books."

"Really?"

"If he's got books."

"What does he do?"

"International trade of some kind. He doesn't talk about it."

Roman broke off when the mayor returned with her friend in tow, and Albert Chu extended his hand first to him. "Good morning, Mr. Franklin. I am Albert Chu. We have met before, in Rotary."

"Indeed we have. How are you?"

The mayor introduced Chu to Eric as they crossed the loggia into the lecture hall located under the upstairs offices. Eric conducted them to the front row of seats and stepped up onto a low stage and waited for the room to quiet. Stephanie quietly set up a video camera at the door and signaled him when it was rolling.

He had rehearsed the speech enough that it sounded relaxed and extemporaneous. They took it as axiomatic that animals in the wild were dying off, and whole species vanishing, at such an alarming rate that captive populations had to be maintained as insurance for their survival. To meet this challenge, zoos around the world had altered their philosophy from pure exhibition and public enjoyment, to coordinating the breeding of rare animals, guided by computer-verified "species survival plans" for each species. For five years The Refuge had existed on its present location building up its physical plant and staff, and most importantly its gene pool of what the species survival plans called founders, vigorous specimens, often taken from the wild, whose blood lines were needed to maintain the genetic variety of animals already in captivity. Now they were ready to admit the public, beginning the next day, partly as an educational resource, and partly, very frankly, because they needed the revenue that would be generated by doing so.

Eric Jackson had also anticipated many of their questions and was able to dispatch them quickly.

Aren't there enough zoos in the country already, and one only as far away as Houston? Why another?

"Well, understand first we aren't a zoo." He noted a few sardonic smirks and he knew that they knew what a ribbing the Bronx Zoo took when they unilaterally renamed themselves a wildlife conservation park. "But of course," he regained the floor, "old concepts die hard. We are more of a clearinghouse and coordinating center for the zoos that do already exist. Just like when you borrow money from your bank, your bank borrows it from the federal reserve. In fact, you've probably heard the federal reserve called the 'banker's bank.' That would describe more closely what we do."

Where in the world did they find the money for such a place?

"Good grant writing." He smiled, as though he intended that answer to suffice, but the reporter persisted.

"Come on, zoos all over the country have been applying for grants for years without a lot of success. How did you break through?"

"Well, all right. I guess we didn't tell the foundations anything they didn't know already, but perhaps we told it to them in a way that was new to them. I think we finally got them to realize that wildlife preservation was the one global crisis that did not come within the purview of any world authority. Third-world development has the World Bank, disease epidemics have the World Health Organization, and on down the line. But the survival of any one endangered species, be it an ape in Borneo or a lizard in Brazil, is a unique difficulty because it may depend upon the budgetary charity of a local city council in Houston or Denver—or Great Bend, Kansas, for that matter, because that's where zoo funding comes from. Look at crime, and homelessness, and education, and inner-city infrastructure; municipal zoos simply cannot, even taken as a whole, mount a sufficient effort. They're all getting by and making do on budgets of usually less than half what they really need. And that's aside from the fact that they are getting so full that they have to neuter and even destroy animals that are endangered in the wild, just because there is no damn room for them in the zoo."

Another hand went up. "Larry Davis, University of Houston." Eric made a mental note of his name; he intended to speak at that school next fall. The boy was of medium build, with curly black hair and gray eyes framed by steel-rimmed glasses. Eric guessed he was about twenty, a sophomore or junior. "On that very point, wouldn't it be better to try to save them in the wild, in their own habitats? I mean, you may say you're not a zoo, but I don't see any representatives here from animal rights groups to back you up on that. Do you think it was appropriate to exclude them?"

"Yes." Eric Jackson glanced across the room at the chairman of that school's biology department, who had lowered his head, his hand covering his eyes. Always count on some bratty college reporter to try to create a story other than the one you were giving him. Fortunately Eric had anticipated it. "Or rather, there wasn't any question of including or excluding them. The tour that we are going to be giving you—"he glanced at his watch and smiled "—very shortly now, I promise, is just for you press, to show you what we have done, and what we are making available to the public. I will say, to try to address your question, that we here at The Refuge believe that the so-called animal rights groups play a very important role in the conservation of endangered wildlife, by keeping the debate focused where it should be—on the preservation of natural habitats around the world."

Eric wondered if the other reporters could sense the level of bullshit suddenly rising. He couldn't very well call the animal-rights people a parade of tennis-shoed goonballs with too much time on their hands. "We believe with them, in principle, that a wild animal's place is in the wild. We do differ with them on certain points. They believe that if a species is in danger of extinction, that fact should be used to increase pressure on the government involved to take steps to ensure its survival, and that to remove some to a captive setting lets those authorities off the hook. That point of view has some validity in theory, but we believe it is playing chicken with the survival of a species, and is misapplied to a government that may not give a damn or may simply be unable to cope with the economics of the situation. We also believe that the case for saving an endangered species cannot be made without studying their biology, and this really cannot be done in the wild. Their ecology, of course, by definition has to be studied in the wild, but their biology really can't be."

Eric glanced around the room, thinking, Thank God there aren't any field biologists in the room; they'd probably start a fist fight over a statement like that. "We also believe," he went on, "that the educational aspects are of vital importance. Most Americans will never be able to travel to New Guinea, or Antarctica. For them to be able to see and smell and in some cases touch wild animals in a naturalistic—if not totally natural—setting, is crucial to gaining their support for saving the world's habitats. Watching television, even if all they watch is 'Nova' and 'National Geographic,' just is not enough. Why aren't you taking notes?"

Larry Davis held up a tiny cassette recorder. "Got it all on tape."

"Good." Eric smiled, gesturing to Stephanie at the rear of the hall, with the video camera and tripod. "So have we." A titter from the crowd rose and fell. Eric expected Larry Davis to call PETA for a response—People for the Ethical Treatment of Animals—and felt no threat that a comment from them might appear next to his own. The animal "ethicists" were aesthetes, who had adopted as a philosophical value the idea that no animal should be captured, for any reason. The Refuge was involved with saving real species from real extinction, and Eric Jackson and his people could not afford such snottiness.

As soon as Larry Davis sat down several other hands shot up, but Eric raised his own hands to delay them. "I know you have a number of other questions, and I will be happy to answer them as we give you the tour. We have quite a large installation here, and we'd really like to get started. So if you will follow me . . ."

He led them out of the lecture hall back into the loggia. Off to their left, or to the right of the entrance as you entered the building, was a wide door that led into a long, narrow, dimly lit exhibit area. By very deliberate design, the only way for the public to get out onto the grounds was to pass through a series of three such halls. There was a large plaque over the door from the loggia that read SILENCE, and one of the reporters pointed to it. "You mean you don't want people talking in there?"

Eric laughed. "No, it's a description, not a command. You'll see." He had been aware of the ambiguity at the time they designed the building, and considered having the plaque read HALL OF SILENCE, but decided against it. If people thought they were being told to shut up, that would be appropriate enough, considering the hall's contents. The order of the scheme would eventually become apparent to them when they saw the plaques over the doors of the other two halls. Eric led them beneath SILENCE into the hall, where glass cases set into the walls faced each other across a width of twenty-five feet. It was a hundred fifty feet long, and in a thin line down the middle a set of bench-chairs, like what you see in the boarding gate of an airline terminal, backed up to each other, facing the glass of the cases from about ten feet away.

The reporters fanned out down both sides of the hall, soberly staring into cases that contained re-creations, or when possible, actual remains of extinct animals. The exhibits began by depicting the human-aided extinctions of prehistory—one contained bone fragments and a whole tusk of a woolly mammoth, scattered around a mock fire pit. Primitive stone weapons leaned against the back wall, which was a mural of feasting Cro-Magnon troglodytes. Small placards in front of the glass recounted evidence that in the most remote areas of Siberia the woolly mammoth may have hung on into the nineteenth or even the early-twentieth century. Sightings, reported by babbling, bug-eyed tribesmen of the area, had not been uncommon then. Indeed, it was possible—unlikely to be sure, but possible—that some still survived. It is hard to hide a herd of mammoth elephants, but in a dense taiga forest the size of the continental United States, it is possible.

The case opposite the mammoth remains told the story of the end of the giant moa of New Zealand, a ten-foot-tall emu-like bird whose bones, old but not fossilized, and rarely even some feathers, are found in caves that were used as Maori native campsites. Further down the hall the dates of extinctions became more recent, passing into the so-called Age of Exploration. There one case held remains and a model of the great auk, a seabird of the North Atlantic, and others told the stories of the blaubok antelope and the quagga, a zebra-like horse of Africa. One case contained a re-creation of the most famous extinction of all time, the dodo bird of Mauritius. Discovered by Portuguese navigators in need of replenishing the larders of their ships, the dodos waddled fat and flightless and curious, right up to the sailors who clubbed them down at will and laughed. For this trust they were extinguished in 1685. What a comment, thought Eric, that a creature so naturally trusting of human beings should be remembered by its name as a synonym for stupid. The largest case in the hall, forty feet long, contained a whole titanic skeleton of a Stellar's sea cow, an Arctic form of manatee. The mural on the back of the case depicted what appeared to be a whaling ship, only the men in the long boats were dodging icebergs to harpoon not whales but sea cows.

As the reporters made their way down the hall, the Age of Exploration gave way to the Age of Exploitation, and American history was not let off lightly. One case told the story of the Carolina parakeet, which until its extermination was the only native North American parrot. In the adjoining case was a re-creation of a passenger pigeon, stitched together from skins of domestic pigeons and mourning doves to get the right colors, and stretched onto a mold of the proper shape. While exploring the frontier, John James Audubon once saw a single flock of them a mile wide that flew over him all day long with the sky never lightening. The last one, a female named Martha, died in the Cincinnati Zoo in 1914.

In the back left corner of the SILENCE hall, instead of an exhibit case was a door similar to the one they had entered before, only over this one was the single word, STUPIDITY. It was the same size and configuration as SILENCE, and doubled back on it. Set in the wall, right in front of the door, unavoidable, were two cases, each surmounted by an eleven-figure odometer with numbers a foot high, similar to the one the tourists see in the Census Bureau in Washington. Only here, the first case depicted the plight of the world's rain forests, which produce much of the oxygen on which all life depends, whose warmth drives the world's weather patterns, and whose diversity of plants and animals is so rank that virtually every island and every valley contains life forms found nowhere else on earth. And the vast majority of it has not been examined for medicinal potential or other economic benefit—species are lost every single day before they can even be classified. In this exhibit there were no painted murals, but photographs, with explanatory text, of logging, and mining, and slash-and-burn agriculture, and why rain forest, once it is cut, cannot regenerate naturally. Once gone, it is gone for good. The odometer was set to register their diminution, accurately, at 55 acres every minute. 3,300 acres per hour; 79,200 acres per day. An area five times the size of Manhattan, every day. 554,400 acres per week; 28,828,800 acres per year, an area nearly the size of New York state.

The case next to it showed the salient facts of world population growth. Its odometer had to be specially built to stand up to speed, for beginning only with the third column from the right—hundreds—did the figures spin slowly enough to be seen with the naked eye. It had been expensive, but in Eric's judgment, worth it.

He had even considered, briefly, a separate case dealing with the Catholic Church and its teachings on birth control. In his own mind, even as an ex-seminarian, he had no difficulty finding his Church's stand primitive and ignorant not just as a matter of public policy but theologically as well. But as the political issue heated up, as it was bound to continue to do for years, one could never tell when a new bishop would arrive like a Knight of Malta with sword and shield to battle any opposition. It was hard not to be amused, in a dark sort of way, at how the latitudes of right and wrong varied from one diocese to another; the Church might preach absolute values, but in practice took on the countenance of the local prelate—which further eroded the rationale of their stand. It was also possible, he had to admit, that to create such an exhibit would be making too personal a statement. The Refuge needed all the support it could get, and to gratuitously alienate anybody was something that had to be avoided. Eric Jackson had found a way to compromise, however; he had attached a small amplifier to the population odometer, and when the hall was quiet you could stand in front of the case, and hear the tumblers whine. That was statement enough.

Most of the exhibits in the hall STUPIDITY dealt with the ongoing animal slaughter—poaching, black marketing. In this hall as much as the first, Eric had taken care to show that Americans, for all their ignorant jingoism and we're-number-one, were among the most heinous offenders. One case contained grainy photographs, surreptitiously taken, of a "canned hunt." In this enterprise, centered in the Southwest, entrepreneurs can buy, at great discounts, old or decrepit circus animals or exotic pets no longer wanted. Then some urban "hunter" with several hundred or even a few thousand dollars to spend drives to a remote ranch, where he can walk up to a walled enclosure or even a cage, gun down his bear or lion, and have a trophy for his den. If it weren't for the photographs, he knew, no one would believe such a thing could happen. But it did happen, all the time.

Another case showed how political lobbies for the ranching industry maintain bounties for predators, in whose pursuit far more nongame animals are killed than bounties are ever collected. In front of this case, instead of a section of bench-chairs, was a freezer, with a tag attached to the handle, reading, "You may open it." Eric stood by and watched as the brunette from Channel 10 regarded it for a minute before yanking the handle and hefting up the lid. A frozen fog spilled out into the room as she recoiled from the sight; it was filled to the brim with bald eagles—the National Symbol in addition to being an endangered species—who had swallowed poisoned bait set out for coyotes. The U.S. Fish & Wildlife Service had been happy to provide the carcasses. The brunette grimaced and motioned to her cameraman. "Dwayne! Dwayne, shoot this!"

The case—or rather, two cases—on which Eric had spent his closest personal attention were those showing the black market trade in rhinoceros horns. He had crafted them, not just out of affection for Ethel Mertz, but because, of all the black marketing in animal products, the trade in rhino horn was the most prominent, the most insane, and the most likely to succeed in causing the actual extinction not just of a species, but the entire genus of all five rhino species. The background mural in the first one was a black-and-white photograph, blown up to life-size, of the inside of a Chinese traditional apothecary, with its strings of dried herbs and bins of mushrooms and desiccated seahorses, and the inevitable cabinet with dozens of tiny unlabeled drawers, like the card file in a public library. A small oak table stood before the mural, and on it a pan scale; one of the pans held a severed rhino horn, and the other balanced its weight with gold. Beside the scale were four more identical piles of ingots. The text made it more explicit: rhino horn is now worth five times its weight in gold. Beside them a second horn and coarse wood rasp lay on a piece of white paper, with a small conical pile of shavings.

Eric was not surprised when one of the reporters looked back at him and asked, "Are they real?"

"No, but we don't think the point is lost." The texts explained how Chinese culture persisted in its tradition, which dated back millennia, that rhinoceros horn brewed as a tea was an aphrodisiac, a magical potion that restored sexual potency to the man who drank it. The medical evidence against this belief was overwhelming and irrefutable, but its position in Chinese witchdoctory was unshakable.

The background photo-mural in the adjoining case was an outdoor panorama of the ancient palaces of Sana'a, the capital of the Yemen Arab Republic at the southern tip of the Arabian peninsula. A heavily gewgawed table, authentic to the region, displayed a huge ceremonial dagger. It was partly drawn from its exquisite scabbard, which appeared to be filigreed in pure gold, and the dagger's grayish-amber handle was polished to a low luster. The handle, the cards explained, was crafted from a rhinoceros horn.

The most sickening thing about the trade for dagger handles was that it lacked even the traditional history that the Chinese herbalists could claim. In Yemeni society a man's dagger—his *jambia*—was his ticket to adult acceptance. Commonly given by a father to his son at the time of the boy's circumcision, his wearing of it all his life was fraught with social implications. It not only had an important role in ceremonial dances, but if two men had a dispute to argue before the local sheik, both gave their *jambias* to him as symbols of their submission to his authority. (It was symbolical only; both men were sure to have real daggers concealed elsewhere in their garments in case the dispute was not resolved amicably.) A dagger's style and decoration identified a man's tribe and region: a scabbard done up with green-dyed sheepskin and studded with brass conchos, for instance, showed him to be a mountain man. The most lavish ones, overlaid with the fine gold filigrees, identified a member of a *Sayed* family—a man of the proudest line, descended from Mohammed himself. But for as long as anyone could remember, the significance lay in the decoration; the handles of all of them, whether humble or magnificent, had been crafted from the horns of zebu bulls. It was only after the influx of Western oil money in the late 1960s that the haughtiest of the Sayed families began casting about for new and more showy ways to express their social position. It was only then that rhino horn became the jambia of choice, and during the height of the hellish trade, from 1970 through the early eighties, Yemen imported at least thirty *tons* of rhino horn, first from Somalia and Ethiopia, and then as those populations were killed out, from East Africa and further south. As the population of black rhinos plummeted from 65,000 in 1970 to only 4,000 in 1986, the price of a first-rate jambia at the market in Sana'a soared to $20,000—enough for even a Sayed man to wear with the satisfaction that lesser men envied him.

Under Western pressure, Yemen had banned the import of rhinoceros horn in 1982, but undercover studies in Sana'a had shown that the only real effect had been to increase by eight times the cost of the necessary bribe to get the raw material through customs—which of course only added to the prestige of acquiring one. Eric Jackson could not show the jambia in its glass case without damning the arrogance and self-indulgence of it, and damning the admission that it was the American and Western European and then Japanese thirst for oil that had financed the whole wicked business, as their money engorged the egos as well as the Swiss bank accounts of the Arab princelings.

In designing this building, Eric Jackson had saved the hall whose door was super-scribed with the legend HOPE for last, because what visitors would see in STUPIDITY was depressing to the point of exhaustion, and he wanted them to enter the grounds in a more positive state of mind. HOPE was the largest of the three in that it was much wider, and extending down the whole length of the middle was a table, like a map in a war room, containing a large-scale representation of the world. The countries' political boundaries were marked off, with national parks and conservation areas set off in green. Americans are so insular in their world-view that few have any notion that other countries have national parks, but many have systems in every way comparable to our own. Around the edge of the table texts described some of the most ambitious and promising of the projects, such as the concept of international parks, where a habitat that extends into more than one country is protected jointly at respectively less cost to each individual government. Canada and the United States had pioneered the concept with Waterton–Glacier International Peace Park, and now Iguaçu Falls was protected jointly by Brazil and Argentina, and the great W bend of the Niger River by Niger, Dahomey and Burkina Faso.

The wall displays in HOPE concentrated on such developments as the signing of the CITES Treaty—the Convention on International Trade in Endangered Species—which for the first time regulated or outlawed animal products derived from poached endangered species, and on the forgiveness of Third World debt by Western banks in exchange for secure parkland. Others detailed the studies of little-known plant and animal life being undertaken at an increasing rate by pharmaceutical companies, who had discovered and developed drugs derived from species as disparate as the Pacific yew tree, the Madagascar periwinkle and the South American kokoá arrow-poison frogs.

At the end of the third hall were large glass double doors out onto the grounds of the park proper, and these doors flanked a large bronze bust of a bewigged and medallioned, decidedly rococo-looking figure, identified on a bronze nameplate as Joseph II, Emperor of Austria.

It was at the vast yellow palace of Shönbrunn, outside Vienna, with its pillars and putti and long enfilades of gilded drawing rooms, in the year 1759, when the Holy Roman Emperor, Francis I, built in the palace garden an octagonal baroque pavilion. It was a present for his Empress, Maria Theresa, Archduchess of Austria and in her own right Queen of Hungary and Bohemia. It was in this pavilion that every morning in summer the majesties of Austria would take their breakfasts, and through the high-paned French windows that looked out on every side would gaze out upon the vast barred crescent of his menagerie. As they were waited upon by liveried footmen who genuflected coming and going, they would point out and chuckle at the elephants and zebras and camels, pacing or galloping the length of their generous pens.

The grounds were modeled on the menagerie of Louis XIV at Versailles, which design had been appropriated by Prince Eugene of Savoy for his own menagerie at the Belvedere Palace just across Vienna. Prince Eugene, though he despised Louis himself, shared his fascination for wild animals, and in turn, many of the specimens from the Belvedere later found their way into the Emperor's collection. Francis also employed his own collector, Nicolas Jacquin, and sent him abroad, and then hired an Italian artist, Gregorio Guglielmi, to cover the interior of the pavilion with paintings of the animals and birds that Jacquin brought back to Schönbrunn—parrots from the East Indies, trumpeter swans and scarlet ibis from America, and Cape hartebeest from Africa, the latter now as extinct as the Austrian monarchy itself.

In 1765 their son, the enlightened Emperor Joseph II, coruler with his mother and patron of Mozart, dispatched further collectors to the distant reaches of the globe, in the name not just of Austria, but of science, and then brought that science to the common people by throwing open the great gates of the Schönbrunn menagerie to the public. That was why, at The Refuge, the glass double doors that led from the exhibit halls out onto the grounds flanked a bronze bust of Joseph II, founder of the oldest existing zoo in the world—a zoo at whose heart Maria Theresa's muraled marble pavilion still reposes in its music-box serenity.

It was Eric who reached the glass doors first and pushed down the bar latch, beckoning the others to follow.

5

IMMEDIATELY BEYOND THE DOORS the reporters found themselves on an outdoor cafe terrace, with half of the small cabriolet tables sheltered beneath a green-and-white-striped tarpaulin, and others standing in the sun. Beyond them a broad grassy picnic area ended at a sand beach; a gravel path threaded its way to the edge of the water, where it inclined up to become the catwalk floored with two-by-six planks in a metal frame, six feet wide, that stretched across the water, narrowing in the perspective of distance almost to a point by the time it touched the shore of West Africa a hundred and fifty yards away. Eric gathered the tour around him and suggested they open their maps of the park.

"Now," he began, "The Refuge contains three thousand acres of public viewing area, which is a lot more than we can cover today. So what we are going to do is walk you through several of the exhibits that contain a representative sample of what we think is some of our most important work. Depending on how long you want to stop and talk about each one, this should take between two and three hours." Framing the cafe area, opposite the water, the kitchen was contained in a one-story extension of the building with a large roll-up window, to which Eric directed their attention. "If any of you would like to refresh yourselves before we start, please carry a Coke with you, on the house, and then when we get back we'll give lunch to as many of you as can stay."

He led them over to the kitchen. "I probably ought to confess we had some discussion about what kind of containers to serve drinks in. The aluminum cans are recyclable, but inevitably we would be the ones to have to pick them up, or fish them out of the water. Styrofoam is cheap but not very 'green,' if you take my meaning, and some people would try to feed paper cups to the animals. So, beverages are served in reusable plastic souvenir cups depicting various endangered species on them, for you to take home to remember us by."

Larry Davis from the University of Houston was at the head of the group when it reached the service window. "With the extra cost to be passed along to the consumer, I suppose."

Eric decided not to take him head-on. "Only partly. Those of you who return in the future as paying guests will discover that our prices will not be as high as at commercial outdoor amusement parks, which we admit do prey on the desperation of people's thirst." He handed Larry Davis a Coke. "Here, collect a whole set," he urged, and won a smirk. "Trade duplicates with your friends."

As they neared the shore, Eric directed their attention to a chain-link fence that stretched beneath the catwalk the whole distance to Africa. "Now if you people will follow our vet over to Africa, I will follow along in a minute."

Jake led them up onto the bridge, and when they were about half-way across, Eric saw them stop, and knowing that Jake was giving the instructions, they all grabbed hold of the railing. At Jake's signal, Eric turned a key in a control box and the center section of the bridge turned on a pivot, opening the fence between the two watery "pastures" beneath them. He gave them several seconds to regard this event, then turned the key back, closing the bridge, and joined them out on the span.

"One of the shortcomings of any modern zoo," he said as he drew near, "is that it cannot possibly construct water tanks large enough to give adequate housing to large aquatic species. This land used to be a marsh, which we drained, but the large ponds are scooped out to as much as twenty feet deep, and their size is measured in acres, not gallons. Only some of the smaller ones are occupied now, but as what we have here is so much closer to nature than what a zoo can provide, we have pretty high expectations of our success at breeding some rare and wonderful creatures."

Albert Chu, the mayor's friend, leaned over the rail and looked at the spot where the chain-link gate of the water pen had swung open like a side-swing drawbridge. "I wonder," he asked Eric, "does it make you feel like Moses to part the waters?"

He laughed. "I guess maybe a bit, yes." If anything, he felt more like Noah with his animals two-by-two. Looking back toward the administration building, Eric caught sight of two more figures emerging. Richard came out first, short, almost fat, with a round face and straight, strawberry-blond hair. He held the door for Liz Ann, who stepped out in a trimly cut business suit. Two of the unlikeliest-looking caterers he had ever seen, thought Eric, although in part he was responsible. In his six years of single-minded labor to create the park, Liz Ann took up gourmet cooking to pass her time. She had always envisioned herself as a homemaker, not employed outside the house, but she at least discovered when she left that she had acquired a marketable skill. She and Richard had met in a cooking class and become friends; when she left Eric she moved in with Richard, although Eric was almost certain he was gay and was not concerned whether she might be unfaithful, at least with him. In fact it gave him enormous relief when it was she who volunteered to leave and not fight him for the house. If she did ever file for divorce, they would have to work it out, but he still had some hope it wouldn't come to that. He watched them step off the terrace onto the picnic area and head toward the bridge. "Looks like we have a couple of late-comers, folks, so we'll just give them a chance to catch up."

Stepping onto the shore of Africa, Eric explained that the various animals were kept in natural-looking dioramas, the largest of them seven acres in size, covered with vegetation appropriate to the species. "What happens when the animals start eating their cover? Don't you wind up with just a big, bare cage?"

"No. Replacement plants are always grown over on the farm, or are used in landscaping along the paths. Those in the paddocks are replaced as soon as they get thinned out. In fact, that is better for the animals, because rather than depending on a bin of hay for their food, they learn to sniff about and find their favorite stuff. That way, those that can eventually be transplanted to the wild will have a smoother adjustment and better chance to survive. Like these black rhinos here."

They had arrived at the first sequence of dioramas, containing a total of nine black rhinos that ate or wallowed, and seemed otherwise oblivious to the human presence across the dry, fenced moat. "Black rhinos are browsers, which means they eat bushes, not grass. If you will look closely along the path—" he held aside some low branches, revealing that several had been pruned away. "Out in the paddocks, some of what looks from here to be brush are really posts, sort of like artificial Christmas trees, which keepers load every morning with fresh branches."

From the path they were on, deep cul-de-sacs radiated both to left and right, revealing glimpses of various antelopes, aviaries and small ancillary buildings that housed reptiles and fish. Eric kept the group on the main path, and as they rounded a tight curve, an enormous African elephant loomed into view, with a sweeping lyre of thick, seven-foot tusks.

When he caught sight of the people the elephant approached aggressively, stopping at the edge of the dry moat ten feet deep that separated him from them. He probed the drop-off with his trunk to see if it could be crossed, and when he discovered that it could not, he bellowed and lashed out with his trunk. If you've never stood—or tried to stand—next to a trumpeting bull elephant, you cannot possibly appreciate its bone-jarring volume and force, the vibrations that can literally make the gravel dance on the ground as it trembles. Your knees go weak and you don't know whether to stumble away in terror, or worship the beast.

There was an audible gasp from the reporters as the elephant swayed and rumbled, and then their motorized cameras began clicking and buzzing like a swarm of insects. One of them nudged Eric to the low chain-link fence at their edge of the moat, which he backed up against obligingly so his and the elephant's picture could be taken together.

"How tall is he?"

"A shade under twelve feet."

"Jesus! Where in the hell did you find him?"

Eric's answer was quick and even. "We won't tell you that." Actually they had found him in one of the former Portuguese colonies of southern Africa, one of those benighted, faction-torn, guerrilla-ridden "republics" where tribesmen now armed with automatic weapons slaughtered each other as they had since their prehistory, only now blaming the white man for it all. With their long history of welcoming Portuguese sportsmen, they still had more land tied up in hunting leases than in national parks, and their commitment to conservation was perhaps the weakest in Africa. The former British colonies had found it merely difficult to enforce game laws but those lands once Portuguese all but exulted in the fact that rich Europeans and Americans could come there to shoot animals protected everywhere else in Africa.

Eric Jackson's operatives had paid ten thousand dollars for a hunting license good for one bull elephant, and with a license to kill him, the government had little interest in whether he was taken out of the country alive or dead. By concentrating their search in a region where the government did not exercise its control with any great energy, and by making friends with, and some well-placed donations to, the local rebels, it proved not particularly difficult to get a sedated animal the short distance to the coast. By felicitous planning, this was also the same region that produced the largest elephant ever found, a thirteen-foot-tall, twelve-ton behemoth shot by a Hungarian trophy hunter in 1955.

Eric got the reporters' attention. "His name is Sobhuza. We named him after a Swazi king who had sixty children, which is just what we want from him, too. You see, throughout the colonial white-hunter era and increasingly to the present, with all the poaching for ivory in Africa, the total population of elephants has been reduced by about ninety-five percent. Now, obviously, the ninety-five out of a hundred that have been killed already were those with the largest tusks, and you don't have to be a rocket scientist to figure out that the gene pool for dominant tuskers—like this one—is all but gone. There are only a couple of places left in Africa where guys like this hang on, mostly in areas where tsetse flies were never eradicated and which remain pretty much unpopulated and untraveled—except of course for the ivory poachers.

"This particular animal has been registered as what they call a founder with the elephant Species Survival Plan, which means he comes from a gene pool not already represented in the captive population. What that means is, he's going to have just as active a sex life as we can arrange for him. That's pretty tricky with elephants, for reasons that Jake can explain to you as we walk on, but the most important and most difficult thing was to get him here, which we've done."

They had chartered a small freighter with a reinforced hold—that was how P. T. Barnum had handled the enormous Jumbo in the 1880s—arranged for their truck to drive right up onto the ship, and it was done. And legally, albeit with a little finesse. But the true history was, that finessing him onto the ship, with a lot of help from a powerful immobilizing drug called M-99, had been less tricky than finessing the paperwork. Eric did not think of his largesse to local insurgents as a bribe. The governing authority of the American zoos and animal parks—AZA, for the American Zoo and Aquarium Association—had very specific ethical strictures against inducing official corruption in the acquisition of animals from abroad. That, he agreed, was a good and necessary measure. But it was also true that in the nineteenth century, if the Duke of Bedford had not greased some strategically outstretched palms in the Chinese royal court in his fervor to acquire some Père David's deer for his collection at Woburn Abbey, that species would be extinct today. The last ones in China were slaughtered during the Boxer Rebellion, by starving peasants who stormed the imperial hunting park. Instead, today these deer thrive in captivity, and are so abundant they are farmed as a source of meat in New Zealand and have even been reintroduced in their native wild, at the Da Feng Milu Reserve in China. Bribes, Eric Jackson agreed, are a bad thing, and as such, are to be made sparingly. Injecting the vitality of a founder like Sobhuza into the gene pool was a priority, however, and there was no need for AAZPA to know the details of his acquisition. And with AAZPA's endorsement, there was no complication getting an import license.

"How in the world can you handle him?" asked one of the reporters.

"We can't handle him," said Eric. "He's quite utterly wild."

"Except for the fact that he's here," muttered Larry Davis. "Sure it was dangerous out there, but at least he was free."

Eric was going to ignore the barb, but Jake was finding young Davis ridiculous and swelled up at him. "I'll tell you one thing this elephant did get in the wild, and that was shot at. When we had him sedated for transport we took X-rays. Found seven bullets in him. He knows all he wants to about people, and he hates 'em; I mean anybody ever gets in there with him is gonna be dead meat. He's a killer."

Eric was anxious to regain control of the conversation. "The fact is we move most of the animals—especially the really wild ones like Sobhuza—also by a series of remote-controlled gates. In fact, trying to use keys here and remember which one opens what would be such an encumbrance that all the buildings and paddocks are accessed using electronic passcards. Unless animals are captive-born, we try not to handle them at all if we can help it. Our goal is to make their adjustment easier for them if their natural habitats are ever safe enough to transplant them back to the wild."

Larry Davis had put away his recorder and was jotting notes. "That's your goal?"

"Yes, but we're not waiting up nights for it to happen."

Davis gave him a grudging nod.

With her catering partner Richard, Liz Ann had watched nervously from the back of the group as Eric posed for the photographs with Sobhuza, not entirely convinced that the moat was wide enough to prevent the beast from reaching out with its python trunk and snatching him. But as the tour pressed on they arrived at an exhibit containing two white rhinos that were impossibly huge—at least four tons apiece. The bull seemed even larger because his forehorn curved upward into a majestic four-foot spire, not a record, but infinitely larger than is seen since the population became so reduced.

"The bull's name is Shaka," said Eric, "named after the great Zulu king, and he is also registered as a founder. Two of his children have been born here, to different mothers, and we've let this cow honeymoon with him since she showed her interest. As far as we know they haven't done the deed yet, but we are very hopeful."

The mayor stopped to gaze at them, her little mouth open as she shook her head. "Just look at that. Most vicious and treacherous of all the big game," she said, her tone revealing that she had seen one too many bad travelogues.

Setting one hand on the chain-link fence, Eric gave her a quick smile and then vaulted over it. "Heads up," he yelled suddenly to the others, "photo opportunity!" He descended steep concrete steps into the dry moat and then up the other side. Facing the two rhinos from about twenty feet away, he clapped his hands softly and spoke to get their attention, then picked up a handful of alfalfa and shook it at them. Shaka stood aloof and then retreated a few steps, but the cow regarded him for several seconds before starting toward him, unhurried, seeming bashful and slightly tipsy, an effect caused in all rhinos when they walk slowly, by juggling and resettling the weight with each pace. Next to him she looked as big as a truck.

Black rhinos have the hooked upper lips that enable them to pull leaves and twigs into their mouths. White rhinos are grazers, with upper lips that are wide and blocky to gather large hunks of savanna grass into their maws. And when Eric fed her, the whole of his forearm disappeared under that wide meaty slab of a lip.

At the back of the group, none saw Liz Ann squeeze Richard's hand. "He knows better than that," she whispered.

Backing away, Eric threw a second armful of hay toward the bull, and backed almost to the edge of the moat before turning to rejoin the reporters.

Liz Ann clenched her teeth and squeezed the blood out of Richard's hand, hissing unheard by the others, "That stupid son of a bitch!" He patted her hand and she shook herself out of it. "I'm sorry," she said as they started to walk on. "It's just that, how many women lose their men when they go off looking for their dream? I lost mine because he found it."

Eric pulled a handkerchief out of his pocket and wiped his hands off, ambling over to the mayor, who looked up at him with her mouth shut tight and her eyes wide. "Don't believe everything you see on television," he said.

Larry Davis sidled up to him. "How in the hell did you do that?"

"Off the record?" asked Eric.

"Sure."

"Strictly, off the record?" He glanced down disapprovingly at the notepad, and Davis put it away.

"All right."

He smiled slowly. "I raised them."

"As you can see," he continued where the others could hear, "many of our animals are captive born and are quite gentle. They are not good candidates for transplant back to the wild, because they don't know how to be wild. But until we see some genetic deterioration, which we try very hard to avoid, they are the best possible breeders."

"Listen," said Davis, "could I talk to you after the tour? Maybe I could like do a feature story or something?"

"Sure." He was only partly listening, scanning the group to keep up with where Richard and Liz Ann were.

They walked on to the next paddock, a large one of about five acres, thickly planted with native grass and bushes. "Now I want you to notice that we have several different dioramas with white rhinos in them. This may seem a little extravagant, but for years, zoos would keep a pair of them, and try to figure out why they were not breeding. We now know that white rhinos, unlike black ones, are herding animals, and don't mate as solitary pairs. We don't have the largest herd of white rhinos in the world, but we rank right up there, three bulls and twelve cows, which we switch around, both within our own herd and by swapping individuals out with other institutions. Right now we have five calves and yearlings, which is one of the highest success rates in the world."

"How quickly can you get them to reproduce?" asked Albert Chu. Once again Eric found himself listening for any trace of Asian difficulty with l's and r's, but detected none.

"A few of the cows have been bearing every other year, which is about the same rate as ideal conditions in the wild."

Eric led them across the rest of sub-Saharan Africa, out onto Madagascar, across to Australia and then north to Indonesia. Especially on the smaller island of Madagascar it was apparent that the landscaping in the park was done with plants native to the region exhibited, and Madagascar, as one of the world's evolutionary "deep-freezers," was a botanical throwback that held plants of a visual weirdness that was nothing if not surreal. And from the number of shutters he heard snapping as they crossed the island, Eric Jackson expected to see at least a couple of photos in local papers devoted to these species.

But the group did not stop for exhibits there or in Australia, and did not stop until they crossed a short catwalk from Australia to Indonesia. Eric stopped them before they exited the bridge. "What I'm going to show you now is in some ways the heart of the park." He pointed behind some trees on the Indonesian island at a large, unfinished structure with a rounded oblong loaf of a roof that rose nearly a hundred feet above the shore. "If you know your geography you know that north of Australia is Indonesia, and Indonesia is home to some of the most endangered wildlife in the world. We are in the process of building an integrated indoor-outdoor habitat for them. It begins here, at the water, where we have already assembled a breeding colony of saltwater crocodiles. You'll see one just over there, under the mangroves." They made out a mud-brown, knobby reptile at least fifteen feet long, lying on the bank with its massive, yard-long jaws closed in slumber.

The idea of exhibiting wild exotics in zoogeographically accurate indoor-outdoor habitat areas was not unique to The Refuge, nor was it even a particularly new concept, but it was surprisingly new in application. For generations zoos had, for convenience in managing the animals, exhibited related species together, regardless of where they came from. Their living requirements were usually similar, their diets were usually similar, and one keeper could tend them all within a few yards of each other. Thus Indian elephants and African elephants were housed together; big cats from all over the world were shown in the same place; all the bears were all in the same place. There had always been an awareness that from an educational point of view this was unsatisfactory, but surprisingly, it was not until 1989 that the San

Diego Zoo opened its $6-million Tiger River Walk, which was the first to actually embody the concept.

Eric Jackson's explanation of all this gave them a suitable appreciation of what he was attempting in his Indonesian house. Inside it was still raw metal and concrete, but the structure was complete and the dome was sealed, and it was not hard for them to imagine what the finished product would look like once it was planted to jungle density and home for tapirs, orangutans, proboscis monkeys, pygmy buffalo, Komodo dragons, and above all else, the Javan rhinoceroses. They passed through it on an elevated walkway, with the indoor exhibit areas on both sides, each one having access to a similarly landscaped outdoor area. Eric pointed out the concrete pillars that supported the dome, which was a metal framework lit by hundreds of translucent skylights. When the pillars were fleshed out with greenery as trees, several dozen different species of Indonesian birds would have the freedom of the building; entry for visitors was through an airlock of two sets of doors to keep the birds inside.

They exited on the other side. "If you find all this impressive," said Eric, "and I hope you do, go back to your newspapers and magazines and write about it as extensively as your editors will allow. I have to tell you quite honestly that, while we are making progress, our acquisition of the Javan rhinos is not a done deal, and I tell you with no shame that our Refuge here needs all the press coverage you can generate. Now there is one more thing I want to show you."

He led them mostly in silence through South Asia and China, pausing patiently as they photographed tigers and two large pandas lolling placidly in a bamboo thicket, across a short catwalk to Japan, and across Japan to another bridge. "What we have over there is the veterinary compound. You probably saw its loading docks as you drove down 521; in fact 521 is just on the other side of this complex. This is Jake's bailiwick, so I'll let him explain it."

Jake's domain consisted of an animal receiving area and quarantine, a clinic with an X-ray and surgery bay large enough to accommodate any animal brought in, an open courtyard with a truck-sized commercial incinerator where they did a necropsy on every animal that died. They cared for them lavishly but life spans being what they are, several died every year, and no corpse went into the incinerator until every avenue of study was exhausted to add what it could to the body of knowledge. Neither Eric nor Jake saw any point in showing them the necropsy yard. Instead, once across the bridge, they entered the clinic and turned down a white-tiled hall lined with offices and labs.

Jake paused by an open door just long enough to say, "Now I'll invite you to just glance in here, but we won't bother her, that surprised-lookin' young thing workin' at the computer is Lucy Conner. She is the associate veterinarian for genetics. She's the one who lines up the chromosomes and decides who gets to make whoopee with whom." Inside they saw a young woman in a white lab coat, working before a green phosphor computer screen. She looked up and waved as Jake pulled back out the door. "Back to work, darlin'." He walked further down the hall, saying, "I don't know, I guess that makes her the head matchmaker around here. Not that it ever did me any good."

He paused at double doors that he stopped to unlock with his passcard, and turned on a light. The central feature of the room was a bulky round device bolted to the floor that might have passed for a spaceship's propulsion device in a bad scifi movie.

"This," said Jake when they had all entered, "is a liquid nitrogen freezer. In fact I'm sure you've all probably heard the expression 'frozen zoo'? Or at least you've seen *Jurassic Park* where that fat guy tries to make off with frozen dinosaur embryos? Well, this here is the real McCoy. What we have in this room is the single-largest repository in the world of frozen eggs and sperm, and some embryos, of endangered wildlife. Mammals, birds, fish, reptiles—even insects. And in that next lab through there is a tissue and pollen bank of endangered plants."

"Have you tried cloning any of them?"

"Boy, you are a quick one. Yes, we have, but just plants. Not animals."

"But what would happen if the power should ever fail?" asked Albert Chu.

"That is an excellent question," said Eric. He surmised that Chu must be very rich, and felt encouraged from his interest that years of currying political favor might finally bear useful fruit. "As you see, the park has some machinery—not just these freezers but, for instance, incubators in the nursery, that should not ever be without power for more than a few minutes. There is a security office in the administration building, and if any of the important equipment should ever fail an alarm will go off in there. Plus, we're sort of set up like a hospital. If the whole power grid goes down, we have backup generators that would kick in automatically to keep the most critical functions going, and there is a line to the closest utility substation that would trip an alarm over there to get repair crews moving."

"You have taken very detailed precautions."

Eric nodded. "Yes, we have." He motioned the press closer in. "We take our mission here—our calling, if you will—very, very seriously. It is entirely possible, in fact it is probable, that one day a species that goes extinct in the wild will be recalled into existence from frozen storage banks like this. Maybe in a better time, when the world is safer and people are wiser, we can fertilize an egg and implant it in a suitable host. That's a tricky business, and we have lots of failures and miscarriages, but we are experimenting continuously." Eric looked at Larry Davis. "Now it's true that the animal rights people find this approach obnoxious, but I tell you, for some species it is the only hope for survival."

"Some people are writing now that if the only way for some species to survive is in captivity, it is better to let them pass from existence. You are aware of that?"

Eric shook his head. "Of course. That's a bunch of crap written by people who need to get real jobs." He smiled vaguely as he recovered his composure. "But, you don't want to get me started on them. I'll tell you one thing, though—the ethicists have pushed things in one positive direction. In addition to collecting sperm and ova from zoos and wildlife parks all over the world, we even take sperm donations from wild specimens. That way we preserve genetic variety in the freezer, but don't capture the whole animal." He pointed in emphasis. "In the whole world there aren't many freezers like these, and most of them are in commercial sperm banks for rich lonely hearts. Only a couple are devoted to endangered wildlife. This is one, and we are on a continuous data link with every accredited member of the AAZPA to take advantage of every possible opportunity to keep animals going who are nearly all gone. That's how serious it is."

He relaxed somewhat. "Now, if we have succeeded in putting the fear of God in you, we're going to lead you back to the cafe and give you a nice lunch. Rather than retrace what you've seen already, we'll give you a choice of ways to get back. If you're dog tired or in a hurry to go, Jake will take you to some golf carts that we keep to get around. If you stick with me, we're going to take you up through Asia and down through the Americas. Feel free to take whatever pictures you like. I won't stop to harangue you with any more lectures, but you may ask whatever you like as we chat on the way back."

"What's for lunch?" asked Larry Davis.

"Fish and fries. Or salad, if you're a vegetarian."

6 🌿🌿🌿🌿🌿🌿🌿🌿🌿🌿🌿🌿

ERIC JACKSON'S OFFICE was off a short hall running west from the reception area, the side opposite the hall to the Board Room. After the press tour he collected his briefcase from Stephanie, stopped in the kitchen next to his office for a cup of coffee—God bless Stephanie, he thought, she always has some fresh—and put his feet up on his desk to look over the month's numbers that Roman had given him.

ENDOWMENT, Balance forward $86,247,512
  Grants received 65,000
  Donations, net. 14,160
ENDOWMENT, Current total. $86,326,672

INCOMES, FOUNDATION RELATED
  Endowment Interest $718,729
  Sale of Bred Stock. 77,250
  Stud & Dame Fees 4,720
  Sperm & Ova Sales. 1,920
  Venoms, Pharmaceutical. 1,215
  Plant Products, Pharmaceutical. 3,600

INCOMES, ANCILLARY COMMERCIAL
  Excess Farm Produce, Retail. $2,470
  Fish, Fresh Wholesale to Market. 1,126
  Plants, Wholesale to Florists 1,745
  Bait, Wholesale Minnows, Worms, Crickets 850
  Fertilizer, "Zoo Poop" Wholesale to Nurseries . . . 2,228

INCOMES, TOTAL FOR MONTH $815,853

Overall their figures seemed pretty much on track. A big urban zoo needs about twelve million a year, but few ever get it; most eke by on seven to ten million and give thanks for it. The Refuge was bigger and had more animals, but he had to spend less on salaries up to now because the public had not been admitted. That was all about to change, and the need for additional income would become, in the short term, acute.

Apart from foundation interest, their largest source of income was sale of excess animals, and that usually meant to commercial ranches. The ostrich industry had exploded in the past few years; chicks were delicate and hard to raise for small-time operators, but once you had a method down, the big, fast-running birds were a cash cow. Chicks fetched $500, six-month old pairs $3,500, and one cock with three hens might produce three hundred young a year. Adult breeding pairs could be sold for $10,000, but Eric and Roman had decided against letting go of any of them. The market for ostrich leather and a growing demand for ostrich meat would have made it even more profitable to set up their own abattoir, but the potential negative press could have been disastrous. The feathers, however, they could process on their own, and get up to $150 a pound for the best of them when the cocks were ready to molt. There was not so good a market for the hens' feathers, but they could be dyed and ratted, and sold as novelties at the souvenir counters for much more than the $40 a pound the bulk buyers offered. That would help the figures a bit. The Refuge also sold its overstock of bison to ranches and some of them were eventually slaughtered, but they drew the line at selling any animals to commercial hunting ranches.

The fertilizer number will go up, too, thought Eric. Since the year of his San Antonio visit, a number of zoos around the country had entered the fertilizer market with great success, capitalizing on what traveling circuses had known for years: where there are elephants, gardeners will surely gather with pick-up trucks. And as this sideline was developed he had discovered that, contrary to what he had once supposed, no federal rules hindered them. It was still just spring, and this was the first year they had offered composted dung. Once people got their gardens going, and word got around, they'd buy a lot more.

Supplying it would not be a problem, God knew. Two whole acres of the farm were devoted to composting experiments, trying to find the best combination of droppings to produce the best possible fertilizer. Elephant stuff made by far the best soil conditioner, because their digestion was so inefficient they passed through large volumes of straw and chewed-up leaves virtually unprocessed. But, for the same reason, it was pretty short on available nutrients.

The big cats' shit was useless, so acid it burned up anything you threw it on. Cat turds they hosed straight on into the sewer to go to the treatment plant. By far the best quality dung came from the hippos—with fourteen stomachs apiece, it should—but the problem was getting to it. The hippos would only take a crap in the water, and even then would beat it to smithereens with their tails as it came out, so that basically all they got was dirty water with bits of stuff settling to the bottom. They had cleaned the water somewhat by growing talapia in the hippo pools. The big, goofy-looking silver fish added interest and authenticity to the exhibit, ate for free, and helped clean the water. As usual, nature knew best.

They also planned on serving talapia in the cafeteria. Boy, Eric would have loved to tell the reporters—to say nothing of future visitors and the fish market they wholesaled to—how their golden-fried crispy fish had matured and fattened having eaten nothing in their entire lives but hippo shit, but the County Health Department would have had a conniption. Talapia for human consumption came from their own ponds on the farm, properly grain-fed, sterile and American.

Eric looked over the expense side of the sheet and saw they had not quite broken even for the month. But the next statement would have more on it—admission fees, food concession, gift shop retail, stroller rental, all kinds of things. There would be more expenses, too: extra security and groundskeepers, guides. They should make money, though. And the Javas, when they got here—postcards, mugs, T-shirts, stuffed dolls—they should do at least as well capitalizing on the Javas as the National Zoo had done with the pandas after Nixon opened China. These were sentiments that he knew he must never even intimate to the Indonesian government. They were not in the least bashful about their outrage toward it—the only comparison to it was, in the last century, the way Greeks and Egyptians felt about the British looting archaeological sites to stock their impressive museums and country houses. To pay money to ogle Javan rhinos in an American game park was, in Indonesian eyes, one more little rape of a culture the Ugly Americans had no respect for. The education argument had been articulated for them many times, that all the endangered species on earth, east and west together, had no prayer of survival without the motivated enlightenment of enough of the general population to make a difference, but it got nowhere with them.

Eric thought ahead, to the following month, when the Indonesian ambassador would arrive from Washington and they would fly the Conservation Minister over from Jakarta to inspect the new Indonesian facility. It was important for them to find it already stocked with orangutans and proboscis monkeys, tapirs and pygmy anoa buffalo and babirusa wild pigs. They must be able to walk through the high-domed structure on its elevated walkway, and see the animals utterly unaware of the human presence. And when they saw that the only empty section of it, with its five-foot-deep stream of sluggishly flowing water, heated to 78 degrees, its banks and secluded nooks lushly planted with the Javan rhinos' own favorite native plant foods, they would be compelled to conclude that Indonesian fauna was not being presented in any carnival atmosphere. And more than that, they would leave *wanting* to see Javan rhinos there. If only Stan would find a fax machine and tell them what proportions to plant in.

Two sharp knocks on the door rapped Eric out of his thoughts, and he looked up to see Larry Davis standing in the doorway. "Can I come in?"

"Please." Eric stood partway up and pointed to a chair, but as he sat back down saw Davis's attention arrested by a photograph on the wall—three eight-by-tens spliced together into about an eight-by-thirty—of Eric in jungle dress, in the rain forest, posing with an enormous anaconda being stretched out to full length by five assistants.

Larry whistled. "Geez, you caught this thing?" He went into sort of a TV imitation. "While Eric wrestles the giant snake in the river, I'll set off into the interior, to see what other wildlife might be in the area. In fact, I'm going to get as far fucking away from him as I possibly can."

Eric smirked. Marlin Perkins had been an idol of his. It had been months since he had seen any "Wild Kingdom" reruns, still among the most popular shows in cable syndication, deservedly so. "All scenes," Eric answered, "whether actual or re-created, depict authenticated facts."

Eric had done the Frank Buck "Bring 'em Back Alive" bit before; he hated it, but he had to know how to do it. In fact, he had videotapes of all those movies from the thirties and early forties, with Frank Buck standing there with his potbelly and safari shorts, brandishing his riding crop, directing teams of bumbling dark-skinned "boys" in building one type or another of traps and cages. The barbarity of such primitive animal capture was as offensive to watch as the ridiculous anthropomorphizing about carnivores being "bad" and herbivores being "good." Eric figured he was the only person alive who had noticed that Buck recycled the most manipulatively precious scenes from film to film—that the baby mouse deer standing in the palm of his hand in *Wild Cargo* in 1934 was the very same footage used again in *Jungle Cavalcade* in 1941. Eric still sat through these films occasionally, with their endless tootling Winston Sharples big band music that strove mightily for exotic effects but managed only to sound like the Shriner Ballet from *Bye Bye Birdie,* sat through them because it was important to remember what zoos—and animal "collecting"—had been, and must never be again.

The sad fact was, however, that few of the endangered species had adequate gene pools among only captive animals. The ones already in zoos could reproduce for a few generations, but eventually and inevitably they would inbreed into defects and still-births. Even lions get dish-faced and stupid after about the fourth generation. If the rare ones were truly to be saved from extinction, some few more of them had to be caught wild, for the good of their own kind. Thus it was necessary to be able to do it with a minimum of trauma to the animals.

And, there was a thrill in it; Eric couldn't deny that. Those same emotions that drew people into theaters in the 1930s to watch Frank

Buck movies, no matter how silly and how artificially they were staged, those emotions were still viable. Every time one of the shuffling "boys" dropped the cobra basket that cracked open at Frank Buck's feet—you could bank on it in every film—the audience still gasped. Perhaps it was, that to have their urban invulnerability stripped away, however vicariously and for however brief an instant, and to be vulnerable even to death, to once again be an animal among animals, could not fail to recall senses far older than the altruism to preserve wild things. It unsettled Eric that the chase could make his own blood race, himself of all people, and to lure himself out of that state and calm himself down, he acquired the habit after a difficult capture of repeating to himself, only partly in joke, the disclaimer buried in the small print at the end of every "Wild Kingdom": All scenes, whether actual or recreated, depict authenticated facts.

Larry Davis had just seated himself when the phone on Eric's desk warbled and he picked it up still on the first ring. Larry only heard half the conversation. "Hello? Hello, Clarence. No, it's okay, what do you got? Usual stuff. Well, hell. No, we still have time today. Hang on, we'll be there in about an hour." He hung up the phone and looked at Larry. "If you want more interview we'll have to do it on the road."

"I can wait, if you'd rather."

"No, you come, too. I want you to see this." He punched his intercom and Stephanie answered. "Get Jake on the phone and tell him to bring the van. We have to go see Clarence."

Her voice crackled back. "Oh, no. Shit. Okay."

"Tell him to meet us out front."

Eric got in the front seat of the van beside Jake, and Larry got in the back, seeing a bank of small holding cages and a case of medical supplies.

The first thing Jake said to Eric was, "You know you don't need to go."

"I know. But I thought it would be good if we could give our cub reporter here a look at the real world." He looked back at Larry and raised his voice above the engine noise and Jake's country music tapes. "The Customs Service got a bad shipment of animals over at the airport. Houston is a big port of entry, and we have a deal with them to care for any sick or injured exotics that come into the country here."

"I thought they did their own quarantine," said Larry.

Jake turned the music down and took over the topic. "Usually they do, but we got a deal with them now, it was his idea." He pointed a thumb at Eric. "We got them to license our own quarantine at the park, so that now whenever wild animals are imported into the country, if there's evidence of abuse or a fly-by-night operation, we take over the quarantine at our place. We're allowed to recoup our expenses for caring for them, and if in my judgment these people got no business having the animals, then my care is very, very expensive. If they don't want to pay, we just keep the poor things permanently."

"That sounds almost like an illegal seizure."

"No, it ain't illegal. But you need to understand, maybe half of all the animals sent to this country die in transit. With some species it's a lot higher, but the law takes no notice of them, and a lot of people in the animal-importing business don't give a rat's ass how many die in the cage. What we've worked out is a way to discourage people from getting in the business who shouldn't be there. I'll grant you it's an artful interpretation of the existing regulations, but we keep a lot of animals alive who would die otherwise."

Jake steered the van up to the big metal doors of the U.S. Customs Warehouse near the airport. Jake was out first. "Howdy, Clarence."

"How you doing?" The officer was a big meaty black guy. "I'm sorry to bring you out this late, but I think I got some real sick ones, by the look of things." He took notice of Larry and held out his hand. "Clarence Hudspeth. How you doing?"

Eric took a deep breath. "Well, let's take a look. When did they get here?"

"Three o'clock. Called you first thing."

Sounds in the vast building echoed repeatedly, with parrot screeches and monkey chatter growing louder as they entered the barred quarantine and approached a line of crates, mostly unopened. "Don't smell real promising, does it?" said Jake, and he gave the van keys to Eric. "If you'll back the truck in here we'll get to work."

The lading bill on the first one listed five small boa constrictors. Hudspeth muscled the lid off the crate with a crowbar as Jake pulled a pair of rubber gloves from his pocket. "Okay," he said as he looked them over. "We got seven small constrictors, four dead, three still alive."

Eric parked the van and slid open the side door. He approached with a burlap sack over his arm as he pulled rubber gloves onto his own hands. Jake lowered the three live snakes into the sack, and Eric took them to the truck.

The second crate had been opened and the lid laid back over it. Inside were two dead blue-and-yellow macaws. Jake asked, "Any of them make it?"

Hudspeth pointed at a row of cages. "Yeah, five. We opened the ones with birds and monkeys in them because they were fussing so."

They worked their way through the boxes; more with monkeys than anything else, a couple of woollies and some tamarins but mostly young capuchins, the ones most commonly associated with organ grinders. More were dead than alive, and the survivors stressed and dehydrated. As Jake did his in-the-boxes triage Eric carried those who were salvageable to their small cages in the truck, hiding his disgust and pain with less and less success.

Once most of the crates were opened, Hudspeth returned briefly to his office and returned with an Instamatic camera; he went down the row of containers, photographing the dead contorted contents in their hay and kapok. He looked up and saw Larry Davis giving him a questioning look. "Evidence," he said.

"You'll prosecute?"

"Who knows? Not my union."

They got to the last crate, and as Jake worked up the lid with a crowbar Eric finally cried out. In it were six squirrel monkeys; five were dead, the sixth one in convulsions, slimy from the feces of the others. Eric lifted it out tenderly in his gloved hands, and Larry Davis saw tears finally rolling down his cheeks.

"Jake?"

"I can't save him, boss. I'm sorry."

"Do it quickly." Eric carried the shivering monkey to the van and sat in the door, and spread a towel on his lap, as Jake pulled a dose of T-61, fast and painless, into a small syringe. The monkey was too weak to resist the shot, but squealed as it was stuck. Eric put one hand over its face. "It's all right, baby, you'll sleep now. You'll sleep." He held it until it grew still and emptied its dying bowel onto the towel. He laid it back in the box and watched as Hudspeth took a photo of the contents.

Larry Davis laid a hand on Eric's shoulder, but he cast it off so violently he popped Davis in the face, sending his glasses spinning to the floor.

"Hey, hey, hey!" Hudspeth caught Eric's arm. "I think you better go wait in my office." Jake pulled off his rubber gloves. "You go on in and sit down. I'll finish up out here."

Davis recovered his glasses and tested the frame hooking them back over his ears. He heard a soft step and turned partway, then jumped when he saw Jake glaring at him, impaling him with contempt, from a foot away. His drawl was even slower and more penetrating than usual. "Well, at least they was free out there, wasn't they, son?" He turned on his heel and returned to the van.

Davis gazed down into one of the first of the crates they had opened, containing four dead boa constrictors, and noticed in the kapok packing, the shipping label on the lid. Instinctively he pulled his pad from his shirt pocket and scribbled the address.

Hudspeth's office was small and quiet, connected to the warehouse by a glass wall and door. Eric had seen monkeys die before, from the majestic plummeting stoop of an eagle in Malawi, and from the sudden flashing emerald strike of a tree boa in the Amazon. He didn't like it then, either, but he accepted it. That was nature; there was order to it, there was a purpose. But this—to be trapped and hauled and frightened half to death, then be suffocated in a dark wooden box, covered in its own feces and the staring, gaping-mouthed faces of its species—and then be finished off by one who would have saved it if only he could. Bleeding Jesus on the cross, where is any order, any purpose, any serenity in that?

Eric looked up and saw a Styrofoam cup of coffee steaming in front of him. As he took it, his eyes followed up the arm that held it and saw Larry Davis. "Thank you."

Larry pulled up a chair and sat by him, reporter-style, leaning forward, like he was ready to take an interview.

Eric sipped the coffee. "I'm sorry I hit you. I didn't mean to. Really."

"Forget it. I've been an asshole. I had one coming."

Eric looked up at him again for this admission, seeing less the color in his curly black hair and gray eyes than the intensity in those eyes. Whatever the boy believed, he believed with passion—strong clay that might be molded one day. "I didn't break your glasses, did I? If I did—"

"No. No." Larry's intense face relaxed for a second as he wiggled them on his nose. "Steel frames. They're tough." He grew serious again. "How often does this happen?"

"Three times last year. Two this year, so far. It's getting worse."

Larry shook his head. "Man, that was awful."

Eric wanted to change the subject. "So, what are you, in school? A sophomore?"

"Junior."

"Ah. What are you studying?"

"Journalism."

Eric laughed. "Yeah, I guess you would be. What do you want to do with it? I mean, print, media, be a news anchor?"

"Print. I don't know, I'm not that great a writer, but maybe it's something I could do that would make a difference. Somewhere." He shrugged. "I guess I want to be useful, but I don't know what to do yet."

"You care a lot about animals. Have you thought about wildlife work?"

"Yeah, that'd be great." His face seemed eager, as though he were hoping the conversation would steer that way. "That's why I asked to cover the story today."

"Even though you thought we were the enemy."

"Yeah. But you can't take any animal courses down here. All the wildlife biology is up at A&M. Have you ever been there?" He whistled. "Bunch of Nazis, man. But yeah, I'd love working with animals, you know, the way you do it, not just caging them up to show people who basically don't give a shit."

"So," Eric mulled the words, "you want a job or what? It's almost summer, we could work out some flexible hours until the semester is over."

"You'd do that?"

"I've been thinking of taking on an intern. Maybe we could work out some credit for it with the Biology Department in the fall. We do that all the time."

"Oh, wow. Let me do this story, and think about it. Would that be okay?"

"That's fine."

"Would you care if I follow your people around for a couple of days? Background for the piece?"

"Sure."

Jake Teal stalked through the door and heaved a sigh. "Well, that's all done. God damn." He picked up the phone on Hudspeth's desk, punched a number and waited. "Hi, Steph. Jake. Ring Lucy, would you?" He waited again. "Luce? Jake. Yeah, it was pretty bad. Get some quarantine ready. We got—" he looked down at a list in his hand"—nine small snakes, two big ones, all constrictors, six macaws, various. Got fourteen small monkeys and tamarins. 'Bout thirty didn't make it. Yeah, I know, darlin'. 'Bout an hour." Jake started to hang up the phone but whipped it back to his ear. "Luce! Listen, it might be a good idea, why don't you take Babs up to Eric's office for a visit? Yeah. Listen, when was the last time you checked on Lakshmi? Goddamn, I don't like the way she's taking her time. All right, we'll just wait."

They drove back mostly in silence, with Jake at the wheel, Eric beside him and Larry Davis in a rear seat. The whole way back, Larry could not take his eyes off the cages in the back, with their tiny frightened wretches swaying as the van swung and turned in the traffic. He couldn't remember ever wanting so badly to be somewhere else, anywhere else. He wanted to turn away but couldn't, feeling crucified by every terrified little shriek from the caged monkeys.

Jake dropped off Eric and Larry at the administration building, then gunned the van down the gravel perimeter road to the vet compound far out on the east side.

Upstairs they found Stephanie typing at her processor, half watching an infant chimpanzee rolling on the floor with a large red rubber ball. When the chimp saw them enter she abandoned the ball and headed for Eric, walking on her legs, her long hairy arms suspended over her head.

"Hi, sweet baby," Eric scooped her up in one arm and took his mail from Stephanie with the other. They entered his office, with Babs bouncing piggy-back on Eric's shoulders as he sat at his desk.

"She doesn't seem to be one of your wilder animals."

"Babs is a special case. She was orphaned and hand-reared by somebody who didn't know any better. Chimps have a highly evolved social structure. If we just threw her in with a family group, she wouldn't have a mother, she wouldn't know how to behave. They'd murder her. Literally." Eric dangled her high above his head. "You don't think man is the only animal that will kill one of his own kind just for being an outsider, do you? Ants do it; lions do it. Chimpanzees do it, too. Maybe we're not so highly evolved as we thought. At any rate, we'll have to introduce her gradually when she's old enough. We've already got her in a play group with other infants and juveniles. She's coming along."

Babs tumbled off Eric's desk, and again walking nearly upright with her arms held cranelike over her head, walked into his bathroom. Larry watched dumbly as the light switched on; he heard wet plunks in the toilet bowl, and a flush. She ran out on all fours and rocketed screeching into Eric's lap. He tickled her, at once playing with and controlling her. "Sorry," he told Larry. "Would you catch the lights? Sometimes she forgets."

Larry complied, and then said, "Listen, I need to go home and work on all this. What I'd like to do tomorrow is come back with a photographer and cover the opening day. I'd like to see you for a few minutes, and maybe you could, like, give me a pass or something so I could just wander around and interview some more of the staff?"

"I think we can work that out."

About an hour after Larry left—it was after five—Lucy Conner entered Eric's office to collect Babs. Her title was associate veterinarian, but the duties she tended, as geneticist, were often independent of Jake's and just as important. She stood five feet six, had delicate features and long, honey-blond hair. She was convinced she was not pretty, on the grounds that her mouth was too small and she had freckles, but Eric had fallen for her at first sight. It was a moot point to him, whether he would have been tempted had he and Liz Ann not already been in trouble. He loved her, and was smart enough to know he needed her. He got up from his desk, closed the door to his office, and greeted her with a kiss that was not returned.

She collected the chimp frostily, and Eric saw from her posture and that certain set in her delicate jaw, that she was angry and meant to have an explanation. "I saw Liz Ann on the tour."

He thought, Oh God, not a fight. Anything but a fight.

"Did you ask her, or did she come on her own?"

He sighed, and leaned back on the front of his desk. "I asked her."

She stared at him like a stone statue, and he reached out to her waist and pulled her closer. Babs thought she was about to be passed back, and snaked a lithe, furry black arm back around his neck. When Lucy didn't hand her over she sat between them, connecting them in ways she didn't understand, making her contented infant chimpanzee syllables.

"Eric, you can't keep doing this."

"I know. I know, it's just, really hard for me right now. I'm sorry."

"I thought it was over."

He raised his hands. "I don't know."

"I can't be the other woman, Eric."

"I know." His voice had become quick and anxious, not quite panicked. "I'm sorry."

Finally she put Babs on the desk and let him hold her and draw strength from her. She felt that, felt some of her store of strength flow into him, and felt how hard it was to give an ultimatum when you knew how much someone needed you.

When she took Babs up again, he held the door open for her. "Dinner? My place. I'll pick up Chinese on the way home."

She pursed her lips and gazed at the floor. "All right."

He raised her chin and kissed her. "I do love you."

"I know you do."

He squeezed her one more time and let her go.

7 🌿🌿🌿🌿🌿🌿🌿🌿🌿🌿🌿

IT WAS AFTER SEVEN when Lucy turned her white Civic LX into Eric's driveway, still annoyed that Liz Ann had been at the park but determined not to bring it up again. She knew Liz Ann was a carp, and knew, if she wanted to win, not to exhibit the same trait. She had been to her own house already and had changed out of her khaki and sneakers into an airy Mexican dress of white cotton with colored bands of rick-rack stitched around a deeply cleft front. She was not at all above stopping at vacant lots where a van had pulled in with a "Mexican Dresses" sign strapped to its side. They were comfortable, and she counted the one or two racks of homemade dresses that rolled out of the truck as as worthy as what she saw in some expensive shop. It was all off the rack to her. Nor was she unaware that it was Liz Ann who was the denizen of the boutiques, and that Eric had crossed words with her about the expense. That she had put on less comfortable shoes—white leather flats—was no matter, for she habitually kicked them off as soon as she and Eric got comfortably nestled. She mounted the front porch with light, scooting steps.

Eric Jackson's house was in one of those upper-middle-class subdivisions that ringed Houston in the real estate boom of the early eighties, and then changed hands at large discounts when the bubble burst—nice houses, but tract houses, all similar looking. Eric's was at the lower end of the scale, three bedrooms, two baths, a one-story house but with a high-hipped roof sliced away over the front door to give the illusion of a second story. There was only one attic room, really more a loft, but it lent some justification for having an elegant, full-height entry with a staircase up to it. Lucy knew that Eric and Liz

Ann had intended it as a playroom for their children one day, but having children had proved a problem—whether his or hers they had not yet investigated, but she knew they had tried, at least up until their marriage began to fail.

She punched the doorbell perfunctorily, even as she slid her own key into the deadbolt. The light was on in the foyer with its tall white sheet rock and white terrazzo floor. A couple of plants and art prints, beige carpeting up the stairs and the polished brass of a small chandelier provided the only color. The room seemed tall and white and—empty, not for want of wife and children, particularly, but Lucy had always thought it odd that as passionately as Eric was devoted to animals, he had no pets.

He had, however, told her once about his last one, an old, long-haired tabby named Isabella. During 1992, the five hundredth anniversary of Columbus's voyage to America, people would ask if she was named after Queen Isabella, and she was, but not that particular one. While Eric was still a student at the University of Texas at Austin, his apartment had backed up to the Barton Creek Greenbelt, an expansive, semiwild park that swarmed with abandoned and feral cats. He'd noticed her for several weeks, peering at him from undergrowth beyond the parking lot as he pulled in, steady green eyes that seemed to be waiting on him day after day in the dapple of tapestry. It was the same look he saw later in Ethel: fear, suspicion, curiosity—the desire to be touched. At length he purchased a box of generic dry cat food and began leaving a bowl of it beneath the front bumper of his car, taking care every evening to shake the box before pouring some out, so she would learn to associate the sound with the presence of food. He needn't have worried, for she found it the first evening as he watched from his bedroom window, and over many months the ritual continued. He got her used to his presence when she came out to eat, whether he sat on the curb near his car or on his doorstep. The months extended to three years, during which time Eric watched her raise, and mostly lose, no fewer than five litters of kittens. It was then that he named her Isabella, not after the patroness of Columbus but for her descendent, Isabella II, the hefty royal slut of late nineteenth-century Spain who was removed from her throne for moral turpitude.

With graduation and with the end of his lease imminent, the question pressed of what to do about her, for abandoning her now was impossible. He moved her food bowl, a couple of feet a day, toward the mat at his door, to get her used to his smell. This succeeded, and late one night he was awakened by a loud thump in her bowl, followed by the dry scattering sound of her food. When he opened the door he saw lying athwart her bowl a huge bloody rat with its death grimace and tiny curled claws. Isabella retreated quickly a half-dozen steps and turned and sat down and meowed, loudly and proudly like, Hey, I can help out around here, too. Eric slid down the wall and laughed till he cried, and all that remained when he left for school the next morning was a brown-red stain on the cement. Over time he began thinking to her as hard as he could, perhaps even speaking, that she simply had to become domesticated, or be thrown back on her own resources. In the evenings he began sitting closer and closer to her as she ate, until one evening he reached through the metal rods of the balustrade and stroked her neck and back. From there it was easy.

The first time he picked her up he was wearing blue jeans fresh from the drier, and for her remaining nine years, denim was the security base she clung to, purred against and slept on. No dog ever proved more faithful; through four moves until he settled into his present house, she never complained and seemed to understand what was, for her own good, required of her. Indeed, as time passed, that was the greater part of Eric's fascination with her, the detail with which they seemed to be able to communicate, to negotiate the terms of her domestication.

When her health began to fail—the vet said she looked like she must be fifteen—if she had been in pain he would have had her put down, but she wasn't; she just seemed slowly to slide into that next state, whatever that is. During her final crises, bladder infections and kidney failures, Eric spent over six hundred dollars on her; he was married by now but Liz Ann dared not object. On her last trip to the vet she stayed three days, and came home with shaved patches on both forelegs with tiny bruises from intravenous tubes, and a look in her eyes and a hollowness in her voice that told Eric in that secret but sure communion they had that she wanted to go.

He knew by then that cats prefer to die alone, but he hoped he could prevail on her to stay inside, so he could be sure she had gone peacefully. He dug a deep hole in the backyard under a spreading pecan tree and showed it to her—it was lined with denim, with the catnip mouse with which she'd learned to play, as far as he knew, for the first time in her life. He really did not want to scour the bushes for weeks, wondering, and he asked her to forego her nature and die in the house. During her last week she ate absolutely nothing and drank little; she lay in the yard during the day, and at night, when she was too weak to jump onto the bed, he folded blue jeans on the floor so she could sleep by him. Sometimes she soiled them as she slowly lost control of her functions, and he changed them without telling Liz Ann. One evening he found her casing the storm drain beneath the curb and gathered her inside. It was obvious that she was failing. That night she slept deeply and limply against his chest as he read, but every time he got up she wobbled over to the door and cried hoarsely to go out. He found her in the morning, not on her denim but by the front door, hanging grimly onto life until she could go out, and he relented. He knelt and stroked her, asking, "Is that the way you have to do it? You've been a good girl. Do what you have to do." He unlocked the door and closed it after her, giving her her privacy. He did not look to see where she went, and he never saw her again.

He asked himself, What imperative did she heed? Whose voice did she have to answer? He prayed that it was easy for her, and stopped looking for her after a week, and filled in the grave under the pecan tree. But he took an oath to himself that never again would he form an emotional attachment to a creature of shorter life span than himself. The Refuge was not a reality at that time, but the process had begun and there were daily meetings with foundation executives and engineers and lawyers and contractors. He knew his life's work by now, but never again, he swore, would he bond with an animal. And, he knew, it was not just because of the pain of loss. What shook him was the knowledge of communication, the certainty that with Isabella he had given, and received, conditions and understandings as exact as they were unarticulated. It was this surety that animals we regard as lower than ourselves are far more sentient than we credit them to be, that when they are abandoned, or frightened, or stalked, they feel acutely abandoned and frightened and stalked, that drove him nearly mad with rage at how animals are treated. And, if that was true of a cat, what then of the whales, and elephants, and wolves, and apes and other highly intelligent and socially structured animals? That seared him to his core, and he could not think too closely on that and keep his sanity, let alone be effective in his job.

Liz Ann had tolerated Isabella because Eric was so fond of her, but Isabella had never warmed to her and there was always a certain strain there, even a kind of jealousy between them. The old wive's tale was that animals sense a person's bearing toward them, and certainly it proved true in their case. After Isabella died, Eric never articulated his feelings about it to anyone except Jake, one night over a beer after Eric had interviewed him for the job, and later, in more earnest, to Lucy.

It was Lucy's intention, if she prevailed, to involve him with her own pets. Her own house was a small menagerie, in which death was treated tenderly but not out of context of the life it is part of. She felt the pathos of abandonment as keenly as he did, and she accepted readily that what he and Isabella had understood of each other surpassed the boundaries of master and pet. But what she knew that he did not yet, even for all his brilliance and commitment, was that grief is sharpened in isolation, and that his fault was, not that he had grown too close to his pet, but that they had been too exclusive. She offered him no simplistic blather about needing a new kitten to take her place, because she knew very well such a place could not be taken, but it would be her way of teaching him that death is not unbearable if it is sufficiently diluted with enough life.

Lucy's shoes echoed through the white foyer into the family room. Eric had risen at the sound of the bell and greeted her with a kiss. "Moo shoo pork," he said, "and vegetarian deligth." It was a private joke between them, the typographical error on the menu on their first date that had rendered delight into deligth.

"Smells great."

He had brewed a pot of jasmine tea, imported from the P.R.C., of which Lucy was so fond, and steamed some extra broccoli, of which she never found quite enough in the platters of vegetarian delight. She pulled cushions from the sofa and arranged them around the low glass coffee table, as he shuttled dinner in from the kitchen. It was also a joke between them now, that on their first date they had tried to impress each other with their use of chopsticks before admitting simultaneously that they were frauds at it. He laid out forks for the vegetables and rice, and a steamer tray with pancakes for the moo shoo pork.

At the top of the hour Eric stretched back to an end table and picked up the remote control. "Catch some news?"

"Sure."

He blinked on the television to "Headline News," to which they listened silently while eating. They sat up in surprise and pointed approvingly at a story about the birth of a lowland gorilla in the Atlanta Zoo. They knew it was impending, but had not seen the announcement yet on their E-mail. On CNN it was the kind of warm fuzzy story that usually ends the half-hour or precedes a commercial, but not this time.

"In a related but sadder story, officials of the San Antonio Zoo today are mourning the deaths of two rare African Black Rhinoceroses. The animals' bullet-riddled bodies were found this morning, with their horns cut off and missing. This leads authorities to suspect the killings were carried out by poachers, who are known to traffic illegally in rhino horns abroad. Their import into the United States is forbidden by federal law."

Lucy put a hand to her mouth. "Did you know about this, honey?"

He shook his head, his eyes wide. There was video footage of a dead rhino, seen indistinctly lying in its concrete block shelter. "That's Ethel," he whispered. "Oh, God, that's Ethel." Lucy took his hand and leaned against his chest. He swore, after Isabella, he would never love another animal, but he had forgotten about Ethel.

The story continued, "Rhino horn is believed by traditional Chinese herbalists to be an aphrodisiac. Medical experts say there is absolutely no truth to the claim, but demand for the substance in the Asian community is so heavy that prices on the black market have skyrocketed. The value of the two dead animals' horns alone is estimated at four to five hundred thousand dollars. This incident is the first known killing of rhinos in a zoo in this country, but with illegal poaching driving the wild African and Asian populations to the brink of extinction, the environmental community fears it may not be the last."

Eric picked up the remote control and turned the set off. They lay together on the sofa cushions without speaking for twenty minutes. Lucy had wondered if Eric was going to want to make love tonight, and if he did whether she would. She wanted to, but didn't know whether it was best to acquiesce or to put him off and tell him to make up his mind about Liz Ann.

Now neither of them was in the mood. She looked up at his face, unutterably sad. She stretched her neck up and kissed his forehead, then his lips. "I better go. Will you be okay?"

"Yeah."

"Are you sure?"

"Yes. See you tomorrow?"

"Sure." Jake got his whole weekends off; she worked Saturdays and they alternated being on call on Sundays. But tomorrow they would both be there, because it was the public opening and they needed to be prepared if any of the animals became overstressed, especially since they weren't sure exactly when Lakshmi had mated or when she would go into labor. "I'm sure I'll see you sometime during the day."

8

SATURDAY SHIFTS WAS A SETUP that Luís Barilla was familiar with also, only he didn't always get a weekday off if the store was really busy. Today had been the law of the jungle; it seemed like nobody was satisfied, and tomorrow—Saturday—promised to be worse for it was always their busiest day of the week. He stood under a hot stream of water, and turned the Shower-Pik to massage and let the hard wet darts drum onto his meaty chest and shoulders. He thought, Man, that's fine; when he ever moved out on his own, he would have to get one of these.

Luís got out of the shower, and as he dried himself ran his fingertips lightly over his chest, enjoying his own idle feathery caress. He had fleshy, sensitive nipples—whose legacy they were he could not imagine, but he judged them far superior to the taut little unfeeling pencil erasers you see on indigent shirtless mestizos. When he was first old enough to start having women, the rich ones in Nuevo Laredo that he did yard work for, he began by letting the lonely ones seduce him, and he discovered they couldn't leave his nipples alone. And the more skilled ones could drive him wild with their licking and flicking. Then they would finish and pay him, and compliment him on the job he did on their lawns, and then they would wiggle into their girdles and cross the river to shop.

He regarded his image in the mirror. He wasn't too dark, really, only when he looked down at his nether regions did he get unpleasantly, almost tribally chocolate. He thought, Hell, nobody sees that in the dark, anyway. He splashed himself with Aramis, rather too much, and got dressed. Uncle Ramón was having someone over to grill faji-tas, only he had forgotten to tell Aunt Ellen and she'd had to drop everything and run to the store, so Luís was going to help her get things ready.

In Houston, West Pasadena is a good neighborhood for an ambi-tious Hispanic to live in—nice brick houses, quiet streets; close enough to Deer Park to feel your ethnicity when you wanted to, but without the blight and crime and the relentless next-door stink of the chemical plants. Ramón Barilla lived in a four-bedroom house on the southwest side of Pasadena. He and Ellen had no children of their own, so when Luís moved in it was a blessing all around. Esteban and his wife and their children—Juan was the oldest—lived two blocks away.

From the kitchen counter Luís glanced out the window into the backyard and saw Ramón turning slabs of flank steak on the gas grill, which was in the yard beyond the patio, which was covered with a translucent, green plastic awning. Esteban and Juan were sitting and drinking beer at the picnic table out in the yard. There was a large four-bowl lazy Susan on the counter before him, and as his Aunt Ellen spooned sour cream and *pico de gallo* into two of them, Luís peeled and mashed some avocados and mixed them with lemon juice to keep them from turning brown, and grated a lump of cheddar. Ellen thanked and dismissed him as she stirred a pitcher of lemonade. He slid the patio door aside and joined them, taking a Dos Equis from an ice chest by the picnic table.

Soon after, they heard the patio door slide again and saw Albert Chu on the patio with a glass of lemonade in one hand and a leather valise in the other. He joined them out in the yard.

Ramón crowed, "Hey, you just in time. Oh, look at that, I think they done."

Chu had just sat down when Luís went back into the house. Ellen opened the door for him and followed with her own lemonade as he carried the loaded lazy Susan and a basket of warm tortillas. They ate leisurely and pleasantly until Ellen excused herself and returned to the kitchen. They watched her figure recede, and once the patio door had slid shut, Albert Chu lifted the valise he had brought from beside his chair and handed it over to Ramón. "I sense you are perhaps somewhat anxious to receive this."

Ramón hefted it a couple of times and grinned. *"Aí,* is pretty heavy." He snapped open the brass latches and peeked inside.

"There is a hundred thousand dollars."

"That is more than we thought you could pay."

"Yes. Well, I included additional money in the hope that you would take it as a down payment. There is another service I wish you to perform for me. Are you willing?"

The four Barillas grinned more broadly, but each in his own way— Ramón greedily, Esteban expectantly, Jean eagerly, and Luís in amusement at the other three. "Sure," said Ramón, and opened his hands upward. "All you got to do is tell us."

Chu did not break his eye contact as he reached into the chest pocket of his jacket and extracted a folded brochure that he handed across. Ramón was farsighted, and held it well away from him as he read, " 'Welcome to The Refuge.' What is that?"

"Open it. It is not really a zoo, more like a wildlife park, very large, that is opening tomorrow, southwest of the city. They have more rhinos than I have ever seen in any one place, at least twenty-five, of all the different species except one. It is incredible."

Ramón unfolded the map and laid it open on the table. "They got it all done up like a map of the world."

"Yes," said Chu. "It is the only place like it in the world."

Perhaps it was inevitable from Luís's upbringing that he studied over Chu's map as though he were living a scene from a made-for-TV terrorist movie. It was the only frame of reference he had for such a situation. He tapped a finger on the southeast corner of the map, over The Refuge's service yard. "We cut their power and telephone lines, they can't do nothing to call for help."

"No!" It was the first time any of them had ever heard an alarmed excitement in Chu's voice, and they stared at him as he waved his hands back and forth over the map in a way that made Luís think: Incomplete pass, no good. "Their alarms and backup systems are very sophisticated," Chu continued. "I don't know if they have radio or wireless phones, but if you cut their power, emergency generators will come on and alarms will go off all over. There is even one in the electric company station."

Ramón Barilla was concerned that such elaborate precautions had been taken. "Are they expectin' something like this?"

"No," answered Chu, "but they have a great deal of intricate machinery. If the power is cut, their equipment will assume there is a power failure, and there is a secure line that will trigger alarms with the utility company. You must not touch their power lines. What I would suggest is that you cut their communications and—" he grew very serious "—neutralize their security guards. Then you should have enough time to do what is needed."

Ramón Barilla looked solemnly around the white wrought-iron table at his brother and nephews, and nodded slowly, sipping at his beer. This was the first time Chu had ever talked about killing people. It did not offend him, but it made him realize what kind of commitment they were talking about.

"Take your time," said Chu. "You must get to know the place well, and it is a very large park."

"That's right," said Ramón slowly. "Is this the place you said you were going on some VIP tour or something?"

"Yes." He gestured toward the valise of cash. "Buy tickets. You see I have given you enough money for quite a few admissions. Their rhinoceroses are not all in one place. They have different kinds in different areas—and, in a couple of months, they will have two big new ones from Indonesia. Or, rather, they are trying to make the deal, and I would proceed on the assumption that they will succeed. I recommend that you wait until they get here."

Chu did not emphasize further the importance of waiting until the Javas arrived, but it was a vital link in his projected chain of income. In the throbbing, affluent Chinatowns of the Far East, in Singapore and Kuala Lumpur and Bangkok and Djakarta, Asian horn is worth far more than African. The horns of Javan, Sumatran and Indian rhinos are almost universally slender and somewhat eroded and rounded, even stumpy. Such a horn, quietly wrapped in a drawer in a traditional pharmacy in that part of the world, was worth well over fifty thousand a kilo already, substantially more than the far larger, but as they imagined, less efficacious, horns of either the black or white African rhinos.

It was his plan, simple and effective, to provide his Far Eastern pharmacists with whole Asian horns for the richest echelon of his clientele, and pregrind the African horns into the medicinal teas at his health products plant in Los Angeles, for export to the foreign markets. For African horn used in this way he would receive less per gram than for fresh-cut Asian but far more than their bulk market value. The only weak link in the chain, and it was a crucial one, was that the traditional doctors in Asian Chinatowns would naturally be suspicious of rhinoceros products prepared as far away as the mainland United States. With all those ranches and cowboys, the horn in Chu's teas might just as well be from beef cattle. Chu knew full well that Chinese doctors had cheated their own clientele in this manner for generations, using water buffalo horn. It was imperative that he generate confidence in his product.

None of this did he share with the Barillas. Nor was it their business that they were getting paid the same rate for Asian horn that Chu could coax into six or eight times the return on the African horn. He was prepared to pay them adequately for the role he would let them play; that should be enough for them.

They heard the slide of the patio door, and Luís rose and took from Ellen a tray of bowls of lime sherbet, one of which was only half full, which he handed to Chu. Like many Chinese he had never acquired a taste for heavy sweets, but he enjoyed a small bowl of sherbet as a palate cleanser.

As they ate, Ramón Barilla slid the map off the table onto his lap and nodded, as he imagined, sagely. "Look real good to me. You bet we gonna think about it. I mean, if is gonna be dangerous, we like to talk it over. That okay?"

"Yes, of course. I imagine you will only be able to hit the place once, and you must take out as many as you can, but I would hope not before the new animals arrive and certainly not before you are completely prepared. Other than that, I leave it in your hands. Study the park as long as you like, do your job, and get away clean, and I promise you the reward will be very, very substantial."

"Okay, we let you know real soon."

Chu put his napkin to his lips, then glanced at his watch. Nine P.M. in Houston meant ten A.M. the next morning in Singapore. "Now, I would like to go inside and thank your wife for a delicious dinner, and if I may, borrow your telephone. A colleague of mine is awaiting a call from me."

All four Barillas rose and shook hands with him, instinctively in their established order, Ramón first, then Esteban and Juan, and Luís last.

From the kitchen Ellen Barilla heard the shuffing slide of the patio door and was drying her hands as she entered the den. Chu took her hands in his. "Busy old businessmen like me are not often treated to such a meal. Thank you very much."

"You have to go already?"

"Yes, in a few moments. But I wonder if I might make a telephone call first."

"Oh, sure." Ellen pointed toward the door to the hall. "Why don't you go back to our bedroom. You can have some privacy."

"That is very thoughtful."

It was a ritual of theirs. Ellen had let it pass through her mind without it registering too heavily that Chu used their house to call numbers he did not want on his own phone bill, but he always gave a generous sum of money—to her, not Ramón—and she trusted he was clever enough not to get them into trouble.

Chu turned right, down a short hall into the master bedroom, closing the door gently behind him. It was furnished with a suite in a Spanish style with walnut veneer; beneath the windows was a round side table with a cloth that fell all the way to the carpet, flanked by two small, blue velvet swivel rockers; two-for-one sale at Sears, probably a hundred and fifty dollars for both of them, Chu assessed and shook his head even as he settled into one. Ellen furnished the house as nicely as she could, within her budget.

Chu twisted in the chair and removed a small address book from a hip pocket and flipped to the page he wanted. He picked up the receiver and turned it in his hands, punching quickly 011 for an international line and then 65, the country code for Singapore, before sliding his slender finger under the number in his book. The listings there were in the American style—a three-digit prefix, followed by a four-digit number. The privacy of closing the door was unnecessary, as the conversation was in Mandarin Chinese. He had closed the door not because Ellen might understand him, but because he disliked his language being heard as some amusing curiosity.

"This is Albert Chu. I believe Mr. Wang is expecting a call from me at this hour. Is he available, please?"

There was the distant clicking of hold buttons and call transfer before his party answered.

"This is Chu. Can you tell me that the job has been completed?"

It was a reasonably good connection, not the best; Wang's voice was clear, but scratchy and distant-sounding. "Yes, we are ready for your visit."

"It would be helpful if you could give me a summary of what has happened." There was no reason for the line to be tapped, and Chu was unafraid to discuss business.

"We recruited a party of Malay hunters in a village outside of Ipoh," Wang began. "They were successful in penetrating the Taman Negara National Park, and about two weeks ago brought down a fine bull rhino, two horns, small but full."

"Good. Were the authorities alerted?"

"Yes. The leader of the party got word to our tourists staying at the park lodge at Kuala Tahan, who happened to discover the body and alerted the park guards. There was quite a stir."

"Excellent," said Chu calmly. "Has it been in the newspapers?"

"Not yet. The story was suppressed because the government there does not want that kind of publicity." "There" meant Malaysia, which was trying its best to observe the CITES treaty.

"But what about in Singapore?"

"There was a little story in the English papers here. The editor of the main Chinese paper is a friend of ours, and he is covering it in greater detail."

"But not in enough detail, I hope, for the authorities to question him about his sources?"

"There is no danger of that. But we can make certain that copies of that issue will find their way into the other Chinese communities around the region."

"Kuala Lumpur and Djakarta?"

"No problem. And Bangkok and Rangoon—all of them. We can make sure that the doctors in those communities will know who is supplying them, and that the product is genuine."

Chu paused for a moment, thinking. It all seemed very simple up to this point. "What about the hunters from Ipoh?"

"They were liquidated as soon as they arrived with the horns to collect their pay."

"Good. And the tourists in the lodge were ours?"

"Yes."

"Very good. I will arrive later in the week, probably Thursday, with some package samples of the products we are preparing in Los Angeles. Between what we show them and what they know from the papers and the street talk, it should make a very effective presentation."

"I agree completely," said Wang.

"I will call you Thursday from my suite there. Good-bye." Albert Chu hung up the phone and leaned back in the blue velvet swivel rocker, replacing the address book in his hip pocket and crossing his legs. Here he sat in the West, he thought, looking around the quiet Westernness of the Barillas' bedroom—Am I so inscrutable?

Of all the Asian stereotypes that annoyed him, inscrutability was the worst offender. Life is simple. Life is about the acquisition of money, and therefore power, and therefore face. If any got in the way—well, they should know better. The collective intelligence of the world would not be noticeably diminished by the disappearance of a few Malay natives who were stupid enough to involve themselves in such affairs. There is nothing inscrutable in that. Chu nodded, satisfied.

Nothing at all. He stood and took a fifty-dollar bill from his wallet and slipped it under the telephone.

He found Ellen in the kitchen, rinsing dishes before loading them into the washer. He tapped on the wall to get her attention. "Thank you again for your kind hospitality."

Ellen shut off the water and dried her hands again as she saw him out the door. "Well, it was so good to see you."

"I'm afraid the phone call was long distance. I left enough money on the table to cover it."

"Oh, you don't need to do that."

"Please," he shook hands with her. "I insist." It was the end of their ritual. "Good-bye."

Back out in the yard, Ramón Barilla took up his beer again after finishing his sherbet. "You know, money goes a lot farther back home. If we had a lot of money, like a million dollars, we could walk away from all these gringos and taxes and shit. Go back home and disappear, live like kings."

Luís was astonished. So, beneath all that Americanization, beneath all that Jaycees and Republican party and passing as Raymond Berry, Uncle Ramón's own seed of hatred at always being the servile one had finally taken root.

Esteban laughed. "You live too high, a million dollars maybe won't go too far."

Ramón leaned back and crossed his legs. "Well, you know, there's more. You remember old Chino's ranch?" Ramón almost never mentioned anything of the days when Joaquín had been alive; it startled the others for him to dredge up the memory of their family spread up in the Sierra Madre. "He tol' me, he hire a—" he couldn't pick the right word and waved his hand in the air "—a geology guy, he tell him he got lots of silver and even a little gold in his hills. Chino don't want to go to the government to get a mine started. Then he got to pay taxes and—" he rubbed his thumb and fingertips together "—las mordidas and all that, you know. But he tell me if he had some money to start a little smelter, he don't mind startin' small to see what he really got."

Esteban seemed dubious. "How much does he need?"

"He say maybe half a million."

Esteban shook his head. "Silver's not worth a whole lot right now."

"Right now, yeah, but that probably gonna change. Plus some gold, too. Maybe lots. It's a big ranch. They didn't take samples from all over."

"When did you talk to him?"

"He call maybe a month ago."

"You never told us."

Ramón shrugged uncomfortably. "Well, he don't want too many people knowin', but I'm telling you now. I think maybe we ought to do it. Look around you, man, ain't you even a little tired of all this shit?"

Esteban considered it. Certainly the lure of the familiar, once you've known it, remains potent. To be on their own again, without interference, no more dressing up and going to the mall and saying "Yes, ma'am" and "No, ma'am," no more paperwork and tax forms. It was attractive. "What makes you think the job for Chu is going to be worth a million dollars?"

"Well, let's figure it out." He sent Luís into the house for his little calculator, whose tiny buttons Ramón had difficulty striking accurately with his thick, leathery fingers. "We don't know for sure how many rhinos he got—Chu says at least twenty-five." He punched 25 into the calculator. "If they like what they got in San Antonio, we guess maybe five kilos apiece." He multiplied by five and got 125. "If he give us ten thousand a kilo, that's—*aí,* shit yeah, man, that a million and a quarter." He started laughing.

"If we get them all."

Ramón nodded. "If we get them all." He turned to his youngest nephew. "What do you think, Luís? If we had a million dollars, you want to go back home?"

The question struck Luís as strange; Ramón had rescued him from Nuevo Laredo when he was sixteen, and that was six years ago. He thought of this as his home but it was going stale, and better to be a somebody among nobodies than to be a nobody here any longer. Some portion of that money was bound to wind up being his, and certainly the pussy, back in that ranch home he had never been to, would be easier, if for no other reason than that. "Let's go; I'm ready."

Ramón popped the top on another beer, running his hand over the map of The Refuge on his lap. "Well, I guess we gonna start going to the zoo on Sundays." Then he remembered something. "Only, now listen, don't tell none of the women about this. I want to tell Ellen about it my own way. Let's just see how things go."

9 🌿🌿🌿🌿🌿🌿🌿🌿🌿🌿

ERIC WAS UP EARLY SATURDAY MORNING, his eagerness to open the park to the public almost instantly tempered by the groggy memory—no, he had not dreamed it—that Ethel was dead. On his way into the kitchen he stopped at the crucifix and knelt, crossing himself. At first he had no words and just meditated, visualizing Francis and his compassion for the animals. Then eventually he whispered, "Father, as you have put it into my heart to believe that animals have in some way some spirit, and since you have told us that not a sparrow falls but you are aware of it, humbly I beseech your care for Fred and Ethel, and all who are slaughtered in greed. And I ask Your peace for myself, to believe that You are infinite, and to believe that I serve You in what I do. *In nomini patri, et fili, et spiritu sancti.* Amen."

It was impossible to pray so and not feel his throat tighten, and he left the house early so he could drive slower and glance out the windows of his new Saturn at the egrets in their marshes.

The first thing Eric saw as he opened the door to the reception room was Stephanie in one motion vaulting from her chair and snatching a paper from the in-basket. She jogged across the room, waving the paper and almost singing, "Fax from Stan! Fax from Stan!" She wiggled it in front of him like a doggie treat until he grabbed it from her and read intensely. "It's all there," she said. "The Javas would do fine on what we're already growing. We just need to concentrate a little more on forest floor roughage and fruits and stuff."

"Hallelujah," he whispered. "Get Millie up here right away."

"I've already called her; she's on her way over from the farm right now. Yeah!" Stephanie reared back to give him a high-five, but when their hands met she caught his and held it. "We all saw on the news last night about San Antonio. I'm really sorry."

He squeezed her hand. "Thank you, sweetie. Is everybody here?"

"Rearing to go—well, sort of, considering it's Saturday. And when you're done there, that guy from the college newspaper is here."

"What, already?"

"He asked if he could wait in your office. I didn't think you'd mind."

He thought, Wow, talk about your eager beavers. He must take care what kind of monster he created with this one. His thoughts turned back to his chief botanist, Millie McMillan, whose job included not just landscaping the continents with appropriately authentic greenery but keeping the animals' enclosures planted with the right food, and growing enough extra on the farm and in its greenhouses to supply them. He handed the fax back to Stephanie. "Make some copies; original for me, one copy for Millie, one for Jake's file, one for Ernie, one for the kitchen. When Millie gets here tell her to get to it on the double. The Indonesian conservation minister and ambassador are coming next month. The Javas' house has got to look like a rain forest and there's not a minute to lose."

"Gotcha."

When Eric entered the conference room he had already said good morning when he noticed something different about the arrangement of people around the table. As he seated himself he noticed his chief of security, Sam Rutherford, sitting next to Jake.

He began in his habitual way. "Jake, you want to go first?" On the staff chart Jake Teal was just the veterinarian, but in reality, if The Refuge had an assistant director and lieutenant general, it was Jake. Eric had not found Jake; Jake found him. When the park was still only a gleam in Eric's eye, he had attended an annual AZA conference. Jake was the vet at one of the small Kansas zoos—Kansas has for its population far more small municipal zoos than any other state in the union. At the conference the major zoo players whom Eric had sought out for advice to the last one had offered encouraging platitudes and then, he knew, chuckled behind his back at his naïveté and wide-eyed earnestness. One of those players, smiling and shaking his head, had told Jake about him, and Jake literally collared him in a crowded room and said, "We need to talk, buddy." They had dinner, after which Jake told Eric that if he could make the park happen, he should call him.

"Jake, you want to go first?"

"Okay. Now, boss, I don't want you to get upset, but I took it on myself to get Sam and Ernie here early this morning so we could talk about what happened in San Antonio yesterday." In addition to being the head keeper for mammals, Ernie Lange had personal charge of the elephants and rhinoceroses. Ernie sat placidly in his usual place at the table. He was a large, baggy old guy with baggy eyes, and always seemed placid; maybe it was something he got from his elephants, like the way pets and owners come to resemble one another over time.

"Now," Jake went on, "I don't need to tell you we all feel terrible about what happened up there. We know you've had an interest in Ethel for years, but beyond that, we thought it was prudent to review our own security capability. And, we're all agreed that we want you to hire an extra guard. Sam?"

Sam Rutherford was fifty-five, ex-HPD who had worked the Fifth Ward until he couldn't stomach the human misery and predation any longer. He was still tough and fit, and had ordered people about for so long he was plainly uncomfortable at having to explain and persuade. "The problem is," he began slowly, "that we're outside anyone's city limits. If, and I say *if*, we were faced with a similar situation here, we couldn't get major police help until a county sheriff's deputy arrived on the scene and requested it."

Eric tapped his pen on his pad. "How long would that take?"

Sam shrugged. "I would guess fifteen to twenty minutes for the sheriff's department to get here, a while longer for them to investigate the situation and determine if backup was required, and if they did make a call to HPD I would guess another thirty minutes for backup to arrive. At least an hour, altogether, before a situation could be gotten in hand."

Eric rose from the table and walked slowly over to the tilted-view window that looked down onto the grounds. It was now after nine, and groups of tourists had begun to arrive. The double doors flanking the bust of Joseph II were directly beneath him, and he watched as groups of visitors, unfolding their maps and pointing, emerged as though from the carpet beneath his feet. "So what you're saying is, if we ever had to protect our stock, we'd be on our own until it was too late?"

Sam Rutherford nodded. "Even if perpetrators were apprehended, there would still be dead animals."

Eric stared down at the tourists, frightened to discover how Ethel's death had altered his own frame of mind. "Hire an extra guard," he said at last. "Don't go the classifieds. Use the placement service at a security academy. Give hiring preference—well, try to find a veteran with a background in marksmanship."

Rutherford pulled in his breath. This was more of a response than he had expected. "Are you saying shoot to kill?"

Shoot to kill. There were certainly precedents for it. The poaching in Africa had become so prevalent that some countries there had been issuing shoot-to-kill orders for years. Once he had even seen it himself, in Zimbabwe, at the Chete Game Reserve on the Zambian border. Its rocky thickets were considered the best rhino country in Africa, and had once teemed with them. Eric had been there a couple of years before, to observe the game guards in tracking and darting the last twelve surviving Chete rhinos for removal to Australia. Once while tracking rhino they came upon a camp of poachers. The soldiers he was with approached as stealthily as if they were nearing a wounded lion, until one who was close enough to see pressed his palms together against his cheek and closed his eyes. The poachers were asleep. They stalked the camp without so much as the snap of a twig, until with a single, native-accented "Fire!" the guards shot four of them in their bedrolls. No "Give up, you're surrounded," no "You're under arrest." Only the loud-bursting staccato of a half-dozen Kalashnikovs, a few plangent shrieks, and the slowly quieting uproar of nearby birds and monkeys. The corporal explained that poachers apprehended in the bush very, very seldom surrender, and even when cornered in the most helpless position, if offered a chance to give up usually manage to take at least a few soldiers with them. Warnings were now considered not only pointless but foolhardy. Eric helped pull the bodies from their riddled blankets. Of all there was to make an impression, the gore, the smell, the fact that one of them had expired with a titanic erection—what struck him was the fact that they all wore socks, black dress hose, dirty and heelless. He felt sick and had wanted to feel compassion, but was unable to conjure it. He who might have been a priest had tried and failed to feel pity for them.

Shoot to kill? Eric Jackson pointed to the newspaper on the table in front of his chair. "They do, don't they?" They had never seen him like this.

"What about you?" challenged Sam Rutherford. "Could you kill a man to protect an animal?" Eric stared at him, surprised to find himself without an answer.

Jake suddenly interposed himself. "Hell, boss, you'd get buck fever and couldn't shoot straight, anyhow."

There was grateful laughter around the table.

"No," said Eric heavily. "No, Sam, I couldn't do that. Just make sure you hire somebody who can." He recognized a moral contradiction in what he had just said, but there was no time to ponder it now.

"If what happened in San Antonio becomes a trend," said Rutherford, "I'll need more than one."

"Eric nodded. "If it becomes a trend, you'll get them."

"There may be another way," said Jake.

Eric resumed his seat and knew what was coming and knew already he didn't want to hear it.

"You know, some of the national park services in some of the African countries have begun programs to dart the wild rhinos they have left and saw their horns off, to take away their value to poachers. I suppose if it's necessary we could do the same thing here."

"Ernie," said Eric, "you've been doing the breeding. Do you and your people usually observe the nuptial sparring and things that courting rhinos are supposed to do with their horns?"

"Affirmative."

"Jake, do you know of any follow-up studies in any of those African studies to indicate that removing their horns has had no adverse effect on their breeding?"

Jake ground his teeth, knowing his answer would settle the issue. "No, I do not."

"Well, guys, considering that our only purpose in having rhinos here at all is to breed them, I would like to avoid doing anything that might tamper with their natural process any more than necessary. So for now, just hire a new guard, and we'll monitor the situation." Eric forbore giving vent to his first thought, which was about the Indonesians. The last thing they needed to hear was that The Refuge was so spooked for the safety of their animals that they had taken such an extreme measure. Damage control from the San Antonio killings was going to be difficult enough to manage without further jeopardizing the effort to get the Javas transferred.

They finished their business, and Eric entered his office, forgetting until he opened the door that Larry Davis was waiting for him, standing at his wall of bookshelves, leafing through a copy of Karl Hagenbeck's 1909 *Beasts and Men*. As Eric headed for his desk, Larry sat in the chair opposite, with the book still in his hand. "Looks like there's quite a history to animal collecting."

"Ancient Egypt, Rome. Yeah."

Eric expected the interview to take the slant of a feature article, but it was apparent from Larry's attitude that the student's mind had turned to other things. "When we went over to Customs yesterday," he said at last, "I copied the address down from one of the shipping labels." He handed it over. "I'm a reporter, let me track it down."

Eric looked at the paper and read Bark 'N Purr Pet Center, with an address in Pasadena. "Track what down? Nothing there was illegal."

"But you said that was the third shipment of dead animals this year."

"Yes, but that's not unusual." He returned the slip of paper. "We went over there purely as a mercy mission. If you want to write about animals dying from being mishandled in transit, that's one thing and it's not a bad story. But that's not the same as violating the Endangered Species Act or the CITES Treaty or trafficking in any kind of contraband. None of those animals were on the endangered list. You have to figure out what your story is going to be."

"But they must have broken some law to do that."

"Nope. Legal as can be. That's what is so sickening."

Larry Davis stared at him. "Then that's a story itself."

"Wait, wait, slow down. Be careful you don't get ahead of yourself. The last time we talked you were going to do a feature about the park."

"Oh. Yeah."

"I appreciate your sense of outrage. And, you know I know how you feel. But get your feet wet first, learn the lingo and who the players are. Learn how the animal park business works. I think you will find that you'll be better prepared to write an angry exposé after you at least learn the vocabulary."

Larry Davis felt like he was being patronized until he heard the last sentence. "Okay, I guess you're right."

"Have you thought about that other thing we talked about?"

"You mean a job?" He smiled. "Yeah, I'm leaning. Can I still cruise around today and talk to people?"

"Yes. How did you get past the counter? Did you pay an admission?"

"Yes."

Eric reached for his billfold, but Larry said, "No, that's okay. Think of it as a donation."

"Well, see Stephanie on your way out. She'll give you a press pass so when you come out you won't have any trouble at the register."

After Davis left, Eric felt curious how things were going downstairs. He descended the stairs at the rear of the entry hall, observing for several minutes that the two turnstiles were both busy—not mobbed, but with a continuous line from four to ten deep. He exited the front door to have a look at the parking garage, satisfied to see car windows already as high as the third level. He recrossed the loggia back to the staircase, and then on a whim turned into the Hall of Silence to see how people were reacting. In the dimness of the hall, he made out five to six dozen people wandering from one lit case to another. Indeed they were quiet, and only sporadically did he hear an echo of, "Come look at this." And he thought: It's working. It's working.

★　★　★

For Jake Teal it began when he was six, at the CenTex Zoo in Waco. His parents had a farm between Mount Calm and Birome, and every two weeks his mother would drive in to Waco to see her sister Wanda, who ran a beauty parlor in the closed-in garage of her house. Mom could get her hair done for free, or sort of free, because she always took in a big sack of fresh vegetables from their garden.

Aunt Wanda had always seemed to like Jake, perhaps because her own marriage had given her no children, and Jake was too young to wonder how anyone who looked like Wanda could spend all day running a beauty parlor. She was a big, hippy woman who wore her hair up in impossible pompadours, and in her home and business gave herself to gossip, chocolates, and tabloid newspapers with headlines like, ARMLESS TOT FIGHTS OFF ALIENS WITH TEETH. She adored Elvis.

That one weekend Mom drove in to Waco and asked Jake, in front of Wanda, if he would like to stay there and visit a couple of days. Aunt Wanda seized him and set him up on her soft double-knit lap and said, "We can go to the zoo. I'll bet you've never been there." It was only years later, after his own divorce, that Jake realized that his parents needed the house to themselves to work some things out.

Jake did know what a zoo was. There was a picture book in the library at his primary school, and he had seen Tarzan and some other jungle movies on television, so he had an idea what waited for him there. After Mom left, Aunt Wanda had put him in her car, a big white 1959 Chevy with an automatic transmission and yard-wide fins that made him feel he was riding in a spaceship. They drove out through Waco's west side, and then he thought they were back in the country, with its rolling pastures and hackberry fence rows, but then they turned in to a park and Wanda stopped the car on a gravel parking lot. It was a blistering July day, and he kept getting grains of chat caught in his sandals like tiny hot coals, but when he began to see the animals, the rest of the world faded into the July haze.

The CenTex Zoo in Waco had an Indian elephant, just more than half grown, but at that time Jake was so small that she loomed as large before him as Sobhuza did now. Jake was electrified. The smell, the size—Jake had seen Belgian horses before and couldn't imagine that animals got any bigger than that—and the incredible delicacy with which she accepted peanuts from him with that long, bristled firehose of a trunk. Then, after Jake had fed her half a dozen peanuts, she put out her trunk to his hand—and blew out a blob of mud and mucous that stuck to his hand like warm jelly. Jake jumped back and shook his hand, but the stuff stuck fast. He thought it was kind of neat, but Wanda had a fit. "Oh, my God," she gagged, "elephant boogers!"

She dug a Kleenex out of her purse and wiped off the worst of it, then marched him over to the drinking fountain, almost running him, so that the hot July gravel kept getting in his sandals and burning his feet. He had to hold down the button of the drinking fountain with one hand while she scrubbed at the affliction, and he remembered saying, "Aunt Wanda, we have to tell them. She's sick. She might have a cold. They won't know if we don't tell them."

She tried to hush him but he simply would not be satisfied until they found somebody to tell. He insisted on it and made himself a nuisance, until finally they saw a groundskeeper and Wanda pushed Jake forward to speak up. The groundskeeper told them where to find the elephant keeper; he was just finishing his lunch break when Jake came up and in his little six-year-old voice said, "Excuse me, I think your elephant is sick. It sneezed in my hand."

"Well, we'd better go see about it, shouldn't we?" the keeper said. They walked back toward the elephant yard, the keeper questioning him seriously and, when Jake could not see, giving Wanda a wink and a smile. When the elephant heard the door to her house unlock she turned from the yard and entered, and the keeper let Jake give her a drink of water from a bucket, explaining that elephants get boogers just like people do, only more of them because they have to drink by sucking water up their noses. He turned on a hose and let Jake scrub her crinkled back with a push broom. The elephant made a whinny-ing little trumpeting sound. "Oh, she likes that," said the keeper. "She likes that." Aunt Wanda had stayed at the back wall, by the door, looking worried but not interfering.

That, for Jake Teal, was the beginning. Aunt Wanda had died when he was in high school. She had complained about her hiatal hernia so often and had to lie down so often that no one suspected she might be having a heart attack. So she went to lie down, and she died.

Jake last saw her in the funeral home, lying in repose in a pink taffeta gown of the kind she would not have been caught dead in while she lived. But he remembered her more clearly standing nervously by the door of the elephant house. "Now Jake, you be careful with that thing. You be careful." She was a simple and silly woman, but she, as much as his mother, had given him his life, and he kept her memory for that.

Jake had married, had two children, divorced, and married again. He had turned forty and was getting thick through the middle. He wore wire-rimmed glasses not for fashion, but because they suited his freckled, aging ex-hippie's face under his unruly red hair. His accent was still so rural Texan that it turned heads, even in Dallas and Houston. He had gone to vet school at A&M, which he found was the beginning, not the end, of a zoo vet's education. Even though he was now the vet at the finest wild animal facility in the world, he still spent more time than he ever would have imagined just keeping in touch with other zoo vets around the world. It is a close fraternity, for most of the knowledge of wild animal doctoring is not found in books, but in long years of experience. That was the one thing Jake lacked, the long history of experimenting, jerryrigging, saying, "I'll bet we could do this."

That was why he needed to stay in touch with older vets and they were willing, because they knew Jake Teal was a brilliant innovator himself. He had certainly come a long way from the time he was ten, when his dad ran over a terrapin with the lawn mower, clipping off the top of its shell and laying open its greenish, oozing back. Jake was inconsolable, and Dad had helped him wash the wound with hydrogen peroxide and seal it with duct tape. When it got infected they tried Campho-Phenique. Jesus, the suffering that poor animal must have gone through before it died. Jake still shook his head at the memory.

At least he and Dad had been on the right track. When he was in college he read one zoo vet's memoir and made a note card of his method of treating a tortoise: ethyl chloride freeze spray to kill the pain, arnica disinfectant, and then seal the hole in the shell with virtually anything—in that case a rubber patch intended for a bicycle tire. That was the kind of improvisation that lay at the heart of successful zoo practice. It's the kind of thing you learn from older zoo vets. There are even lineages of study, like taking piano lessons from somebody who studied with somebody, who studied with somebody who studied with Liszt. But now he was one of the very best at what he did, and now everything Jake learned he passed on to Lucy, who was making her own note cards, on a computer.

It was early in the afternoon when Larry Davis crossed a short moat from the east side of Japan and entered the veterinary compound. He didn't need to inquire which office was Jake Teal's, for as he made his way down a tile corridor—noiselessly, wearing canvas sneakers—he could hear Jake's grinding accent around an open door several yards ahead of him, dictating notes.

He was curious to see if he could understand any of the lingo and waited outside the door, listening as Jake said, "The purpose of this experiment is to record the Extremely Low Frequency vocalizations (hereafter referred to as ELF vocalizations) of a cow African elephant *(Loxodonta africana)* in estrus. By comparing the sound graphs of these rumblings to the ELF vocalizations of a nonestrus cows, we hope to determine which of these vocalizations are the ones that are responded to by musth bulls, and especially to see whether overt mating interest in the bulls can be elicited by playing recordings of certain estrus-cow vocalizations. If the results are positive, it may be possible to determine the breeding-cycle status of both bulls and cows by remote microphone surveillance, without disruptive examinations. Musth bulls could then be introduced to estrus cows in a dynamic similar to the call-and-response that takes place in the wild.

"A successful result of this experiment would be the more important in view of the fact that attempts to collect semen samples from live bulls have not shown much promise. Resultant births and rearings could then be observed for what improvements, if any, in the mother's maternal skills might be related to this more hands-off approach to elephant breeding.

"Since all the vocalizations are below the range of human hearing, recordings will be made on a Nagra IVSJ Recorder, using two Sennheiser MKH 110 microphones. All the equipment will be calibrated using a Model 14230 B&K Acoustic Calibrator . . ."

There was a knock, and Jake looked up over the toes of his snakeskin boots, saw them framing Larry Davis standing in the door, and pointed to a chair on the opposite side of his desk. He switched off the recorder. "Come on in."

Larry headed toward the chair. "Man, I had you pegged for a country horse doctor. I guess I was wrong."

As Larry sat down, Jake slowly plopped his feet on the floor. "Yeah, well, you were a real horse's butt yesterday, I guess you know that."

Larry laughed. "Yeah. I know."

Their eyes met; Jake said, "He offered you a job, didn't he?"

"How did you know?"

"I know Eric. You gonna take it?"

"I don't know. Maybe. He agreed to let me follow the staff around for a couple of days to see how things are set up."

"Is that so?" Jake was not impressed.

"I don't know about Jackson, though. I think he enjoys his work but—" Larry shook his head vaguely. "He seems, I don't know, driven, or something. Tell me about him. What makes him tick?"

"Reporter wants a capsule characterization, huh?"

"No, not for print, just for me."

Jake eyed him suspiciously. "All right." If Eric was going to trust the boy, he should do the same. He put his feet back up on his desk, pointing at Larry over the scuffed knees of his khakis. "Now, if you ever tell him I told you this, I'll skin you alive."

"I won't."

"I remember the first time we went over to Customs to get some smuggled exotics they got hold of."

"Like yesterday?"

"No, those yesterday were mishandled, but they weren't smuggled. Anyway, they usually send 'em out to their own facility near Cotulla, till they got so full they said they didn't know where they'd put any more. They asked us if we'd take some over, and we did. You ever been over in the Spanish *barrio* by the ship channel?"

"No way." Larry Davis was a liberal but he wasn't stupid.

Jake Teal's lips curled into a knowing smirk, which made Larry wonder if it was because Jake didn't believe him or because he did. Either way, it made him feel undressed. "Well, if you ever do, one thing you'll see is, about every fifth house has a big ol' parrot or macaw in it. Now, you can call me a racist if you want to, but the Mexicans just love bright colors like that. It's a cultural thing. A lot of these birds, it's not against the law to own 'em, but it is against the law to import 'em without a permit 'cause they carry psittacosis and shit like that. Plus, a lot of them are endangered species and don't have any business bein' in private homes.

"It was about a month after we got set up, the Customs guys called and said they got a pickup truck. Couple of damn *fayuqueros* had taped about twenty birds all inside the thing. The damn truck was so old and beat up it could hardly run—finally popped a radiator hose and pulled over. Highway Patrol stopped to see if they could help and smelled something weird. Damn idiots had birds taped everywhere—wrapped 'em up in newspaper baggies, except their heads. Taped their beaks shut so they wouldn't squawk. They hid 'em under a false bottom in the tool box, inside the bumper, inside the spare tire, ever'where. There was three behind the front seat in the cab. They was the only ones still alive. Shit."

"It was the birds they smelled?"

"Well, they towed the truck in. We got over there, lifted up the hood. They had three parrots strapped under the hood got scalded to death in the steam."

"Oh, Jesus!"

"Eric took it real quiet but I could tell he was upset. We put the live ones in the van and started back, Eric was driving. We got about a mile outa there and he started to lose it, started crying. He had to pull over; I'd never seen a grown man bawl like that. You see, he knew about poaching and smuggling and all that. He knew it went on, but he'd never seen it. I mean, dead rhinos in Kenya is one thing, and that's bad enough, but scalding helpless little birds to death—he just never had to look at it with his own eyes that anybody really could be that cruel and that stupid." Jake was quiet for a second. "Don't you ever let on you know about that."

"I won't." He thought briefly. "That's why you—protect him. Like yesterday, doing all the paperwork, having that chimp waiting for him in his office. You try to make things easier for him. Don't you?"

"Yes, sir, I do. We all do. You need to understand now, don't think he's weak, 'cause he ain't. Eric Jackson is a strong man and a brilliant man. My God, boy, how many people do you think could have put a place like this together—and more than that, made it pay for itself? But you see, he's tender. And when he has a bad experience or needs some downtime, you bet we step in to take up the slack. And we don't think the less of him for it, neither. Not a bit."

Larry Davis nodded quietly, not breaking eye contact.

"So what does he want to hire you to do?"

"Intern," he said. "I guess that means a little bit of all of it."

"Well," Jake glanced at the clock. "You want to get a little hands-on experience?"

Larry smiled dubiously. "Sure, I guess."

10 🌿🌿🌿🌿🌿🌿🌿🌿🌿🌿

JAKE PICKED UP THE PHONE and punched a three-digit extension. "Ernie. Jake. You got Junior ready for his one o'clock? You give him his happy shot? Good, we'll be right over." He punched in another number. "Miss Lucy. We're on our way over to collect Junior's donation. Think you can pull away and give us a hand? Naw, no hurry. We'll start without you." He repeated the process. "Say, boss. We're goin' over to see Junior and give him a good time. Want to come? Good, see you in a minute." He hung up and slapped his knees. "Well, let's get going. Did you walk all the way out here?"

"Yes." He wondered what in the hell Jake was talking about but didn't much like the sound of it.

"Well, let's give you a ride in a cart; show you how the executives move around this place. Takes a lot of miles off the old dogs." As they passed through the door, Jake snatched from a small hook a chain with a magnetized ID card on it.

They walked down the white-tile corridor and turned a corner into the quarantine section, and out a back door. "Those boots look so comfortable, I wouldn't think you'd mind walking."

"They are, actually."

"They look like ostrich skin."

"Yup." He guessed what was coming.

"It doesn't strike you as odd that a wildlife advocate would wear those?"

"Not a bit. No species of animal on this earth is going to be saved unless it can pull its own weight economically. That's sad and I don't like it, but that's a fact, cold and hard. You pick one of them, any one of them, and I'll tell you half a dozen reasons why they should be preserved and I won't never touch either the ethics or the aesthetics."

"I didn't think ostriches were endangered."

"They ain't." Jake locked the door behind them and they climbed into his camouflaged golf cart, which started forward with a jerk. "But if you preserve their habitat, you also preserve the habitat of other species that are. Besides, ostriches are about the most useful big birds around. The feathers are good, the leather's good, obviously; the meat's good, even the eggs are good. They don't serve 'em in the cafeteria yet, but chef is working on a way to make them taste less oily. Now, I told him he ought to try deviled, so he can use some of their own oil and cut down on the mayonnaise."

He glanced over at Larry Davis, who said, "You're a fraud. You're no hick."

"Well, ever'body's got an act, don't they?"

From the vet compound they drove south on the perimeter road that surrounded the park, turning west along the south boundary of Australia and then Africa. To their left was the green wall of shrubs and vines that screened the park from the road, and on their right a continuous wall of loading docks and access doors, each clearly marked as to which diorama was being accessed, the whole looking not unlike the back side of a shopping center where the trucks make their deliveries. After every third or fourth entry way, a long alley pierced into the complex, giving access to the enclosures toward the interior of the park.

Jake stopped abruptly at a metal door that had two other carts parked outside it. They approached it, and Jake inserted his card into a box by the door. There was a hum and a thump, a red light turned off and a green one switched on, and Jake opened the door, standing aside for Larry. " 'Come into my parlor,' said the spider to the fly."

Inside, Jake introduced Larry to Ernie. They crossed the cement-floored service area and rounded a corner to see a bull black rhino being held in a tight squeeze-cage. Larry Davis had never been so close to one and was instinctively frightened, but then saw that the animal's attention was fully focused on Eric, who was standing at the front of the cage, cutting slices from an apple which the rhino was consuming so eagerly that he had one piece chomped and down, and his mouth gaping open for another before Eric could finish slicing it. When it was all gone, Eric patted the rhino on the side of the face, saying softly, "They killed your mama, Junior. I'm so sorry, they killed your mama."

Larry heard Jake ask, "You right-handed or left?"

"Left."

"Hold 'er up." He fitted a latex surgical glove onto Larry's left hand.

"What are we going to do?"

Jake handed him a jar of KY jelly. "You, my boy, are going to masturbate a rhinoceros."

"Like hell."

"Just dab this around his foreskin until the real thing comes out. Then just carry on like you was doing your own."

"Bullshit!"

It was true that other male animals could donate semen by the much more sanitary, not to say aesthetic, method of electrode stimulation, but pachyderms had no accessible testes. Junior was one of the few in captivity who tolerated the indignity of manipulation. Jake sympathized, but neither could he deny that he enjoyed the show of delegating the old-fashioned way to a novice.

Larry looked to Eric for help, who turned up his hands helplessly. "Jake's in charge here."

Larry Davis shook his head as he dropped to one knee, laughing softly, "Oh, fuck me." He had just reached through the bars and touched Junior's side when he slammed his horn into the side of the cage with a tremendous crash that echoed through the room. With rhinos it is easy to think they are being vicious when they are merely eager, and Larry jumped back. "No way, man! No fucking way."

Eric strewed some fresh alfalfa in a removable bin under Junior's nose, and Jake pushed Larry on the shoulder. "Aw, go on, get down there. We've given him a little sedative so he won't get too worked up. You'll be fine reachin' in. Just don't get carried away and roll under there."

Larry Davis had never suspected how threateningly nasty a large mammal's privates are; in size, odor, sight—everything is on a scale all their own. Steeling himself, he dabbed small streaks of KY around the opening of the foreskin, finally grasping as much of it in his hand as he could get. What began to emerge truly made him sick.

"That's good," encouraged Jake. "Keep goin'."

After several minutes they heard the hum and thump of the lock on the access door and Lucy entered, her attention on the clipboard of forms to record the sample and prepare the bill. She didn't know Eric would be there; when she looked up her eyes flickered a greeting, but she said nothing.

"Luce," Jake said broadly, "get down there and help this city boy out, will you?"

Larry heard a girl's laugh, high but husky, the last sound on earth he was at that instant expecting, then through the rhino's legs he saw a pair of boots, jeans tucked in, and the hem of a lab coat. She knelt, and then beneath the rhino's belly he saw one of the loveliest faces he had ever seen, a feminine coy smile partly obscured by that turgid brown-black salami. "Hi," she said.

Larry Davis had never been so embarrassed in his life. He answered, "Uh, hi," absently loosening his grip.

She reached out quickly and caught it. "Be careful. Try not to bump it on the floor. It'll get dirty." She had blue eyes, her honey-blond hair pulled back in a short pony tail.

"Sorry." He resumed the stroking as she held it off the floor.

"Is this your first time?" she asked gently.

"What?"

"Don't be nervous." She touched his hand. "I'll help you."

He thought, Oh Christ!, and saw a glass beaker in her other hand. He kept doing it, glancing back up over his shoulder. "How long does this take?"

Jake snorted. "I don't know. If you was his missus it might take ten minutes, sometimes an hour. Sometimes he don't come at all; that's just the way it is with rhinos. I guess it depends on whether you turn him on."

"Yeah, thanks a lot, buddy."

"Naw, really, it's true," Jake went on. "You know, people think the Chinese believe in rhino aphrodisiac because the horn is shaped like a phallus, but that's just part of it. When a bull rhino mounts a cow he might really stay there for an hour and he might come fifteen or twenty times. Impressed the hell out of the Chinese. Impresses me, too."

"Well, you tell me how the hell the ancient Chinese figured out how many times a rhino comes, and *I'll* be impressed."

Larry saw the blond girl getting tickled. "What's your name?" he asked.

"Lucy."

"Lucy. I'm Larry." He kept doing it, squeezing a little harder.

"Pleased to meet you, Larry."

"I remember you from the press tour. You're the geneticist, right?"

"Associate vet—and geneticist."

He continued for several more minutes, trying to think up what the hell to say. "Don't you think he'd rather you were doing this?"

She laughed. "Nah, you're doing fine."

"Does the vice squad know you do this for a living?"

Lucy felt a surge of extra tension in the rhino's penis. "You better keep your mind on what you're doing. When he gets close he won't thrash and yell, 'Oh, my God,' like guys do. It'll just kind of ooze out."

"What do you—" Larry started to ask her, but then saw what she meant. "Oh, God! Aww, J-e-s-u-s!"

Lucy was under there helping him. "Careful! Here, let me catch it. Keep it up, keep it up!" She grabbed hold deftly, her hand over his, and guided the opalescent drizzle into the beaker, then let Larry take it away.

He got to his knees and then his feet, looking like he was going to throw up. He gave the beaker to Jake, who took it over to a metal box. "You're sure this is his, now?"

"What do you mean?"

"Well, hell, boy, the way you was carryin' on down there, we weren't sure which one of you was gettin' off, you or him." Eric was sitting on a bale of hay, laughing.

Larry stood with the KY-lubricated gloved hand up in the air like a mitt full of leprosy he didn't know what to do with.

"Here, let me help." Larry turned around, looked down at Lucy's taut figure under her lab coat, in tight brown jeans and khaki shirt with her name stitched on the pocket. She skinned the glove easily off his hand, inside out, leaving no mess and only talcum powder to rinse off. "There's a sink over here; we can wash."

She led him to a large zinc double basin next to a long rubber hose coiled on the wall. They washed and shared a towel, and he couldn't take his eyes off her.

"So," she said softly, "was it good for you, too?"

He couldn't believe she was doing this.

Jake hovered over the metal box. "Whoa," he said. "Six milliliters. That's a helluva load, considering. Good job." He sealed the sample in a vial, closed the box and gave it to Lucy. "Why don't you go check the motility and get this right into the freezer. Give Roman the papers so he can get it off air freight to Edinburgh right away." Of course there was more to it than that. A mixture of glycerinlike liquids would have to be added to the semen to keep the sperm from exploding when they were thawed. It was different for each species, and often different even for different races within a single species. The trial and error had taken years and still went on; the list of species whose semen could be dependably frozen was growing, but there was still the greater distance yet to go.

Jake took another apple from Ernie—Ernie always brought some treats when they squeezed Junior in the cage—and approached the rhino's head slowly. Junior stretched out his long, hooked upper lip, showing the bright pink of his tongue and gums. Jake placed a slice in the inner curve of his upper lip, which closed about it and pulled it into his mouth. Jake patted him on the side of the jaw and pulled gently on the ears as he chewed. "Boy, you'd like to get laid more often, wouldn't you? Well, that's all right, so would just about ever'-body." He looked up. "We all clear?"

Lucy glanced around the area outside the squeeze cage, in the passage that led out to his enclosure. "All clear."

"I'm turnin' him out." Jake inserted his same card into the same kind of metal box that had gained them access to the building, and pushed the button to open the gate to the pasture, and released the catch on the outer side of the squeeze cage. The instant Junior saw it move he banged against it with his horn, sending it flying open, and then with his head down and veering side to side, sped outdoors in that rolling trot, his long blackish-brown dick slowly reeling back inside the foreskin. Through the concrete floor they felt the whump-whump-whump of his two-ton hoofed trot recede.

"Uh, listen, Lucy," Larry pretended he was still drying his hands. He saw one of her blue eyes had just a fleck of brown in the iris, and thought she was adorable. "Could I . . . see you sometime? You know, to talk about this? I'm working on a couple of articles."

Eric saw her look up and meet his own eyes for just a second, over Larry's shoulder. "Sure," she said. "I'd like that."

"Great."

She picked up the box with the sample. "Come back over to the clinic with me, I'll give you my phone number."

At first Eric couldn't believe what he was hearing but then knew there was a message in it, that there are all kinds of ways to turn the heat up on a guy.

Larry repeated, "Wow, that's really great." He meant Lucy but knew somehow that translated also to the whole experience, to this whole little world they had here.

"Thanks, Luce," Jake's voice followed her out the door.

"Larry," Eric called after him.

"Yes, sir?" Larry couldn't believe he just called him sir. Lucy turned around, too. "Come back around to my office before you leave, we can talk." He looked evenly at Lucy as he said it, leaving her to wonder what it was they would talk about.

As they left Jake washed his hands, and as he dried them walked over by Eric. "Well, boss, I guess we all know what's going on here."

"Yeah—except the boy."

"You want me to talk to her?"

Eric sucked on a piece of alfalfa straw. "No, don't make a big deal out of it. We'll work it out."

Jake made a gesture in the direction of the back door. "You know a good timber wolf would know how to handle a rival like that."

Eric shook his head and smiled. "Wolf? Hell, I almost became a priest."

Throughout the day, through three surgeries—two of them were sterilizations, which Jake hated, but nonfounders outside the SSPs were not favored for breeding or for taking up room for those that were needed—and several dozen injections, Jake Teal thought about it, and as he worked at his desk near closing time bellowed out, "Luce!"

When she appeared at his door he pointed to the chair on the other side of his desk. "Sit down, darlin'."

Jake knitted his fingers together like he was playing here's-the-church. "You know why I hired you?" He didn't give her a chance to answer. "I hired you because you were the best prospect on the market to turn into a first-class zoo vet. So, I feel like I've got sort of an investment to protect. So, I'll just ask you straight out if you think it's a good idea to get involved with the boss?"

"I haven't let it affect my work."

"No, that's right, you haven't. But there ain't a job in the world where dating the boss ain't risky."

"I know that."

"Do you really think Eric's ready to give up on Liz Ann?"

"Do you think that's any of your business, Jake?"

"If it don't work out and you wind up quittin' the job I've been trainin' you for, hell, yeah, you bet it's my business. Besides," he flopped his hands on his stomach, "I don't want you to get hurt."

"I know."

"Now look here. I don't care if you go out with him. And I don't particularly care if you use some poor dumb college boy to make him get jealous. I don't like it, but that ain't my call. And if it works out between you and Eric, nobody will be cheerin' louder than me. But if it don't, and you need some help or someone to run interference for you, or anything—" he pointed at her "—you come to me and I'll do what I can. I mean it. He won't fire you and I don't want you to quit. Understand me?"

She closed her eyes and nodded. "Thanks, Jake."

"Now, how's our girl Lakshmi doing?"

"I just checked a half hour ago. No labor yet. I'm getting worried, too. We don't know positively that she's term yet, but my hunch is she shouldn't be carrying this long."

"Yeah, I know. Phone Sam. Have the night watch check on her and make sure she's got plenty of hay, not just in her bin but on the floor. If she scoots too much of it around he needs to throw some more in with her. He needs to look in on her every hour and phone me if she goes into labor. Can I reach you if I need you?"

"If I'm not home I'll plug in the call-forwarding."

11 🌿🌿🌿🌿🌿🌿🌿🌿🌿🌿

AFTER WITNESSING THE PROCEDURE WITH JUNIOR, Eric returned to his office and regarded a pile of folders on the left side of his desk. He glanced through the top one and saw that Stephanie had finished going through the day's newspapers, and saw that her scissors had been busy. The Refuge carried subscriptions to the *Houston Post,* the *Wall Street Journal, New York Times,* and *Christian Science Monitor;* one of her first tasks every morning was to scour through them, gleaning the day's stories concerning wildlife and habitat conservation, and environmental issues in general. After he had a chance to look them over she filed them, by topic, in a cabinet behind her desk.

The second one was from Wallace the lawyer; in it he found a completed draft of articles of incorporation for a membership society to serve as an auxiliary for the park, and thought, Good, and proceeded to read them carefully. Eric regarded him as a very lucky find indeed, the hottest young ace at one of Houston's largest firms, who also harbored a passion for wildlife. Wallace needed to take on some amount of pro bono work to look good in the firm, but detested working with poor people, not because they were poor but because they were ignorant, and nothing on earth depressed him like ignorance. The Refuge needed a good legal eye to look over its shoulder, and the match was natural.

The park itself was chartered as a private foundation—tax-exempt but not burdened with having to heel to a meddlesome membership. Before his vision of The Refuge cleared to him, Eric had belonged to other conservation-related causes, and saw firsthand the kind of havoc that could be wreaked by even a couple of busybodies with too much time on their hands and a passion for *Robert's Rules of Order*. As a student he had belonged to an outfit lobbying for protection of a dense primitive swamp that was a literal Pleistocene relic deep in southeast Texas. That organization had been formed when Herbert Hoover was President, and for decade after decade their fratricidal bickering had sabotaged every attempt to organize a national park. The goal was almost accomplished when Eric joined—he was just out of high school—but at the couple of meetings he attended, all he witnessed was a nightmarish progression we're-going-to-do-it-my-way, my-acre-is-more-important-than-your-acre, I-want-to-lead-the-parade; small-time wannabe-hero egotists. They meant well, but they were idiots. It was a formative experience. No more of that for him.

He had dodged requests for a membership organization before, but now with the public being admitted, the increase in offers of willing hands meant that much good work could be done—if they could be prevented from interfering in the operation of the park. At a big urban zoo their utility lies foremost in lobbying the zoo's interest before the city government, which the zoo itself cannot do. But at The Refuge there was a wide variety of tasks done by staff that could as easily be done by unpaid volunteers. Eric was still studying over Wallace Gibson's draft charter for "The Friends of The Refuge," appreciating the cleverness of good draftsmanship, when Larry Davis knocked at his door and entered.

"Well, have you about recovered?"

"I think so."

"It's a dirty job, but somebody has to do it. I've put together a packet of some reading materials you might find helpful in getting acquainted with the business."

Larry Davis seated himself. "Great. So listen. Tell me about that 'associate' vet, Lucy?"

"What about her?"

"She's fine."

"Yes, she is."

"Is she dating anybody?"

Eric gave him a long look. "She didn't tell you?"

"No."

"Well, I thought maybe she was, but I don't know." Dimly from his college days he recognized that Larry Davis was looking at this as a kind of male-bonding thing, and leaned back in his chair. "So, did you ask her out?"

"Yeah, I did."

"What did she say?"

"She said yes."

"Really," he nodded. "Well, I guess that would give you something of a reason to stay, wouldn't it?"

"That's cool, isn't it? I mean, do you have rules about employees dating each other?"

"That's none of my business."

"Great. So, if I took a job as an intern, what kind of things would I be doing—I mean, other than, like, jerking off rhinos?"

"A little bit of everything until you learn how it all works. But don't take it on unless you're really serious about it. I don't want to find out later I've been wasting my time."

"No, no," Larry Davis was quite serious. "I think maybe this could be it for me. I can't know till I try it out, of course. But, like I was saying the other day, I want to make some difference, and I think you are making a difference."

"How would you feel about hanging around with Jake a few days a week? He's the most honest guy I know, and he can show you our wheels and gears better than anyone." He had already spoken when he realized that meant he would be closer to Lucy as well but he let it stand. If he suddenly put Larry Davis in the kitchen chopping carrots for the gorillas it would be obvious to Lucy that his insecurity was showing. Better to meet it head on.

"Trial basis?" asked Davis.

Eric nodded. "Say, twenty hours a week, minimum plus four bits. That's our usual entry wage."

"Okay."

"You'll need to see Consuela, our personnel manager, and sign some papers. Her office is out Stephie's door, then turn right down the hall."

"Um, one other thing."

Eric waited.

"Could I tell you something?"

"What is it?"

Once again Larry produced the note with the Bounce 'N Bark address on it. "Those monkeys yesterday, I can't get them out of my mind. The whole way back in your van, I felt like they were—I don't know. It sounds weird. But I feel like, if I don't tell people about them, nobody will. Does that make sense?"

The boy had no idea how deeply Eric Jackson understood. "All right."

"I mean, I can do it on my own time, but I want to at least start checking out what is going on."

"Okay. But—" he held up a finger "—be aware you're jumping right into deeper water. It may not be something best suited to your school paper. No offense, but if the story affects you that much and you want to tell a lot of people about it, don't preempt that by having it appear where nobody will see it. I'll tell you what, you work on it gradually. Approach it as a big—maybe three or four installment—investigative feature. When it's done, we'll give you some photographs from our quarantine, and get you some more from the Customs Service. With us behind you you might be able to get it syndicated and sent out on the wire."

Larry Davis said quietly, "Okay," giving no hint of the fact that this was the moment he first felt he had walked onto the field where the big boys play. It quieted him and awed him a little.

"Only one thing, we'll need to go over the finished piece for legal liabilities. We've never been sued yet by anybody, and I don't want, whoever they are, Bounce 'N Bark, to be the first."

After all the excitement at the park on Saturday, Eric Jackson slept in on Sunday morning. He thought about going to Mass, but could not face it. He had only been a couple of times since Liz Ann had left, and felt uncomfortable being around people who managed the facade that their lives were all together. Father Laurence was understanding enough, and Eric was aware that perhaps the discomfort was shaped mostly by his feeling humiliated but yet . . . the other parishioners who had been their friends—his and Liz Ann's friends—seemed somehow different in their reaction to him as a "single again," as they said. Eric had married late enough in life to have experienced how, when his buddies got married one by one, bachelors are, sometimes subtly and sometimes not, left off the social calendar; married people pal around, when they pal around at all, with other married people. Now it was his turn to experience the unmaking of that process, how married people who had been "their" friends were now indefinably, but perceptibly, more distant. He understood their awkwardness, that they were sympathetic but must not appear to take sides, yet there remained that certain unspoken nosiness and vague superiority of those who had worked out their problems and kept their lives together. It was not difficult, on most Sunday mornings, to talk himself out of treading onto such a minefield.

It also preyed on him that his animals were his life now, and Christianity was not a kind religion to them. This was true not so much in its intrinsic values, although any religion descended from a suffering, hard-scrabble desert tribe was bound to look around and see more a banquet-on-the-hoof than all the marvelous life that God had infused into His creation. Rather Christianity had become unkind to nature through centuries of incrementally added social attitudes that the Church, and other equally unthinking churches, had enfolded into the overall Christian ethic. For God to have given man dominion over the world was a trust of stewardship, but as man replaced God in his heart with greed, it became a justification for plunder. "Go forth and multiply" was a benediction, but ignorant people had turned it into a command and turned most of the world into an impoverished, overcrowded, pestilence-ridden, smelly—and increasingly resentful—hell. And in the most recent years, the back-to-the-fundamentals, bornagain Bible thumpers had had their say, reading scripture with their ignorant, superficial eyes, utterly devoid of the historical and cultural contexts in which it was written. Surely no people had ever skimmed so artfully through the Bible, picking verses like cherries one here and one there to justify preconceived social prejudices and goals. Their high point in the United States came in the early-to-middle 1980s, when one of them reigned long as Secretary of the Interior, an idiot savant who truly could calculate the price and profit of anything wild but who understood the value of nothing. And then he had the effrontery to justify massive clear-cutting and sweetheart deals to maximize short-term industry profit by lecturing that it was Christ's will that resources be utilized. And still atop that, they had the effrontery to call themselves conservatives, they who used resources in the most liberal and ill-considered and short-sighted ways. The most conservative position one can take is to care for resources, to husband the finite ones against that day when they might really be needed, and to renew the renewable ones so that their use can be sustained. Where do people think the word "conservation" comes from, anyway? How easily people are gulled by the crafty.

But if not Christianity, what? The other major religions of the world are, at their best, neutral in their regard for nature, popular misconceptions notwithstanding. Eric knew of only one discipline that rooted itself in the protection of nature—the Bishnoi sect of India, the followers of a holy man named Jambeshwar, who about the time Columbus was sailing to America had a vision of human ruin resulting from environmental callousness, and enunciated his twenty-nine principles for respectful and conscientious living. And his followers, no less than those of Christ, had their martyrs. In 1730, more than three hundred of their women died trying to protect a forest from destruction, hacked to death under the axes of woodcutters sent by the Maharajah of Jodhpur. And in the modern Indian state of Rajasthan the sect still follows its conscientious way.

Eric supposed their American equivalent to be the radical environmentalists, sallow-cheeked and sandaled vegetarians who, like the Bishnois, hug trees. Of all the world's belief-systems, it struck Eric Jackson that the one that found a balance, the most sensible, was that of the Native Americans. He knew perfectly well that skillful public relations in the era of political correctness had transformed popular perception of American Indians into something little resembling what they had ever actually been. Like all other peoples everywhere they were capable of the most wanton waste—slash and burn agriculture, stampeding buffalo over a cliff, in the process killing far more animals than they could utilize. And their cruelty to each other, long before the arrival of Europeans, was unspeakable. What appealed to him rather was the widespread native philosophy that every thing was useful, that every thing was here for a purpose, that no thing was waste. And within that worldview what appealed to him was the sense of individual ethic—that a resource could permissibly be used, provided it was used gratefully and respectfully. An animal killed for meat and hide was apologized to and given honor. Because the Native American saw himself as an integral part of the Creation and recognized in that a responsibility, he had, in his scheme of things, no need for guilt.

And that is what, in his own hagiography, led Eric Jackson to an affinity for St. Francis—not just that he is the patron saint of animals, and cheap plaster or concrete statues of him adorn seemingly every garden pond and birdbath in the Western world, but that Francis saw so clearly his own individual place in the natural world—neither vegetarian nor glutton, neither martyr nor judge. It made him easy to pray to, like a warm friend and brother, far in concept from some Awful Presence, and he gave Eric the reassurance he needed that there is no sin in believing that the plants and animals whose extinction he was warding off ought in their turn to be useful. Not just useful in the sense of selling worms for bait, or orchids for corsages, or raising talapia to sell in the cafeteria. Beauty is useful in itself, and wonder is instructive. It is important to have mysteries as well as solutions. And however much Eric might believe that plants and animals have a right to exist that is independent of our by-your-leave, the fact is that their survival will not be vouchsafed until average people, ignorant people, are made to understand that the utility of nature—its benefit to us—is measured as fully in beauty and wonder as it is in food or clothing or medicine. If any Western saint could admire and smell and bless a flower before pressing its oil, it was Francis. And on those Sundays when going to Mass and having to deal with people he didn't want to see was more than he could face, Eric always devoted a few minutes, kneeling on the velvet footstool, to Francis.

Lucy Conner also slept in on Sunday. For her it was hard to say exactly when it all started, for her maternal instinct had always been triggered by animals. Even when she was a toddler, at an age when most girls were discovering the simplest of dolls, her excitement—it almost seemed like a need—to care for them all, kittens, puppies and rabbits, indiscriminately, was so gentle and mature in its nature that her parents had allowed her to have pets at an age far younger than most children. And unlike most children, for Lucy the newness of it did not wear off after a few weeks. It had never worn off. In her adolescence she was smitten with the love of horses, in all its pseudo-Freudian innocence, no less than other girls her age—her National Velvet phase, as Eric liked to call it. But when she outgrew it, instead of outgrowing the love of horses, she gained instead a love of everything else besides.

Lucy awakened when the sun was high and bright through her bedroom window, and she lay awake and wondered if she was doing the right thing about Eric. He must eventually choose, she thought. She knew how unhappy he had been with Liz Ann; no, it wasn't likely he would ask her back. Then when Larry Davis called, she made the date and thought, If Eric doesn't like it, let him deal with it. Let him choose.

The brilliant Sunday sun found the Barillas in a different frame of mind. Ramón had told Ellen they wanted to make a trip out to the new wildlife park, and she made a special trip to the Walmart to buy a pair of light canvas sneakers for walking. Esteban brought his wife and Juan brought his girlfriend, a happy-natured young Hispanic girl named Cecilia, so there was no shortage of girl-talk. But the whole expedition was a surprise to her; Ramón had never taken an interest in such things before, indeed he wasn't even that attached to his pet store, whose management he left to the employees. She took it as a good sign, however. Ramón had needed some kind of hobby for years, although he was not one to take suggestions.

After passing through the doors beside Joseph II, Ramón unfolded their map, and they decided to make their way through Africa and Australia, then up to Asia, back to Africa via the Middle East, and then have lunch at the concession. If there was time and the girls were not too tired, he said, they would go up and do North and South America.

They lingered long in front of the large mammals, seemed to record a passing appreciation of the birds in the large, walk-through aviaries, and all but ignored the fish and reptiles. Nothing unusual in that, that's the way with most tourists in a game park. The men seemed particularly fascinated with the rhinos and read all the signs describing their habits and ecology. They passed over to Australia and had some good laughs at kangaroos and kookaburras before making their way up to Indonesia.

Eric had decided to open the vast, domed walk-through of the Indonesian house to the public, had directed Millie during the week to smother it, if she had to, with potted plants, so they could get the bulk of the residents in quickly—tapirs and orangutans, anoas and Komodo dragons, proboscis monkeys, and a profusion of birds. The indoor-outdoor area for the Javan rhinos was still bare and sterile when the Barillas saw it, and understood this was the arrival they were waiting for.

There were a couple of times during the day when Ellen saw Ramón and the other men peering into service alleys and pointing out transformers and electrical and telephone wiring. When she asked him about it he said, "We just looking. Must take a lot of work to keep a place like this going. See how they plan it all out? Boy, this is something."

It was all good news to her but the park was larger than she had anticipated, and as Ramón figured, she and Esteban's wife decided over their late lunch of talapia and French fries that the one partial circuit of the park had been enough. With only a five-dollar admission, she said, they could, if he wanted, come back and see the rest next week. She didn't want to dampen their enthusiasm but needn't have worried; it did not occur to her that it was Ramón's intention to have a return visit seem like her idea.

Larry Davis negotiated his hours with Jake at 12 to 5 Tuesdays through Fridays. When he arrived at the vet compound on that first day he found Jake scrubbing to operate on a big male chimpanzee. Larry asked where Lucy was.

"She's gone out to dart him and bring him in."

"You have to dart chimpanzees? I thought you could just hold them and give them a shot."

"Yeah, I'd like to see you try," said Jake. "Did you ever wonder why all the chimps you see in circuses and on TV are babies? An adult male is almost as big as you are and about four times as strong. He's smart, mean, aggressive and nasty, and if you even tried to give him a shot, you'd get about two steps into his territory before he'd pull your arm out of its socket and beat you over the head with it."

"Wow. Sounds like a couple of truckers I met in a titty bar once."

"Same principle. Never, ever screw around with adult chimps. Even the smaller ones have a wicked bite, and their mouths are so nasty you can die from the infection."

"What about Jane Goodall and thirty years among the chimps and all that?"

"Jane Goodall had the sense to work herself into their social setup so they'd accept her. And even then—well, read her books. When she finally got to contact one of the boss males, she was terrified. She knew exactly how dangerous they are." Jake nodded his head at a door across the hall. "Now go into the storeroom and get three jugs of sterile saline and take them into surgery, please, sir."

They heard Lucy's cart pull into the dock and went out to meet her, arriving just as she, the chimp's keeper and two vet techs were heaving the limp animal onto a gurney. Larry glanced into the cart and saw the small blowgun they had used to drug him, then walked alongside as they wheeled him into surgery. He had never seen a large male close up before, and it shook him that it bore a much closer resemblance to a deformedly muscular, hairy, bald-headed little man, about five feet tall, than it did to tumbling little Babs he had seen in Eric's office. And his most prominent feature, lying on his back, was his wet-looking, gray-white spike of a dick flopping over two large, tightly packed testicles. Larry could not help but find it demoralizing in a way that although it was more streamlined and had no swelling at the glans, the whole assembly was half-again larger than his own, and he was not noticeably underprivileged.

"You weigh him yet?" asked Jake.

"Fifty-five kilograms," said Lucy. "Undoubtedly some of that is fluid buildup."

Jake was already prodding the belly gently with his fingertips. "Yeah, shit, this is gonna get mean. How much drug did he get in the dart?"

"Ten milligrams."

"Well, I think we'll give him a little bonus so he don't wake up and ask questions." Jake crossed over to the refrigerator, and Larry heard the bottles clinking lightly as Jake searched for the right one, reciting idly, "And who remembers Doctor Snow, he ain't with us no more, 'cause when he reached for H_2O, got H_2SO_4. Ha, there you are . . ." He measured five more milligrams into a syringe and surveyed the operating theater: Lucy, two techs, the keeper, and Larry. "All right now, we all set?"

The techs had already shaved the area of the chimp's belly where Jake needed to cut and swabbed it with bright orange disinfectant. Lucy was placing a ventilator in the chimp's mouth, and the techs had lain sterile sheeting over all the body except the swollen orange balloon. "Guess so."

"Now, I remember when I first started out—"

"Look out," said Lucy, "we're about to visit the good old days."

"—all we had to do was thump a chimp with some phencyclidine and start to work."

"What?" Larry was bemused. "PCP? Like angel dust?"

"Same stuff," answered Jake. "Different formulation."

"Cool!"

"They thought so. Sweet dreams, partner." Jake administered the injection. "In fact, I'll bet you didn't know this. One side-effect of using phencyclidine on apes is it gives them erotic dreams. Triple-X hard-core."

They could tell from the wrinkles at the corners of Larry Davis's eyes that he was about to crack up behind his surgical mask. "No way! How could they know that?"

"You won't think I'm tellin' the truth, but I am. Like with a bunch of other things back then, they tested phencyclidine on humans without tellin' 'em what it was. I guess when the guinea pigs came back with smiles on their faces and asked for more, the authorities figured it was something they'd better ban."

"Did they?"

"Almost." Lucy saw a twinkle in Jake's eye. "The government doesn't want people to think it's even produced anymore, but some of us still have our ways. I only keep a little in case I get an ape that can't tolerate the stuff we use now."

Larry shook his head. "Wow."

"Yup, and here's something else, if you think about it," said Jake. "You know there's less than a one percent difference between this guy's genetic material and ours. I'd bet you a dollar to a doughnut that if somebody put his mind to it, it'd take maybe a year to make up a formula for a bedtime phencyclidine pill that could keep you lovin' for hours. There you got the Chinese running around the world trying to knock over rhinos to saw up their horns as an aphrodisiac, and here we got the real stuff in our fridge, all along. I think that's what you college boys would call an irony."

Larry Davis stared back over at the refrigerator. "That's fucking incredible."

"Well, don't you go getting no ideas about raiding my private stock before a hot date. We don't know what all this stuff might do to humans. Phencyclidine—especially that kind—is extremely dangerous, and there ain't no antidote. If you overdose, you die. That's all."

"Yeah, but what a way to go!"

"Well, I finally gave up usin' it unless I have to. It's bad form to come during an operation, anyway. I had an orangutan shoot all over me once while I was working on him."

Lucy scowled. "Jake, don't tease him!"

"Hell, I ain't teasin'. I nearly let the son of a bitch die. Wasn't even my type." Jake pinched the skin over the ape's tight belly and made a quick incision, and then began working at the underlying muscles. "Now the trick is to get into the abdominal cavity without touching the membrane inside, 'cause if he's got a belly full of amoebas in there it's under a lot of pressure. If I nick the membrane it's gonna be the biggest mess you ever saw."

Larry and Lucy and the keeper watched him intently until he spread apart the muscle wall and they saw an ugly, veined pinkish blob. "Well, Lucy, my dear, it seems you were correct. Now if you can draw some of that out without turnin' it into Old Faithful, we'll have a lot easier time."

Lucy inserted a huge syringe quickly and deftly into the small exposed area of the sac, pulling the plunger back so quickly that little of the fluid escaped from the wound. For a couple of seconds Larry watched the vile, thin pink liquid bubble into the syringe, then turned his head so he couldn't see, which made Jake laugh. "What's the matter, boy? Bet you'll never take Pepto Bismol again, huh?"

With the pressure relieved, Jake enlarged the opening to remove the sac, and Lucy helped him flush the area with sterile saline. Together they rocked the limp chimp back and forth to get a good rinse, then closed him up and Jake left the techs to watch over him until he woke up.

Lucy and Larry washed. "Did Jake tell you I went out with them to get those monkeys Saturday?"

"Yes." Lucy had been the one to settle the refugees from the customs warehouse into quarantine space. She didn't tell him what opinions Jake had offered about him. Nor did she scold him for only caring about the monkeys. She was as worried about the birds and snakes but like most people, and she guessed it was understandable, Larry seemed most drawn to the animals closest to himself on the evolutionary chart.

"Eric said I could start on a piece on animal shipping. I thought I might go over to the pet store where they were headed. Just check the place out. Would you like to go?"

She leaned her head to one side. "I don't think so. I can do zoos, but I don't do pet stores. I get too depressed."

"Really?"

"Yeah."

"God, I'm sorry."

"No, it's okay. I just—well, I don't do humane societies either, if that tells you anything."

"But aren't you sort of a humane society here?"

"No; there is no element here of adopt-or-die. Even when the animals we take in on a compassionate-care basis are so common we can't even give them away—and that's most of them—we would never dream of putting any of them to sleep just because they're in the way. We try our best to establish them in natural groups and give them good lives. Sometimes we do neuter them so the problem won't get worse than it already is."

"Geez." All he had seen of the zoo mission had to do with breeding rare animals—it never occurred to him that animals that aren't rare can get into a captive overpopulation problem.

"Come with me, I want to show you something." They went into her office. "Look at this—" she pulled a large gray-green softcover volume down from her bookshelf. It was the AZA *Annual Report on Conservation and Science,* and she found a suitable page. "See, we know down to the last nest and cage how much room we have for any species in the zoos all over the world. Sometimes it's a problem even for endangered species. Look here."

Larry Davis saw she had opened the book to the section on snow leopards, and followed her slender finger down the page past a table of figures as to whose meaning he was clueless—

Founder Genome Equivalents	12.917
Fraction Wild Gene Diversity	0.961
Fraction/w.g. Diversity Lost	0.039
Mean Inbreeding Coefficient	0.022

Her finger stopped at a section entitled Special Concerns and he read for himself, ". . . the gross population of 247 counting surplus is well beyond the high figure. The Felid Advisory Group is currently addressing the culling-euthanasia issue as it pertains to Felid Species Survival Plans. To date no snow leopards have been euthanized strictly for population management."

Larry Davis could hardly believe his eyes. "Man, they sound like they're proud of themselves for not killing any."

"It's a hateful idea, but what can they do if there is simply no room to keep them?"

Larry's animal rights instinct returned to him. "If they're no longer endangered, put them back in the wild."

"How? A leopard or a lion raised in a zoo doesn't know how to hunt. Have you ever seen *Born Free?*"

"No."

"You know what it's about?"

"No."

"Then there's some homework for you. Go to a video store, rent *Born Free* and watch it."

"So, you want to watch a movie with me?"

Lucy had been reshelving the AZA report but spun around. "Stop hitting on me. I'm not in the mood."

"What's going on? You were sure in the mood Sunday night."

She calmed down for a minute. "You're right. I'm sorry." She wrapped her arms about his waist and squeezed, then let him go. "Hit on me again later in the week—you can't tell what might happen."

He thought, Oh boy, watch her moods and move when she wants me to move. This is going to be more fun than the NFL draft.

Lucy wiped something out of her eye. "So, listen, you want to see the monkeys you brought in Saturday?"

"Are they all right?"

She brushed by him, taking his hand just long enough to pull him after her before letting it go. "Most of them are hooded capuchins. They were so traumatized that they don't seem to remember any of their old family ties, but their bonding instinct is so strong that they're forming a new group. It should go smoothly."

12

IT TOOK A FEW DAYS for Larry to visit the Bounce 'N Bark in Pasadena. When he finally arrived late one afternoon, he thought, What a different place it was, what a different feel than what he had been doing out at the park. There was none of the science nor the urgency nor the sense of mission he was getting used to, and none of the sickening stink of the big animals. Everything here was fuzzy and playful, and the lights were bright. This was the public perception of what baby animals should be. Perhaps it was not the reality to which he was acclimating himself, but it was far more restful.

An older—almost elderly—red-headed lady waited on him.

"This is really a terrific store," he said. "Geez, you even have some little monkeys. Do you own it?"

"No, I'm just the manager." Her speech was slow and pleasant, her accent softly Southern. He pegged her for a Baptist, certainly sang in the choir, probably went to a Bible study group.

"Well, it's very nice."

She thanked him.

He held out his hand. "My name's Larry Davis. I work on the newspaper at the University of Houston. I've sort of been developing some story ideas—maybe something on student summer jobs or, you know, something like that."

She smiled and nodded and said, "Uh-huh."

"Do you ever hire students, like, during the summer?"

She thought maybe he was fishing for a job. "Well, I don't do any of the hiring but you'd be welcome to talk to the owner, if you'd like."

"That would be great. When does he usually come in?"

"He doesn't come in very regularly. You understand, he has other businesses that he has to give his attention to."

Larry pulled a notepad out of his shirt pocket. "I see. Is there any way I could get in touch with him?"

"Well, he spends most of his time at his gift shop in the Gallería. It's called Ramón Barilla Imports."

His face brightened with recognition. "Oh, yes, I've been by there and seen it." That was a lie. "He's the one I need to talk to? Ramón Barilla?"

"Uh-huh." She walked behind the counter. "Would you like me to give you the phone number?"

"That would be very kind, yes." Sweet woman, he thought, simple and trusting, like a cow. Or a dodo. He hoped her world would be safe.

She wrote the number carefully on the back of a business card and gave it to him. He was almost out the door when he turned back suddenly, as though he remembered something. "While I'm here, do you carry Science Diet?"

"Uh-huh, we sure do."

"Could I buy a four-pound sack of the CD kitty crunchies? That's the kind my cat has to have." That too was a lie, but he knew Lucy would reimburse him. She went through three sacks a month.

It took a couple of weeks for Lucy to put any kind of official cachet on her recognition that she and Eric were not seeing each other anymore. Or rather, she knew it and let it go by, that she was letting him slip away. When she first flirted with Larry she had weighed it as carefully as she could, whether Eric might resume negotiations with Liz Ann, but she doubted it. She and Eric had been too right for each other, and he had spoken too often about he and Liz Ann having been wrong for each other.

But after she became involved with Larry, and waited for Eric to pursue her, and waited yet longer without result, she began to realize how she had misjudged him. She had proceeded with him as she would have with any man she loved and meant to have, but proceeded without care as to whether he was like other men, and only now saw how unlike other men he was. Perhaps she thought that Eric, as an animal lover in a contained little world that revolved around animals, would take his cue from the males of other species—even the more primitive males of his own species—and make a stand for her. And only too late, she feared, was she realizing that his need for bonding was as much a need of heart and spirit as it was of hormones. He was not some alpha male who would compete for a female, whether by the ritual combat in which the heaviest antlers won or in the urban jungle of the singles bars. She felt the same need, the very same need, but in a world of find 'em-feed 'em-fuck 'em-forget 'em men she had known, how could she, she thought, how could she have miscued the opportunity when it arose?

This awareness became acute after she and Larry had sex. He was the first lover she had taken who was appreciably younger than she. She was twenty-eight, he was twenty-one, and when they were together she could not help comparing making love to a boy with a mature man. Eric was a vigorous thirty-five, eminently satisfying and youthful, but he no longer had the slim-waisted contour of a boy, or the sweetly forgivable foibles of a boy, or a boy's insatiable appetite that is as much the result of discovery and the tendency to wear out a new toy as it is of his sex drive. Yet it took only one night with Larry for her to realize that Eric was what she needed. That Larry was a good lay was undeniable, as it was undeniable that she was lonely and in need of being loved. But what she needed was the communality of life-purpose she shared with Eric, the shared experiences and shared frames of reference that are part of a real mating, which Larry, for all his youth and vigor and well-meaning heart, could not provide. But he was eager and funny and she did care for him, thus against her better judgment she let it continue, unable to tell him who his favored predecessor was. And so after they made love she would lie beneath him or atop him, their shared musky sweat conveying to him a satisfaction that in her heart was not there. And she would lie awake while he slept, wondering if the situation was one she could retrieve.

From just such a melancholy one night she reached out from under him to answer the telephone, and knew from Jake's voice and the lousy connection that he was on his car phone. "Sorry, darlin'," he said, "but Lakshmi is starting to do her thing. I need you."

She squinted hard and opened her eyes wide, and objects in the room came into focus. "I'll be right out. How long has she been in labor?"

"Sam went by her about eight-thirty and thought she might have been acting a little funny. He went back around at ten and said she was turnin' circles and gettin' up and lyin' down, so he called me. Sounds like the real thing."

"Yeah, it does. I'll be right there." Almost as an afterthought she added, "Have you called Eric?"

There was a pause. "No, I don't think we need to drag him out. I called Ernie and he's coming. Listen, though, you might call that Larry friend of yours; he's been wanting to see some of the real stuff."

"Okay, yeah."

"I'm almost there now so I'll meet you at her house."

She hung up the phone slowly. Eric had not missed a rhino birth in all the time she had known him. Something about it was not right.

Larry rolled off her, wrapping an arm around her and sliding a hand up between her breasts to her face. "Trouble?"

"Rhino in labor. You know how to work the Mr. Coffee?"

"Yup."

"Why don't you make a pot real quick? There's a big Thermos in the cabinet to the right of the sink. Jake wanted me to call you and see if you would come out, too."

"I'm not home."

She smiled and rubbed her eyes. "Oh, God, it's showtime. Here we go."

He caught her back around the middle. "I liked what we were doing better."

She took his hand gently. "Don't be a little boy. This is serious. Let's move."

They drove out in her car, seeing Jake's big Cherokee pulled up at the loading dock of the quarantine. Larry had almost forgotten that the vet compound had its own entrance from Ranch Road 521. Lucy parked and got out, uncomfortably sticky and, in her perception, smelly from the night's sex, wishing she could have taken a shower, but then remembered how messy mammal births are and she was sure to need a shower anyway before returning to bed.

She didn't take anything from the clinic, knowing Jake would already have everything there. They nosed their cart up next to Jake's at the rear of her house; the lights were on inside, but there were only a couple of bulbs and they did not brightly light the interior.

They had just opened the door as they heard Jake say, "Thatta girl! Good girl." They approached and saw Lakshmi turn and sniff at a dark still lump, nuzzling it gently for nearly a minute before she walked slowly to the other side of the stall.

Larry had never seen her this close and was struck by how incredibly ugly she was—or not ugly, that's a subjective term, but how incredibly incongruous and disproportionate, as though fashioned of wet clay on a bad day. The hide, which from a distance afforded the famous riveted, armor-plated look, up close proved to be knobby skin so loose that it hung down about her hind legs like a skirt. But the oddest thing was her face. Black rhinos have hooked lips, and white rhinos' are wide and square; Lakshmi's jaws, when she opened her mouth for a bit of hay, parted like melted wax, the upper almost formless, and the bottom square and thick and rubbery and very flat, much like the old photos he'd seen of Ubangi women with saucers wedged in their lower lips.

Lucy and Jake watched the calf intently, knowing that it could take several seconds before there was an eruption of bubbles from the nose and that first, coughing gasp they waited for.

Lucy was tapping the thick iron bars impatiently, until finally Jake said, "I don't like this." He slid himself his body's width under the lowest bar and reached out to the motionless form, but Lakshmi caught sight of him and charged over with a tremendous deep, belching grunt, her head down, still trailing bloody leathery amnion out of her uterus. Jake knew very well that Indian rhinos, unlike the African, don't gore with their horns, but their huge ugly maws effect nasty bites, and he log-rolled to safety with a couple of yards to spare, spluttering, "Oh, come on, now! We're just trying to help you." Lakshmi smelled again at the calf. She nosed at it gently, but it showed no more muscle tone than a water balloon.

He looked up at Larry. "Hand me that thing." He indicated an eight-foot pole with a lasso looped around one end. As soon as Lakshmi had turned again, he slid the pole under the bars, looped it under one of the calf's feet and pulled it tight. "Help me pull."

With a heave from Jake and Larry the calf slid limply under the bars, and in a flash Jake and Lucy were on it with practiced teamwork. Jake pressed its chest hard and rhythmically as Lucy slapped it lightly on its nose, just like it was a colt or puppy. "Come on," she whispered, "come on," and tapped its nose again.

Larry gazed down at its eye, not open nor closed but rolled up and lifeless looking, and its head oblong and angular, the size and shape of a rugby ball. "Davis, you see what I'm doing?" said Jake.

"Yes."

"Well, take over, same pressure, same speed." Larry got on his knees and pressed his folded hands onto the calf's chest, slimy and pliant and instantly precious, as Jake filled a syringe with what Larry took to be adrenaline, or whatever equivalent you use on rhinos.

Lucy cursed and forced the calf's mouth open, reaching in as far as her elbow, trying to discover if there was an obstruction in its trachea that prevented it from breathing. She had pulled its tongue out of the way, and her hand rummaging around inside the mouth made a nauseating, sucking, wobbling sound, not different from groping around inside a turkey trying to pull out the giblets. Larry turned his head away and continued the chest massage.

"You find anything?" Jake asked Lucy.

"No, it's just not responding."

Jake emptied the syringe and took a quick glance between its back legs. "Well, we got us a little boy here." He touched his stethoscope to its chest and motioned Larry to stop for a second, then shook his head. "Work him some more."

"Well, he's going to be a dead little boy if he doesn't breathe, right now. Come on!" She threaded her fingers up its nostrils as far as she could probe, then popped the nose again lightly. Larry thought he heard her murmur "Fuck" when she stuffed the tongue back in its mouth, clamped the lips shut and covered one nostril with her hands, then sealed her lips over the other one and blew as hard as she could. Larry had now received more sensory input than he could sort, that the lips which an hour before had been sweetly sealed on his own were now fastened grimly to a slimy, probably dead fetal rhinoceros. But he was not about to admit he was feeling faint or sick, and said he felt a slight rise in the rhino's chest. After two more hard breaths Lucy paused and waited.

Nothing.

"Jake," she said suddenly, "can you pick him up? Turn him up."

Jake nudged Larry out of the way. "Get back, son." He heaved the calf up by the back feet and guessed he weighed about ninety pounds—full term and at the large end of the scale—as he held him vertically until the front feet lifted limply off the floor. "Larry," he grunted, "put one hand on his back and press into his diaphragm, just like you was doing before. Go! Go!"

Lucy was under him, her arm up in its mouth again rattling around, and her fingers up its nose, repeating, "Come on, come on."

Jake was able to hold him up nearly two minutes before easing the supple body back down. With the back of his forearm he wiped the sweat from his brow and said, "Well, shit."

"Was there any delay in him getting out of the sac?" Lucy's voice conveyed her determination to be professional and dispassionate, but the quiver was there, giving it away that she wanted to cry.

"No, no, he popped right out of it on the way down." Jake shook his head. "He was just in there too long."

Lucy looked up and saw Lakshmi had lain down against the far wall, expelling a placenta the size of a washtub. "How you doing, honey?" she called loudly. "Boy, that was pretty rough, huh?"

In all of wild animal practice, this moment is the queerest for it seems as if the one emotion you all have in common is a kind of shame. You don't feel ashamed, necessarily, but it is such a shame; you could swear that the mother feels that she failed, and then you feel ashamed for her, and you have to repeat to yourself that animals do not feel shame. Or do they?

Jake was the first over to the sink to wash the worst of the gunk from his hands and arms, and Lucy and Larry were close behind, as Larry looked over his shoulder at the limp, limber figure lying alone on the cold cement.

Jake picked up three towels and handed two to the others. "You okay, Luce?"

She nodded, without speaking, her lips shut tight. She thrust her hands under the cold stream, then bent low and scrubbed her face vigorously, then buried her visage in a towel.

"Well," said Jake, "let's just try to remember she's an old lady. Nobody expected her to breed and she's not part of the SSP anyway. We just thought we'd try it and it didn't work. So no harm done. All right?"

Lucy coughed and nodded. "Yeah."

Jake returned to the bars, speaking to Lakshmi, trying to coax her closer. He had kept a tewpia melon from the last crop frozen in his freezer against just this time, which he had thawed in his microwave at home, and now he offered the half-spoiled fruit through the bars. Reluctantly Lakshmi snuffed her way over, and Jake broke off a piece for her. She ate it eagerly and popped down her great flat black Ubangi lower lip for more. Jake fed her one chunk at a time, patting her below the eyes and under the chin. "You'll be okay. Just don't you go into shock on us. You hear? Huh? You hear me?"

His hands were gunked up again, and before washing he used the time to roll the fetus onto a canvas dropcloth, which he and Larry loaded into the back of one of the carts. They would store it in the walk-in fridge at the clinic and schedule a necropsy as soon as they could. Essentially they were done but waited until Ernie arrived so that Lakshmi would not be left alone.

As they waited, Sam Rutherford walked in with his flashlight and two-way radio riding on his belt. "How'd she do?"

Jake answered him. "She seems fine, but she had a still-birth."

"Aw, damn." He looked at the crumpled, shiny form in the back of the cart and strolled over to the bars by Lakshmi. "That's a shame. You okay, sweetheart?" He offered her his hand, and after she smelled him he patted her face. "Better luck next time."

He turned back around and got Larry's attention. "Eric says you've been working for Jake for a while now. You about ready to come work for me?"

"I don't know, I've got finals coming up and really could use the time to study."

"Perfect. You could work here at night. I can put you in the security office and you can get some studying done while you're scanning the monitors."

Larry thought about it. He certainly needed the money. Squiring Lucy around had not been cheap and he hated going to his parents for a boost. "Yeah, that would be okay. Is it usually pretty quiet here at night? No trouble?"

"Nah, not really. It's not that unusual for kids to stop on the road at night and try to climb the fences—once they find out the barbed wire on top is hot, they get out pretty fast. We don't even call the sheriff over that. You won't be out here alone; if you see a car stop on the monitor, just call me, I'll be on the grounds, plus we got that new guy starting in a couple of weeks. We'll check it out."

"Okay."

"What do you think, Jake? Can I have him for a while?"

"Take him away."

As Sam led Larry aside to make their arrangements, Lucy cornered Jake by his cart. "Jake, Eric should have been the first one here. What is going on?"

He folded his arms and looked at her squarely, and sadly. "Yeah, well, I was afraid you wouldn't let that go." He worked his lips like he wanted to speak but couldn't form the right words.

"Talk to me, Jake."

"You play poker?"

"No."

"Yeah, you do, too. You just don't play it with cards."

She was getting angry. "Tell me what you mean, Jake."

"You bluffed him, and he called you. Eric and Liz Ann worked out a deal to get back together. His part of the deal includes, he can't go flyin' out of the house in the middle of the night anymore. So, he's not here."

Lucy took this quietly but coldly. "How long have they been back together?"

"A week."

"Why didn't he tell me?"

"Why should he? That's part of playin' poker is that ever'body stops talkin'. Ain't it?"

She said nothing.

"You okay?"

"Yeah, I'm great."

The whole way back to Lucy's house Larry could not shake the image of her giving mouth-to-mouth to a dead sticky fetus, but he kept such thoughts to himself. The experience had told him in the most explicit way who Lucy was and what she was about, and he knew he could either deal with it or not. He hoped that he could.

When they reached her house he said he wanted to go home and take a shower.

"Yeah, me, too." They sat without moving for a minute before she added lamely, "Quite a night, huh?"

"Boy, howdy. As Jake would say."

She laughed and patted his knee with understanding. "Well," she said, "now you really know what it can be like. I'll see you around." She had not intended him to be around this long, but with Eric lost, here he was and he would have to do for now.

"I was going to ask. That Barilla guy that owns the pet store also has an import boutique of some kind in the Galleria I thought I might check out. You want to come?"

"Oh." A neglected errand clicked in her mind. "Yes. I have to be in a wedding in Austin in a couple of months. I haven't bought a gift but that might be a good place. Sure."

13 🌿🌿🌿🌿🌿🌿🌿🌿🌿🌿

LARRY DAVIS WORKED HIS NEXT SHIFT in the security station off the Hall of Silence, having become adept at manipulating the remote cameras and chatting back and forth with Sam as he patrolled the grounds. He went home and slept, grateful that after the next night's shift he had a couple of days off. Working nights was an annoyance, but it was quiet and he managed to get some cramming done for finals. He went back out to the park to pick up Lucy when she got off at five, and found her in her office, making inquiries into the ISIS data net as to whether certain specimens whose acquisition they were considering should be allowed to breed with individuals they already had. If the factor of wild gene diversity lost was too great, the pairing would be nixed and other mates would have to be found.

The whole problem would be obviated if more founders could be taken in from the wild, but that set the ethicists and animal rights people on edge. They had yet to come to terms with the fact that a species' survival cannot be ensured with the genetic material from five or ten or even fifty specimens already in captivity around the world. The SSP computer programs were set up to maintain adequate genetic variety for two hundred years, but without new founders more and more proposed pairings would be struck down as the existing captive population became more interrelated. Even then, a two-hundred-years survival projection seemed to her to be too short a time, given the unknowns, but perhaps by then techniques of gamete collecting from wild populations would be more of a perfected art. She hoped so.

She heard the knock on her open door and spun around on the

casters of her chair, and remembered in a flash of embarrassment that Larry Davis had caught her in her glasses. She slid them off her ears as though nothing were wrong. "Hi."

"You ready?"

"Just about. I need to go give a quick checkup to some monkeys we're shipping out tomorrow, then we can go. Come on along; I can use you." From the back door of the infirmary Lucy led him across the courtyard to the quarantine, past the line of cages he was familiar with, and into a tile examination room that was new to him.

The back wall was barred off into two large cages strung inside with ropes and branches. One was empty, and in the other a dozen tiny monkeys leapt and chattered as they approached. Each had black hands and feet, and a bright, interested black face framed by an eruption of metallic orange fur, brilliant and silky, as long and dramatic as the hair on a kabuki mask. Larry caught his breath. "Wow."

"Golden lion tamarins," said Lucy.

He knew that. In the Amazon section of South America he had seen them up in their trees, but never at so close a distance. They washed their hands in a sink, and Lucy gave him a surgical mask to put on, even as she put on one as well. "Are they sick?" he asked.

"No, but you might be." Tamarins are susceptible to a wide range of viruses which, in humans, are usually nuisances but to them are lethal. A tamarin can die of measles or even herpes, if it should reach out and touch a human cold sore.

Lucy took a banana from a tray, peeled it and broke off a piece, and opened the door of the cage and offered it to one of the monkeys, who jumped onto her hand without a second's hesitation.

She set it on the examining table and glanced at its ID band, and after finding its chart logged the necessary data—weight, temperature, pulse, a blood and stool sample. "I'm almost done with this one. Take a piece of banana and reach in. One of them will jump onto your hand. Bring it out and hold it while I put this one up."

A second after Larry reached in, a furry orange comet the size of a squirrel rocketed onto his wrist, and began wresting the piece of fruit out of his fingers. He withdrew his hand and closed the cage door, cradling the tamarin in his arm, letting it have the banana and laying his other hand on its back. It smacked the fruit energetically, taking no particular notice of Larry but curling one of its tiny hands around his thumb to steady itself.

The little black hand amazed him and he studied it, the long, lithe fingers, its knuckles and tiny black fingernails, the whole perfectly formed and no bigger than a dime. It thrilled him to see a wonder so small. The tamarin looked up at him for just an instant with its quick black eyes set in that intelligent little kabuki face, and their gazes met. Then it took another bite of its banana. Larry heard himself cooing, "That's a good boy."

"Girl," said Lucy and took her gently from him and set her on the table. "When you see a boy, you'll know it."

"What's her name?"

"Chiquita," said Lucy, and then her voice took on a high little Shirley Temple sound, with a Spanish accent. "Tell him, don' chu fall in love with me, 'cuz I'm going back to the jungle where my gramma came from."

A flash of alarm swept over him. "You think that's safe?"

She shot him a look—partly amused but quizzical, and just a little contemptuous. "Wait a minute, I thought you were the free-the-animals freak."

It's different now, he thought. It's different after you hold them, and they trust you, and they look into your eyes and show no fear, and take food from you and hold your hand while they eat it. Somehow it seemed a betrayal to turn them back to the wild, with its snakes and big cats and God knew what else. The monkeys didn't know about that, what was waiting for them out there.

He tried to articulate these things to her, and when he was done Lucy looked him squarely in the eye and said, "No shit."

"So, what are her chances, out there?"

"About even, I'm afraid."

Larry Davis looked at the brilliant orange little entity who had searched out his eyes and wrapped her tiny fingers around his thumb, and felt sick. "Is that all?"

Lucy grieved for him a little, too, at losing his naïveté of thinking that animals could be turned back to the wild without cost. Of course there was a cost, and it was a high cost. "If she makes it through the first year her chances improve a bit." She didn't like turning them loose to get sick or be killed any better than he did, but there was no other way to reintroduce them to their natural habitat. To think "natural habitat" justified it, made it easier to take, but of course she worried about them after they left. She turned her back on him to put Chiquita in the second cage. "Get me another one, will you?"

The irony was that the tamarins would be monitored in the wild almost as closely as they were here in their cage. Their natural range, in the jungle along the Brazilian coast above Rio de Janeiro, was almost completely gone. Not enough of it was left even to create a single nature reserve to guarantee the survival of the species. The "reserve" Chiquita was going to at Poço das Antas was really a patchwork of plots and acreages isolated from each other by farms and suburbs. Scientists there had been studying the tamarins since 1984, and discovered that they would not cross the cleared areas to get from one piece of jungle to another. Each group roamed its high little green castle until their inbreeding began to compromise their collective robustness. Now, tamarins were trapped in this "wild" and moved from one plot to another to continue their genetic variety. Not primeval, Lucy explained to him, but it was the best they could do since the habitat was about gone. Theirs were not by any means the last human hands that Chiquita would feel.

On their way out of the quarantine Lucy picked up the Cap-Chur gun, a box of CO_2 cartridges, and a box of blunt practice darts. "What in the world is that for?" asked Larry.

"I need to take a little target practice this evening."

"You're going to dart me and put a radio collar on me so you can follow my migration?"

She laughed. "No. Jake is going to pack up his batteries and collect some semen from antelope on the Serengeti. I've never done any wild collecting so I need to be ready."

"Cool! When?"

"July. The rainy season will be over and the ground will have had a chance to firm up."

"Can I watch?" The next day was his off day; working nights was an annoyance and he was tired, but he wanted to see that.

"Sure."

When they got to the parking lot, Larry realized he had screwed up by coming all the way out to the park to get her. He had to come back out that night anyway to work his shift, but there was no need for Lucy to repeat the trip. She wrote it off as the harmless gaffe of a young suitor, and he followed her to her house, where she stopped to change clothes. They went on to the Galleria in his car, which he turned into the underground parking. When from there they walked into the lower level of the mall, they had to find a map and index to locate Barilla Imports.

It was on the ground level but at the other end of the vast arcaded center. It was nearly a ten-minute walk to get there, but when they found it, they entered a small shop, well-kept and carpeted, with displays of carvings, brass, pre-Columbian reproductions and the like.

They were greeted by a handsome young Hispanic who smelled of too much Aramis. "May I help you?"

"Just looking," said Lucy.

"I see." He thought she was excellent. "If there's anything I can help you with, please let me know."

"I have to be in a wedding, and I'm just looking for a gift, is all."

"Yeah, you know, a lot of people like to get art or something kind of decorative for a wedding gift; they get enough toasters." It was a practiced line that he brought off well.

"Those stone figures over there look nice."

Larry Davis wandered elsewhere into the shop and left them alone.

"Those are Olmec reproductions. A lot of people like those."

She picked one up and found it heavy; the tag underneath read sixty dollars—more than she wanted to spend but within her budget.

"What do you do?"

A personal question took her off guard. "I'm a veterinarian."

He nodded with a smile. "Oh. Dogs and cats, huh? That sort of thing."

She felt increasingly uncomfortable. "That sort of thing."

Larry returned and decided it was time to take control of the conversation. "Are you Ramón Barilla?"

Luís fielded any kind of question suspiciously. It was his instinct. "No, I am Luís. Ramón is my uncle." He was afraid he had gotten out of line and was going to be reported. But no, this guy shouldn't have known his uncle by name.

"My name is Larry Davis." They shook hands. "I visited your pet store in Pasadena recently, and the manager said I might like to talk with your uncle about maybe doing a story."

"What kind of story?"

"I work on the newspaper at the University of Houston. I wasn't sure at the time, but I think maybe about successful minority businesses or something."

"He's in the office. I'll introduce you." They met, and for ten minutes Larry laid the kind of journalistic smoke screen by which, with enough practice, a journalist learns most of what he needs to know.

During his years in the United States Ramón had found recognition a scarce thing to come by, and was not disposed to be suspicious of the young reporter. Indeed he was voluble in his conversation. He mentioned his connections with the Jaycees, his recent activity in the Republican party, and finally concluded that, he was sorry, it was too late in the day for a real interview but he would be happy to talk to Larry later in the week. He handed over his card, and through the whole exposition never noticed that what most caught the attention of Larry and Lucy both was the fact that he had spread flat over his desk a tourist map of The Final Refuge Wildlife Park.

As they left, Ramón chuckled and tapped Luís on the shoulder. "Hey, I think she like you, man. You get her phone number?"

He pulled away. "They didn't buy nothin'."

Lucy also had sense enough to say nothing about the map on Ramón's desk until they were barely down the mall from the shop.

"So, why do you think—"

"I don't know," he cut her short. "I need to think about it."

"Maybe it's just a coincidence."

Larry looked at her sidelong. No, she didn't think so, either. But why?

On the way back Larry drove all the way out on Westheimer, even though I-10 was only a mile to the north. He wanted a chance to talk through the stoplights.

"So, how come you live out here?" he asked her. "Closer to work?"

"Sort of. There's not really that many younger people out here, though. When I first moved to Houston I lived nine months over by Rice University, but I just couldn't take the way the students treated their pets."

"Oh, come on."

"No, really. It's not like they beat them or anything, but so many people have pets who have no business having pets. Some guy puts the dog out and tells him to stay, in a yard with no fence, and goes and eats dinner and watches TV. Or he runs the dog in the park, no leash, and gets distracted by some girl with bouncy tits. That dog's gone.

"That, or they'd move in with a cat, and the next day they'd turn the poor thing out to 'explore' the new neighborhood. Naturally the poor cat tries to go home, wherever that was. Cats are centered on a place as much as on people. When you move you should never let a cat out for maybe three weeks. There were handbills going up all the time on telephone poles about lost pets, 'Heartbroken,' 'Reward,' 'No questions asked.' I'd see some poor kitten with a flea collar and a bell, just cowering on a sidewalk next to a six-lane street and not know where the hell she was. If I couldn't get them to come to me I'd just go home and throw up. Some people even dumped their pets in parks when they moved and figured someone would feel sorry enough to take them in."

"So you did."

"I couldn't save them all. I had to find homes for maybe six or eight of the poor things that wound up at my house. It's weird, how they can tell who will take them in, like there is a network on the street. 'Need a meal? House on the corner, she's a softie.' So I got out of there."

Larry Davis thought, Yes, this is a girl who would attract the homeless, the uncertain and the confused that other people would never even notice were there. Dogs, cats, perhaps that guy Luís, perhaps even himself. He had never dumped an animal but he did lose a dog once; Larry assayed how much of himself Lucy had been describing and changed the subject.

Back at her house she corraled the dogs into the garage—the cats were in the house—as Larry helped her set up a step ladder to the roof overlooking the backyard. It was surrounded by a six-foot privacy fence, and near the back was a pile of four bales of hay with a well-used target on it.

She had explained to the neighbors in previous days that it was not a firearm and there was no point in calling the police. After a few rounds Larry helped her move the hay and target to the corner of the yard, as she repositioned herself at the opposite end of the roof to make the longest shots possible, about a hundred fifty feet, and scored a couple of bull's-eyes and nearly all very close.

"That's good shooting," said Larry. He was making himself useful, scurrying down to retrieve the blunt practice darts.

"I've done longer before, but I have to use the range at the farm. I just haven't had time during work to get over there."

"Would you like for me to go down and stand with an apple on my head?"

Just at that moment she was wishing for Eric and thought, Don't tempt me.

14 🌿🌿🌿🌿🌿🌿🌿🌿🌿🌿

WITH THE VISIT from the Indonesian ambassador and conservation minister looming large, Eric set aside half a day to go deep within himself and plan a line of attack. He knew he had to give an after-lunch speech to the Kiwanis over in Friendswood, but he would give it his whole morning. He was showered and fresh but it was not yet six when he returned to the bedroom and wrapped his arms around Liz Ann, and she responded groggily but with affection. She should, he thought. He had made love to her half the night to earn an early pass.

"You're sure you don't mind my going in now?" he asked.

"No, babe. I know it's important." She was willowy and brunette and he believed he could still love her, but still there were things that seemed arduous and as he left he wondered if God meant for marriage to be arduous. It was barely past six-thirty when he turned his Saturn into the parking garage. Sam Rutherford's car was in its assigned space, and there were a few others that bore temporary stickers. Over the past few weeks it had been Eric's idea, but Sam agreed, to have some of the student volunteers who were doing behavior observation for school credit take turns doing some night studies. There was no need to tell them they were serving a security function, but the garage was never emptied to only one or two vehicles, and Sam had taken to issuing the kids hip radios while they were on the grounds and casually showed them how to get in touch with him if they saw anything unusual. Now that the summer vacation was nearly at hand, the students would be gone; the biology department at the University of Houston would pick it up again in the fall, but during the shorter summer sessions with their smaller enrollment, a summer program was decided against.

Eric's footsteps echoed through the loggia as he crossed and climbed the stairs, turning on lights as he went. He turned on the Mr. Coffee in the kitchen by his office, and as it brewed he dug into the file cabinet behind Stephanie's desk; he remembered seeing some relevant clippings from the rhino files and wanted to refresh his memory. Leaning back in his chair, his feet on his desk, he read each article thoughtfully.

Dateline Gauhati, India, September 1993. PARK'S LAST RHINOCEROS KILLED. The Laokhowa Wildlife Sanctuary, a 30-square mile refuge in the northeastern part of the country set aside for the preservation of the Indian rhinoceros, lost its last specimen to poachers. Two years before there had been fifty rhinos in Laokhowa. A park official leaked the news to the Western press on the condition of anonymity, for the sake of his job, if not his life. India was not unsympathetic to the plight of their rhinos. Indeed, judged over the forty-five years since their independence, the national government had made tremendous strides in wildlife protection. But things could be different with the governments of the various states; Laokhowa was in Assam, a thousand miles from New Delhi but only fifty miles from Bangladesh with its rich, Chinese merchant class who quietly bettered in their superior way the wretched poverty around them. At Laokhowa the countryside was rough and patrols were insufficient—and the people were poor. If they did not know already how much a horn was worth, the entrepreneurs who threaded in on the forest trails from Bangladesh and Bhutan and Myanmar would have educated them in a hurry.

Dateline London, October 1993. RARE GOBLET STOLEN, RECOVERED. A thousand-year-old drinking cup crafted from a hollowed-out rhinoceros horn, dating from the T'ang dynasty, stolen from a private collection, was recovered badly damaged in an Asian apothecary. It had been partially ground up for powder. As an artifact of ancient Chinese civilization it was valued at fifty thousand pounds; as medicinal tea it was worth three times that.

Dateline Washington, November 1993. UNITED STATES THREATENS TRADE SANCTIONS AGAINST CHINA, TAIWAN. Less than a year after China set its pen to the CITES Treaty, cameras concealed on the persons of operatives of an international environmental organization had filmed Chinese soldiers lording over a warehouse trove of severed rhino horns, for sale to whoever would buy. The price even included armed escort of the merchandise to its destination.

Eric Jackson remembered skimming these articles before, but at the back of the file was one new to him. A *U.S. News and World Report* from November 1993, five pages clipped together under the title of "Wildlife's Last Chance." He took a sip of coffee and settled back to read it carefully, surmising that Stephanie must have put it in the file in a flurry of catch-up work. It restated the opposing positions of altruistic preservation of endangered wildlife versus "controlled use," a euphemism for farming, as it were, wild animals and then harvesting them for meat and hides—and ivory or horn, when applicable. Under the title was a large photo—two thirds of a page—of a cow elephant *sans* ears and trunk, hung up with chains by her feet in a tile-floored slaughterhouse that the government of South Africa had opened in Kruger National Park, one of the flagship wildlife preserves in all of Africa. Eric found it familiar; he had visited the place not long before Chete. He didn't like it, but he understood the need for wildlife to pay for itself and had incorporated many of those tenets into his own operation. He had almost concluded that there was nothing new in it, when a figure caught his eye. Rhino horn was then—and that was some months since—going for $28,000 a pound. That was a new figure, and he noted it down. The Indonesians don't know pounds, and Eric pulled a calculator from his desk drawer and multiplied by 2.2. $61,600 per kilo. That they would understand. Eric turned to the last page of the article, where a photo assaulted and nauseated him and in a flash he understood why Stephanie had hidden it from him. It was of a public tiger execution in Taiwan. In an urban square with high-rises in the background, a magnificent Bengal was spreadeagled on its back in a rusted iron cage, its paws roped and drawn tightly to the corners of the cage, its back legs hefted high off the floor. The tiger's roped head was outside the cage, the sliding door pressing down on its throat. Inside the cage was an aluminum saucepan to collect its blood, which, like rhino horn, was an important commodity in Chinese pharmacology, as a crowd of workaday Taiwanese stood about smoking cigarettes in their American bluejeans. Stephanie knew very well that there were some things that Eric just couldn't bear to have inside his head, and wisely she had filed this photo away. But now it was too late, and Eric fought the tears even as they rose. He caught himself in mid-thought—the phrase "stupid fucking slope-headed chinks" had already gotten by him—when he shook his head, not at the photo but at himself. He was the last person on earth he wanted to regard as a racist, and sights such as this set him at war with himself. The Chinese will never change, he thought. They will pretend to, and they will laugh at us, but they will never change.

But this could not be a day he could spare for mourning the stupidity of the human race. He folded the articles back into their file and replaced it in Stephanie's cabinet, determined not to say anything to her, and then glanced at the clock, allowing himself ten minutes to get over what he had seen.

The biggest obstacle to his Indonesian campaign was without a doubt the field biologists already on the ground in Udjung Kulon. Even on this topic, possession was nine-tenths of the law.

Their enmity mystified him, for it seemed to him that the zoo people had no more natural ally on earth than the field biologists, whose studies could tell them how better to rear animals in captivity to safeguard the dwindling wild populations—not just rhinos but all the hundreds of different endangered species. Yet that was not the case, and although they agreed on the necessity to save them, their differing opinions on how to do it had separated them almost into armed camps.

In Indonesia the situation had been damaged enormously by one well-meaning zoo advocate, who showed up with a new computer program. By supplying numbers—all of which even Eric regarded as either problematical or wildly hypothetical—to fill variables such as Javan rhino estimated natural mortality rate, availability of food plants per hectare in Udjung Kulon, and the like, he announced his conclusion that *half* the rhinos in the reserve should be trapped and removed. The Indonesian government was aghast, and the poor man had played right into the hands of the field biologists already on the ground there—and there was an army of them, British, Dutch, and American as well as Indonesian and Indian—whose outrage seemed vindicated when they could point to such an unproven assertion and say, "See? See what the zoo people *really* want?" He had probably set the effort back five years.

Eric had to concede that the field biologists were absolutely right on one point: no matter how much zoos say they are keeping the wildlife going until the wild is made safe again, it is a bare fact that animals born and raised in captivity have no idea how to be wild. Their behavior is as much learned as instinctive. The golden lion tamarins that they were shipping out to Brazil had been through weeks of boot camp, learning how to do for themselves. At first they don't even know how to peel a damned banana. Then, the research station at Poço das Antas blends them gradually and gently back into the jungle, and even then the mortality is at least half. The field biologists should be powerful allies in showing the zoos how to prepare animals better for a return to the wild, but when zoo people pop off like this guy did in Indonesia, it is only natural that the field biologists stake out their turf, too, and that was about what they had on their hands, there and elsewhere: a stupid fucking turf war.

Whenever he thought of this, Eric thought of Eleanor, a cow elephant who was raised from infancy in the orphanage at Tsavo National Park in Kenya. As an adult she left the orphanage and rejoined a wild herd, but strangely, eerily, and unbidden, she began returning to the orphanage. After greeting the human friends who raised her, she would take one of the infants who had been weaned and was ready, would take it out to the herd and teach it how to be wild—she taught it the language and the social order, and how to behave. In all of human history and all that is known of natural history, Eleanor is a case whose implications shatter everything that is known of the boundary between people and animals, and what makes people people and what makes animals animals. Eleanor was now in her middle age and still performing a role that she had taken entirely upon herself, to recognize that the baby elephants in the orphanage at Tsavo had a right to grow up wild but could not because they did not know how—unless she took them out and showed them how.

What the field biologists and behaviorists ought to be fucking doing was studying Eleanor, and how other Eleanors might be cultivated among other species. If they could do that, Eric mused, then the promise would become a reality that when a home can be made secure for them in their own habitats, animals could truly return to the wild from their sheltered captivity.

When he thought of Eleanor, Eric thought inevitably of the other animals who had shown flashes of unsuspected intelligence, like the whales, or Koko the gorilla, who not only learned sign language but transcended what she was taught and began using signs to ask for things she wanted and to communicate how she was feeling. And thinking of Koko and thinking how, yes, they do think and they can communicate, made him think of his old cat, Isabella, and he caught himself and knew he had digressed too far. It was just that there was so much to do and so much to understand, that it was difficult to concentrate.

But he knew he had better concentrate, because the Indonesian conservation minister was coming, and he would want some hard answers to some difficult questions. Eric did have high cards to play. Millie had performed magnificently, and by now the Indonesian house was a riot of tropical greenery, and the paddocks were stocked with populations of orangutans, tapirs, proboscis monkeys, anoa, Komodo dragons—he could even show them videotape of their two Sumatran rhinos doing the dirty deed, as they probably thought, unobserved. The only empty enclosure in the building now was the largest and most elaborate, for the Javas. He would lower a ladder and lead the dignitaries through a habitat virtually indistinguishable from the swamps of Udjung Kulon, with a river five feet deep, flowing sluggishly and heated to 78 degrees, with their favorite food plants growing rank on the banks. It would be unthinkable they could leave without themselves wanting to see Javan rhinos in there.

And if that failed he had prepared a coup-de-grace, and he envisioned himself telling them, "We know from studies at Kaziranga—"

studies, he knew that the field biologists had done "—that Indian rhinos have private dens that they retire to during the day when they're not feeding. The Javas are so closely related that we made an assumption that they might require the same sort of retreat to adjust well." And that was the greatest surprise: they now knew just how closely related they were. Stan Over was with a native team at Udjung Kulon when they trapped and tagged a Javan cow. He had taken a scraping of skin cells from inside her mouth, and Lucy had examined the genetic makeup. Surrogate implanting was the latest thing in zoo technology—implanting a rare embryo into a closely related but common surrogate mother. If a Javan embryo was implanted into an Indian cow, Lucy's chromosome analysis showed the chances of success were at least as great as with other, similarly related, species, where implanting had resulted in live births. If it worked with the Javas, it would be a fast track to a large, stable population that would obviate any necessity of capturing more than just a very few of them.

If they were dealing honestly with him, they simply could not refuse such arguments. But their honesty, he also knew, was not unimpeachable. Even when all this was done, you could never be sure when you had an agreement with these people. He stopped, having caught himself at it again: "these people." A slur. You just can't do that.

Eric had always taken great care to demonstrate cultural sensitivity to the Indonesians, right down to pronouncing Udjung Kulon the native way, with the accents on the second syllables. But the fact was that Miami Metrozoo once thought they had a firm deal for Komodo dragons—the largest and one of the rarest lizards on Earth—but when a new minister took over the post he surprised them with a new requirement: he wanted two gorillas in exchange. It took some very stern talking to convince him that in today's world, with the "new" zoos acquiring animals to save them from extinction and not to just amass a collection, business simply was not done that way anymore. One cannot make racist generalizations, Eric knew, but still they were Asians with Asians' worldviews, and in their world everything was negotiable until it was in the past tense.

That was not to imply that everything and everyone in South Asia was inimical to wildlife. Singapore, for instance, had a zoo that was dazzlingly modern in its philosophy. They even had the only polar bears in their part of the world, in a tank and enclosure that was not just spacious but whose configuration they changed completely several times a year so the intelligent bears would not get bored. They even released live fish into their pool so they could hunt and catch them; no pails of half-thawed mackerel for them. Singapore gave him hope that eventually, once Asian people developed a consciousness of this great new purpose that zoos serve, they would become as innovative and lead-taking as they had been in industry and technology. But God, that could be a long road.

There was a knock at his door, and Eric looked up to see Larry Davis. "Hi."

"Boy, you're here early."

"Big meeting to prepare for." Eric pointed to one of the chairs in front of his desk.

"I'm just getting off my shift."

"How's it going?"

"Pretty good. Meeting with the Indonesians? About the Javas?"

"Yes." Eric was now finding it no easy task to tutor Larry Davis in the wild animal business, but Lucy seemed content with him. To chase after her and find her no longer interested would have raised the specter of harassment, and to vent retribution on Larry would have compromised the sense of professionalism in which he took such pride. Thus whenever Larry appeared now, Eric stewed silently and was correct and helpful—much the same attitude, he realized, with which he would have gone through life had he become a priest when he once felt the inclination.

"Listen," said Larry, "that article about animal trafficking—I went over to the pet shop. The owner is a guy named Barilla who also owns an import shop in the Gallería. Lucy and I went over there; I laid some smoke about maybe doing a story on minority businessmen. We talked to him, and, well, he had a map of the park out on his desk. Parts of it were marked up, but we couldn't tell what. Is there any reason why he would have a map? I mean, other than coincidence."

Eric leaned back. "Well, sure. We're holding a shipment of impounded exotics that he's probably paid for. I'm sure Clarence would have had to tell him where they were."

"Oh." He hadn't thought of that. That was business still pending. "I don't know; I just got a bad feeling about him somehow."

"So are you going to proceed with the article?"

"Yeah. He said if I came back he'd show me around and stuff. I'll find out what I can. I mean, I don't want to sound like an alarmist or anything, but Lucy didn't like him either."

Eric would have just as soon he would stop mentioning Lucy. "Well, talk to him again and see how it goes. Keep me posted. Oh, and after finals are over, I wonder if you would write a little something for me"—he produced a file of newspaper and magazine clippings. "I'm not real happy with the text we have explaining the exhibit on rhino horns and Chinese medicine. You know the one I'm talking about?"

Larry nodded.

"Here's some articles to go on. I know there's a bunch of books in the public library on Chinese medicine, maybe you can check those out. Think you can do that for me?"

Larry took up the sheaf of clippings, wondering when he would find the time. "You said it can wait till after finals?"

"Sure. No rush."

After breakfast and a nap, Larry took a noon exam and then went back to the Gallería to see Ramón Barilla, whose map was no longer on his desk. The interview he conducted seemed for all the world like the profile of a success story. They talked partly in the office, and partly as Ramón toured him around the showroom.

"You must get stuff from all over," said Larry.

"Yes, just about all over."

"Do you keep a large inventory?"

"Pretty big, but not too big 'cause we gotta pay taxes on whatever we got at the end of the year, you know. Come on, I show you the storeroom."

Larry Davis saw the backstock well organized, which he complimented, and read some labels aloud. "Peru—Guatemala—India—"

"India make really nice brass. You saw the trays and stuff outside?"

"Yes." His eyes fell on three wrapped parcels addressed to Imperial Ming Exporting Company, at an address in Los Angeles.

Barilla noticed him notice and said quickly, "Those, I have a friend in L.A. that I send some things on to him. I get a little cut, you know."

"I see. Does he send them on out of the country?"

"Maybe," he said. "I don't really know."

"Well, I mean, I just noticed it was an export company. I guess you got to make a little extra wherever you can, huh?" he gave a confidential smile.

Ramón Barilla laughed. "That's right. It all count the same."

Larry began writing on his pad, as he said, "Well, this really is quite a spread of importing sources. China—Bolivia—" But what he was writing in his pad as he ticked off the countries was the address of Imperial Ming Exporting Company, on New High Street in Los Angeles, and as they exited the storeroom he saw something else on the parcel addresses which he added: "Attention: Personal, Albert Chu."

Back in the office, Larry made himself comfortable in a chair and said, "I have to ask you something, I hope you won't mind."

"No, go ahead."

"You received a consignment of animals for your pet shop that was impounded by the Customs Service. How did that happen?"

"You know about that?" He was not pleased.

Larry laughed it off. "Well, come on, I am a reporter."

"Well, you know, when you get animals from other countries, you never know if they gonna be responsible or not. These people, I never use them before, and I find out they not reliable. I mean, when Customs take the animals, I lose a lot of money, but I can't control how carefully they gonna ship them. You bet on this, I ain't gonna use them again, that for sure."

Larry nodded. "Thanks. I just needed to clear that up. But I can't tell you how impressed I am at what a success you have made of yourself since you came into this country."

"Well listen, why don't you come out to my house and maybe have some dinner. I like you to meet my wife, we can talk a little bit more."

"That would be great. Why don't we wait a few days so I can talk to my editor, and maybe I can give you a better idea just what kind of story she might want me to do. Would that be all right?"

"Sure." Ramón Barilla was very pleased. He had never been in the newspaper before in his life.

15

LARRY DAVIS did something he had not done before, nor was he certain it was his place to do it. He called Eric and asked for a meeting with him and for both Jake and Sam to be present. It took a couple of days to find everybody free at the same time, and even then Jake was a little peeved at listening to Larry's report about the Hispanic animal dealer whom he had, himself, wrangled with over the phone a few times about the impounded shipment.

"Well, there was something else about him," Larry protested. "I was curious as to whether he might have any kind of a criminal record, so I checked that out. There was nothing real bad as far as the police were concerned, but I thought you might be interested to know he was busted three years ago for poaching deer up in the Crockett National Forest."

"People poach deer all the time," said Jake. "That don't mean much by itself."

Larry looked straight at him. "Most deer poachers aren't caught with an ice chest containing seventeen deer tails."

Jake's mouth went slack, his jaw dropping slowly like its weight was held up with chewing gum. "God almighty."

"You remember those books you asked me to read?" he asked Eric. "The ones about Chinese medicine?"

"Yes."

"Well, I've been reading. Deer tails are used in Chinese medicine."

Jake was figuring it out. "You mean he was poaching to supply an Asian pharmacy. Why, that dirty son of a bitch."

Eric asked, "Was anyone else implicated?"

"No one was convicted or anything. But when I was in his shop a few days ago, I saw parcels in the storeroom addressed to a place in Los Angeles, and, I swear to God, it was the same place the deer tails were supposed to go to."

"Do you know what place that was?"

Jake was standing closest to Larry, and he handed his open note pad to him. Jake read slowly, "Imperial Ming Exporting Company—" his voice began to trail off. "New High Street, Los Angeles, Attention— Oh, my God." He handed it to Eric.

"Attention: Personal, Albert Chu." Eric faded back into his chair, white as a sheet. "Oh, my God, what are we going to do? Do you think this means he was involved with what happened in San Antonio?"

Sam Rutherford finally spoke up. "Maybe it's about time we called the sheriff's department. Get them warmed up to what kind of deal might be going down."

Jake crossed his arms and glared at Eric. "You know I still want to take the horns off the rhinos we got."

"Yes, I know you do."

"You haven't changed your mind?"

"No."

"And you still don't want to get the police involved."

"Jake, the Javas aren't here yet. The Indonesians could still kill the deal at a moment's notice. We simply cannot risk word of something like this getting out."

"Well, now, have you stopped to consider that maybe for the Javas' own good it's not the best thing to bring them in just now?"

"Yes, I have. Jake, if anything happens to screw the deal up now, we won't get this close again in ten years and you know it."

Jake nodded slowly. "So, you are perfectly satisfied in your own mind that going ahead with it is the right thing to do?"

"Yes." No, he wasn't. He had prayed about it, and no, he wasn't. He wasn't even certain that his own motives were not tainted with pride and a desire to be recognized as a premier wildlife savior. But even if they were, it did not alter the fact that as far as getting at least two Javas out of Indonesia, it was now or never. "Yes. What we have to do for the moment is sit tight and not panic."

Larry Davis raised his hands. "Wait, wait, wait, wait. You guys are losing me. All I said was that Ramón Barilla got busted for poaching. Five minutes ago Jake thought I was Chicken Little. Will somebody tell me what the fuck is going on?"

Jake spit into Eric's trashcan. "You remember your first tour out here with the press corps?"

"Yeah, I particularly remember getting acquainted with you."

"Do you remember that old Chinese guy, the mayor's buddy, who took such an interest in the rhinos? That was Albert Chu."

"Oh, no," said Larry. "Oh, shit."

It took a couple of weeks from the time of his first meeting for Larry Davis to get back in touch with Ramón Barilla, telephoning him at the store. He explained how exams had sapped more of his time than he wanted, but the school paper was still going to publish during the summer, and he asked if Ramón would like to go ahead with the story.

"You bet," said Ramón heartily. "We got plans for this weekend, but why don't next Wednesday you come out for dinner at my house. We love to have you."

He gave him the address and directions, and then called Esteban into the office. "You remember that college guy I told you about, is going to do a story about me? He call back, and he comin' to dinner Wednesday night. What do you think about Tuesday night we go out to the animal park and see if we can get in?"

Esteban nodded. "That might be good."

"You know, not to try to get anything, just see if we can get in and out okay."

Esteban continued to nod. They had been out to The Refuge three additional times, and thought they had a spot picked where they could make an entry. Certainly the time was drawing near. They had seen it all over the newspapers and in the evening news that the park had consummated an agreement for the importation of two Javan rhinoceroses. Albert Chu had even called them to make sure they saw the story, from which they surmised that he was anxious for them to move as soon as the rhinos arrived.

Tuesday night, Larry was working in the security office off the Hall of Silence, with the surveillance cameras on automatic rotation to view the various parts of the park in sequence. He had with him Eric's copy of the English translation of Heini Hediger's *Wild Animals in Captivity,* one of the first classic treatises to systematize problem areas that had to be overcome for wildlife to feel more at home in a confined circumstance. But knowing what they knew now, he had put it aside and studied each image on the monitor as it appeared.

Between two and three in the morning he noticed a long, dark sedan motoring westward by the entrance. Around the perimeter, one camera was set up to monitor the loading dock at Jake's compound, one at the main entrance gate, and one at the driveway into the farm. When they first installed the system, Eric had judged surveillance cameras too expensive to be able to continuously watch every yard of the entire perimeter, but since their last meeting he had begun to think again. The fact was, however, that the new security guard would take another two thousand dollars out of their monthly budget, and the Javan operation was costing half a million that had to come out of the capital fund. More cameras would simply have to wait until they could find the money.

Sam had told Larry to call him if he ever saw a car pass by more than three times, but sitting through the whole cycle took nine minutes. If Larry overrode the sequence for a long look out the gate, he would lose his view of the rest of the park to watch the road, which might not have another car on it for an hour.

From within the dark interior of Ramón's blue Olds the Barillas watched the fences closely, inspecting the place they had selected to break in. In two passes of the whole length of the park they had not encountered a single other car. Esteban leaned over Ramón's lap to see the dark fence slip by. "Man, there's nobody out here."

After they turned off from 521, about halfway to the entrance gate, a gravel drive extended south across the road from the dual fence. It was the driveway to a large commercial sand-and-gravel operation.

They had spotlights on their rigs but they were several hundred yards from the road, and they decided the car would be well enough hidden by pulling into this drive and edging it right against the mesquite brush that crowded up to the gravel ruts.

It was on their third pass that Ramón told Juan, "Pull in here a little bit and stop." They looked again up and down the flat length of highway. There was no one. Ramón motioned Luís and Esteban out of the car. "See if you can get in. We'll wait here; if anybody come by we say we got car trouble. Don't let nobody see you; just look around and get out quiet."

The two hunched across the road with a clumsy, glopping sound caused by their rubber waders, and at the outer fence Luís reached into his satchel for his wire cutters. The deer fence was not difficult to get through; there was no need to go over it when they could just snip through the wide, four-inch mesh and squeeze through. They found the moat knee-deep and muddy, and ten feet after they emerged they came to the six-foot fence topped by the barbed wire. The lower part was thick chain-link, so Luís grasped the top bar and with his other hand reached up to snip through the barbed wire. From where they waited Ramón and Juan saw the spark and heard the loud snap of electricity.

"Shit!" hollered Ramón. "Start the car!"

Luís flew away from the fence with a yelp, the wire cutters sailing in an arc to splash in the middle of the moat. He landed on his butt five feet from the fence, feeling heavy dull pain from his hand all the way up his arm and then down into his chest. "God damn," he wheezed. Esteban helped him slog back across the moat and through the deer fence. Their car doors weren't even closed before Juan tromped the accelerator.

It was an important aspect of The Refuge's security that the electricity was atop the inner fence and not the outer one. No matter how valuable the property, protecting it with booby traps was illegal virtually everywhere. To have electrified the outer fence would have risked shocking someone who—although it would have been a fanciful story—could have claimed to have come in casual contact with it. The only way to get a shock, and it was not a severe one, was to cut through or to climb over a ten-foot deer fence and wade in the moat. That would not be an innocent trespass, and even then, they had the claim that the electricity was not to keep people out but dangerous animals in. Wallace the lawyer had even had to dig up case law which held that electric fences installed for safety did not constitute booby traps. The things they had to do, Eric once thought, to get insurance.

In the security office, Larry Davis was scanning the overview of the bridges that connected the Pacific islands when the electric alarm sounded for thirty seconds, like the high, flat-pitched squeal of an EKG when a patient dies. The monitor switched instantly to the main gate, then the farm and then the clinic. It settled into that rotation: gate, farm, clinic—gate, farm, clinic—indicating that something had come in contact with the hot wires on the south or east side.

Larry said to himself, "Whoa, that is bad ass," even as he radioed out to Sam.

"How 'bout it," asked Sam. "You get a license number?"

Suddenly Larry felt like he somehow should have, but he had never even seen who it was. "No," he said. "I never saw them."

"That's okay. If they came back up the road we've got them on tape. Keep your eyes peeled and let me know if you see anything else."

Sam came back into the office at six A.M., at the end of Larry's shift. The rent-a-cops they engaged to keep an eye on the crowds would arrive soon, but Sam wanted to stay and have a look at the video. The long dark sedan they saw from the main-gate camera cruised by headed west at 2:37, then again headed east at 2:45. That was the pass Larry had missed. It had not passed in front of another camera before returning and pulling into the drive of the sand-and-gravel company. The camera at the quarantine loading dock saw the same car rocketing by going north at 3:07.

They backed up to the second pass and enlarged the picture, but the license plate was unreadable. "You know what kind of car it is?" asked Larry. Unlike most boys, cars had never been a thing with him.

"GM maybe, couple or three years old. Full-sized, maybe an Olds. Look there, looks like it's got a tiger tail or something on the radio antenna."

"Yeah, I see it. You'll tell Eric today?"

"Oh yes, I make out a report of everything that happens like this. Well, that's that. I'll go out and have a look at the fence tomorrow. You still need tomorrow night off?"

"Yeah, remember I'm having dinner with that Barilla guy."

"That's right. Well, watch yourself. If he's poached for Chu and has a beef running with Jake, for God's sake watch your mouth. He still doesn't have a way to associate you with the park?"

"No, I'm sure he doesn't."

Sam was walking his rounds at eleven the next night when his radio crackled and he pulled it off his belt. It was Larry. "What the hell are you doing here? I thought you were—"

"Sam? Sam, it's the same car. It was Barilla's car. I saw it in his driveway, tonight. Remember? The tiger tail on the aerial. It was the Barillas who tried to get in."

"Holy mother. All right, hang on, I'll come in."

When Sam stalked through the back door of the headquarters, Larry heard the door open and met him halfway down the Hall of Stupidity. "What should we do? You think we should call Eric?"

Sam considered it. "No. We're not supposed to call him at night anymore unless it's a real emergency. In the morning I'll stay around until he comes in. If you're that keyed up, you want to work the rest of your shift?"

"Yes. I couldn't sleep a wink tonight."

They collared Eric and Jake both as soon as they arrived, and told them the certainty that it was the Barillas who'd tried to violate the park. Eric seemed strangely prepared or at least unsurprised by the news, and had an answer ready. "Don't wait on the Javas. Put the new guy to work, right now."

Jake sniped a bullet back into the room as he started to leave. "I don't guess there'd be any point in reminding you what it is I want to do."

Eric hung his head almost like he was about to admit a defeat. "I'm thinking about it. All right?"

"Well, all right." He sounded patronizing, almost sarcastic. "You think about it."

As Larry left he handed Eric a plastic binder. "I finished the thing on Chinese medicine. See what you think."

After they were all gone, he put his feet up on his desk and read.

MEMO

FROM: Larry Davis
TO: Eric Jackson
SUBJECT: Rhinoceros Horn in Chinese Medicine

The history of conflict between the system of medicine practiced in the West, and the Chinese traditional practitioners, is long and involved, and was complicated even further with the advent of a Communist government on mainland China. From the time China was "lost" in 1949, everything Chinese was shunned by the American political establishment during the McCarthy era. In fact, no American doctors or scientists visited mainland China—universally referred to at that time as Red China—from 1949 until 1971. When China finally did open to the West, Chinese films of such things as open-heart surgery on a fully conscious patient anesthetized only by acupuncture, caused a furor in the West and eventually occasioned a grudging admission from our own medical establishment that there "might be something to it."

The scope of this report, on the use of rhinoceros horn as an aphrodisiac, is limited to a different facet of Chinese medicine, that of so-called traditional pharmacology. And in this field the most striking aspect of the use of rhino horn as an aphrodisiac is the total absence of literature on the subject—at least in the English-language sources that I consulted. The first six books I looked at on Chinese medicine had no listing whatever in the indexes for "rhinoceros," "horn," "impotence," or "aphrodisiac." Two did have index listings for "aging," but the texts described only herbal remedies.

I am at a loss to explain this absence, except to note one point—that all the books I consulted were printed recently enough for the practice of poaching rhinos for their horns to have been already widely criticized and derided in the West. Since these books all had as one of their aims the gaining of a wider acceptance of traditional Chinese medicine in Europe and America, the authors and editors may have thought it discreet to just leave the topic out, rather than risk more ridicule.

What I did learn about rhino horn as an aphrodisiac came not from books about Chinese pharmacology, but from books and articles about rhinos. Everybody knows that rhinos are poached and their horns taken for the Asian drug market. Until the adoption of CITES, the Convention on International Trade in Endangered Species, and even for some years thereafter, the product, though expensive, was freely available at any clinic in China. It is still there; although now a black market item, it is not in scarce supply. Understanding the tenacity of this continued Asian faith in and reliance upon it has to be rooted in some grasp of Chinese traditional medicine itself.

The foundation of this discipline was, and remains, the *Huang Ti Nei Ching Su Wen,* or the *Yellow Emperor's Classic of Internal Medicine,* written down by Wang Ping in the T'ang Dynasty (c. 760 A.D.). He utilized other written sources dating back to 300 B.C., and ascribed actual authorship to the Emperor Huang Ti himself, who lived—if he actually lived—c. 2600 B.C. The greatest difference between medicine as it is practiced in the West and the system handed down by the Yellow Emperor lies in the latter's inclusion of philosophy and religion within the medical canon.

Traditional Chinese medicine pictures the healthy man or woman being in harmony with the universe. That universe consists of the five elements of which all things are made— fire, water, metal, wood and earth. Man keeps these elements in proper proportion within himself by striving to live according to *Tao* ("the right way") and by accommodating the differences among the four seasons, which in turn are governed by the balance of *Yin* and *Yang,* the two creative forces of the universe that alternately attract and repel each other. Yin, the force of cold and dark which is the associative female element, dominates in winter. The male-associated Yang, the force of warmth and light, dominates in summer.

Thus for one to remain healthy, he or she must maintain balance with the seasons as they change, but it is equally important to "live right." If you get sick, the first assumption is that, at some level or other, it's your own fault. There are different places in the *Yellow Emperor's Handbook* where it is stated quite explicitly that deviation from social norms will cause sickness or even death. Western medicine is grounded in diagnosing physical symptoms and treating them; a Chinese doctor's inquiry is much broader, extending to his patient's social life, personal habits and even his opinions. This system has given the Chinese traditional practitioner a position of great power in his society, not just as a healer but as social and even political enforcer. Conjunctively, Chinese society has evolved over four thousand years as one which places enormous emphasis on conformity, and one in which social norms are rigidly enforced at the expense of individual expression.

Thus it is no wonder that people who are raised from birth to believe that rhinoceros horn is an aphrodisiac will find it difficult or even impossible to shed this faith merely because Western medicine claims there is a lack of scientific evidence for it. The scientific method and empirical evidence count for very little in Chinese traditional medicine. Indeed, in their history, autopsies and anatomical study were forbidden, but their belief in the five great component elements of the universe was so strong that to this day their charts of the human body depict imaginary vacuoles in the body cavity which are the seat of a person's "fire." Nor has Chinese medicine, for instance, ever recognized any causative relationship between the presence of pneumococcus in the lungs, and the onset of pneumonia. This did not, however, prevent them from developing a seemingly effective herbal remedy for pneumonia. Undoubtedly the greatest asset of Chinese medicine is the patient's faith in it; if you tell him he'll get well, he is trained to believe it and he gets well. Western medicine is only now beginning to understand the role that the mind and the emotions play in physical well-being, but it has been the crux of Chinese practice for centuries.

Thus, an American or European doctor will pooh-pooh the idea of adding rhinoceros horn to one's tea to enhance sexual potency, and say that at best, it is a sympathetic association—rhino horn resembles a phallus, thus its ingestion assimilates its properties. The Chinese herbalist will answer, who cares? If it works, it works. The Western doctor can point to graphs and spectral analyses and computer printouts to prove that rhino horn is worthless. The Chinese practitioner can point to his stack of anecdotal testimonials to the contrary, and accept them as just as valid. There is nothing of the charlatan in it; he believes it just as much as his patients. It is their dual heritage of 4,500 years of history since Huang Ti defined the art of healing.

Eric mulled the paper over and thought, Damn, that's pretty good. He found nothing major in it he wanted to change and laid over it a memo he made out to Garrick Saenz, his exhibits curator who worked out of a small shop over at the farm. He instructed Saenz to weed out the first-person references and research-paper tone, and work the data into a large-type interpretive placard to put in front of the Chinese case in the Hall of Stupidity.

Larry had told Lucy all of the adventure with the fence and the video cameras, and that it was the Barillas who had attempted to breach The Refuge. She had heard most of it from Jake already, peppered of course with commentary about Eric's reluctance to dehorn the rhinos, but she wanted to hear Larry's take on it. There was something in the way Larry related it all that told her he was excited but was beginning to be genuinely frightened as well. Ramón Barilla was now in a position to begin pressing him for some kind of publication date for the story about him—the story that didn't exist—and he had decided that returning to the store would be a very, very bad idea.

With the Austin wedding still pending, though, Lucy felt little hesitation in going back, using the gift purchase to see if she could learn anything else.

It was Luís who greeted her, smiling widely. "Hey, I remember you, the vet lady."

"Yes."

"Remember, my name's Luís? How are things with dogs and cats?"

"And birds. Pretty good."

"Did you get a gift for your friend that's getting married yet?"

"No, that's why I came back. I think she'd really like that Olmec head you showed me, the reproduction."

"Oh, yeah, right over here. We still got it."

"Good, I'll take it."

Luís preceded her over to its shelf. "You know," he said, "I don't want to get out of turn or nothing, but you know, you're a pretty lady. I'd really like to get to know you."

"Thank you, that's very sweet. But, I really can't." She smiled, attempting to make it look as beatific as she could, but it did not strike him as sincere.

"What's the matter, you got a boyfriend?"

"Well, yeah, sort of."

Luís led her over to the register. "Oh, you mean that guy from the newspaper—what was his name?"

"Larry."

"Yeah, I remember him. He's a really nice guy. I liked him a lot— he came back to talk to my uncle about his business."

"Yeah, I know. He's really excited about doing the story." She caught sight of Ramón within his office and traded waves with him.

"You know when it might come out?"

"No. I do know he's just been real busy having to do news stories and stuff. The feature writing always has to take a backseat. I'm sure he'll get to it."

"Yeah, I see. So, are you like, real solid with him?"

Her reserve descended suddenly like a wall of frost, in that practiced way that most attractive women have when they need to use it. "I'm afraid that's personal. Why?"

He shrugged coyly. "Well, you know, if you not real solid with him, I'd still like to show you a nice time, you know."

"Thank you, but no, I can't."

He looked ready to tease her. "Well-l-l, if you sure."

"Look, I don't want to be rude, but I don't think I appreciate being hit on with that kind of persistence when I walk into a store to make a purchase."

"Oh, no, I'm sorry." Luís got defensive. "Don't take it wrong. I'm really a nice guy."

"I'm sure you are."

She relaxed just a bit, and Luís rang up the sale as quickly as he could. "Do you want gift wrap?"

"No."

"Sixty-five oh-four," he said.

When she finished writing the check she automatically pulled her driver's license out of her purse and laid it on top, and handed them both over.

Luís studied the check over for a second. "Everything on here correct?"

"Yes."

He pulled a rubber endorsement stamp from beneath the counter and whacked it on the back of the check. "You have a work phone?"

Lucy froze. She should have known better than this, she should have left as soon as she bawled him out. Noting the work telephone number on a check is a common business practice, and she could not protest without raising suspicion at her balking. She gave nothing away in her expression as she reasoned there was no possibility the check would bounce. "Sure," she said, and gave him the number at the park.

Luís came from behind the counter to give her the package and walked her to the door. "I hope your friends like the gift. If they don't, just keep the receipt, and after the wedding come back and you can find them something they like better."

"That's very thoughtful, Luís, thank you."

"And once again, I am very sorry if I offended you."

"Please don't think of it again. I'm sorry if I jumped on you." She extended her hand and he took it firmly and gently.

"Thank you for coming in. 'Bye, now."

He watched her pear-shaped butt recede down the mall and deep down he thought: bitch. At least she didn't tell on him. Ramón thought it was fine for him to check out the women but didn't like getting complaints from customers. *Dinero* took a very definite precedence.

The showroom was empty after she left and Luís went into the office. "Hey," said Ramón, "I see she came back alone this time. Something goin' on?"

Luís went back outside. "Just lemme alone, okay?"

As soon as she got home Lucy phoned Larry with a report of the encounter.

"When are you going up for the wedding?"

"Not for a few weeks yet."

"Damn." He really wished it was sooner. Larry Davis suspected there were some answers about Albert Chu on file in the state office buildings in Austin. But, if Eric's counsel was to sit tight until the Javan rhinos were safely locked in The Refuge, he could wait if everybody else could.

16 🌿🌿🌿🌿🌿🌿🌿🌿🌿🌿

WITH THE COMMITMENT from the Indonesian government, it did not take a lot of persuading from AZA to convince Fish and Wildlife to issue an import license for two Javan rhinoceroses to The Final Refuge Wildlife Foundation, Arcola, Texas. Holding them in a quarantine stall would have entailed too great a risk of traumatizing the animals, and Jake got around it by making the entire Indonesian house a quarantine, which no animals could leave for sixty days. Thus their adjustment was softened by allowing them into their habitat on arrival. The chance of trying to get them eventually to mate was no greater than it was for any other rhinos—females are choosy, and the process is somewhat similar to plucking any two human beings of opposite sex from a random population and expecting them to take a sexual interest in each other. But, it was a start. And ever prepared for disaster, Jake prepared an emergency kit to keep in the Indonesian house, just as he had for Sobhuza, to excise and preserve fresh gonads if for any reason one of them should die suddenly. And they had to face facts, the mortality rate for rhinos taken from the wild was not insignificant.

In their habitat they proved shy and gentle, and Eric congratulated himself on having provided solitary nooks for both animals; they did not fight but spent most of their time apart, in seclusion, visible to the public only through the one-way glass. Keeper contact was minimized; they did not have to be washed as they virtually lived in their stream, and each section of the enclosure was cleaned and their food-plants replenished on a when-empty basis. From all indications, they seemed to look right at home.

The additional guard they had hired was prominent at the evening gala they hosted to debut the Javas to the public—mostly to the wealthy, social, money-donating public. As Eric had instructed, Sam found a veteran and marksman, Max Parker, who stood by the indoor viewing area in uniform as guests in black tie and cocktail dresses were ushered in, in groups of no more than twelve who were politely hushed by staff as they entered. It was a long walk from the headquarters to Indonesia, and a shuttle of camouflaged golf carts rolled out the service road as far as the bottom of Australia. The exhibits curator had set up a suggestion box—NAME THE JAVAS—whose results Eric was actually looking forward to reading. He expected everything from Bill and Hillary to Beavis and Butt-head.

"Have you been out to see them yet?" Larry Davis turned to see who had spoken and felt the hair rise on his neck. "Mr. Davis, isn't it?" Albert Chu shook hands with him.

They'd had a brief exchange at the press conference several weeks before, but Larry was sure that Chu never saw his name. "Yes. They're really something."

"You are the student, aren't you? I saw your article in the *Post* on animal trafficking. It was very sensitively done."

Larry was flustered. "Thank you, very much."

"Is that what you are going to be, a newspaperman?"

"I don't know. I thought so once. But I've been working here the last few months and I really like it."

"Yes, animals can be very fascinating."

Larry regarded Chu's impassive Asian face and thought he saw an opening. "I've been thinking about moving to Los Angeles, though," he said. "There are courses you can take at UCLA that you can't get here."

"Ah, yes. Beautiful city. I have relatives there, but perhaps it is a little too . . . cosmopolitan, in its atmosphere, for a conservative old capitalist like me."

Larry laughed with him.

"Well, please excuse me," said Chu. "I have not met the guests of honor yet, and I am going to take the next train out. All the best to you." He held out his hand again.

Larry Davis had already been out to view the Javas. He wasn't sure just what he expected them to look like; for some reason he rather thought they would be smaller and furry, like the Sumatran. Zoogeography can lead you to have expectations without your really being aware of it. Throughout the northern hemisphere, similar animals get smaller the further south you go. In Asia, Siberian tigers are twice the size of Bengals; the Javan tigers were the smallest of all, until they were wiped out. The same is true of wild cattle. In North America, deer, bears, and mountain lions all get smaller as the latitude decreases.

Thus it was that when he got his first look at the Javas, he caught his breath. They were just as big as the Great Indian, every inch twelve feet long and six feet tall, but more lightly built and lanky, a bit less than three thousand pounds. The two species had only been distinguished from each other in the 1820s, although they looked distinctly different in important ways. The Javas' thick skin, dark coal gray fading toward fleshy pink within the folds, lacked the armor-plated look of the Indian, appearing instead scaled like alligator hide, and the upper lip, though prehensile in eating, when hanging limp seemed as thin and sharp as the beak of a sea turtle. All their aspects made the Javan rhinos look as much like reptiles as mammals—strikingly primitive and quite utterly arresting. In fact seeing them had seemed to galvanize his own commitment to what he was doing, and made him think that perhaps Eric was right in believing that their presence would do much to marshal public support for the cause.

Lucy elected not to change clothes before leaving Austin. She did her bridesmaid duty, but was too shaken by what she had learned at the Secretary of State's and the Comptroller's Office to dally an instant longer than friendship and propriety required. And it was a Catholic service, a whole wedding Mass with Communion and everything. She thought it would never end. Still it pleased her to notice that when the bride and groom ran the gauntlet to their car they were showered with birdseed instead of rice. Lucy was still flicking some of it out of her hair as she strode across the church parking lot and slipped into her white Civic. She had driven up on U.S. 290; it was an easier drive, but she returned on State 71—shorter and more direct, and by turning south on State 36 in Sealy she could go straight to the park via

Rosenberg and never have to mess with the Houston traffic. There were stretches where the highway was only two lanes and she would have to run some farmers off the road, but she would brave it; if she timed it right she could arrive just as the party got rolling. It was only as she passed through the high whale backs of pine trees around Bastrop that she thought of her dress, and decided that the airy blue floral print would be fine for a garden party, anyway.

The Refuge's drive was lined and the garage was full to the fourth level, but she dug her passcard from her purse and found her own space in the staff lot. There were a few people on the lawn, and the loggia was full of the moneybags and politicos from the curry-favor file, sipping champagne and plucking the catered hors d'oeuvres from their daintily held toothpicks. She had no trouble finding Jake, looking miserable, standing with Ernie and Consuela. He was wearing blue jeans—well, she thought, at least they're new—and a power-red tie under a corduroy coat. "Don't you say nothing," he growled as she came near. "If I wanted a suit I'd be a damn lawyer."

"You look fine. Where's Eric?"

"In the lecture hall, bein' charming. Did you find anything out?"

She took his arm. "Come with me. We have to talk to him. Sorry, guys, I gotta steal him for a minute."

When she turned around she saw Larry coming toward her, for which she was grateful, not to have to hunt him down. The three entered the lecture hall together with purpose, but Lucy froze suddenly in her tracks, as though bucketed with ice water. Framed by the dais she saw Eric, hand in hand with Liz Ann as she made chitchat with the society people, punctuating her conversation with sweeps of her tulip-glassed champagne, standing there tall and brunette in her wine-red velvet formal, strapless and revealing a craning white sweep of her back, standing there, she thought, like the Duchess of Windsor in training. Suddenly she hated her, and hated him. No, she didn't hate him. Whoever she hated, she thought, It's my own damn fault. None of this could she mask from her expression.

Larry Davis saw the emotional component of her face change and turn color like a traumatized chameleon, and for the first time saw the real scoreboard flash numbers a foot high before his eyes. Jake had been between them, but now scooted forward to get ahead, like a car goosing through a gate before it closes. He turned and pointed at one and then the other. "Not now, kids. Later. Go on up, I'll bring the boss."

Larry and Lucy paced awkwardly back out into the loggia, as Jake went over to Eric. Liz Ann was otherwise engaged, and Jake squeezed Eric's collar as he whispered, "Upstairs. Your office. Right now."

Eric raised his hands for quiet. He was sitting on his desk, with the Indonesian ambassador downstairs and the Javas safely—he prayed, safely—in their new jungle, and appealed for calm. "All right. All right, let's go over exactly what we know."

"We know that Ramón Barilla's import shop is really owned by Albert Chu," said Larry. "We know that the Barillas have supplied him with animal parts in the past, and we know that it was the Barillas who tried to break into the park a few weeks ago."

"Look," said Lucy, "when you incorporate or get a sales tax permit you have to list what other businesses you own or are a partner in. I learned today that Albert Chu owns Imperial Ming Exporting, and he owns another business out there, Strength of Heaven Health Food Products. You can't tell me he's not up to something!"

Eric Jackson looked at them all, feeling like a Renaissance monarch cornered by rebellious ministers. "I agree that he probably is; the problem is that the evidence we have is circumstantial, not even enough to get a search warrant. Any hint of an inquiry from the police now, and anything like evidence will vanish long before they could be busted." The publicity, he knew, would also be a disaster. "What do you want to do?"

"Send me out there," said Larry. "I have a friend, from school. He's Chinese and he knows Chinatown. I've already talked to him, he thinks he knows a way to find out some things. If you won't get the police involved you've got to let me track down what's going on out there."

"I think you ought to do it, boss," said Jake.

"Can you come back with hard evidence?"

"I don't know. All I can do is try."

Eric thought hard. "Okay." He circled his desk and sat down, pulling a checkbook from a lower drawer. He made out a check, for cash, for one thousand dollars, subscribing it "travel expenses." He looked at it long and then held it out.

17 🌿🌿🌿🌿🌿🌿🌿🌿🌿🌿

LARRY DAVIS had traveled east before but never west, and took the trouble to get a window seat. Instead of a novel he took with him his library copy—already several times renewed—of the massive Lee Crandall monograph, *Management of Wild Mammals in Captivity*. It was old, published in 1964, and much of the data had been superseded, but little of it was outright wrong and it was still one of the best written introductions to the business.

Almost from the moment he took off, though, his eyes were not on its pages but looking out the window. The chalk and juniper of the hill country slid beneath him, and then the gridlike pegboard of the oil fields in west Texas, the brown thread of the Rio Grande and the rugged mountains of the New Mexico–Arizona border, all as Larry Davis reflected whether he had found himself, or was merely indulging a whim that fascinated him for the moment but which he would outgrow. The time seemed nothing like the two hours that passed before the plane's tires squealed on the tarmac at Phoenix. And then it seemed no sooner were they aloft again than Larry looked out the left window at the Salton Sea and Imperial Valley—All of it, he thought, my God, you can see all of it at once, it's so small—before the plane banked right and began a descent to LAX.

He was met at the gate by Eddie Lu, a fellow journalism major at the University of Houston, who was home for the summer. Larry found himself wishing he could relax and take in Los Angeles because it was such a mecca for journalism and radio-TV-film people, and even more so because, contrary to his expectation, he liked it immediately. The air was bright and cool—Eddie Lu was quick to point out that the smog usually took care of the bright part—but having grown up in Texas the atmosphere here was so palpably different: trees and shrubs he had never seen before, and so many convertibles. The freeway in from the airport was everything he had heard; he had seen from the plane as it descended, long miles of cars eight and ten abreast, moving at a crawl and stopping.

It gave him plenty of time to explain the situation to Eddie Lu as they sped up and braked, and sped up and braked, with Larry looking up at the dark, wide underpasses that he knew could collapse in an earthquake. No earthquakes, he had told Eddie on the phone. Whatever else, he didn't want any earthquakes.

Eddie Lu's parents lived in a stately two-story house near Hancock Park, which had a guest suite over its detached, three-car garage. They sat up late talking as Eddie explained how he thought they could learn what they needed to know.

"Do you really think your grandfather will help us?" asked Larry.

"He said he would."

"But isn't that, like, treason against his culture or something?"

"Not all Chinese Americans are stereotypes, man. Besides, he has his reasons."

"There's something else about this guy Chu that bugs me," said Larry. "He talked to me at the reception and said he had read my articles, but I don't know how he could have remembered what I look like."

"You never met him before?"

"I saw him at the press tour before the park opened, but we didn't meet or talk."

"Did you ask questions?"

"Yes. So did he."

Eddie Lu nodded. "That's not unusual, man. That's just one of the weird things about Chinatown. It's like, you could maybe owe somebody some money, and one day a guy from the neighborhood association will call and ask if you need help. I swear to God, it happened all the time with my grandparents, and with my parents too until they got out. If I was you I'd steer as clear of the guy as you can."

It was not a long drive to Chinatown and it was not late in the morning when they left, but a smog, discernible and brown, had already congealed. Eddie Lu's grandparents lived in that residential enclave contained between the length of Chinatown proper, and the angle that Sunset Boulevard makes with the Pasadena Freeway. When you walk downhill on Alpine toward Chinatown, there is a park and a strip of vacant lots and parking lots along the west side of Hill Street, giving Chinatown a well-defined border, almost like a moat.

"You said Chu's exporting place was on the other side?"

"New High Street, that's right." He swept his arm from left to right. "This first street here is Hill Street, the next block is Broadway—that's like the main drag—and New High Street is beyond that, and that's about as far as Chinatown goes, man. It's about half a mile from north to south, but basically only three blocks wide."

"We won't cause any suspicion just walking down from your grandparents like this?"

"Nah. All the neighbors know my parents are Chuppies who left for the suburbs years ago. It won't surprise them that I would bring someone home from school to meet my quaint little grandparents. They think I'm a shit, but they can gossip about that and not think that anything else might be going on. Besides, you're just another *low faan* to them, man."

"A what?"

"Barbarian. White devil. It's almost like the locals make a study of finding new ways to ignore white people. Unless they think you're the tax man, or from the police or immigration, they'll look right through you like you're not even there. By the time you get done today, man, you're going to have more than you want of being ignored."

"Well, whatever. I guess what we need to do is work our way up and down each street. We need to know where the apothecaries are, maybe go inside and check them out."

"Look like a customer?"

"Yeah."

Eddie Lu laughed out loud. "You won't fool anybody for a minute. The best you can do is look like a tourist. So, I tell you what, let's start down at the foot of Hill Street in the square. Buy some stuff in the tourist traps so you'll have some sacks to drag around. People will be nicer to you if they think you're spending money."

They turned left down Hill Street, looking briefly into a couple of bustling little open-air malls that passed through to the next block. Larry Davis had been a stamp collector when he was a kid and recognized that the signs in bright paint or neon light over the shops were in three and sometimes four languages: Chinese, Korean, Vietnamese, and Thai. Only in a couple of places was there any English at all. One shop just off the Hill Street curb caught his eye because it appeared to be a drugstore, but not a traditional apothecary of the kind Eddie Lu had told him about. Taped to the inside of the display window was a confusion of pamphlets, fliers, and testimonials. The mainstay of their products appeared to be ginseng, but what drew his attention was a stack of brilliant red and gold boxes that read, under larger Chinese characters, DEER'S TAIL EXTRACT / A Tonic Oral Solution / The Changchun Pharmaceutical Works, China. The boxes were the size of small boxes of chocolate, and one of them had the top flipped open and held upright by a red ribbon. Arranged inside on a flat rack of cardboard and foam plastic were ten glass ampoules full of an ugly-looking brown liquid. Larry Davis tried to recall whether he had ever even seen ampoules before—the only ones he could think of were in an old Nick Nolte movie called *The Deep*, which he otherwise remembered only for Jackie Bisset's hooters. One of the boxes was turned around so that the back label was visible, on which was printed carelessly across the top, "SUPERIR QUALITIED NOURISHMENT (to be taken orally)," followed by an extensive list of maladies for which it was "most efficacious" in treating.

"Hey, look at this," he said to Eddy. "I want to go in and buy one of those."

"You go ahead. I'll wait out here."

Inside the store, Larry took a box off the top of the stack and laid it by the cash register, and the clerk, a Chinese who looked about thirty, rang it up and said, "Nine seventy-one."

Larry gave him a ten and took the change, and watched as the clerk dropped it in a small plastic sack and gave it to him with both hands, like it was some minor presentation, then rewarded him with a hurried, but seemingly unaffected smile. "Thank you," he said.

Back outside he caught up with Eddie Lu. "He wasn't so unfriendly."

"Trust me, he was smiling at Alexander Hamilton not you. You missed this." Eddie pointed out a flier listing the benefits of their ginseng, and ran his finger down the long list of diseases and conditions it was good for. The last item on the list was impotence, and it was the only one followed by a question mark. "That tell you anything?"

"That maybe they want to protect themselves against a charge of making a false claim?"

"M-hm. And that, maybe that's the only one that the authorities look for. By adding that little question mark they relieve themselves of a load of responsibility."

"Sort of a cat-and-mouse game."

"That's a good way to put it."

The canister of ginseng, a little smaller than a can of tennis balls, cost $99.95, and Larry Davis made a mental note of the impotence and its question mark, but decided against spending that much money.

As they continued down Hill Street, Larry pulled the red and gold box out of the sack and turned it over to read the back label aloud: "COMPOSITION: This preparation contains the main ingredients: 2% of Deer's tail extract; 2.5% of fresh Royal Jelly."

There was no indication what the other 95.5% was, but he supposed it was alcohol and read on: "INDICATIONS: 1. Most efficacious for neurasthenia, poor appetite, malnutrition, etc., for its efficacy of enhancing physical energy, promoting metabolism, and its high nutrition. 2. Good for stimulating mental and physical energy in case of undergrowth, senility and debility during convalescence. 3. Good for hepatitis, anemia and peptic ulcer. 4. Also satisfactory for rheumatic arthritis and rheumatoid arthritis."

He put the box back in the sack. "Boy, I'd hate to meet the guy who scores a hundred on that test."

"You're going to see a lot more than that today, man."

They entered Chinatown's main square, an open-air enclave of shops mostly oriented to the tourist trade, clustered about a landscaped courtyard whose heart was a seated bronze statue of Sun Yat Sen. The square was full of people, a few Anglos among the Asians, and what struck Larry about the Chinese was: They're so small.

Eddie was chunky and towered over the rest of the Chinese. Well, thought Larry, of course he would. Partly it was Eddie's GI father, but more than that, he got to eat protein when he was a child. He would be the same size as they if he had grown up eating nothing but rice and seaweed.

They entered a souvenir shop off the center of the square. They were waited on by an effusive lady of about seventy, who spoke little English, but Larry removed from a shelf a cherry-wood jewelry chest inlaid with a thin medallion of jade. The old woman put it back on the shelf and pointed to a tiny storeroom. "One in here," she said.

The storeroom was cramped and no bigger than a closet, and she emerged, presenting him with a box, from which he understood that the one on the shelf was for display. When he opened the box and found its jewelry chest to be of rosewood, he pointed out the difference and asked if he could have one of cherry. Nervous and embarrassed, she laughed and reentered the storeroom, opening a couple more boxes until she found the right kind. When Larry produced his Mastercard, the old lady called into a back room, in Chinese—he figured it was for someone to come out and ring up the sale. A second woman whom he took to be the owner, forty-five, petite, businesslike, wearing a beautiful emerald trousseau of stones small enough for him to know they must be real, sold him the box, thanked him brusquely and turned her back on him. As they left, Larry heard an explosion of angry Chinese and turned to see her upbraiding the grandmotherly wraith who had been so nice. Stooped and expressionless, the older woman entered the storeroom and began tidying up the boxes.

As they passed the seated bronze of Sun Yat Sen at the center of the square, Larry Davis kept looking back over his shoulder. "Did you see that? How could she talk to her that way?"

Eddie Lu did not seem in the least surprised. "Welcome to Chinatown, man. That was probably her mother."

"No shit? What was she yelling?"

"I couldn't get it all—it was Mandarin. My people are Cantonese. But something about what would the other tenants say if they saw her being friendly with a white boy like you. The only thing these *low faan* are good for is spending money. Then she told her to clean up the storeroom."

"What a bitch."

"That's nothing, man. My parents know lots of people like her. One ol' biddy they know played poor and got a rent subsidy from the city—six hundred dollars a month. You know what she did with that apartment? She bought plywood, divided it up into what they call a *gong si fong*—a bachelor tenement—for nine single guys, and charged them $200 a month apiece. Cleared twelve hundred a month, then you know what she did? She moved in with her mother!"

"My God."

"She's still in business, as far as I know. Look, man, you will never understand Chinatown unless you understand greed. They don't like money here, they don't even love money. They worship money. They will do anything to get money—especially if they can do it at the expense of you white people."

"Why hate us? We're giving them a home and that capitalist system they're so fond of."

"No, man, Chinese take a longer view of history. You think it's an accident that statue there is of Sun Yat Sen? Ninety-nine percent of these people are still really pissed that China was lost to the Communists. Hell, a lot of them are still fighting the Boxer Rebellion. And that's one reason nobody here would ever turn your friend Chu in. You can bet if people know about the rhino horn deal, he's getting big face out of it. He's upholding a piece of traditional Chinese culture, thumbing his nose at you *low faan,* and making sacks of money doing it. That, man, is about as big as face gets."

They found the outlet of the square onto Broadway and walked south. The staple business of Chinatown seemed to be the tea shops, at least one on every other block, all apparently making most of their living off the sale of ginseng. They entered the first one they encountered; about ten feet inside they met the proprietor, a slim, wired-looking man of about thirty, who thrust tiny white porcelain cups into their hands and poured them freshly brewed samples of ginseng tea, thin, yellow and fragrant. Larry saw his canisters were identical to the ones he had seen before. He blew on the cup until it was cool enough to sample, and he tried but could not entirely suppress a grimace at its rank heavy bitterness. He returned the cup and apologized, sucking in some fresh air, "I'm afraid that's a little strong for me." The proprietor laughed and nodded.

At the end of the nearest aisle was a freestanding display of various boxes of other teas, one stack of which he reached out for, its boxes printed in green and black on plain white cardboard, featuring a stylized, leaping ballerina whose tutu transmogrified into a spiral galaxy. The label read Chunfeng Weight Reducing Tea. "This is the one I came in for," he said as sincerely as he could. He bought it for a dollar-fifty and they left.

The voice of the nervous-looking little proprietor followed them outside. "Sure no ginseng? Today only have two-for-one special. One for sixty dollar." As they left Larry felt like he was being barked at in a carnival.

Back outside he read the side label of the new box of tea out loud to Eddie Lu: " 'Along with the great changes with each passing day of modern science and technology, man has been freed from heavy physical labor and thus has been enabled to have rich food and comfortable living conditions. Therefore, obesity and overweight have become problems which much worry honorable ladies and gentlemen.' " Larry Davis shook his head. "Geez, this sounds like a Charlie Chan movie."

Eddie Lu made no response and Larry read on, " 'Chunfeng Weight Reducing Tea, selected from the distinctive tea of Yunwu Mountain of Guizhou and first-class medicine herbs, is carefully processed by the Chinese old traditional method guided by modern science and technology.' " He looked up again. "Boy, they're really big on modern science and technology, huh?"

"Wouldn't you, if this was what you were selling?" Eddie Lu was looking irritated, caught between embarrassment that so many people of his heritage maintained such faith in primitive remedies but vaguely unappreciative that some part of him was being made fun of. Larry read on, " 'Drinking Chunfeng Weight Reducing Tea will help become strong and handsome, both in body and mind.' Fucking wow. People really believe in all this stuff—don't they?"

Eddie stopped cold and glared at him, then walked slowly on. "I'm just showing you the place, man, I'm not defending it."

"Sorry, bud."

"Forget it."

They entered a few more tea shops—not all of them, for there were too many. In fact there were more of them than any other kind of enterprise, with one exception: there was a plethora of Chinese fraternal and benefit associations, which Larry noticed but did not inquire about.

They had walked about halfway up Broadway, and Eddie stopped again. "These other guys haven't really been apothecaries, just tea sellers. This is the real thing here. You want to go in?"

Beside them was a dirty narrow storefront glass. By now they had entered enough places that Larry was no longer concerned about his motives being suspected, as no one paid them any attention unless they were ready to buy something.

Inside, it was even more crowded and cluttered than the other places they had been, but within that confusion the arrangement of wares was tidy and precise. Most of the length of the shop was taken up by a glass counter, under which lay trays of roots, herbs, whole desiccated lizards and seahorses, and more different kinds of mushrooms that Larry Davis had ever dreamed existed. In the rear of the shop was wedged a small consultation nook with an old Formica dinette table, and on either side of it a heavy oak side chair of the kind seen in old courthouse hallways. Hanging over the table was a framed diploma with the owner's snapshot in the middle. The only English on it was in red, reading, "Society of Hong Kong and Kowloon Traditional Practitioners, Member." The rest of the paper consisted of columns of black Chinese characters, and at the bottom a collection of red stamped cartouches, which in the Orient serve as signatures. Behind the dinette table stood a heavy wooden chest whose front was a mass of tiny drawers, none of them labeled in either English or Chinese, looking precisely like the cabinet in the rhino horn display in The Refuge's Hall of Stupidity. Larry stared at the chest, and took in the ambiance of the place, sensing that he was very, very close to learning what he needed to know.

He bought yet another box of tea and back out on the sidewalk wrote down the address. "This is the kind of place we need to check out. There are others?"

"Six or eight."

By early afternoon Larry Davis had a list of candidates to check out. New High Street does not extend the length of Chinatown, only about half of it, and they backtracked half the length of Broadway to cross over to it. They walked down the west side of it, checking out the addresses across the street—it seemed to Larry's perception that this was really the down-scale side of the enclave. The fish markets absolutely reeked of the live carp in their tanks; they entered a poultry shop which contained only a window behind which the butcher worked, and in the public area a wooden cage about twelve feet long and the height and depth of a bench or football bleacher. It contained maybe twenty ducks, two of which had keeled over dead from apparent heat stress. Larry found himself thinking, Boy, the animal rights people ought to get a load of this.

When they finally saw across from them the address he had for Albert Chu's enterprise, it looked like a filling station from perhaps the 1950s, boarded up, with concrete islands where the gasoline pumps used to stand.

"Looks deserted," said Larry.

"Yeah, I'm sure that's the idea. Haven't you noticed how many 'deserted' buildings there are in this neighborhood? If they were really deserted, man, nobody would bother boarding up the windows."

"What do you mean?"

"You know how to spot an immigration agent in Chinatown? He goes up to the door of a deserted building and puts his ear against it. Most of them are sweatshops, and he can hear the sewing machines."

"Sweatshops?"

"Indentured servants, child labor, the whole bit, man."

"Chee. Well, let's go take a look."

Eddie Lu glanced back up over his shoulder. "Shit, no, man, keep on walking."

"But that's what we came here for." He stepped off the curb to cross the street.

Eddie Lu pulled him back by the arm, hissing, "Fuck, man, don't argue. Walk right with me and don't slow down."

Larry obeyed silently. When they got as far as Sunset Boulevard he said, "You want to tell me what that was all about?"

"Tong, man. Have you noticed how, like, every couple of blocks there is a door with some association name over it? Neighborhood Association, Fraternal Association, Benefit Association, Chinese-American Association?"

"Yeah, I was going to ask you about that."

"Well, they are how Chinatown gets run. They control everything, absolutely literally fucking everything in Chinatown. Who gets loans, who gets leases, who gets protection, even who gets buried right. Some of them, not all of them but some of them, the tongs, are fronts for crime syndicates."

"Like the Mafia."

"Yeah, but instead of the families, we got the tongs. They're bad, man, and I ain't lying. Where the Mafia sends somebody to break your legs, the tong will kill you and your whole family, then come back and kill your dog. Never bat an eye. It doesn't happen very often, because it doesn't have to. You set the community an example like that, the lesson doesn't need to be repeated."

"Really."

"You know how, in black neighborhoods, in Spanish neighborhoods, the teen gangs are a problem?"

"Yeah."

"Well, in Chinatown they aren't a problem. You know why? Because the tongs control them and use them like farm organizations, like minor league ball clubs. Extortion, murder, learn it all in the minors before moving up. Tongs don't let anybody out, either. Once you burn your vows and pray to Gung Gong, that's it, man, they got you by the short curlies from then on."

"But there's an association every couple of blocks."

"I said, not all of them are tongs. Most are legitimate. I mean, they can all pull a lot of strings under the table, but maybe only three are really bad—but one of them is right across the street from that old gas station and looks right down on it."

"Oh, boy, so if we had gone over there and poked around the building—"

"If your friend Chu is up to no good, he is probably associated with a tong, because they wouldn't allow him on their turf if he wasn't. If that's the case, even money says some dude in a business suit would come out of the association building and say, 'May I help you?' "

"Jesus Christ. So what are we going to do?"

"Right now? I say eat lunch. You hungry yet, man?" They had turned right, back up Broadway. "There is a great restaurant right up here. You like Chinese?"

After what he had seen in the local fish and poultry markets, Larry Davis said he was uncertain he could handle anything too authentic.

"It's okay," said Eddie. "This place is world famous. You can tell people you ate there. It's sort of expensive, but you're buying."

Inside, under Eddie's tutelage, they ordered Tsing Tao beer and appetizers of sticky shrimp, with a main course of moo shoo pork. Eddie drew Larry Davis's attention to the other tables, to white people eating delicately with their chopsticks, picking up one item and placing it in their mouths; and some of the Chinese, who gaped their maws and literally flung the food in from the plates. "You ever watch the Discovery channel, man, when they do something about China? Five thousand years of history, developing the most exquisitely prepared and presented food in the world, and even on TV they eat like hogs." He shook his head. "I never got it."

Larry Davis had never thought about what it must be like to be caught between two different worlds, or how that difficult phenomenon might apply to Eddie, or to Luís Barilla, or for that matter to Babs the chimpanzee. But he thought about it now and didn't know what to do with it, and pulled his notepad out of his pocket. There were now six addresses on it. "So," he said, "how are we going to find out about these places?"

"Did you see that park at the south end of Chinatown? That's Presidio Plaza. Cross it, and you're right at City Hall and the Hall of Records. From there, you're on your own."

In an afternoon of research they learned that the owner of record of the building at Chu's address was, in fact, the Hua Hsing Hui Benefit Association, whose own address was across the street from it. They also learned that a previous enterprise that leased a building they owned was shut down for exporting American animal products—black bear paws and musk glands—to the Far East. They checked the addresses of the different apothecaries, and discovered that two of them also leased space from Hua Hsing Hui.

"Well," said Larry at last, "that gives us two places to send your grandfather tomorrow with his little problem."

18 🌿🌿🌿🌿🌿🌿🌿🌿🌿🌿

THREE DAYS AFTER HE LEFT HOUSTON, Larry Davis burst into Eric's office, shattering what had been a quiet meeting with Jake. Stephanie followed in his wake, protesting that he could not see him right then, along with an uncertain Eddie Lu.

Eric looked up at Stephanie and said, "It's okay," and she closed the door as she left.

Larry crossed the room and slapped a manila folder down on Eric's desk. "Guess what Albert Chu is setting himself up to sell all over fucking Asia?"

Eric leaned back. "Don't tell me. Natural aphrodisiacs?"

Larry handed over a small silk pouch, which Eric opened and shook out a small pile of herbal-looking tea into his hand, which he then crumbled onto the manila.

Larry nudged Eddie Lu on the arm. "Tell him, Eddie."

Eric half stood and held out his hand. "Eric Jackson."

He took it. "Eddie Lu."

Eric was vaguely aware that he had probably paid for the guy's plane ticket, but decided for the moment that it wasn't important.

Eddie picked up Eric's pen and pushed the desiccated components around on the paper. "This is the classic recipe for aging and impotence," he said. "It goes all the way back to the Sung dynasty. It's called *liu wei di huang wan*. These are red dates, that is ginger, the yellow strings are astragalus root. There's some other stuff, but look here, this has something different." He separated out some slightly iridescent, gray-white flakes, like fingernail filings.

"New and improved," snorted Larry Davis. "Extra strength."

197 🌿

"That," said Eddie, "is shaved rhinoceros horn."

"How do you know?"

"My grandfather paid three hundred and fifty dollars of your money for this."

"Yes, but how do you know it is genuine?"

"Give it to me," said Jake, "we'll find out in the lab."

"No need," said Eddie Lu. Eric looked up into his round face and the narrow, almond eyes magnified by steel-rimmed glasses. "It is genuine enough. When you trust your doctor, he will sell you these shavings for three hundred dollars an ounce. But sometimes it's just cow horn. If you want to make sure of what you're getting, you ask the doctor to cut you some fresh—that way you don't imply that you don't trust him. But he'll take out a whole horn and file it for you, for about two thousand dollars an ounce. This packet contains one-eighth of an ounce. That was two hundred fifty dollars. The rest was for the other ingredients and the consultation."

"He had a whole horn?"

Eddie Lu nodded solemnly.

"Mother of God." Of course, thought Eric. Rhino horn is too expensive to buy in pure doses anymore. It is blended in.

"That's what happened to your friend Ethel," said Larry. "In fact—" he drilled his index finger repeatedly into the desk "—that probably *is* Ethel. Customs in California looks for that kind of stuff coming *in* from Hong Kong and Macao. They'd never in a million years suspect that it was about to be exported!"

Eric nodded. "And not just exported, but exported in a form that the Customs Service would be clueless to detect. If you export an herbal tea and mislabel the ingredients, they'll never know."

"And get this," Larry Davis waited till he was certain he had Eric's attention. "Herb tea is a food product not a drug. They don't subject it to any analysis. It's brilliant."

"Mother of God."

"Sorry, boss," snarled Jake. "I don't think she's answerin' her phone today."

Slowly and sickly the enormity of it sank into Eric's brain. Of course. Rhinoceroses in the wild were now so scarce and so well protected, and the international ban on trading in horns so vigilant, that poaching in Africa and Asia had become unacceptably risky. It still happened a lot, but at greater and greater risk—and would continue so until they were all killed. Rhinos in American zoos were, at least by comparison, all but defenseless. And the most lucrative market for their horn was not here, but in East Asia. What a wretched, terrible irony, he thought, just now that the zoos and wildlife parks and environmental advocates had come so far in getting rhinos rescued from the wild, that the most profitable future for poaching lay in totally reversing the flow of the trade. The potential for a North American slaughter lay wide open—San Antonio and Ethel, over and over again.

Eric rested his head on his fingertips. How could he not have seen this coming? Foresight was his strongest suit. When he had sent a rhino team into Zimbabwe for specimens from a different gene pool, he had made sure they were provided with guards who spoke not just Swahili, but the local Chilapalapa. And not just guards, but informants in the villages, well paid, to warn them if the poachers were tipped off as to their whereabouts. He had always seen trouble long before it could see him. But to shoot rhinos in zoos, in the United States? It was so simple it was obvious, and so obvious that neither he nor anyone he knew had even considered it. Of course this is how it would happen.

And behind that Eric recognized a second and even sadder "of course." The extinction of species—especially large and important and visible species like the Pleistocene megafauna, the rhinos and elephants—was a cosmic and terrible event that somehow carried with it an assumption that it would be perpetrated by a criminal element so malevolent, so putridly evil, as to be worthy of the deed. But that was not the case, and had never been the case. Except for those very rare occasions when a life form passed from existence as a result of natural processes—as it seemed cheetahs must eventually do—except for those few cases, the extinction of species was usually caused by small-timers out to make a buck or cut a corner. No drug lords, no cartels, just unthinking little bit-players like the Barillas, trying to get a leg up in life. It was so with the sailors who stocked their ships' larders with the carcasses of the dodo birds of Mauritius; it was so with the American farmers who fired their shotguns blindly up into the unending clouds of passenger pigeons to feed their hogs on dead and flopping wounded birds. It remained so with the subsistence farmers of the tropics who slashed and burned the rain forests, and it remained so with people like the Barillas. An unsavory tycoon like Albert Chu, or some other source of investment capital, could catalyze the process, but they would be helpless without the small-time grabbers and users and middlemen, and the ignorant consumers they supplied. Of course this was how it happened.

"How did you get hold of this?" he asked Eddie Lu.

"Larry discovered that two of the traditional apothecaries in China-town are beholden to the same tong that Albert Chu is part of. Based on a suspicion that rhino horn was available there, my grandfather made an appointment at each of them for a consultation for impotence. The first one could not supply him; the second one was able to provide the goods."

"Why one and not the other?"

"I don't know. Maybe the tong had some reason not to trust one of the druggists."

"What the hell is a tong?" Jake barged in.

"An organized crime syndicate."

"Oh, that's just fine and dandy." Jake got out of his chair and started pacing the room.

Eric shook his head. "Maybe after all it is time we went to the police and the FBI with what we have, let them handle it from here." He turned to Larry. "Who else knows about this? Anybody?"

"No."

"Does Chu know that you know?"

"I don't think so. Not yet, anyway. I talked to him at the party last week and he seemed to know who I am, but—"

"What!" Eddie Lu blanched. "I just thought of something!"

"What is it?"

Eddie looked sick and sank into a chair. "That shop must not be busted, man. Understand?"

"He doesn't know about your grandfather. It's okay."

"It's not okay! Man, what have I been thinking about? Look, you bust that druggist, the tong says, okay, who have you sold horn to lately? He tells them. They ask around the neighbors, anything been going on with old Mr. Lu lately? They say, well, his grandson came home with a white boy from school. Really? Where did he go to school? In Texas. What did his friend look like? Oh, about so big, with curly black hair. Don't you see? If you call the cops, my grandfather is toast. He'd never testify, but he'd never live that long anyway. If you get police involved in this, he's dead.''

Jake exploded with an expletive and leaned far over Eric's desk, into his face. "All right, that settles it. This boy's into some dangerous shit. I asked you before to let me start taking the horns off those rhinos before somebody drops 'em, and now you're my friend but I'm telling you, I want to start doing it, now, or you're going to have to find yourself another vet.''

For the first time Eric felt truly without options and said quietly, "All right. But maybe we could work a deal with the FBI so that they wouldn't move, but they could start an investigation.''

"Well, maybe that wouldn't be a bad idea," Jake started to calm down. "We're pretty much on our own out here, unless you do. I mean, they could—" Jake stopped. Watching FBI shows on television had never been his thing, and the truth was, he didn't know what they could do. "—they could, track their bank accounts or something and find out who they pay for the stuff.''

"No way, man," Eddie Lu suddenly stood and gripped his hands together in a kind of Charlie Chan imitation. "Nobody do raundry rike Chinese peopre.'' Then he was serious again. "And that includes money. You go to Chinatown, man, nobody there uses banks. Everything is cash, even the legitimate merchants.''

Jake insisted, "But when you walk into a store you can write a check or use a Visa card.''

"But that's what I'm telling you, man, even the big-time merchants go to the Chinese Associations to get their checks cashed and stuff.''

"You mean you're talking about the—what the hell did you call them—tongs?''

Eddie Lu thought, Here we go again. "Some of the associations are fronts for crime syndicates, but most aren't. But it's one-stop laundering for money at any of them. A merchant may go to the bank every day, but I promise it's only to put cash in his safety-deposit box."

"Well, all this is beside the point," Eric said abruptly. "If you're right, and if what we're thinking is true, we may not have time for a federal investigation to get set up."

Eddie Lu breathed a sigh of relief for his grandfather's sake, relief that the facts were going his way. "And even if there were time," he said, "I doubt they would help you much."

"Why not?"

"There is only room for so many undercovers in Chinatown, and they are all after drugs. Do you really think the FBI is going to pull people out of heroin cases to check up on the ingredients in herbal tea? Come on, man."

Jake's voice drilled Eric again. "The goddamn horns have got to come off, *now!*"

"Jake, Jake, I already said yes." He didn't know how he would square it with the Indonesians, that the precious Javas they had entrusted to his care outside of Houston, Texas, were in greater danger than they were back in Udjung Kulon, but he would have to find a way. Maybe they didn't need to know—maybe they could take off the horns and replace them with prostheses of some kind. But if it were done in secret the animals would still be in danger. He would figure it out some way.

"Larry, one more thing," he said. "Until we can hire more guards, I want to put Sam and Max both on the grounds at night; I'll need somebody inside for dispatch. Can you handle that awhile longer?"

"Sure, I can do that."

The pager on Jake's belt suddenly began its urgent beeping, and he unhooked it and looked at the number. Reaching for Eric's phone he punched in the three-digit extension and waited. "Jake here." After a long minute he said in a dark whisper, "Well, God damn it to hell, anything else gonna go wrong today? We'll be right there." He hung up. "That was Ernie. He says Sobhuza's limping real bad on one foot. I need to go take a look at him."

Eric stood up. "I'll come, too. Eddie, you've been very helpful," he extended his hand. "Do you have a place to stay?"

"His place," he inclined his head toward Larry.

"Well, I don't think we need detain you any longer."

"He's my ride. Can I hang out until he leaves?"

Jake had already called Lucy to have her meet them at Sobhuza's enclosure and was headed for the door. "More the merrier. Come on."

19 🌿🌿🌿🌿🌿🌿🌿🌿🌿

THE FOUR OF THEM went downstairs and passed quickly through the exhibit halls, out the doors that flanked Joseph II, and turned right into a small side lot where carts were parked. Jake drove, not out the catwalk to Africa—the bridges were too narrow for carts—but down the gravel road that serviced the back doors of the animal houses.

"This is cool," said Eddie Lu. "Does the public get to rent these?"

"No," said Eric. "They're too expensive."

"That, and the insurance," said Jake. "Plus, we don't really want people drag-racing in them."

Jake fell silent, to all appearances thinking about Sobhuza, but then suddenly looked back at Eddie Lu. "Just tell me one thing I'm curious about. Why was your grandfather willing to help us out?"

Eddie did not look back at him, but watched the greenery roll by. "He got to Chinatown seventy years ago. He was ten. He spent six years as an indentured servant, then went to work for somebody else. He lived in a flophouse owned by his employer; his rent was held out of his pay. He scraped and saved for fifteen years before he could go into business for himself, and once he did, he had to turn right around and start paying protection money to the Hua Hsing Hui. If he hadn't taken their insurance they would have burned him out. Nobody knows better than my grandfather how Chinese people treat each other in this country, and nobody knows better how the culture is used to keep people down. So now he's old, and I guess he figures he's old enough to strike a blow for change, you might say." Now he looked at Jake. "That answer your question?"

Jake shook his head. "Well, I'll be goddamned."

The first building they passed at the rear of the African paddocks contained the eight houses for the black rhinos; Sobhuza's was the first entry of the second building, and beyond him were the rest of the African elephants and white rhinos. Ernie's cart was already there, and as they piled out and trotted up steep, concrete outdoor stairs they saw Lucy approaching in her cart from the opposite direction.

When she joined them she handed Jake a pair of binoculars she'd brought from the clinic, and he studied Sobhuza grimly. As he did so Eric and Lucy exchanged a searching look, each now so trapped in the silent quicksand of suspicion that they no longer even smiled at each other. She figured Jake had told him that he told her that Eric and Liz Ann were trying again—there it was, the whole sucking mire of she knew he must know that she knew this or that. And both of them in looking long and painfully at each other realized the brutish truth that in the absence of honest, artless speech, events took on a momentum of their own that had now carried them both to places they did not really want to be.

Jake felt the chill gusting behind him as he held the binoculars tight to his eyes. Sobhuza was chewing fronds out of his morning pile of acacia branches, milling as he did so, noticeably favoring his right hind leg. "He's leaving a little blood out of that foot," Jake said with the binoculars still raised.

"What do you think happened?" asked Larry. "Did someone throw in some glass or something?"

"Well, it's possible but it ain't likely. If he stepped on enough glass to break the skin he would have pulled back before he put all his weight on it." The soles of elephants' feet are thick and callused, but supremely sensitive.

"Shit," Jake said at last. "I'm gonna have to put him down so I can look at him. Luce, go back to the infirmary. Get the Cap-Chur gun. I want enough M-99 to take him down and M-50/50 to wake him up. Take this boy with you—" he jerked his head in Larry's direction "—and have him load up that padded stanchion so we can prop his foot up. Ernie, round all your people up; looks like we're gonna need 'em." Placid-looking Ernie hustled downstairs.

Lucy's camouflaged cart left a cloud of dust rising behind it as they sped around the perimeter road and pulled up at the vet compound. Lucy pointed out the stanchion Jake wanted, a sawhorse of two-by-fours with a thick wrapping of foam rubber wound around the cross bar, and as Larry loaded it she ran into the clinic. She put two syringes in a case and out of the refrigerator took a bottle of M-50/50. She reached back in for the M-99 and froze when she discovered they had only one small bottle of it left.

M-99 is a morphine-based narcotic, and as such is heavily regulated and not even manufactured in the States anymore. It was a bitch to get hold of. For a split-second she considered substituting acetylpromazine. They had plenty of it because it was unregulated, easy to come by, and they used it on a wide variety of animals, but Sobhuza had never been exposed to it, or to the other possibilities, and at least they knew he had no reaction to M-99. With M-99 Jake could regulate the dosage more strictly, and the only real side-effect was several hours of pronounced irritability on the part of the patient. God, she thought, I hope it's enough, and tucked the small bottle into the case.

Back atop Sobhuza's house Lucy watched as Jake assembled the gun, and then she held out the M-99. "This better do it," she said. "That's all we have."

Jake skewered her with a look shot from under his heavy red brows. Ordering drugs was her department, and as she watched the line of his lips narrow to a thin white crease, wondered if he was going to chew her out. "Damn!" he said at last. "You need to order a bunch more right away. We're going to start de-horning the rhinos as soon as we can get some."

"He's going to let you do it?" Her voice registered her relief, but then she fell silent, letting him concentrate as the plunger's vacuum sucked the M-99 out of the bottle. Filling a syringe is the most menial of tasks, but M-99 is so powerful that even the tiniest slip of a needle prick would be almost instantaneously fatal to a human. Only after he slipped a CO_2 cartridge into the Cap-Chur gun and snapped the breech shut did she continue, "If you want to do it in a clean sweep we'll need to get a couple of the wranglers to do some overtime. Is that a problem?"

"Naw, get 'em on the schedule."

"Great. Ralphie and Chang have been asking if they can work some extra shifts." She looked around the gathering on the roof of Sobhuza's house and saw Ernie had begun assembling his crew of keepers and helpers. "Chang, did you hear that? Can you do some overtime?"

"Cool," he said, "sign me up whenever."

Jake thought he was an odd sight, Asian but punk-looking with his cereal-bowl haircut above close-shaven temples. She could call Ralphie that night. Lucy turned back to Jake and saw to her consternation he was holding the Cap-Chur gun out to her and knew instantly this was her punishment for letting the pharmacy run low on M-99. "Jake," she whispered, "that's all we've got. What if I screw up?"

His gaze penetrated her own. "You ain't gonna screw up."

She told herself, Take it like a big girl, and turned her back on him, dropping to one knee and bracing the gun barrel on the top of the chain-link fence.

Behind her she heard Jake's voice growl, "God damn, I hate using this stuff on him. Makes him meanern' shit." He patted her on the head twice like she was about to fire a bazooka. "Take him down, girl."

Sobhuza was no stranger to M-99; in the middle of the African bush Eric had darted him with it, but Jake had to manage the logistical problems from that point. No elephant this size could have been wrangled limp onto the flatbed of a truck, and what Jake managed was one of the first operations of its kind. Once the beast was down, hawsers were secured to each of his legs and tow lines ran from his tusks to the winch on a Land Rover. Jake gave him just enough nalorphine to wake him up—M-50/50 was not on the market yet—followed by tiny doses of M-99, enough to render him woozy, but conscious, and in this state he was *walked* into his captivity. It was a technique sometimes used since, with rhinos, but his accomplishment of landing Sobhuza with it he regarded as a gem of his career.

Lucy squeezed the trigger and there was a loud *pap* as the CO_2 cartridge exploded. The dart was propelled almost too fast to see its bright-red plastic tag arc through the air, but suddenly it materialized square in the middle of Sobhuza's right butt, a solid, dead-on hit.

Sobhuza greeted the stick with a bellow and a pirouette, and Jake patted Lucy on the shoulder. "Girl, I'm gonna take you duck huntin' with me this year."

She couldn't help a proud little laugh. "Not likely, but thanks." They watched Sobhuza for five or six minutes before he began to wobble on his feet. Most elephants wandered and staggered for some time more, but seconds after his first unsteadiness Sobhuza's back legs crumpled and he sat on his rump like a big terrier.

Erupting, "Shit fire!" Jake tore at a gate in the chain-link fence and snatching up a sharp prod, lowered a counterweighted aluminum ladder down into the paddock, yelling, "Come on! Bring them ropes!"

Everyone followed, making a terrific clatter down the light aluminum steps, following Jake in a dead run across the yard to where the great elephant sat, as Larry rightly supposed, groggy but still dangerous. What he shortly learned was that the single most mortal danger for a drugged elephant is that he will go down on his chest, with the mammoth bulk crushing down onto the lungs, causing hypostasis and then suffocation.

As he ran Jake reached back and took a coil of thick hawser from one of the wranglers, and on reaching the elephant, coiled a loop around the left pillar of a foreleg that rose above him, careful not to touch it until he threw the excess length of it under the animal's chest, behind the other foreleg. Ernie motioned everybody else to line up holding the rope like in a tug-of-war, and when they were ready, Jake pulled the noose tight and jumped back to avoid a backward sweep of tusk. With Sobhuza glaring at the little figures on his right, Jake jabbed the prod into the lower part of the left leg. Just as the elephant blanched enough to take some weight off it, Ernie yelled, "Pull!" and the left leg swept behind the right. The giant rolled smoothly onto his left side with a groan.

Jake and Lucy both knew they had been lucky. If Sobhuza had not cooperated with the physics of the maneuver, if he had fought them with the last of his muscular control, it might have been curtains for him. Jake looked out past the moat at where tourists were gathering to watch. Sobhuza had become their most popular draw, and from the hubbub they had created, Jake saw close to a hundred people pointing and talking and taking pictures, and he knew that, come right down to it, if Sobhuza had crashed down onto his chest, he would not have hesitated a second before drafting volunteers, at gun point if he had to, to swarm the moat and help push him over.

Lucy pulled hard to remove the dart, and then swabbed the wound with disinfectant. M-99 sedates the animal but it leaves him aware of his surroundings, and to minimize the stress two of the wranglers stretched olive-drab sheeting over Sobhuza's eyes, which they wet so the evaporation would cool him.

Once they got the foot up, it took Jake only a few seconds to find on the inside toe an angry-looking pus-filled whitlow—the rough equivalent, in elephants, of an infected hangnail, and proportionately more painful when seven tons of weight is pressed on it. In zoos it is usually a preventable malady; tame elephants can be groomed regularly, but Jake would have liked to see somebody try to trim Sobhuza's toenails. Dealing with things like this was one cost of trying to keep them wild.

"That's simple enough," grumbled Jake. The complication was that the only way for Jake to get to it was to lie flat on his back almost under the padded sawhorse. It was awkward, but not difficult, to lance and drain and disinfect the whitlow. Jake finished by dusting the bloody cuticle with an astringent powder to keep it from oozing too freely until it clotted over.

"Now," breathed Jake finally, "while we got him down I want to go over his other feet to keep us from having to go through this again." He took a large pair of tin snips from his case and handed Lucy a big woodfile. "I'll do the trimmin' and you come behind and file. Okay?"

"Right behind you."

Larry Davis watched fascinated as the pedicure proceeded smoothly for some twenty minutes before Jake replaced the implements in his kit and snapped the lid down, saying, "That oughta hold him. Let's wake him up." He handed Lucy a large ball of cotton and a bottle of alcohol, and she got Larry to help her raise Sobhuza's ear. He propped it up like a stiff heavy flap of sail canvas, almost hidden beneath it, and bent it forward over the shaded eye.

Jake began filling a second syringe. "Now, I'm going to give him a nice little squirt of this M-50/50 here—"

She peered over his shoulder and noted the dosage. "You think that'll do him?" Lucy had found the principal vein in the back of his ear and swabbed vigorously with the alcohol. Jake was fussy about not pumping more chemicals into the animals than they absolutely needed, sometimes to the point that Lucy worried he might be a little too conservative. But in this case it was a close call, especially since they had shorted him a little on the M-99 to begin with.

"It's a little shy, but it'll do the job. He'll just be in a shitty mood for a day or so." He held the needle against the sky and squeezed the air out of it.

"How shitty is that?" asked Larry.

"Well, why don't you hang around for about thirty seconds and find out? All right, now, all you people get out of here, I'm gonna wake him up." Jake slowly emptied the syringe into the vein and when he withdrew it, Lucy pressed the wound with the alcohol-soaked cotton, where a small scarlet stain rose to the surface after several seconds.

Suddenly the ear flipped back, throwing Larry off his balance.

"Uh-oh, time to go," Lucy backed away and took Larry by the hand.

"You people get out of here, let's go!" Jake was leading them, not following them, to the door of the elephant house.

Sobhuza convulsed from the middle of his back in the first attempt to get to his feet, rearing his head full in the air and flinging his trunk out to its whole length with a vile, rumbling grunt, both right legs swinging through the air for leverage. Larry had stumbled and dropped the padded stanchion, and stooped to pick it up but fell over it as he dodged the right front foot like a Sunday punch.

Jake was already in the door, beckoning him. "Leave it there, you idiot!"

With another effort Sobhuza wobbled to his feet, distracted for a second by a burst of applause from the gallery of now nearly two hundred tourists. When he saw the scurrying figure halfway to the door of his house, he bellowed and took after him, but the second time he put weight on his right hind foot he shrieked and stopped cold.

Larry regained the doorway, limping from a slight twist of an ankle. "You all right?" Jake asked him.

"Yeah. That stuff works pretty fast, doesn't it?"

Jake's eyes narrowed at the crow's feet and they knew he was smiling beneath his mustache. "Yup."

They watched Sobhuza explore his pains, gently smelling out the wounded toenail with the tip of his trunk, then his flank and then up to the back of his ear, rumbling wickedly at the human-smell all over him. He caught sight of the stanchion and gimped the couple of steps over to it, plucking it up with his trunk and holding it high over his head before shattering it on the ground. Then he picked up one of the pieces and flung it a good thirty yards through the air, and picked up the largest piece, the padded crossbar with one leg still attached, and headed toward his pool of water, dragging the stanchion with him and smashing the ground with it, half trophy and half weapon, trumpeting.

"Jesus," wheezed Larry.

Jake pointed at the ear-splitting commotion. "Mighta been you. I'm sure he'd rather it was you."

Larry Davis had not been inside Sobhuza's indoor area before, and the scale of its security was overwhelming. The bars that separated them from the space where the titan lived were solid iron, eight inches thick, buried deep in reinforced concrete, and even then there was no guarantee that his continued pushing at it might not fatigue the metal one day and bend the whole assembly over. Other elephants had done such damage in zoos before; one in Los Angeles had torn a two-inch-thick steel door from its hinges, twice, before dying under sedation when they tried to move him to a larger area. Elephants can react unpredictably to drugs; that was why Jake was so chary in dosing them, and they kept an emergency procedure ready just in case: a kit was ready, not in the clinic but here in Sobhuza's house, that, if anything should happen to him, contained everything they needed to cut out his testicles and milk them of semen before it could have a chance to deteriorate. It would be a hideous job when they came to it, for a bull elephant's testes never descend, but remain high up in the body cavity, closer to the spine than the belly. But if they planned it right, Sobhuza could continue to be a founder, *in vitro,* long after his earthly days had come to an end, which they hoped fervently would be peaceable, natural, and a long, long time hence.

From their vantage, Sobhuza's pond was obstructed by vegetation and a low hill, and Jake pointed for a second toward the back door. "Let's go upstairs and make sure he comes out of it okay."

The group gathered again at the point from where Lucy had shot him. Sobhuza had taken no cognizance yet of the aluminum ladder that descended from the top of his cliff, and Jake quickly raised it as quietly as he could. They saw Sobhuza at the water's edge, from where he flung the remnant of the stanchion as far as he could, sending it crashing into the brown, sprayed cement that formed the backdrop of his enclosure.

"Come on, boy, take a nice big drink and calm down." Sobhuza waded gingerly into his pool, stuck his trunk into the water and squirted four or five gallons into his mouth. Jake was satisfied. "Yeah, he'll be fine. Darlin'?" he walked over beside Lucy. "You know I don't like running out of stuff we might suddenly need."

She spun around. "I know. I'm sorry." She looked about quickly— Eric, Larry, Ernie, Chang, all the handlers—suddenly seized with the terror of being bawled out in front of people.

"Well," Jake nodded his head back toward the stairs. "It's still early in the day. Why don't you fax off an order to Germany right now."

"We still can't be sure how long it'll take."

"Yeah, I know. Call the AAZPA people and tell them what it's for. Maybe they can run some interference and cut some red tape with the feds about getting it into the country." Making his life miserable was one of the least foreseen side-effects of the perennial War on Drugs. The U.S. Fish and Wildlife Service had begun listening to the AAZPA on matters of import permits, but the Drug Enforcement Agency was not quite on board yet.

"Sure, right away." She knew he was pissed, but left grateful he had still never blown up at her the way she knew he was capable of.

Jake walked with her over to the stairs. "You can figure it out.

We'll need enough M-99 to take down all thirty-one rhinos, and M-50/50 to counteract, and some resin to dab on the stubs. We'll start makin' time to get their horns off as soon as it gets here. Whenever the hell that is."

"Right."

"Let me know if AZA can help us."

Lucy nodded again, and Larry helped her lug the kits and equipment into the cart and drove her back to the infirmary. "Listen," he said, "Eric wants me to work some more night shifts in security so Sam can stay out on the grounds with Max. If you're free why don't you come back out; call it a cheap date."

"Oh, I don't know."

"He also wants me to take some behavior notes using the remote cameras. He thinks some of the condors and wisents and some others are showing mating interest, and there's no students to stand watch with a notepad. You could show me what to look for."

He watched the breeze blow through her hair as he drove. "Okay," she brushed a honey-blond strand out of her face. "Yeah, okay."

20 🌿🌿🌿🌿🌿🌿🌿🌿🌿

LATE THE SAME AFTERNOON at Barilla Imports in the Gallería, Luís sat in the office, flipping through the Rolodex until it stopped at the card with Lucy Conner's name on it, and the sting of that encounter rose in him again. In this job he had the opportunity to talk to—he refused to think of it as hit on—a lot of women, but this one struck him as special. She was delicate and beautiful, intelligent, sophisticated, professional. Any number of women had declined to get acquainted with him, although, as he reminded himself, several did, but when this one acted like she was too good for him, that really hit him all wrong.

His eyes came to rest on her telephone numbers—work and home. It was his job to make sure all their customers who paid by check got their addresses and telephone numbers recorded on their mailing list. That was just good business.

He glanced out into the showroom and saw he would be alone for at least a few minutes. He picked up the receiver even as he realized he didn't know what he would say. Perhaps she would pick up the phone and say, "Pasadena Animal Hospital" or something—then what? Then he remembered—some new pre-Columbian reproductions had come in, similar to what she had bought. Perhaps she would be interested in them.

He punched the first three digits of her work number and stopped. No, that wasn't good enough; she'd know he just wanted an excuse to call her. He laid the receiver back in its cradle.

At his house he had a mutt named Paisano. It was time for his shots—that was true enough, Paisano had never had shots in his life. That would do.

The sound rang twice distantly at his ear, and what he heard was Stephanie's cultured voice. "Good afternoon, Final Refuge Wildlife Foundation, how may I direct your call?"

He was stunned. He sat there in total silence, frozen and stupefied.

"Hello? May I help you?"

In slow motion Luís laid the receiver back in the cradle. She worked there! She said she was a vet, but he never imagined—there! Shit! All he'd been trying to do was break in and kill her fucking animals! He sat there silently, letting the hurt, and the hatred, build. If he left a message she wouldn't call him back, the bitch. Goddamn, he could really like her, too.

Luís looked up suddenly and saw both his uncles and Juan and wondered if they'd seen him on the phone, and if he was in trouble. Then he saw Albert Chu behind them. "Listen," said Ramón, "you remember what we talk about? About if we had enough money we could get out of this damn country and go back home? Do you want to do that?"

"Sure," said Luís, and meant it.

Ramón looked at Chu. "Tell him."

"My friend who works in the wildlife park tells me they are going to saw the horns off all the rhinos there, as soon as enough sedative is delivered. He has no idea when that will be. For all we know it could arrive as early as tomorrow. I will pay you fifty thousand dollars per kilo, cash, for every horn you can take out of there tonight. That is the full market price. If you want to do this you have to move tonight. How do you feel about it?" In part he had lied. Fifty thousand was no longer the full market price. But it was a round number and it was sure to impress the Barillas.

Luís looked at Ramón. "Is not gonna be easy," said Ramón, "but all the rhinos they got, we get just half of them, it still be over ten million dollars. But we can't just sneak in there like we tried before. We got to take them head on, cut their phones and kill some guards. Is gonna be dangerous. If somebody get hurt, we got to be like soldiers—" he made a sweeping motion with his hand. "We take casualties, we got to just go on."

"What about Aunt Ellen?"

"She don't know nothing yet," Ramón answered. "Once it's over, she can come with us, if she want to. This means we got to leave everything, the house, the store. We leavin' tonight, right after the job, and we never comin' back. Just walk off and leave it all. Are you in?"

The timing cannot be an accident, thought Luís. It must be the stroke of God. "Yeah. Hell, yeah, I'm in. How do we get the horns to Mr. Chu?"

"I will go in with you," said Chu calmly. "But there is something else you have to know. I want you to know everything so you can make an informed decision about whether you wish to proceed." He reached inside his coat and produced one of The Refuge's magnetic passcards, and handed it to Luís. He turned it over in his hand, seeing on the obverse the photo and social security number of a young Chinese named Chang, and a magnetic strip across the top of the back. He gave it back. "All the buildings in the park are opened with these cards," said Chu. "My contact could only supply me with this one. It is his own, and we must not use it because if anything happens it could be traced to him. You must acquire your own."

"You know what that means," said Ramón.

"It means," said Chu, "that you will of necessity have to neutralize the security guards before you can do anything else."

Luís nodded. Killing. He looked up at Ramón. "You think we ought to go for it?"

Ramón looked at the others, less for reassurance than to make certain they were really behind him. "Yeah, I think we ought to go for it."

"Once we are finished inside," said Chu, "we will drive to my house, where you will unload, and I will pay you. I can pay you up to two million in cash, and if you get more, the rest in securities. Then you can go to your house, collect your belongings, get out of the country and get on with happy—and very wealthy—lives."

Luís knew better than to ask an impertinent question like whether

Chu had ready access to those kind of assets. Of course he had. He looked at Ramón instead. "Do you think Aunt Ellen will come?"

"I don't know."

"What about the pet store?"

Ramón looked at him vapidly. "What about it?"

That was when Luís realized most clearly that Ramón did not mean to be quibbled with, and would not accept anything less than a whole commitment. He wanted to ask, Don't you want Aunt Ellen to go?, and he wanted to ask, What about the puppies and kittens in the pet store?, but he knew better. A smile slowly creased his face. "Okay," he said. "Fuck, yeah, let's get it on."

"All right then," said Ramón with some impatience. "Now I want you to go with Juan. Go someplace and buy a good chainsaw. Then go to a different place and buy another one. Then go to the auto supply and buy some gas cans; once we get goin' I don't want to stop anywhere. I got some Mexican plates we can put on the car before we cross so nobody will know across the border. And one more thing, nobody does any drinkin' till we out of the country. I mean it, we got to be able to think straight tonight."

"Where will you be?" Luís asked Chu. "You aren't going to stay around here, are you?"

"No. I will go to Los Angeles to tend to some business, then Singapore. Of course, I'll go down to San Diego and visit the zoo there for perhaps some use in the future. But after this transaction I will be living in Singapore."

21

EVER SINCE he had talked Liz Ann into returning Eric had found their relationship altered, for the worse, in a way that he began to think he could not overcome. It was not that they fought; indeed they were both so conscious of not fighting, that not fighting seemed to have become their principal goal. It was the feeling that was altered. He knew he had acted from the most commendable of motives—for the sake of their marriage, out of respect for their families and church. But even when they made love, her attitude seemed to him to be a kind of lay-here-and-let-him-do-his-thing. But it was subtle. Not that she pretended not to enjoy it, but it was as though she would rather he have to ask, and then have to be grateful, or at least more grateful than she. It was after they moved back in together, and again began going to church together, that he realized that whatever the sources of her motives, manipulation was so woven into her personality as to have become inextricable. And Eric found himself unsure if he could spend the rest of his life gambling at her emotional card table.

From that standpoint it seemed fortunate to him that the day of Larry's return from Los Angeles, with its uproar over Sobhuza's foot, had left him too worn and depressed to want to fill out an application to do Liz Ann that night. He went to bed early and she joined him later, as he barely noticed before returning to a sleep so sound that the telephone, when it rang, seemed too distant to reach out and pick up. But even in sleep he found it.

"Sam said to call and let you know something's going on." There was a certain tension in Larry's voice he hadn't heard before.

"Tell me exactly." His voice was groggy, but his mind cleared rapidly.

"Max called in from the gate and said a car full of guys had stopped. I radioed out to Sam and he said he would come in, then—"

"Wait. Where was he?"

"Uh, up in the Arctic, checking on the polar bears and musk oxen. Then about five minutes later he called back in and said something's not right. He doesn't think it's kids this time. He said to call you and call the sheriff for some backup."

"Yes, do that right away. I'll be right out."

He hung up the phone and slipped his feet out from under the covers to the floor and sat up, creating as little disturbance as he could. He knew Liz Ann had heard it; if she hadn't wakened at the ring of the telephone, he was certain she heard him say he was coming. Her ears were tuned to it, like a test pattern.

"What is it?" Her voice was thick and muffled.

"It was Larry, at the park." He hesitated. "One of the animals is sick."

She groaned. "Oh God, Eric, it's after midnight. Don't tell me." She conveyed as much despair as menace.

"Yeah, I'd better go out."

He expected the storm, but the suddenness of her fury astonished him. "I thought we worked all this out! Eric!" Her open hand slammed down onto her pillow.

"I'm sorry, honey. I really have to."

"No! It can't even throw up without your having to be there to wipe its mouth?"

He thought fast. "It's one of the Javas." They both knew she couldn't fight that.

He closed the door of the walk-in closet before pulling the chain on the light bulb, and in the cramped space pulled on blue jeans and sneakers and reached for a shirt, but then stopped and took out a black pullover instead. When he returned he saw Liz Ann sitting up in bed, glaring at him; she had switched on the lamp on the night table, the light raking shadows across her face. She was livid; she had been sleeping soundly, and the puffiness of her face made her seem even more enraged.

He sat by her. "Let's see, if this was the movies, this would be where I ask, will you be here when I get back?"

"This isn't the goddamn movies, Eric."

That's right, he thought, goddamn movies. Liz Ann never swore merely because she was angry; she swore only when she wanted him to *know* how angry she was. It was something he had learned to listen for. Still he tried to cajole her. "Is that a yes?"

She reviled him with her look, breathing hard, her chin trembling.

This is fine, he thought. My life's work is in danger of going down the toilet, and the most this woman is concerned about is that I prove my love for her by not letting the sheets get cold. It is a curious sensation, he thought, to feel the last reservoir of your affection for someone draining away, even as you sit there talking to her. He had never felt it before, like water with its tiny whirlpool draining out of a sink, making a tiny sucking noise just as the last of it disappears, and when it's gone, it cannot be recalled.

Like extinction.

He nodded. "Well, I'm sorry. I have to go." There was too much to do to think about it now in great detail, but at that instant he was certain that the next time the moment was opportune, he would ask Lucy, even if he had to move into her place, to begin a real life together.

Liz Ann knew that, too—perhaps it was the coolness with which he said he had to go—but for all her faults she was a woman with a woman's intuition and she knew it was over, too, and spat after him, "Bastard!"

In the hall he brushed quickly by the crucifix, intently fingering his keyring for the smallest one. In his study he unlocked the bottom drawer of his desk and pulled out a .38 revolver, and, just noticing his hands begin to shake, opened a box and dumped out a handful of bullets, which he stuffed into his pants pocket. He opened his billfold and removed his electronic passcard, which he thrust into the other pocket. He turned out the light, but then before leaving the study first glanced through the den because he didn't want Liz Ann to see him leaving with the gun. He saw the light in the bedroom was off again, and he exited quickly from the kitchen into the garage.

From Westheimer Eric sped south on State Highway 6; most of the interminable stoplights had switched to constant flashing yellow at midnight, and only at the main roads were they still in their daytime sequence. When he came to the first red one he was right on it before he stopped abruptly, quickly scanned in all directions and gunned the car through it. The worry that a highway patrolman might see him lasted only a second; yes—maybe one would, so much the better. If ever there was a time when Eric Jackson wanted to be pulled over, it was now, and his speedometer edged through sixty and seventy and crept up on eighty. He was old enough to be getting a little night blind, and dared not risk going any faster. Plus he never drove this fast during the day, let alone in the dead of night; he felt wildly out of control and so turned on the bright headlights and eased the speed back down to seventy, knowing it would only mean a minute or a minute and a half difference in his arrival time.

Perhaps it's nothing. Perhaps it is kids again, after all. Sam and Max can handle it. Eric approached another light that was red and slowed to forty before blasting through it. He wished he had a cup of coffee, then no, he had forgot to use the bathroom before he left the house. Alone and afraid, speeding on a dark road it was screwy, the things that streaked through your mind like shooting stars.

In Arcola he turned onto 521, leaving rubber on the pavement both stopping and going, but in checking the rearview mirror saw no police following him. Well, yes—of course: never a cop when you need one. Rank pastures and soggy rice fields glided by all black and gray and silver in the moonlight outside the new Saturn's windows, and for the first time Eric realized he was uncomfortably hot and close. He had forgot to open the windows, and now opened them halfway to circulate some air.

And he had forgot to pray and wondered if God could hear him if he was not kneeling on the velvet stool under the crucifix. Father, he thought, Father, please don't let this happen. If it is Your will . . .

No, he mustn't get stopped! Oh, Christ, if a trooper pulled him over he would see the gun and take him in and then he would never get there.

It was then that The Refuge's fence came into view, the northeast corner, and he slowed somewhat, looking for signs of disturbance, marking time and distance by the repeated bright white rectangles that caught the headlights and blurred by on his right:

DANGER/WILD ANIMALS
PELIGRO/ANIMALES FIERAS

He slowed even more as he approached the back side of the veterinary compound, inspecting the driveway down to the loading dock and its huge metal garage door. He could see everything in the glare of its spotlight and spied no hint of trouble. Eric turned right down the south fence toward the entrance, straining closely to see cuts in the fence or barbed wire, but there were none.

He was almost to the entrance drive when he heard, faintly but distinctly, the sharp pop-pop-pop, pop-pop-pop-pop of automatic weapons fire; he jumped and nearly steered into the ditch before regaining control of the car, his heart racing as in that instant he knew Sam's worst-case scenario was unfolding.

It was Juan Barilla who had studied the electrical and telephone lines and knew what to cut to sever The Refuge's communications without disturbing their power. They knew from their first attempt that only the barbed wire at the top was hot. It was no great challenge, as the others waited hot and close inside the car, parked in the drive of the sand-and-gravel company, for Esteban to snip an opening in the links of the inner fence, then sneak up on the guard at the gate and twist the cord around his neck.

Albert Chu waited nervously in the backseat of the blue Olds as they motored through the gate and Esteban pushed the button to close it again. Chu's feet nestled among extra cans of gasoline on the floor—enough to get the Barillas to Matamoros without stopping. His gray jogging shoes looked odd beneath his expensive black slacks; lightly he fingered a tiny .22 snubnose beneath his black silk shirt. On the seat beside him were soft lumpy valises. There was one machine pistol for each of the Barillas, and their backpacks bulged with extra fifty-round clips. Atop the valises rested two oily new Poulan chainsaws.

Ramón clambered out of the front right door; like Esteban, he was wearing old blue jeans. Both boys wore denim cutoffs, for it was a warm night, and dark shirts and sneakers. All the clothes were old; they expected to get blood on them and had brought a change of clothes for each in the trunk.

Luís glimpsed Max Parker's body slumped inside the kiosk, and felt his pulse quicken with the realization that what was happening was real and he was part of it. But as he slipped the dead man's passcard out of his shirt pocket and into his own, he felt a triumph within himself, a surge, a massive getting even with everything and with everybody. With her.

Silently Luís slipped into the back door of the administration building, creeping on tiptoe down the dim corridors of Hope and Stupidity, and finally Silence, at whose far end he turned carefully into the side hall, toward the security station, its door open, its light beaming into the hall. He paused to make sure the safety was off, then spun into the room. Larry Davis jerked away from the monitor he had been watching, which held the image of the walk in front of the condor flight cages. Luís recognized him in a flash, from the store, and who he was with, and took a savage exultation in splitting open Davis's forehead with a single shot, then shooting up the whole bank of electronics in a deafening crash of glass.

As Larry Davis lay back in his chair wall-eyed and dead, Luís advanced on him, feeling into the chest pockets of Larry's shirt for his passcard. Not finding it, he flipped the body forward with a thump onto the papers he had been studying. He fished Larry's billfold out of his rear pocket and found his passcard in one of the pockets. There were no credit cards, but as he muttered, "Yeah, you can suck my dick, hombre," Luís found twelve dollars which he stuffed into his own pants pocket.

It was after he returned to the gate that he saw his uncles and cousin had overwhelmed the other security guard and were extracting his passcard from his wallet. Luís had expected to see killing on this night; what he had not expected was that he would enjoy it.

22 🌿🌿🌿🌿🌿🌿🌿🌿🌿🌿

Eric slowed as he passed the entrance gate, and the first thing he noticed, other than the fact that it was closed as it should be, was that he saw parked on the driveway just past the kiosk the long dark sedan he knew must be the same as from the tape Sam and Larry had shown him. He looked further in but saw no sign of life around the headquarters building, and motored on without slowing further. He did look far ahead and in the rearview mirror for some sign of the law, but Sam must have been right; a response could take forever.

If the power was off he could get over the fence, but then it registered that the landscaping lights were on around the building, so chances were that the fence was still hot. It was a half mile to the farm's gate, and when he turned in he saw the lights off in the office but the ultraviolets on in the greenhouses. He turned a hard right down its perimeter road, not turning into the interior of the farm until he reached the last drive, which he motored down until it dead-ended at the field where they grew bamboo for the pandas. He seized the revolver and jumped out of the car, remembering even in his haste to disconnect the alarm. That would have been all he needed, for the alarm cricket to start chirping. Using the tall cane as cover, he sprinted down the rows until he gained the gate that connected the farm to the park proper. Immediately he backed out of that road, back into the bamboo, and knelt and pulled a handful of bullets out of his jeans pocket, spilling some on the dirt as he tried to steady his hands.

He inserted his passcard into the farm gate and it clicked open. The shortest distance to the administration building was along the catwalks through the Pacific Islands, but if a lookout was posted he would be instantly visible in the moonlight. The perimeter road was shielded from sight, but the noise of tires on the gravel would have alerted the intruders all the same. So there was no help for it but to run, and that was what he did, in a crouching lope the half mile from the farm gate to where he could see the condor flight and parking garage coming up on his left. Already he was winded, more from the emotional strain than from a half-mile run, but he thanked God it was not more and as he reached the corner of the garage, knelt in the shrubbery to catch his breath while figuring out how to get into the administration building unseen.

The sidewalk from the garage went to the front door, but that was out of the question as it would put him in full view for at least forty yards. Circling the building and entering through the tourist doors at the end of the Hall of Hope was equally dangerous; if the Barillas had managed to gain control of the security system, any one of them still inside could be manning the surveillance cameras. The only other door was the food delivery to the kitchen; it was hidden, it was isolated from the rest of the building, and surely they would not think to guard it. From within the shrubbery Eric eased himself over the waist-high concrete wall into the darkened parking garage, and ran down its length to the gate to the staff lot, where he paused, still within the cover of the garage, to survey.

There were three cars in the lot, Larry's and Sam's and Max's. Larry inside and both guards on the grounds—good. He could see the whole south front of the administration building, its stark white marble seeming to glow in the moonlight, the front door as visible as it was unapproachable. From the corner of the staff lot a cart path snaked down the west side of the building toward the kitchen: no windows, no moonlight, no cameras. Keeping under cover of the greenery, Eric hunched his way around the edge of the staff parking toward the cart path. When he reached it, he gave a final glance over his shoulder for some sign that he had been seen and with the .38 over his shoulder, raced through the deep shadow toward the kitchen delivery door.

A single pass of his card through the box clicked it open, and as he slipped inside and pressed it shut he raged at himself: be careful, be careful. Though he had designed virtually the entire park himself with only structural consultation from the architects, the kitchen was an area he'd left to them. He knew nothing of restaurant design or the equipment specifications, and the kitchen was the one area of the building he was relatively unfamiliar with, and the prospect of bashing his head into a hanging, clanging line of soup pots was not an attractive one. Once inside, however, he saw that the east windows, from where food was served onto the patio, were closed but not shuttered, and this twenty-foot stretch of glass admitted enough light to see the dim little hazards—the rubber mat that the dishwasher stood on that might be tripped over, the metal carts that could be sent rolling into a wall. A quick study of the patio betrayed no sign of movement.

The other door of the kitchen, catty-cornered opposite from where he had entered, opened into the lecture hall, a design feature intended to make receptions easier to serve and break down. Listening as far ahead of him as he could, Eric padded through the lecture hall, which truly was pitch-black for it had no windows. As far as he could remember, there should still be chairs rowed across the middle of the room, so keeping to the edge, literally feeling his way, he finally gained the double doors into the high, two-story loggia. He cracked one open a few inches, into a silence so thick that the tiny click of the latch echoed through the marble like a wrench had been dropped. There was no sound whatever, and the moonlight streaming in the high south windows showed no one anywhere.

Then he thought of the balcony above him, that there was no way to see that it was empty without exposing himself to fire from there. He thought of his first goal, the security room, reached through the corridor that opened off the Hall of Silence. Quietly he sidled along the back wall of the loggia, his eyes trained on the bottom of the balcony above him, but glancing to the staircase, which remained empty, and to the door Silence, which opened dark and, indeed, silent as a sepulcher.

From the back corner of the loggia he gathered his nerve, and finally sprang the dozen steps into the Hall of Silence, gripping the fingers of his free hand on the door-facing to propel himself in a tight arc into it, low, training his .38 down the hall long enough to see it was empty, then cautiously looking back out into the loggia and up at the balcony, which was also empty.

Eric looked back down the hall, which was dim but not pitch-black, for there were 15-watt night lights in the corners and every twenty feet down the length so night security could get out onto the grounds and back. In that dim glow he made out the painted cavemen in their heavy-browed contentment on the back wall of the first case, skinning and flensing their mammoth kill with their flint scrapers and knives. Knives, shit! Why hadn't he gotten a knife in the kitchen? Then he knew why—he didn't know where they were.

From the open door that said EMPLOYEES ONLY over it came a some-what brighter glow, and in peeking down that corridor he saw light streaming brightly into it from the open door of the security center. With the .38 steadied in both hands and with his back to the wall, he crept toward it. Those who knew him only socially or from church would have been taken aback by the adequacy of his stealth, but in jungle and thornscrub he had stalked quarry far more intelligent and elusive—if not more deadly—than human beings. If there was one thing he could do, it was stalk, and that was the one thing that kept his terror under control.

Eric stopped in the shadow just short of the broad yellow stripe of light cast across the corridor floor, gathering himself, listening. He spun into the room in a crouch, the .38 held out at arm's length, and saw it empty. But then no—empty, except for the form of Larry Davis, slumped forward over his notebook.

In a muttering whisper Eric repeated, "No, no, no," as he ran to him. He started to lift him by the shoulders to lean him back in the chair, but discovered his black curly hair matted to the paper by a mucilage of blood and drool and spilled coffee.

"Oh no, Jesus, Larry . . ." If his eyes had been closed, Eric might have believed he was unconscious. But they were open, and there was a bullet wound above his left eye, and there was no question that he was dead. "I'm sorry, I'm sorry . . ." He laid him gently back down, squeezing his shoulder in a kind of good-bye, when he spied the telephone and he yanked the receiver to his ear as he punched 9-1-1 with violent precision and waited.

"Come on, come on . . ." His eyes scanned the small bank of video monitors and saw them shot to pieces, and realized there was no possibility of remotely scanning the grounds to find where the intruders were. In his ear the connecting tone and clicks and ring did not come and did not come, until he realized the problem. He smashed his hand down on the cradle, waited a second and released it, and found there was no dial tone at all. It was dead.

"Shit!" First peering around the corners, Eric raced back out to the Silence Hall and then across the loggia to the front desk and yanked up the phone there. Again there was no dial tone, but—he didn't know phones—maybe, he punched a 9 for an outside line, but was met by the same flaccid silence. The line had been cut outside. "God damn it!" He started to slam it back down but then slung it silently back in the cradle, then he remembered the guns.

The guns—the cabinet in the security office, last-case use in emergency only—he sprinted back there, squeezing around Larry Davis's body, and pulled open the cabinet and swore again as its empty back wall stared back at him. Both the 30/30 and the .416 Rigby were gone, and the boxes of ammunition. Not even Sobhuza could stand up to the Rigby—but no, they were after the rhinos. If they didn't know how to fire the Rigby they would only use it once, for the recoil would kick them senseless.

He needed stuff. With a quick shake he emptied Larry's backpack and ransacked the room in a search for anything that might be useful. He found a flashlight, and a short coil of rope, then suddenly remembered the upstairs kitchen across from his office. He didn't know where things were in the restaurant kitchen, but the little kitchen by his office he knew had at least a paring knife and he remembered an ice pick.

Back across the loggia he bounded up the stairs two at a time, down the left into the reception area, left again down the corridor to his office. He turned into the kitchen, careful to close the door before turning on the light, which he had to do because it was an interior room and had no window. He opened the top drawer next to the under-counter refrigerator. The ice pick he grabbed up and flung into the backpack, but the paring knife was not there. He rammed the drawer shut and opened the one beneath it, shut it and opened the next one, all the way to the bottom.

Maybe, he thought, maybe on a shelf in the pantry—he didn't remember leaving it there, but maybe Stephanie had. Eric crossed the small room to the door of the closet-sized pantry, silently upbraiding himself for his inefficiency—a cop told him once after his house had been broken into that thieves who know what they are doing start with a bottom drawer so they don't have to stop to close them. So thinking he pulled open the pantry door, and the scream and flash of the knife were too sudden to evade completely. Even as he jumped back he heard the sleeve of his pullover rip open.

But with the downward slash finished, Eric pulled the figure out of the pantry and spun behind it, burying his face in the familiar clean scent of Lucy's straight blond hair, pinning her arms at her sides. She started to shriek again but it was cut short by Eric's had cupped over her mouth as he whispered loudly right in her ear, "It's okay, honey. It's okay, it's me. It's me. All right?"

She nodded, he let her go and she turned and faced him, and upon seeing who it was crashed limply into his chest, not weeping, but with great, heaving sighs as he held her. "They shot Larry," she moaned at last.

"I know," he said. "Who was it? The Barillas?"

"Yes. I saw Chu with them."

Her face was still buried in his shirt until he held her out. "Tell me what happened."

"Larry asked me to keep him company while he worked his shift."

"Where's your car?"

"We came in his car. Sam called in to say something was going on, and I thought he might want us to come out and help him look around, so I came up here to use the bathroom first. I was coming back out when I heard them crossing the lobby. I ran back into Stephanie's office to call down and warn him, but the phone was dead, and then I heard gunshots. What about Larry—did they—"

"Yeah, he's dead, sweetie."

It was then she began crying, and he comforted her for a moment before he held her away from him. "Larry was going to call the sheriff. Do you know whether he did before they got him?"

"No, I don't know."

"Shit!" Why hadn't he himself called from the house to make certain? "Okay, we'll just have to assume he didn't. Come on!"

Eric grabbed her hand and they ran back through Stephanie's reception office and down the opposing corridor to the Board Room with its large picture window down onto the grounds. They looked across the moonlit ripples of the Atlantic and saw five figures on the catwalk, almost to Africa, walking fast but cautiously, turning repeatedly to look behind them.

Then the figures paused; three stepped onto the African shore, and two returned at a dead run back to the building.

Esteban Barilla was not amused at having to retrace the hundred and fifty yards of the catwalk. "I think you full of shit, man," he muttered. They reentered the administration building beneath the blind bronze gaze of Joseph II.

They ran quickly through Hope and Stupidity and Silence, but Luís was adamant. "No, man, I'm tellin' you I saw somebody in the window."

Esteban motioned him into the corridor to check the security office, while himself scanning through the loggia and lecture hall and cracking the door to peer into the kitchen, but finding nothing. They met in the loggia and sprinted up the stairs, Luís to the left and Esteban to the right. He found nothing in Consuela's office nor Roman's, and joined Luís in the Board Room. Together they looked out the picture window and saw the catwalk now empty. They ran back down the stairs to the front doors; they exited onto the porch and returned, walking briskly back toward the door to Silence. "You fucked, man, there ain't nobody. No cars, nothin'."

"Man, I sure thought I saw somethin'."

Their footsteps receded through the exhibit halls until the silent building echoed with the crunch of the push-bar on the doors out to the grounds. When the latch had snapped shut again, Eric's face slowly rose above the souvenir counter in the loggia, his eyes wide, the .38 ready. Lucy slowly rose beside him. "I know that voice," she whispered lowly. "That's Luís. Larry and I met him in the shop. The other one is his uncle, I don't know which one."

"Oh, God, it's all true," he said, and sank back down. "It's all true." She drew near to comfort him, but when he looked into her eyes he whispered suddenly, "Sam!"

Eric jumped to his feet, turning once, and twice, confused. "Sam, come on, Sam, where are you?"

Lucy stood beside him. "When he called in he said he was going to check the front gate; that's the last I heard. Can you get him on the radio?"

"No, they shot it up. I have to go out to the gate. Get back down there and wait for me. Okay?"

Lucy nodded and sank back beneath the counter, then slid back one of the doors on the rear of the display case, to see Eric, framed by tiny, molded-plastic elephants and rhinos, push his way through the front door that the Barillas had unlocked.

He ran in a crouch, keeping in the shadows of the foliage, toward the front gate. As he loped past the strange car he slowed to glance inside. He tripped and fell over a large dark lump, and when he raised up found himself looking into Sam Rutherford's dead open eyes.

"Ah, God!" He lurched backward before creeping back and checking Sam's throat for a pulse. "No, Sam!"

He got to his feet and ran on until he caught himself on the window railing of the kiosk, and knew that the body slumped inside must be Max Parker's. Only when the headlights of a passing car raked through the glass did he see Parker's face, swollen and purple, the garrote still biting deep into his throat. Eric looked away and fought back a heave from deep in his stomach.

Headlights—Eric leaned across the narrow space in the kiosk to push the button that opened the gate but in so doing dislodged Max Parker's body, which fell off its chair with pure limp gravity and rolled onto Eric's feet.

He ran out onto the farm road and saw the red taillights receding. He jumped up and down and waved his arms, but dared not shout. "Come back," he pleaded quietly. "Please, come back." He looked long but there was no more traffic visible in either direction.

A staccato burst of gunfire came from deep in the park, in Africa. Eric nearly jumped out of his skin at the suddenness of it, but it was only then that his terror transmuted into rage—a pure rage, unlike anything he had felt before, unlike what he had felt even for the poachers in Chete, the poachers in their filthy old black dress socks. Their attitudes were framed by a lifetime of deprivation and colonial inequity; the Barillas were in it purely for the money. Even Chu could not hide behind his culture; he was in it for the money he could make off his culture. But Eric knew that at the root of it, these were his rhinos and this was his work, and the rage that it kindled in him was new—but could he kill?

Sam had asked him that. Could he kill? The rangers in Chete had told him: poachers almost never will be taken alive. But that was Africa. Would he even have to kill? Jake had told him he'd get buck fever.

It took a second short burst of gunfire to ignite him, glowering, "Fucking bastards!" He reentered the drive, swearing and fumbling in Larry's backpack until he pulled out the ice pick as he knelt beside the long blue Oldsmobile. "Sons of bitches, let's do it!" Without thinking whether the tires might be steel-belted, he buried the pick up to the handle into the side of one and then another, which hissed audibly when he withdrew it. "Get away now, by God!"

He burst back into the kiosk and closed the gate, and ransacked the interior looking for Max's two-way radio, which he found, ground up, on the floor, and for Max's passcard, which he did not find. He dragged the body partway outside and, ignoring the balloonlike face, went through his pockets for the passcard but pulled out only a wad of Kleenex and his keyring.

Keyring . . . *keyring!* If they took his and Sam's and Larry's passcards that gave them three, any one of which would get them into any building in the compound. The electronic passcards accessed everything but the bridges. When they designed the park, the architect had told him the only drawbridge controls on the market were activated with keys.

The bridges . . . Eric held Max Parker's keyring up to the moonlight, his fingers frenzying through them until he found the bridge key, and his fist closed around the ring as he hissed, "Yes!"

He went through Sam's pockets and found the keys, including his bridge key. "Yes!" he repeated, and yanking up Larry's backpack, ran full bore back up the drive, ignoring cover now, until he burst through the front door.

Lucy had seen him coming from her peephole under the counter and ran out to meet him by the turnstile. "Eric, they're shooting. I think they're shooting the animals."

He took her by the shoulders. "I know. They're after the rhinos, maybe the elephants, too. I don't know." During the firing he had listened for the deep cannon boom of the Rigby but had not heard it. He saw she was scared—as scared as he was. "I'm sorry you're in this."

"What can we do?"

"There's no time to get help. We've got to try to stop them. Do you think you can help?"

"I'll try. But how?"

"Do you have your card?"

She checked her pocket. "Yes."

"Come on." He took her hand and they ran into the Hall of Silence, where Eric stopped abruptly. He had to make sure. "Wait here." He entered the corridor to the security office and heard behind him that Lucy was following. He turned and pointed at her: "No!" She knew from his ferocity that he would not be disputed and returned to the Hall of Silence. Eric went through Larry's pockets and breathed, "Thank God," as his fingers extracted his keyring with the bridge key still on it. First checking his own pocket to make certain he had his own bridge key, he tossed the other three keyrings into the wastebasket and scattered atop them papers he had emptied from the backpack.

He rejoined Lucy and they raced through Silence and turned the corner into Stupidity, passing the whirling odometers, one of world population and the one in reverse that counted off the decimation of the rain forests. They turned again through Hope and skidded to a stop at the glass doors by Joseph II. Eric took her by the shoulders again. "Listen to me. They've got passcards and they can get into the houses. We've got to get the animals out into the paddocks. The rhinos will hide in the brush. All right?"

She nodded.

"Now. They've got cards, but they don't have keys—they can't open the bridges. They are on the African island now. If they just shot a couple of rhinos it'll take them maybe fifteen minutes to get the horns sawed off. I'm going to take a cart down the perimeter road and try to get the others out, and then open the bridges from the other side and try to isolate them in Africa. I want you to take another cart up the north road, come down into South Asia from the other side. Park the cart where they can't see it. Turn the Asian rhinos out—Javas first, then the Sumatran and the Indian. I think I can keep them out of Asia that long. Then get the hell out of here and get help. Do you understand?"

She nodded again, and holding hands they ran out to the yard where the carts were recharging. Eric had just unplugged two when he raised up and smacked himself on the forehead. "Oh, God, that's no good. What if they split up?"

Lucy saw she was now his partner in this and considered it. "No. There's no other way. We saw all five on the bridge from upstairs; none of them went up the north road. Just try to keep them off me as long as you can."

"You're right." Eric studied her face and held out the .38 to her, and she looked at it and up at him.

"No. They may find me and they may not. But you can't do anything without it."

Eric laid the revolver on the seat of the golf cart and fumbled with his keyring before handing one key to her. "My car is at the farm. It's parked in the pandas' bamboo, just across the gate. Turn the Asian rhinos out and then don't screw around—get to my car and get help."

Lucy's fingers curled tightly around the key before she buried it in her jeans pocket. Agilely she swung into her cart, which jerked forward with a whine, and Eric watched her disappear into the dark maze of exhibits up the north road.

23

THE CART Eric selected creaked under his weight as he jumped in and started it, then steered it down the perimeter road, thinking even as the motor reached the highest pitch of its whine that he could run faster than this. That would leave him out of breath, though; so he coaxed the cart along, unconsciously leaning and leaning against the steering wheel. Dark greenery spun slowly by at his right, obscuring the east end of the administration building, then its front lawn. At the point where the path took a sharp left to parallel the ranch road outside, he knew he was only a few shrubs and a fence away from the kiosk where Sam's and Max's bodies lay. He resolved to grieve for them, and Larry, later, but first he had to survive the night himself and save as many of his rhinos as he could. The gravel crunched under the tires of the cart and he raged at himself: For God's sake, think!

He had heard two bursts of gunfire, the first as he drove by initially—that must have been when they killed Larry and destroyed the surveillance system—and the second only a few moments before, from inside the building. The African paddocks were designed with the rhinos and elephants serviced directly from the perimeter road because they consumed the largest amount of food. It was the interior space that held the smaller mammals and the aviaries and aquaria. From where Chu and the Barillas crossed the bridge, all the African rhino paddocks would be on their right. If they intended to clean the rhinos out in one night, it would stand to reason that they would begin with the first one and simply work their way through. They would not know whether the rhinos were indoors or outdoors; in fact, he didn't know himself what Ernie was doing with them. Knowing Ernie, the keeper had left them to their own hook, to stay out and browse or come in to sleep in shelter. Then there was that second burst of gunfire, and Eric figured he had to concede the loss of two rhinos in that one, a black rhino cow named Uhura and her nearly grown calf. Since the Barillas had not split up, they might probably tag-team the operation; sweet Jesus, that was the worst possibility, that maybe two of them would work their way through, killing as they went, and leave the other two to saw the horns off as fast as they could. He just couldn't know until he got there. How to investigate, and quickly, and without giving away his presence, were questions he did not have time to answer before the tall cinder-block mass of the eight connected rhino houses hove up on his left.

Eric nosed the cart into the bushes along the fence until it was, at least to casual observation in the dark, concealed, and leapt off. Each "house" had its own back door to the service road, and the whole line were connected to each other, but it was impossible to know where the Barillas were. But at each end of the building that was the rhino complex and at a couple of intermediate places, for it was a very long building, there was a steep, narrow concrete stair up to the walkway that ran along the roof, from where a view was had into each of the paddocks. Eric bounded up this stair, crouching as he neared the top to conceal himself in the bushes that were planted along the rim to make the sprayed concrete walls of the dioramas look more like natural cliff faces.

In the first paddock it was a hundred yards from the back wall out to the fence where the tourists looked across, and two hundred eighty feet wide, forming an enclosure some two acres in extent. The back was high enough that Eric, on his knees in the bushes, had a good view of its grounds, and there were no animals in it, and no one on the path in front of it. He had almost concluded that he was, indeed, too late, when suddenly he felt a vibration through his knees, of all things, and thought he heard a faint hum.

Crawling from the shrubs back onto the walk, he pressed an ear to the asphalt and heard distinctly the buzzing spit of a chainsaw, or two chainsaws. He thought, Oh no, oh Christ, I'm too late, but on rising up, he saw a movement in front of the second paddock, which was less than half as deep as the first but much wider, for it was more of a display enclosure.

He crept quickly nearer and saw three men, two of them with machine pistols hefted over their shoulders. From his perch Eric could just make out the dark, lumpy form of Junior, lounging in a crescent of brushy cover and unaware that he was being stalked. He realized that he was right, they were working in two parties, one to do the killing and one to do the sawing. Burrowing on his belly through the lowest branches of the shrubs, Eric moled through to the chain-link fence that ran along the rim, and from where he looked out he figured he was only a hundred and twenty feet from the men searching out the interior of the paddock. Two were burly Hispanics, one in blue jeans and one in cutoffs. The third, the unarmed one who stood back a little from the others, seeming to observe them as they went about their business, was older, a lean man wearing black trousers and a black turtleneck. The third man turned from the Barillas, walking quickly further down the rhino paddocks to scout them out in advance, and when he turned just right in the moonlight Eric saw without mistake that it was Albert Chu, but he was beyond sight in a few seconds and Eric turned his attention to those at hand. Resting the barrel of his .38 on a link in the fence, Eric aimed carefully at the chest of one of the armed men, forced at last to confront whether he could shoot, praying Please, please, God, don't make me do this. For a moment he considered firing into the air and yelling at them to get out. No sooner did the thought cross his mind than he knew that was not only futile but stupid. Not only had the rangers in Chete driven the point home to him repeatedly—poachers must be shot with the intent to kill—he was now, like the rangers, playing not just for the animals' lives but for his own. They outnumbered him and they would kill him if they got the chance.

Juan Barilla raised his machine pistol and aimed into the paddock, at a movement he thought he saw. Eric sighted him carefully in the .38, his finger touching but not squeezing the trigger, then squeezing just enough to cause a tiny backward movement of the hammer. It was then that the bead wobbled in the sight, and Eric realized his hand was trembling, and more than that, his arm as far up as the elbow went as weak as water. His focus changed, from Juan to the revolver to his arm starting to shake weakly, as if from a fever. In an absurdly detached way he regarded his trembling limb and thought, Jesus, Jake was right; buck fever is a real thing. Yes, thought Eric, detach. Detach and refocus. Eric's gaze measured Juan's aim outward into the paddock and saw that whatever he saw, it was not Junior. He gave thanks, that at least for that instant he was spared having to take that awful step.

No, wait, he thought, that's a stupid game. Are you going to wait and let him shoot first? What if you miss and he doesn't—dead Junior, dead Eric and maybe dead Lucy.

His attention went back to the two men, one of whom was gesturing into the thicket and who then knelt on the path.

It was Esteban Barilla, who had whispered, "Look, man, I'm gonna throw a rock in those bushes. Maybe he's in there." He laid his own weapon aside and selected a handful of large pebbles from the gravel of the path, briefly gauged the distance to the clump of bushes, and threw like a pitcher as hard as he could.

From his perch Eric thought, Oh shit, no—Christ. He watched the white pebbles of gravel slowly spread out like great, slow-motion buckshot and pepper the brush, one of them hitting Junior in the belly and another bouncing up against his flank. Junior vaulted to his feet with a sirenlike moo, turning an angry half-circle, raking his horn into one of the bushes, creating a disturbance clearly discernible to Esteban and Juan. Junior advanced a couple of steps to the side, exposing his profile from the side of the thicket.

Esteban tapped Juan on the shoulder. "There, man, see it? He just comin' out."

Juan raised his weapon tentatively, until he was certain of what he was seeing, even as Eric sighted him again, steadily, down the barrel of his .38. You son of a bitch, he thought, I gave you a chance, why didn't you take it? He aimed at the center of his chest, but then lower—he would have a greater chance of surviving a gut shot than one at the heart. He found himself now cool and patient and alert, like a leopard at night, waiting, until he saw Juan suddenly tighten his aim.

Esteban saw the flash and bang at the top of the paddock the same instant that Juan twirled backward and writhed curling on the ground with a gagging kind of groan. Esteban whipped his machine pistol from where it lay against the fence and sprayed the top of the diorama. Eric flattened himself against the ground, but one of the bullets hit close enough that chips of concrete raked into his scalp like tiny brands of fire. If anything in this entire night disenthralled him and aroused him to a pitch of awareness, it was the wet burning of blood in his hair.

Perhaps one will be enough for them and they will leave . . . Eric raised up and saw Esteban trying to awaken Juan and fired again, a miss, at which Esteban at one time screeched, fired a second burst into the bushes near Eric's head, and fled past the first paddock and toward the door that accessed their house.

With a quick glance Eric saw Albert Chu returning in a running crouch with a small gun drawn, but did not wait on him before vaulting down the outdoor stairs at the rear of the building. He zipped his card through the lock to Junior's house, his gun drawn and eyes wild, assaying every corner with the quick precision that is born of anger and fear. Finding it empty, he heaved a pitchfork from Junior's store of hay and sprinted across the room toward the door to the first house, praying hard he would reach it before Esteban reached the other two men there. As soon as he entered he heard the chainsaws at their work and knew they must not have heard the gunfire outside.

The noise of the chainsaws was very loud as he neared the door, but still as quietly as he could he jammed the handle of the pitchfork through the bar of the door to hold them back a few precious seconds. He had reasoned that must be the way of it, that the Barillas had entered the first house, killed the two rhinos, entered Junior's house, but finding it empty had sought him outside. They probably had not investigated the other six houses; that was why Chu had gone ahead to scout the paddocks.

Eric dashed full bore back across the room, and halfway across it the buzzing roar of the chainsaws abruptly ceased. He slashed his card through the lock to the third house; he swung open the door but as he propelled himself into it, he tripped over a bucket and mop that one of the keepers had left leaning there. He hit the cement floor hard, on his side, but fortunately with the .38 pointed high in the air. But the metallic clatter of the bucket crashed through the stillness and echoed and echoed again, and Eric had no sooner pushed himself to his feet than he heard the Barillas trying to force the door into Junior's house from the other side. At least the mop was at hand, and he wedged it into the bar just as he had the first.

Number Three held a single cow, a loaner from Portland who was ripe to breed but who had spurned bulls in two other zoos, and whom they hoped Junior would charm into submission. He found her standing in her hay-lined stall, next to a great depression in the hay that showed where she had been sleeping until a moment before. Eric saw Ernie had left her door open to the outdoor paddock so she could go out if she wanted. He thought, How to get her out?, and an inspiration it was—taking advantage of her near-blindness, Eric ran at her low, waving his arms, making from the deepest part of his throat his best imitation of the guttural, squeeze-belly roar of a lion. The ruse worked before he was halfway to her bars. By the time he had a view outside after her, she was galloping with her tail high into the thickest part of her brush.

In any other circumstance Eric would have thought, Damn, I'm good, but he had just chased her out when a burst of gunfire and the crash of the door told him the Barillas were into Junior's house, and he moved on in the same manner. The next two houses were empty; Eric had not thought to close the gate after the Portland cow and lock her out, but these two empty ones he took time. If they were safer in the paddocks, he did not want them wandering back inside. Number Six held another bull; unlike Junior he was a founder, taken in from the wild, from the W National Park in Niger, who was still quite skittish and it was no problem to shoo him outdoors and lock the gate after him. He was grateful to find Seven and Eight empty, their residents, one with a cow and the other a cow and calf, were spending the night in their paddocks. Eric paused only to lock them out before racing on, feeling like he might be gaining a little time on the Barillas, who were following but were forced to check out each house to see if he was lying in ambush.

When he was finished with the black rhinos, Eric exited the building and dashed across a narrow alley to the next row-house, the one where the elephants and white rhinos were kept. Sobhuza was the only elephant he intended to free into his yard. He suspected the Barillas were only after rhino horn, but of all the elephants Sobhuza was irreplaceable, and he simply could not risk their shooting him just for the thrill of killing something so massive. God knew, better men than they had succumbed to the same temptation, and he had seen nothing of the Rigby.

Eric slipped his card through the lock and eased himself inside, and knew from the low—very low, almost subsonic—angry rumble that Sobhuza was inside and alerted to his presence. Eric approached in the gloom, not turning on the light; even after three years of captivity, standing in close quarters, right next to a Goliath of such raw majesty it made his stomach quiver. His sense of instinctive terror was heightened even more when Sobhuza bellowed and lashed out with his trunk, which smacked into the gateless iron grid. But rather than back away, Eric repeated the lion trick, rushing at the startled behemoth with the most guttural belch-groan-growl he could manage. The display of defiance, however silly it seemed, was still the first Sobhuza had seen in a lifetime of maybe thirty years, and he jerked back as though slapped. Eric repeated the maneuver again, louder, with no effect, when he seized a chair by the door and, yanking the lights on and off like a strobe, flung it into the bars with a crash. This finally sent Sobhuza shooting outside with a screech, his tail high in the air and his back feet pushing as far forward under his body as they could swing.

The delay had cost precious seconds, and Eric realized with a gasp that there was nothing at hand to block the door before he heard the last door from the rhino house crash open and footsteps scoot rapidly across the alley. When two of the Barillas entered, the brothers Ramón and Esteban, their guns were drawn and they moved lithely, cautiously.

Esteban looked into the great empty, hay-strewn stall where Sobhuza had been. "This one is empty too, man." There was an edge to his voice, an anger, or madness, beyond frustration. The death of his brother-in-law had been little compared to that of his son, but not even that gouging agony clouded the realization that he was committed now to a course from which there was no turning back. He had committed a murder and was an accomplice to two others. Flight to Mexico was now not just the plan but an imperative of survival, and they had to leave with all the money they could get their hands on.

"Yeah," whispered Ramón, "but I think that guy may still be in here somewhere." That possibility kept him from turning on the light, and dimly he made out the back wall of the house, the hydrant and sink, the coiled hoses, a vast stockpile of baled hay and before it a pile of loose hay heaped into a mound. He found a pitchfork and thrust it deep into the stack, first at one place and then another. His other hand held his machine pistol ready, and at the first thrust he hissed barely audibly, "I gonna stick this up your ass, you cock-sucker." After Esteban satisfied himself that Eric did not lurk in a corner, he yanked open a metal cabinet, empty except for the cabinet which contained the emergency surgical kit Jake kept there just in case.

It was then that Luís burst in, out of breath, having sprinted through all eight rhino houses to catch up with them. "Listen, Chu says fuck him. Here's what we gotta do. I'm going to go with him and try to get to those other Asian ones before anything else can happen. He wants you to stay here and see if you can find this guy and take care of him. If you lose him and can't get any more of these rhinos, then you come on up and help us. You understand? All right, he says, do it, now! Let's go!"

They ran out together. There was no need to retrace their steps through all the rhino houses, for the alley between the rhino complex and the elephants' extended into an access corridor that went right out to the pathway from where the visitors viewed all the animals. No sooner had their footfalls receded than Eric rolled to the edge of the twelve-foot-tall wall of hay bales and scanned the floor beneath him. Thank you, Lord, he thought, thank you for showing me what to do.

His first destination was the roof, from where he saw Chu and Luís Barilla press deeper into Africa, and Ramón and Esteban separate each into a different cul-de-sac, apparently on the hunt for him. He was running back along the roof of the rhino complex, back the way he had come, as he thought, I think I've got enough time. As he ran along the roof of Number Two he saw Junior still safe in his thicket, and also saw what he had hoped to see, Juan Barilla's machine pistol lying by his body. He descended the stairs behind the building, sprinted through the back of Junior's house and then into Number One, where he skidded to a stop at the sight of two rhinos, the young cow Uhura and her offspring, lying dead in a slop of blood, into which were impressed a confusion of athletic shoe prints. Their noses were bare, mangled messes where their horns had been. He stared at them only a second before dashing out onto the visitor path to Juan Barilla's body. He had not intended to kill him, but guessed from the volume of blood that the bullet had cut a major vessel. Avoiding the dead face, Eric snatched up his gun.

Then he was out the rear exit of Number One, backing his cart out of the bushes and pressing further down the service road, concentrating as hard as he knew how. He wanted to stop and make sure the white rhinos were outdoors, but then they habitually were, and though he loved them they were not the highest priority, for of the five species they were now the least endangered. What was paramount now was the Javas, and from the African rhino paddocks there were three ways for Chu and Luís to get to them. One was overland, across the Middle East and down through China. They could stay more under cover, but it was arduous as they had raised high artificial hills to simulate the Himalayas and they would have to be crossed. And there were two bridges, one from east Africa straight across to India—the most likely candidate—and the second route, a short bridge from southeast Africa to Madagascar, and then a longer one from Madagascar to Australia, and then another short bridge from Australia to Indonesia. Counting all the bends in the tourist path, Chu and Luís would have to cover at least a mile and a half before they reached the likely bridge, the one to India, and if he could speed an end run around them and open it, thus denying them the Indian route, he could possibly buy Lucy enough time to get help.

The doors blurred slowly by on his left; he knew from long experience that the last one at the end of the last building was the roost and tank for jackass penguins, loud, saucy braying little penguins endemic to the coast of South Africa. Like the dodos they had no natural fear of man and were headed for the same fate. At the end of that building he nosed the cart into the bushes again, gained the interior and sprinted up the east coast of Africa, lit by the moonlight reflecting off the large pond of the Indian Ocean. He slowed as he approached the first bridge that crossed the moat to Madagascar, and then ran another quarter mile to the long, quiet stretch of catwalk that led straight as an arrow to India.

Of Chu and Luís there was no sign, and when Eric turned his key in the control box, he felt the bridge assembly vibrate as the turnstile out in the middle rotated open ninety degrees, leaving ten feet of open water lapping on either side of it.

On his return he approached the Madagascar bridge again, still unsure in his mind exactly what was best to do with it, but his indecision was rendered moot when, once he was there, he saw the two older Barillas a hundred yards away, approaching in a jog, making their own way to the Javas as Chu had told them. There was no sign they had seen him; Yes, thought Eric, leave it connected. They would be hung up for at least five minutes twisting their way through Madagascar before even reaching the long bridge to Australia. Then, he thought, Come on, boys, come on across. He regained his cart outside the South African penguin roost and drove still eastward, skirting the two hundred yards of open water between Africa and Australia.

Ashore in Australia, Eric sprinted up the west coast, keeping a sharp eye on the long bridge from Madagascar, passing its control box and, at last conceiving a plan, decided firmly now to leave it usable, and waited a few minutes to see if they appeared. Dimly in the moonlight he saw them hang about the opposite shore, and then enter the bridge in a cautious trot. He preceded them, further up the west coast of Australia all the way to the short bridge that connected it to Indonesia, whose high dome he saw rise from the vegetation across the strait. But rather than cross it, Eric vaulted the fence and made his way down to the shore, where he knelt and agitated the water hard with one hand, then took a couple of handfuls of pebbles and scattered them out into the water. Then he returned to the path, crouching amid ferns and lobelias planted along the fence, waiting.

24 🌿🌿🌿🌿🌿🌿🌿🌿🌿🌿

LUCY HAD STEERED HER CART— it seemed to crawl, but she knew it would have been impossible for her to run the whole distance—the long way around, up through North America, across Europe into Asia, down through China, then Southeast Asia, and had just reached the soaring dome of the Indonesian building when she began hearing the gunfire across the park—a single pop, then a burst of automatic weapons fire, two more pops and then another burst, and periodically several more. The only conclusion she could draw from the pattern of gunfire, from the fact that Eric's revolver had fallen silent, was that they had killed him and were slaughtering their way through the African rhinos. She had to physically fight down the nausea, concentrating hard on working rapidly and precisely and thinking clearly. She turned out the Javas and then the Sumatran rhinos before driving back up to India, noting that there had been no gunfire at all for several minutes.

She released Lakshmi and the other Indian rhinos into their swamps, then regained the tourist path and headed back toward the headquarters the same way she had come. She had her cart at full speed as she topped the bare rocky crest of the Himalayas, unable to stop before she made out Luís Barilla and Albert Chu far downhill in the moonlight, coming toward her at a fast walk. Luís stopped and pointed at her, then Chu pointed at her and Luís broke into a run uphill at her as Chu followed, slow and labored. Lucy U-turned on the path, knowing even as she did so the cart would never outrun Luís in this short a distance.

When Luís topped the rise he scanned the topography as carefully as he could, saw her empty cart nosed into one of the fences, saw the paths that forked down to India or over to China, the cul-de-sacs as far as he could see into them, as many of the enclosures as he could dash by, but by the time Chu joined him at the crest of the hill Luís had not found her.

"Did you see her?" Chu gasped as he gained the top.

"No, man, it's like she fucking disappeared. I looked in the yards and everything. She's not there."

"So there are two to deal with instead of one." Chu's almond eyes set in his oriental face flicked to all different directions and showed plainly his processing the various factors. "She can do nothing," he said at last. "The rhinos in Indonesia are the most valuable. We will go there now and take them, and then if all is still well we will come back to India for those." He had spoken with one hand pressing on his diaphragm.

"Are you okay?"

"Yes. I only needed to catch my breath a little. We must hurry now."

They had this conversation by one of the rank patches of tewpia melons that were grown in abundance in this part of The Refuge, as they were the Indian rhinos' favorite treat. As their footsteps receded down the Indian fork, Lucy's head rose slowly out of the dark greenery. As soon as she could no longer hear them she disengaged herself from the clinging, musk-stinking tewpia and ran down the China fork toward Japan and the clinic.

She paused for a second at the edge of the causeway to make sure she was alone, then entered the darkened compound. There was enough moonlight streaming in through the windows for her to make her way to her office, where leaning across her desk, she yanked her phone off the hook and put it to her ear.

Nothing. She had assumed the veterinary phones were on the main circuit but couldn't be certain until she tried. Through the dark corridors she ran and crossed the courtyard to quarantine, where she hardly broke her stride as she grabbed the Cap-Chur gun from its rack. She made her way to surgery, where she jerked open the refrigerator door and in the cold yellow light stared hard at the shelf of tranquilizers and immobilizers. M-99 would kill them instantly, but they had used the last of it on Sobhuza. She was not in her panic certain how big a dose of T-61 would be required or what acetylpromazine would do, but before she could think about it her eyes focused on the phencyclidine Jake held in reserve for the apes and she reached for it.

She left the fridge door open for the light and turned the cold little bottle upside down, inserting a syringe into it. She guessed that Chu weighed about a hundred fifty pounds, any of the Barillas a hundred eighty to two hundred. No antidote, she thought quickly, overdose and you die—but she had to be sure she got enough, one of them might weigh 220, the needle might get hung up in their clothing and not inject the whole load. She took a couple of hard breaths and pulled the plunger out until the chamber was full, then put the bottle back. "This might kill you," she whispered as she squeezed the air out of the dart. A tiny geyser squirted from the needle. "But you'll go out with one hell of a wet dream."

She glanced back quickly at the drawer of syringes but ruled out taking an extra. She couldn't run carrying both the gun and a case, and in whatever maneuver she'd have to do to get a shot, she could not wrap it securely enough to be sure of not sticking herself or bending the needle, or both.

She slipped the phencyclidine dart into the barrel, followed by a CO_2 cartridge, and clicked it shut. She headed toward the door, stopping only to wrap a handful of tissues around a scalpel and slip it into her blouse pocket. Then constantly checking ahead of her to make sure the way was clear, she made her way down South Asia to the Indonesian house.

Eric lay in hiding in Australia, at the south entrance of the bridge to Indonesia, waiting and hoping that his plan would work, and knowing that it was within his grasp when he saw the two of them— Ramón and Esteban—approaching in their cautious trot, about eighty yards away.

Eric jumped from the bushes full into their view, firing a short burst at them from Juan's machine pistol and then, shaking it as though it had jammed, ran out onto the bridge to Indonesia. About halfway across he turned and tried to fire again, and again shaking it violently, dropped it onto the two-by-six planks and fled onto the island. Esteban, a little ahead of Ramón, stopped and fired a short burst at his receding form, the bullets clipping leaves from their branches as Eric dodged into cover.

Seeing him drop the gun, the two took after him. Halfway across the bridge they stopped to pick up Juan's gun, and so did not see Eric lean out from the bushes, reach and turn his key in the bridge's control box. There was a thump and a hum as the central pedestal where he had left the weapon began its ninety-degree turn.

"What the fuck!" exploded Ramón. He sprinted back to the widening gap and vaulted across to the Australian side. Esteban was caught more by surprise, and when he followed the breach was too wide. Like a trapped animal he ran to the other end, but lost his footing as the catwalk continued to shudder and rotate beneath him, causing him to spill Juan's machine pistol into the water with a loud splash. He looked backward and forward and back again, stranded in the middle, water in front of him and in back of him.

Leveling his .38 as best he could in sighting Esteban's legs, Eric fired, but the bullet spit off one of the metal posts that held the chain link and Esteban flattened himself onto the planks of the walk.

As loudly as he could Ramón rasped, "You got to wade back over, man. He shoot you out there."

Eric fired again, without careful aim, onto the catwalk, and this time Ramón replied with a burst from his machine pistol. "Come on, man, I cover you."

Eric pulled the trigger of the .38 again and heard the hammer snap down onto the spent cylinder. "Shit!" He opened the cylinder and spun out the empty shells, then dug into his pants pocket—deeper and deeper until he felt it was empty. "No! Shit!" He looked back out onto the catwalk, at Esteban staring hard and frightened into the dark water.

"Hurry up, man! I cover you!" He fired in Eric's direction. "Throw me your pack."

Carefully Esteban rose up far enough to pitch the backpack, containing the horns they had just collected, across the thirty feet of open water to Ramón. The throw was only a little short, and Ramón was able to lean out and catch it before it fell into the pond. Only its straps trailed into the water before Ramón hauled it up to safety.

Shaking, Esteban crawled to one of the open ends of the bridge, set his gun on the edge and slowly lowered himself into the water. Finding it deeper than his waist but not up to his chest, he reached back up to the planks and seized the gun and waded toward Ramón, holding his hands above his head.

Esteban did not look back to see the shallow, V-shaped wake arrowing slowly toward him, a wake that stopped eight or ten feet from him as the saltwater crocodile submerged to take its prey, and then at the last second turned on its side and opened wide the daggered snout as large as a man's outreaching arms. All Esteban felt was an irresistible pressure on his leg, which then spun out from under him as neatly as a judo flip. Only when he surfaced again did he scream with all the power in his lungs, only to have it cut short with a gurgle as the croc was suddenly atop him. It was log-rolling, spinning in the water, the usual method by which a crocodile stuns and dismembers prey too large to swallow whole. Esteban surfaced maybe eight or ten times, each time with a different timbre of shriek. Or maybe it was all one long shriek, Ramón couldn't tell as he aimed his machine pistol at the maelstrom in the water, but he couldn't fire because it was a blur of man-croc-man-croc-man-croc as they spun churning the surface.

Then suddenly there was a tremendous lashing *wham* on the water of the massive, plated ten-foot tail, as the crocodile took him down to the bottom. The calm was abrupt, the waves and chop radiating slowly outward with a hissing calm from where the tail disappeared.

Ramón crouched electrified by the sheer silence, not snapping out of it until the calm was broken by the audible blooping gurgle of bubbles on the surface of the water, as Esteban's exhausted lungs gave up the last of his air.

"I kill you, you bastard," screamed Ramón, leaping from his crouch out onto the bridge that went nowhere, firing a long burst into the bushes at the water's edge. "Son of a bitch, you dead!"

Eric mashed himself into the dirt, covering his head, as leaves and twigs rained about him, but he knew that as long as Ramón was trapped on the other side, his rage was impotent.

Making his way through the jungle of vines and creepers, Eric regained the visitor path around the first bend from the water's edge, at a spot out of Ramón's line of vision. He had just peered back to make sure of that when he heard the pop of a small handgun and simultaneously felt the buzzing whine of a bullet whiz by. He spun around and saw Albert Chu walking toward him with a quick, regular stride, reaching up with his other arm to steady his aim.

Eric cleared the fence from the path in a single vault, but then slid helplessly down and down the muddy embankment into the shoreline mangroves, where he lay motionless and silent, hoping the saltwater crocodiles were still occupied out in the pond.

He heard Chu's footfalls approach and pass above him, and a moment later the thump and hum of the bridge being closed. Eric groped in his pocket for the keychain and only then realized he had left it in the control box. Stupid, he thought, stupid, stupid.

He heard the quick thumping of the planks as Ramón Barilla ran across. "Did you see that?" he cried as soon as he descended onto the gravel path. "Fuck, man, did you see that? He killed my brother."

"I came as soon as I heard the screaming. Your brother was a good man. I am very sorry."

"Fuck, man, we got to get out of here."

"No. We knew it would be dangerous. I just saw Jackson for a second, but he fled from me. I think perhaps he is out of ammunition."

"No, man, he ran from us, too, but it was a trap!"

"You must try to calm yourself. Now it is even more important to leave here with horns, or your brother and his son will have died for nothing. Did you get any of the African rhinos?"

"Two."

Chu pointed at his pack. "Do you have the horns?"

"Yes."

"Good. Hurry then. Luís is already in the Indonesian house." They hustled away as Chu added, "We did see someone else, a female security guard or something, but she was unarmed and ran away."

Lucy entered the Indonesian house by a service stair and ascended high into the flight cage, unseen, using the grips and handles that the keepers used to hide food in the tree branches. The massive tree trunk was artificial, but the vines and creepers strung through them were quite genuine, supplementing the ropes that the proboscis monkeys swung about on. Screened by this foliage, Lucy wedged herself in a tree fork and surveyed below as carefully as she could. The tree rose from the tapir pit, on the other side of the elevated walk directly opposite the indoor part of the Java's enclosure. In this perch she heard first the outer doors and then the inner ones open and close. Lowering a stair into the Javas' jungle, Chu and Ramón Barilla descended, and Luís emerged into the clearing, his machine pistol over his shoulder. Blessing her luck that she had released them outside, she unshouldered the Cap-Chur gun and laid it across her lap.

One shot, she thought. One lousy shot, and then she would have to get away somehow and then somehow think of something else—too many somehows. Her eye followed up along one of the ropes to see where it attached to the top of a second, taller artificial tree in the adjoining enclosures, the one for the Komodo dragons. Gauging that the tree it was attached to was about as far away as it was tall, she unwrapped the scalpel, sliced through the end that was above her and twisted it about her wrist. Jesus, she thought, oh Jesus, what am I doing?

Silently she raised the dart gun to her shoulder, as Chu led the others into the foliage of the Javas' jungle. It was Ramón who offered the fattest back, and she aimed quickly and squeezed the trigger. The sharp *pap* of the Cap-Chur gun was followed instantly by a squealing bleat from Ramón as he leaped sideways into the air, not unlike a lion or gorilla or any other animal she had ever seen darted. "Shit, man, I'm hit!" he wailed as he crashed into the greenery.

In a flash Luís was beside him, pulled the empty syringe out of his back and held it up for Chu to see.

"It's that bitch!" cried Luís. He fired a burst up into the treetops in her direction, but with no chance of seeing her he succeeded only in shattering several skylights.

Lucy covered her head against the rain of translucent plastic, then with the dart gun slung back over her shoulder, breathed a final expletive and let herself fall from the tree, and the rope carried her in a long, swinging arc down and away from it.

This Luís did see, and he fired another burst after her, lighting her descending swoop like a strobe until she disappeared on the opposite side of the elevated walk. He grabbed Chu's arm. "Take care of him. We can't do nothing till I get her. Wait here."

Lucy landed in a crushing whump of greenery but felt a sticking pain in her shoulder and wished she had dropped the scalpel before attempting the swing. Opening her blouse, she saw it was not a deep cut, though it was starting to bleed, and she stretched out her wrists and ankles to make sure there was no other injury. Hearing a quick movement in the bushes nearby, she expected to confront Luís, but instead saw she was being investigated by one of the Komodo dragons—she didn't know which sex the lizard was but it was ten feet long, probing the night air with its forked, blue-black tongue. She knew they fed the Komodo dragons whole goat carcasses so they could maintain their natural behavior, in tearing them apart with their powerful jaws. This was one den she did not mean to dally in.

She got to her feet and swung out at him with both hands and a hissed, "Hyah!" and it crashed off. Swiftly and silently she got out of there, and not seeing Luís on the walkway, she ran along the wall of glass herpetaria and halfway down it whisked her card through the lock of a doorway marked EMPLOYEES ONLY. She clicked the door shut behind her and found herself in the service area from which the reptiles in the glass cases were fed.

The room was pitch-black and silent, and she tiptoed slowly across it, trying to feel for any furniture before she dislodged something. She was halfway across it when the door clicked open again and the lights flashed on, and she spun around and saw Luís in the door, covering her with the machine pistol in one hand, the other holding a passcard coyly in the air. "Well, lookee here," he said. "The vet lady."

He pushed the door closed behind him with his hip and approached her slowly, motioning her with the gun barrel, "Now, you put that down."

She obeyed, laying the Cap-Chur gun on the floor, backing up. "Luís—"

"How you doing, vet lady? Remember me?"

Terrified, she nodded.

"Did you kill my uncle with that thing?"

"No. It was a drug called phencyclidine. He'll sleep for a while but he'll be all right."

He came on, slipping the passcard into a shirt pocket, then his free hand found and played with the button at the top of his denim cutoffs. "So, you too good to go out with a Mexican boy, huh?"

"No," she almost whimpered, still backing up.

"I think you are." He kicked a chair aside with incredible violence, sending it crashing into and bouncing off of the wall. "I bet you not too proud to fuck a Mexican boy now, are you?"

She had backed up as far as she could go, into a cabinet counter.

"I get you naked, I don't need this." He laid the machine pistol on the floor, well out of her reach, and grabbed out suddenly and squeezed her breast.

She was petrified. "Luís—why—are you doing this? You're not like the others."

"Oh, yes I am, lady. Everything you ever said to me told me I am, just like the others."

"Luís, how could I? I was dating somebody else."

"That's bullshit, lady! I was just as good as him."

Suddenly her eyes flashed from his face to the door over his shoulder, and when he looked around she made a grab for the scalpel in her pocket. She had already started her motion to drive it into his neck when his meaty hand clamped about her wrist like a vise.

He laughed. "That's pretty good, lady. Oldest trick in the book, and I almost went for it. I really did." He shook her hand and she dropped it.

He angled his lips closer to hers, pinning her arms behind her, and then mashed his mouth onto hers, working his jaw around for several seconds before he felt her go supple in his arms and even kiss him back.

He pulled an inch away. "Well, that's better. Yeah—"

He kissed her again, snaking his tongue under her lips. She opened her eyes and saw his closed, and then she kneed him in the groin with every ounce of strength she had. He bent double and she kneed him in the face, stunning him backward a couple of steps, not past the gun but far enough for her to elude him and flee down the long narrow corridor—only to discover as she neared the end that it had no other exit.

The light from the room did not fully brighten the hall all the way to the end, and she was in shadow when he came down the corridor after her. "Oh, you gonna get it, now." He unbuttoned the top of his shorts, and slowly pushed the zipper down with a distention of his stomach muscles.

With a great heave Lucy pulled a glass case off its display shelf and hurled it at him. It knocked him back but not down and fell to the floor and shattered. Two, three, four and five of them she flung at him as fast as she could, grunting and hollering, in a long, loud crashing of glass and gravel. When the last one was gone he was still there, his hands up to shield his face. She glanced down at the floor.

"All right!" she screamed. "All right, you want to fuck me, Luís? Here I am!" She grasped her breasts lewdly, and bowed out her knees in a kind of squat. "You fuck me! Let's see how big a man you are!"

He rasped, "Oh, you bitch!" and came down the dim corridor at her. Three steps, four steps, she heard the shards of glass snap beneath his sneakers. If he touches me at all, she thought, he'll kill me.

Then in one motion Luís yelped and leapt high, his arms wild in the air, and he stared down at the floor to see it alive with long black snakes, one of which had fastened onto him, chewing hard into the calf of his leg. He bounded screeching out of the corridor, and in the light pulled the snake off his leg. Lucy heard a spurt of gunfire as he killed it, but when he reentered the hall to kill her, she was gone.

Pulling the cases off the shelf had left openings to the outside hall the size of the tanks, one of which she wriggled through and fled.

Luís took up the scalpel from the floor and lurched his way back through the door and down into the Javas' jungle where Chu awaited him. "What has happened?" asked Chu.

Luís was unable to answer, only grunted as he ripped his shirt into a strip and made a tourniquet tight around his knee, and with a squealing grimace drove the scalpel deep into his calf and pulled it across the bite. His last act before he fainted was to reach out to Chu and plead, "Help me!"

Of all the night's horror, this was the first thing to penetrate Albert Chu's resolve. He wanted out, he wanted away. He shook off Luís's hand and through the jungle made his way to the outdoor area, grateful after a few yards that Luís's retching choke had faded behind him. Outside, he caught sight of the fence he had to reach and fastened his eyes on it, but then felt his bowels liquefy in terror as he ran smack against one of the Javas, which humped and bucked to get out of the way and just as quickly disappeared, visible only for a second in the moonlight and then was gone from sight as soon as it was back within cover.

Breathing hard, Chu mounted the steps out of the pit and clambered over the low chain-link onto the gravel tourist path, his little .22 in his hand, turning left and right, unable to think where it was best to go.

"That's right," said Eric. "Game over."

Chu could not see him and aimed the gun at different bushes.

"Lay the gun down, now, and step away."

Beaten, Albert Chu complied. When he had backed several feet from the gun, Eric stepped from the covering that concealed him. After falling and sliding down into the mangroves, Eric had lain perfectly silent until Chu and Ramón Barilla were out of sight before daring to move, and once they were gone had had to lay hidden awhile longer as the saltwater crocodiles began to emerge from the water. As they scented him he saw one and then another of their huge toothed snouts turn in his direction, from one of which trailed shreds of Esteban Barilla's denim jeans.

Backing slowly out of the mangroves and eluding the crocs had necessitated exiting their pen at its far end, and still more time was required to make his way back to the Javas' outdoor jungle. Eric had just swung one leg over the outdoor fence to descend into it when he heard Albert Chu crushing through the vegetation to make his way to the steps.

Now he rose from the low bushes across the path, the .38 held in both hands, at arm's length. His face was sick and sad and angry and scared. He crouched down to pick up Chu's .22, clicked on the safety and put it in his pocket.

Chu straightened himself and slowly raised his hands. He was winded, but again calm and polite. "There is no need to shoot, Mr. Jackson. I am, as they say, your prisoner."

Eric's voice was an enraged croak. "Look what you've done! You piece of shit!"

"Yes, but still, I think you will not kill me. Fortunately, I know you are a Christian, maybe even a philosopher. You hate the thought of taking life even more than you hate me."

Eric aimed at Chu's forehead. "How sure of that are you?"

Chu smiled evenly. "Not sure enough to try to take your gun away from you. But surely, you would not harm me while we are holding your young lady."

Eric's face went blank. "Where is she?"

"With my other young friend. Come now, the odds were not all that good for you from the beginning, were they? If you want us to spare her, perhaps it is you who should give me the guns."

Eric lowered his revolver uncertainly, and Chu took just a step forward when Lucy's voice roared, "No!" from down in the Javas' jungle. Eric snapped his revolver back up and Chu stopped cold. Lucy mounted the steps and swung over the fence, then covered Chu herself with the machine pistol she'd taken from Luís's body.

Eric embraced her for a second. "Are you all right?"

Shaken but unhurt, she nodded.

He touched the blood on the shoulder of her blouse. "Are you sure?"

"Yes, it's just a scratch."

"Where are the other two?"

"A viper got Luís."

"Is there time to get him a shot of antivenin?"

She shook her head. "No, he's dead. I don't even know what kind it was. There's a whole bunch of them loose in there."

"Not with the Javas!" The thought of banded kraits and cobras loosed in that vast indoor-outdoor tangle, and having to search them out one twig at a time, was not a pleasant one.

"No, no, they're just in the service room. I closed the door when I left."

"Thank God. What about the old man?"

"I got him with the dart gun."

"No!" He shot her a quizzical, amused look and she started to laugh, finally able to release some of the night's horror.

"I sure did. Call me Annie Oakley."

"What did you use?"

"Phencyclidine."

"Oh, Jeez!"

"No, he didn't get a full dose. It won't last but I went back and tied him up."

"Did he have a hard-on?"

"I'm sure I didn't check." She lied. She had, and he did.

Eric turned his attention back to Albert Chu. "Well, let's take in this piece of filth."

"Yes," said Chu. "You have me after all. But don't you see? So what! You still lose the game!"

Eric's face registered just a second of confusion.

"Yes, Mr. Jackson. I will go to prison. But, do you really suppose I am the only one interested in what is here? Use your head, Mr. Jackson! If a rhinoceros horn is worth a quarter of a million now, in a few years it will be worth a half a million, and then a million. Time is against you!"

Lucy advanced a couple of steps and spit on him.

Chu insisted, "How long do you think you can protect these poor animals of yours? Hmm? How long! Not forever!"

Eric's vacant sorrow, and the sick exhaustion of the night, began to show through. "You're right."

"He's not right," snapped Lucy.

"I even respect your motives and your determination," Chu continued, "but ultimately your effort will be futile, because it is the whole world you must change, and not even you can do that."

Chu lowered his arms just a little, but Eric snapped back on guard. He and Lucy stepped back, motioning Chu back down the path toward Australia. When they came to the catwalk Eric stopped and retrieved his key from the control box. When he put it in his pocket, with a look of surprise he pulled out two .38 bullets he had missed in his haste before.

A stunned Albert Chu watched as he opened the cylinder and slid them in, then snapped it shut. Eric smiled and shrugged. "Um, I was out of bullets."

From Australia they crossed the Indian Ocean and Madagascar, and entered Africa at the east coast.

25 🌿🌿🌿🌿🌿🌿🌿🌿🌿🌿

ERIC SQUEEZED the .38 into his belt and Lucy handed the machine pistol to him, happy to be rid of it. They paced nearly a mile, passing the cats' and antelopes' enclosures, a few of whom were visible milling in the moonlight. Then with the gun he pointed Chu into a covered alley at the end of the antelope paddocks. They climbed a flight of stairs to emerge onto the service walk that ran atop the complex that housed the white rhinos and elephants, for Eric wanted to make a quick visual survey of the whites to make sure they were unharmed.

The first paddock they passed above held three cows and two calves, all sleeping peacefully in their tuft grass, and the second was that of Shaka, their founder Southern White bull with his majestic forehorn, who heard the footsteps above him and trotted to a clearing beneath the wall. He lowered his head, threatening the people he heard and smelled but could not see, and thrust his horn upward into the air. Eric found it impossible to see him even in these circumstances—standing there seven feet tall at the shoulder and capable of gouging a ten-foot ceiling—and not be in awe of him.

Chu felt it, too, and said abruptly, "I can offer you an alternative."

Eric did not want to hear it. "Just keep walking."

Instead Chu stopped short and turned, careful to keep his hands in the air. "What if I could guarantee the safety of your animals here?"

Lucy gasped. "You nervy bastard!"

Chu was suddenly so very Chinese in his politeness. "Mr. Jackson, even among people like me there is a kind of honor, a code. If I make it known among my . . . colleagues that your one preserve here is, shall we say, sacrosanct, they will respect my position in this matter."

Eric found the offer offensive, but it took him so by surprise that the known ciphers of worldwide rhinoceros survival raced through his brain despite himself. In the last two decades the world population had declined by more than ninety-five percent, the African black alone from 60,000 to only 2,300, and the rate of slaughter was faster, not slower. Putting them in national parks had not helped. Outlawing the horn trade had only driven up the price, and China's signature on the CITES Treaty was a joke. De-horning wild rhinos had not helped; poachers shot them anyway to spike the price of the existing product—five times its weight in pure gold and still rising. Shooting to kill the poachers had done nothing; since Zimbabwe and the other countries had instituted this policy they had hunted down more than three hundred of them and still they came in their dirty black dress hose with no heels in them, lured by the promise of gold watches and automobiles.

Chu's offer was intrinsically offensive, but if he could deliver . . . the animals—keeping them alive—had to come first.

Lucy slapped his shoulder to snap him out of it. "Eric, don't listen to this!"

Chu sensed him waver, too. "I can do this, Mr. Jackson. Let me go, now, and everything here will be ensured from poaching. Rhinos, elephants, all of them. Then your park will truly be an ark. Forever." He smiled, his hands still in the air. "You can even change your name to Noah, if you like. What do you say?"

Lucy was horrified. "Eric!"

He was near-hyperventilating when he finally yelled out, "I say fuck you, you son of a bitch! Move!" He motioned him with the machine pistol to turn and walk on. Lucy slipped an arm around his waist as they followed.

Shortly they passed above a paddock with a cow white rhino and a juvenile calf. They stood idyllic in the moonlight, their noses up to scent the people as they passed above, reminding Eric for all the world of Ethel Mertz and Junior, years before. It was the first time that night he had thought of Ethel, and he gazed down at them, his sickness and despair growing. Chu was right and he knew it; their horns would only become more and more valuable, until they were all dead and rich Chinese squires would be reduced to warring over the dwindling powdered elixir like the spice in *Dune*. There was no hope.

Midway across the next paddock Eric suddenly called out, "Stop!" and Chu turned around.

Eric laid a hand on Lucy's shoulder. "I want you to go on over to the farm. You still have my car key?"

"Yes."

"There's a twenty-four-hour convenience store about two miles back up 521. They have a pay phone. Call 911 and get the county sheriff out here. Then call Jake and get him out here; I don't want those snakes loose all night, they might find their way out."

She faced him, squarely and angrily, not budging.

"Go on. I'll be outside the headquarters when you get back."

"What about him?"

"I'll handle him. Go on, get going."

Lucy backed away from him, unbelieving, before she turned and strode quickly away. She turned around once, walking backward as she did so, and saw Eric still watching her, with his arm motioning her onward. She turned around and broke into a run, and he watched her until she disappeared.

"Is that your promise?" he asked quietly. "I let you go, and The Refuge will have your protection from the rest of them?"

Chu nodded solemnly. "Yes, that is my promise. You have my word." In the deepest part of his bowels Eric thought: You monster.

From their place on the wall they saw a pair of headlights, distant but approaching from the west. Eric wondered if Larry had managed to phone the sheriff before he was killed, but the headlights passed the gate without slowing, then passed their position and the taillights quickly receded.

With the machine pistol still lowered at Chu, Eric moved to his right and opened a gate in the chain-link fence. He lowered a counterweighted aluminum ladder with a bang down into the paddock, a large grassy pasture studded with high rounded boulders meant to suggest the granite *kopjes* of the African savanna. "Follow this paddock out to the fence," he said. "You'll come to a ditch. Go down into the ditch and you'll see steps going up the other side. Then you can go out the same way you came in."

Chu displayed no emotion but walked to the metal gate and paused. "I do have respect for you, Mr. Jackson. I am very sorry we cannot be friends."

"Go on." Then he added with a meaning that only he knew, "This is your chance to be free."

Chu descended the twenty or so steps of the aluminum ladder with a small metallic bang-bang-bang of his footsteps, and when he was down Eric raised the ladder again with a creak and a hollow clang as it clamped into place.

From atop the wall he saw one of the huge boulders seem to move . . . "Mr. Chu!" Chu faced him, looking up.

Eric said softly, "God forgive us both."

Chu turned to leave, but had time only to raise his arms and scream as the elephant Sobhuza crashed full tilt into him.

Sobhuza hit him, flinging his trunk out in mid-stride like a batter leaning into a pitch. The trunk belted the whole length of his torso from crotch to face, hurtling him back into the concrete wall with a sickening crunch, his two feet a yard off the ground.

Chu slid down the wall and stood frozen on his feet, uttering a pleading squawl that sounded almost like some huge baby's bawl as Sobhuza came at him. The elephant tried to gore him but Chu dodged, standing screaming and clinging to the wrinkled trunk between the two seven-foot tusks that the animal gouged into the sprayed concrete of the cliff, prying out chunks of it that fell from the steel mesh lathing underneath. Then Sobhuza backed away and raised his trunk, and answered Chu's shrieks with a bellowing trumpet that made the building vibrate so hard that Eric found he could no longer stand and sank to his knees, hooking his arms over the fence. He could look down into Sobhuza's great black mouth and see the big pink slab of a tongue seeming to ripple with the force of the sound.

The trunk smashed down on Chu like a monstrous, suffocating blackjack, cutting a scream short into a kind of grunt. It was then, when Chu pushed himself up to his knees, that Sobhuza managed to gore him, low in the belly, not vital, but the pain must have been indescribable. Eric leaned over the fence and saw Chu's face. It reminded him of the two masks you see in the theater—comedy and tragedy—Chu's face twisted into the very mask of tragedy, his mouth contorted into a down-turning slit, trying to sob but instead choking and spitting blood. With his tusk still embedded in Chu's belly, Sobhuza vaulted his head upward, throwing the man high over his back, a cartwheeling mess that squealed and spewed black blood like paint from a sprayer until he landed with a whump on his stomach, and Sobhuza wheeled and stood over him. Groaning and grimacing, Chu slipped a hand under himself, into the hole where his belly had been, his face in the dirt, not looking up at the mighty foot that loomed over him.

No one who knows elephants thinks that they are clumsy; the truth is they know acutely, precisely, how much pressure they exert on something. The great toenails raked down Chu's back from his shoulders to his hips, taking clothes and hide together, skinning him as neatly as a chicken thigh and leaving black, naked meat exposed to the night air. At this Chu managed one last screeching bawl that gurgled into a blood-puddle under his mouth. Then Sobhuza gored him again, low in the back, below the kidneys. As the monster foot crushed his legs, the great stained tusk ripped upward, popping out gray-white ribs one after another like stitches in a sack of dog food. Chu's only movement now was the frantic involuntary jiggling of his hands, one of which disappeared beneath a slough of meat and organs that dropped wetly off the end of the tusk.

Once the sheriff got here, Eric didn't know how they would get Sobhuza away from Chu's body. He knew that an elephant in the wild, if sufficiently enraged, could worry and savage a corpse for hours, perhaps even stop to rest or snack before returning to it and remembering his rage afresh. The big elephant had stomped and knelt on him repeatedly, and now snaked the end of his trunk around Chu's neck and pulled, taking the head off the top of the spine as easily as a ripe date slips off the pit. Sobhuza flung it behind him and it hit the wall with a wet cracking sound like a cantaloupe.

It was then that Eric could watch no more, and he made his way over to the main gate to wait for Lucy. She would return long before the sheriff arrived, and they would have time to get their stories straight.

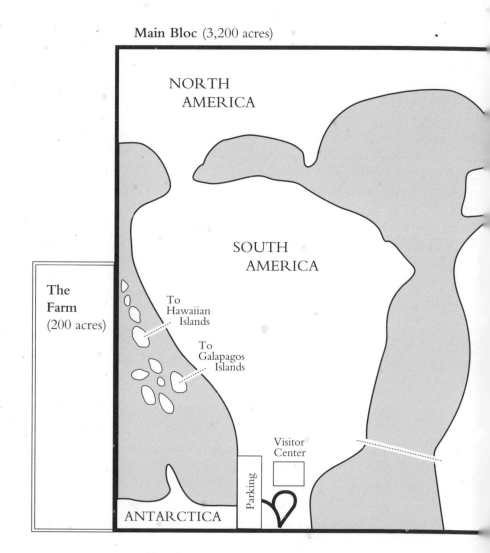

Main Bloc (3,200 acres)

NORTH
AMERICA

SOUTH
AMERICA

The
Farm
(200 acres)

To
Hawaiian
Islands

To
Galapagos
Islands

Visitor
Center

Parking

ANTARCTICA

Final Refuge Wildlife Park